P9-DUK-576

WITHDRAWN

JUN 2 7 2024

DAVID O. McKAY LIBRARY
BYU-IDAHO

AN OLD CAPTIVITY

Books by
NEVIL SHUTE
———

MARAZAN

SO DISDAINED

LONELY ROAD

RUINED CITY

WHAT HAPPENED TO THE CORBETTS

AN OLD CAPTIVITY

LANDFALL

PIED PIPER

PASTORAL

MOST SECRET

THE CHEQUER BOARD

NO HIGHWAY

A TOWN LIKE ALICE

ROUND THE BEND

THE FAR COUNTRY

IN THE WET

SLIDE RULE

REQUIEM FOR A WREN

BEYOND THE BLACK STUMP

ON THE BEACH

THE RAINBOW AND THE ROSE

TRUSTEE FROM THE TOOLROOM

STEPHEN MORRIS

AN OLD CAPTIVITY

by

NEVIL SHUTE

HEINEMANN : LONDON

William Heinemann Ltd
15 Queen Street, Mayfair, London W1X 8BE

LONDON MELBOURNE TORONTO
JOHANNESBURG AUCKLAND

First published 1940
This edition (reset) 1951 (twice)
Reprinted 1952, 1953, 1955, 1957, 1959, 1961, 1964, 1972

434 69906 3

Printed Offset Litho and bound in Great Britain
by Cox & Wyman Ltd,
London, Fakenham and Reading

AUTHOR'S NOTE

This book is a work of fiction. None of the modern characters have any existence except in my imagination, and no reference to any living person is intended.

But Haki and Hekja were real people, the first explorers of a great country.

NEVIL SHUTE

THIS case came before me quite by chance in the spring of last year. I was travelling out to Rome for a consultation. I might have saved time and fatigue if I had gone by air, but it was early in the year and I had decided against it on account of the high winds and rain. Instead, I booked a sleeper in the first-class *wagon-lit*, and left Paris on the midday train.

The journey was a normal one as far as Dijon, and a little way beyond. But as the darkness fell and the line began to climb up into the Jura mountains the train went slower and slower, with frequent stops for no apparent reason. It was that difficult hour in a railway train, between tea and dinner, when one is tired of reading, reluctant to turn on the lights and face a long, dull evening, and conscious of no appetite at all to face another meal. It was raining a little; in the dusk the countryside seemed grey and depressing. The fact that the train was obviously becoming very late did not relieve the situation.

Presently we stopped again, and this time for a quarter of an hour. Then we began to move, but in the reverse direction. We ran backwards down the line at a slow speed, for perhaps a couple of miles, and drew into a little station in the woods that we had passed through some time previously. Here we stopped again, this time for good.

I was annoyed, and went out into the corridor to see if I could find out what was happening. There was a man there, a very tall, lean man, perhaps thirty-five or thirty-six years old. He was leaning out of the window. From his appearance I guessed he was an Englishman, so I touched him on the shoulder, and said: 'Do you know what's holding us up?'

Without turning he said: 'Half a minute.'

There was a good deal of shouting in French going on outside between the engine-driver, the guard, the head waiter of the restaurant car, and the various station officials. I speak French moderately, but I could make nothing of the broad, shouted vowels at the far end of the platform. My companion understood, however, for he drew back into the corridor and said:

'They're saying up there that there's a goods train off the

lines between here and Frasne. We may have to stay here till the morning.'

I was irritated and concerned, and immediately thought, of course, that I must telegraph to my colleague in Rome to tell him that I had been delayed. I exchanged a few remarks about French railways with my new companion, and then said:

'You must speak French very well. I couldn't understand a word of what that fellow was shouting.'

He nodded. 'I worked for some years in the French part of Canada, in Quebec. I got used to queer sorts of French out there.'

Presently the conductor came down the corridor and repeated to us the substance of what we had already learned. He passed on, and we stood chatting together for a few minutes. Then I said:

'If you're travelling alone, we might have dinner together.'

He smiled. 'I'm all by myself; I should like to. It seems about the only thing to do—to have a damn good dinner and make the best of it.'

I nodded. 'Well, I'll join you presently. I must see if I can send a telegram.'

He said: 'They'll send it from the booking-office for you.'

I went and sent my telegram, and came back to the train. My new acquaintance was still standing in the corridor; from a distance I had time to make a quick inspection of him. He was dressed quietly and well, in a dark suit. He was a tall man, six feet or six feet one in height, of rather a slender build. He had black hair, sleek and brushed back from a high forehead. His face was lean and tanned, and rather pleasant. I judged him to be of a highly strung, rather sensitive type, probably with a very short reaction time. I took him for an officer on leave, possibly in the Air Force. It was no surprise to me when I heard later that he was of a Scotch family.

We chatted for some minutes in the corridor; then they came to summon us to dinner and we went through to the restaurant car. Darkness had fallen; there was nothing to be seen from the windows of the train but the little station platform on one side, and the swaying of the branches of the trees on the other. We were marooned right in the middle of a forest, miles from anywhere.

I pulled down the blind beside our table, and turned to

2

the wine list. 'It's a great nuisance, sticking here, like this,' I said absently, studying the card. 'I ought to have gone out by Imperial Airways.'

'So ought I.'

There was a turn in his voice that drew my attention from the Burgundy and made me raise my head.

'Do you usually go by air?'

He hesitated. 'I ought to explain. I'm one of the Senior Masters in Imperial Airways. I'm going out to pick up a flying boat at Brindisi.'

I said: 'Indeed? I should have thought you would have flown out.'

'I would have done normally, but all the boats this week are leaving with full loads. We're doing a lot of business these days.' He paused, and then he said, 'I don't suppose you know my name. It's Ross—Donald Ross.'

I smiled. 'My name is Morgan. I'm going out to Rome.'

The waiter came to my elbow, making an interruption; I turned again to the wine list, consulted Ross, and gave our order to the waiter. Then I turned back to the lean tanned man opposite me. 'That's really very interesting. Were you with Imperial Airways when you were in Canada?'

He shook his head. 'They don't operate in Canada. No, that was with a much smaller concern, some years ago. In Quebec. We used to run down as far as Rimouski, and up to Eastmain and Fort George in Hudson Bay, and on to Churchill. Those were the regular routes. On special trips, of course, we used to go anywhere—all over the north.' He smiled. 'That's where I learnt my French.'

'But were there many passengers up there?'

'Not many. Trappers and prospectors, mostly, and hunting parties in the summer.' He paused. 'But then, we carried everything they needed: kerosene, mining machinery, sacks of flour, tinned foods, petrol, dresses for the squaws, pigs and goats—everything you can think of.'

'Extraordinary.'

'It's cheaper to take those things in by air than by canoe, with a portage every ten miles.'

The waiter came and took away the soup plates, and brought the fish. We ate in silence for a time. I was thinking, not for the first time, of the wide lives open to the young men of today. With their experience behind them, the world should be well governed when they come to power.

3

In the end I remarked: 'I've lived a very different life to you. I'm a psychiatrist—a doctor, of a sort.'

He said hesitantly: 'That means a brain specialist, doesn't it?'

'That's right.'

'I suppose you're on holiday now?'

I said: 'Not a bit. I'm on my way to Rome for a consultation.'

He digested that in silence for a time, probably wondering how much I got for going out to Rome. The fish plates were taken away, and they brought the *gigot*. When the waiter had gone, he said:

'You'll forgive me, but I don't know much about these things. Do you do dreams, and all that?'

I smiled. 'To some extent. Dreams are useful, if you don't try to read too much into them.'

'I see.'

We went on with the meal in silence. From time to time I shot a glance at my companion; he now had something on his mind. I was convinced of that; he was in a brown study. The courses came and went; he ate them mechanically, and several times refilled his glass with Burgundy. He was not the type to grow irresponsible or excited under liquor, but presently I knew, he would begin to talk. He did.

Over the dessert he said suddenly: 'Would you say that dreams—exceptionally vivid dreams—meant that a chap was mentally unstable?'

I was very cautious in reply. I know that method of approach so well. I said: 'It depends. If a patient reaches a condition when his dreams have more reality for him than his waking state—then, of course, he may be getting to a point when he will want some help.'

For all my care, I could see that he was worried by my answer. He was silent for a minute, and then he said:

'This only happened once. But it was all so real and vivid that the chap thought it was true, although, of course, it was really only a dream.' He paused, and then he said: 'Would that mean that the patient was abnormal mentally?'

I replied: 'Not necessarily. Many of us have strange experiences once or twice in our lives, and we don't call ourselves abnormal. When did this thing happen?'

'Nearly five years ago.'

'And since that time, has the patient been quite normal?'

4

'Absolutely.'

'No other realistic dreams, or delusions?'

'Nothing at all.'

I smiled. 'Then he should set his mind at rest. Whatever his dream was, he's quite all right.' I paused, and then I said: 'The mind heals like the body, you know.'

He stared at me across the table; there was a strained look about him, and I knew we were coming to the root of things. 'You don't think he'd be likely to go crackers as he got older?'

I met his gaze. 'Not in the least.'

'I see.'

I said gently: 'We've got a long evening before us. Would you like to tell me about it?'

Donald Ross is the son of a solicitor of Scotch descent, who was killed in 1915 at the battle of Loos. His mother was an Irish girl, from somewhere in the neighbourhood of Athlone. She did not survive her husband very long, dying of influenza in the epidemic of 1918. The young man therefore is of Celtic ancestry on both sides of the family, and he was left an orphan at an impressionable age, facts which may be significant.

He was brought up by his aunt, Janet Ross, a tall gaunt spinster who lived at Guildford and eked out a tiny income by teaching mathematics at a girls' day school. She made great sacrifices for him, being Scotch. Out of her small means she gave him a good education, keeping him at school till he was nineteen years of age. It was not possible for her to find the money to send him to a boarding school; during his adolescence they lived together in a small house in a row upon the outskirts of the town. He seems to have been fond of her, so far as was permitted by so bleak a character as hers.

She would have sent him on to Oxford had the funds permitted, but that was quite impossible. So she did what seemed to her to be the next best thing, and one which coincided with his own desires. She sent him into the Royal Air Force for five years, on a short-service commission.

'Ye'll live with folks of your ain station in life,' she said, 'which ye'll nae do if you bide with me in Guildford. And mind ye make gaid use of the time, for it's costing a mint of money.'

He passed into the Royal Air Force without difficulty, for he was intelligent and well educated, and superbly fit. He became a pilot officer and learned to fly; after a year or so he was promoted to flying officer and sent to Egypt. He spent practically the whole of his service in Egypt and Iraq. During this time he flew about a thousand hours. He had one or two small accidents, but nothing serious; he suffered no injuries. He had one slight touch of sunstroke at Basra due to going out without his topee; with this he was in hospital for about a week. He had no malaria. Being of so spare a build, he was not much worried by the heat.

He left the Royal Air Force with a small gratuity early in 1929. At that time aviation was booming in the United States and Canada. The rise in stock values brought a great flood of money to the speculative aviation market, and enterprises were promoted and subscribed for companies and air lines of all sorts, the majority of which had very little hope of making profits. This flood of money meant the purchase of new aeroplanes in great numbers; with that there came the need for men to fly them. For a few months there was an acute shortage of experienced pilots in the States and Canada.

Donald Ross went forward on this tide. With his gratuity he crossed the Atlantic economically, and had no difficulty, the day that he stepped off the ship, in securing a position as one of seven pilots of the Quebec and Hudson Bay Air Services Incorporated. He was business-like and efficient as a pilot, and well liked by the management. He stayed with them for four years until the Company, having lost the whole of its capital and a good deal more, was finally wound up.

In those four years Ross learnt a lot about his job. He learnt to fly an aeroplane on skis in winter, and on floats in the summer; in the awkward intermediate seasons of the break-up and the autumn he learnt to dodge the floating ice when putting his seaplane on the water, and to match his floats when he had failed to dodge it. He learned to operate an aeroplane in the incredibly severe conditions of the Canadian winter. With temperatures of thirty below and more, he learned that if the oil was not drained from the engine and the oil tank within five minutes of landing the machine would probably stay where it was till spring, because no power on earth would make the solid oil move in the passages and ducts. He learned to get his engine started up each morning in the short time of an hour and a half, with a firepot in a tent over the nose of the machine, a pint of ether, and oil steaming in a can upon the stove ready to pour into the tank when the engine fired.

He learned to deal with drunken French-Canadian and Slovak labourers, usually making their first flight, usually sick. He learned to deal with stretcher cases going out, with tourists coming in, and with imminently pregnant women rushing to the hospital at Churchill. He learned how to take live goats and pigs and calves in his frail aeroplane without mishap. He learned to speak a little Indian and a little Eskimo, mostly by signs, and he learned to repair the structure of his aeroplane when it had been damaged by some awkward piece of cargo in a spot remote from all repair facilities.

He learned all these things and a good deal more, but he did not learn how to save money. His flying background militated against his Scotch descent. Being a pilot he drove a very large two-seater Packard round about Quebec; apart from that he had an ice yacht and a sailing boat. In the four years that he was in Canada he had two love affairs, neither of which touched him very deeply, both of which cost him a good deal of money. As he put it, it was a good time while it lasted, but it didn't last long enough.

It came to an end in 1933. The Air Line had been declining for some time as Canada grew poorer in the slump. As it became more difficult to make ends meet the pilots were laid off one by one till only two of them were left, Ross and the managing director. Then the end came; the machines were seized by the creditors in partial payment of their claims, and the Company became a memory of a good effort stultified by world conditions.

With many other pilots, Ross decided to go home. Internal air lines were beginning to spring up in England; the depression did not seem to be so violent over there. He put his affairs in Canada in order. The Packard went back to the overstocked, disgruntled dealer who had given it to him upon hire purchase, the sailing boat paid off his debts, and the ice yacht bought his passage back to Liverpool upon a cargo boat. He landed in England with a good outfit of clothes, a slight American turn of speech, a vast experience of flying in the frozen north, and seventeen pounds, six shillings, and fourpence in his pocket.

He went straight to Aunt Janet at Guildford, glad to be back with her again. She greeted him unemotionally but made him genuinely welcome. He told her his situation on the first evening and counted his money in her presence; it was a trifle under sixteen pounds. She reached across the table and took eight of them.

'Ye'll not be needing these,' she said; 'I'll keep the money by me. Eight pounds will pay your food and washing for the next three months, Donald—maybe four. If ye get another job before that time I'll gie ye back the change.'

'All right,' he said. 'But can you do it on that money?'

'Oh aye.' She sighed. 'I'd like fine to have you free, Donald, but things are deeficult. The lassies dinna take the mathematics as they used to. I have but the twa afternoons a week to work, this term.'

He saw that she was looking tired and frail. He was very sorry that he had not run a Chevrolet in Canada.

It was late in March. He made several journeys up to London on a workman's ticket; within a fortnight he succeeded in getting a job as pilot to an air circus. It was not a good job, and it was poorly paid. The circus was a very small one, a thin imitation of the highly successful National Aviation Day run by Sir Alan Cobham. It was financed by an East End clothier, and managed by an unsuccessful theatrical producer. It was badly advertised, badly equipped, and badly managed. It started operations in the Midlands at the end of April; within the first week two children had been killed, wantonly and unnecessarily, at Leamington. At the end of the second week Ross left the show, without his money.

He went to see his friend Clarke at the Guild of Air Pilots.

'The thing's a regular menace,' he declared indignantly. 'There's no discipline, and no maintenance, and no money in the show. The ships aren't even airworthy, let alone the rest. They're trying to run on motor gasoline.'

' "Petrol" in this country, old boy.'

' "Petrol," then. And there isn't an air-speed indicator working in the whole outfit.'

'Why did you leave them? What reason did you give?'

'I told them I was afraid of being killed. And that's the truth.'

The other smiled. 'They still owe you fifteen pounds, do they?'

'That's right.'

'I'll ring up Morrison and see if he can help you. What are you going to do now?'

'Anything that I can get.'

The other nodded slowly, tapping his pencil on the table. 'You're a bit late for this season, you know. Most operators have booked up the pilots they want this year.'

'I know that. But I couldn't stay on in that show. Better to be a live coward than a dead hero.'

'Of course new things are always coming up. I'll let you know if I hear of anything.'

'Good enough. Let it be soon.'

The other glanced at him keenly. 'It's like that, is it?'

'A bit.'

'All right. I'll let you know the minute that I hear of anything that would suit you.'

Ross went back to Guildford, and began writing letters in answer to the advertisements for pilots in the flying papers. For want of other occupation he took to the domestic life. He got up early in the morning and cooked breakfast for Aunt Janet before she went to work at the school; he swept and dusted for an hour after breakfast, and washed the kitchen floor. Later in the morning he went marketing with her shopping basket, and returned in time to lay the lunch. The work amused him, and kept him from worrying too much about the future. She had sense enough to realise this and acquiesced in this disturbance of her household, grumbling and finding fault with all he did.

'I doubt ye'll never make a housewife, Donald,' she would say, 'buying butter at elevenpence the pound.'

'What ought I to have got, Aunt Janet?'

'Why, Sunray Margarine of course. Threepence three-farthings for the half-pound. There's no reason to go buying a whole pound at once.'

A fortnight later, when he was worrying about his future a good deal, a telegram arrived from Clarke. It read:

CONTACT LOCKWOOD PAUL'S COLLEGE OXFORD FOR JOB PILOT GREENLAND EXPEDITION.

He sat down in the kitchen on a chair and stared at the message. A great feeling of relief swept over him, succeeded by a pleasurable anticipation. His first reaction was that a Greenland expedition would suit exactly the experience that he had. He knew all the hazards of flying aeroplanes and seaplanes in the north, the difficulties of maintenance. Very few pilots in England had the knowledge of such things that he had. He could hold a job like that if anybody could, and do well in it. Perhaps the pay might not be very good, but then the cost of living would be practically nil. It would be difficult to spend much money in Greenland.

In his later reflections there was solid genuine pleasure. That was the time just after the successful British Arctic Air Route Expedition, and very soon after the tragic death of its leader in Greenland in the following year. Greenland was in the news; Ross, and the world with him, knew all about these Greenland expeditions. They were recruited from young men, very young; at the age of twenty-nine, Ross might well be older than any other member of the party. It would be a light-hearted affair of youth, a brave business nonchalantly carried out. It would probably be a year of freedom from anxiety and of good fellowship; a time that he would look back upon with pleasure for the remainder of his life.

The name Lockwood meant nothing to him. At that time he had very little knowledge of the universities. From the first he was prepared to find that this man Lockwood was much younger than he was himself; he would have to adjust himself to that. He did not think he would have any difficulty in doing so.

In any case he must get on with this at once. There was no time to be lost. He mustn't let a chance like this one slip away.

His aunt's house had no telephone, of course. He went and changed into a dark lounge suit, packed a dinner jacket and a few things for the night into a suitcase, and caught the next train up to London. He telephoned to Clarke from Waterloo.

'I don't know any more about it than I said in the telegram,' Clarke told him. 'We got the letter in the post this morning, and I thought of you at once. The letter just asks if we can recommend a pilot for an air expedition to Greenland. It's a funny sort of phrase to use—an air expedition.'

Ross frowned. 'Who is this chap Lockwood—do you know?'

'I've no idea. I've never heard of him before.'

'Well, anyway, I'm going after it. It's just the sort of thing I want.'

'I thought you'd feel like that. Would you like me to send him a telegram?'

'If you would. I'm speaking from Waterloo; I thought of going down to Oxford right away.'

'That's the stuff. Nothing like getting after these things right away. I'll send him a wire to say you're coming.'

Ross went by underground to Paddington, and took the next train down to Oxford. He got there about five o'clock. He did not know the city and he had no money to spare for a taxi; he enquired the way to St. Paul's College, and walked up from the station carrying his suitcase.

It was the middle of May and a warm, sunny afternoon. The streets seemed to be full of young men and young women dashing about on bicycles. It struck Ross as a very pleasant town. The grey stone walls of the colleges stood cheek by jowl with very large shops and enormous cinemas; before them the streets were packed with cars. On that sunny evening there was an atmosphere of wealth, virility, and youth about the place. It seemed to Ross to be a busy, cheerful town; he wished that he knew more about it.

He was amused to see a hansom cab, the first that he had seen since he was ten years old. He stood and watched it as it ambled down the street.

He found St. Paul's College and asked at the lodge for Mr. Lockwood.

'I don't think Mr. Lockwood's in his rooms, sir. You might find him at his house.'

'Where is that?'

'In Norham Gardens.'

'And where's that?'

The porter told him. 'I'll ring up the house, sir, if you like, and find out if he's at home.'

'Thanks a lot.'

There was an interval while the porter telephoned. Ross stood by the lodge and looked around him. He had never seen a college before. He saw a grey stone, cloistered quad with a carpet of very smooth green turf in the middle; in the centre of this there was a little round pond with goldfish in it, and a fountain of weathered stone. Above the cloister there were rooms with open windows; on the window-sill a young man was carefully painting golf-balls white, and arranging them in a row to dry. At another window a young man was talking earnestly to a girl, a very young girl with a queer black cap upon her head. Somewhere there was a gramophone playing dance music.

The porter came to him. 'Mr. Lockwood said, would you go down to his house, sir?'

'All right.'

He turned and walked down through the pleasant streets still carrying his bag. He found Norham Gardens after walking for a quarter of an hour, and stopped for a moment before the house. A puzzled little frown appeared between his eyes; this was not at all the sort of house he had expected. It was a very large, brick house half covered in ivy; the brickwork was ornamented at the corners with stone insets. It had a Gothic stone porch over the front door, giving it a half-hearted mediæval effect; before the house there were a few clipped laurels. The path up to the door had been newly laid with gravel; the steps were very white, and the brass upon the door was very clean. It looked a solid, prosperous, substantial house, built in the more spacious Victorian age, and kept in the manner that its style demanded. It was not quite the house that he had expected to find as the home of the young leader of a Greenland expedition. Unless, of course, there was a son.

His immediate reception did nothing to encourage him. A grey-haired old servant, infinitely prim and neat in a black dress and a white cap and apron, opened the door to him.

Ross said: 'Can I see Mr. Lockwood?'

She eyed him severely. 'Mr. Lockwood is giving a tutorial,' she said. 'You can't see him now.'

Ross said mildly: 'I think he's expecting me. They rang him up from the college a quarter of an hour ago. He asked me to come down here.'

She looked very doubtful, but motioned him to enter. 'Wait here,' she said, indicating the exact position on the hall carpet. 'I'll see how long it will be before he will be free.'

She went up to a door opening off the large hall, and knocked reverently. A murmur of voices inside ceased, with a clearer invitation to come in. The old parlourmaid slipped inside the door, and closed it behind her.

Ross was left standing in the hall alone. He was bewildered. This was like his headmaster's house at the Guildford school. He must have come to the wrong place.

The elderly maid came out again, and closed the door softly behind her. 'Mr. Lockwood will see you in a little while,' she said primly. 'Now, will you wait in here? No, leave your bag there.' She led him to a drawing-room, opened the door, and showed him in. The door was closed carefully behind him.

The drawing-room was unoccupied, and a little cold. It was a large white room opening with french windows on to a garden. Deep brocaded chairs and settees stood about the room, each cushion uncreased and most beautifully smooth. Ross felt that it would be a social blunder to sit down on any of those chairs. The room itself seemed hardly meant for use. It was too precious. A fine gilded clock under a glass bowl swung a low pendulum upon a pure white marble mantelpiece; in a corner a white marble head of Justinian stood five feet from the ground on a white marble column. A long case of Sèvres china stretched along one wall. A fine oil painting of the Colosseum at sunset occupied another wall. It was a fine, wealthy room, furnished in advanced Victorian taste. It was a room in which one could have entertained royalty, and it looked as if it had never been used for anything else.

The pilot moved over to the window, and looked out into the garden. It was a large suburban garden between high brick walls, with a couple of fine old beech-trees at the end of it. It was infinitely neat and tidy. The flowers stood regimented in the beds in neat array. The lawn was mown and trimmed as primly as a tablecloth. In the shade of the beech-trees two cane chairs and a cane table stood mathematically arranged upon the lawn, with a polished brass ash-tray precisely in the middle of the table. The centre of the lawn was laid out for clock golf, the figures beautifully white.

Ross turned away depressed. He was sensitive to atmosphere, and this atmosphere was far removed from that of flying seaplanes in the north. However, he took a small grain of comfort from one feature of the place. It might be frigid and schoolmasterly, but it was not a poor house. Seaplane-flying cost a lot of money. No one knew that better than Ross.

He waited for some time, puzzled and a little worried.

Presently there was a sound of movements in the hall outside; a door opened and closed. A few minutes later the elderly parlourmaid came to him.

'Would you kindly step this way?'

He followed her out into the hall. She knocked at the study door, waited for a moment, and then showed him in.

Ross went forward into a large room. The walls were lined

with books and the furniture was dark, but the room was light and airy from very large windows opening on to the garden. A man got up from the desk and came to meet him, a man about fifty-five or sixty years of age. For his years he was a well-set-up man, tall and broad-shouldered, with iron-grey hair thin on the top but still not bald. He was clean-shaven, with a firm, slightly humorous expression; he wore rimless glasses.

He came towards Ross, holding the glasses in one hand.

'Ross? Good afternoon—I'm sorry you had to wait so long. It's Captain Ross, I suppose?'

The pilot shook his head. 'Plain Mr. Ross,' he replied. 'I was only a flying officer.'

Lockwood said vaguely: 'Oh, really? I thought all you flying people were captains.' He motioned to a chair. 'You've been very prompt in coming down. I only wrote to the—the —er—the Guild or something or other yesterday. Or was it the day before? No, it was yesterday.'

Ross smiled. 'I was very interested when I heard what you had written to them.'

'Capital—capital. Have you had tea, Mr. Ross?'

The pilot hesitated. 'Well, I haven't. But don't bother about that for me. I don't often take it.'

The other pulled a watch, a silver hunter, from the pocket of his rather shabby waistcoat, opened it in his palm, and looked at it. 'Oh, it's only six o'clock.' He rang the bell; the parlourmaid appeared almost immediately. 'Tea,' he said. He turned to Ross. 'Do you like Indian or China tea, Mr. Ross?'

'Well, as a matter of fact, I like Indian. But it really doesn't matter.'

'Indian for Mr. Ross, Emily, and China for me.'

He made the pilot sit in a deep leather chair, and sank down himself into the chair at his desk. 'I understand that you know all about aeroplanes, Mr. Ross,' he said conversationally.

The pilot said cautiously: 'I've been messing about in them for quite a while. I was in the Air Force for five years, mostly in Iraq. Since then I've been flying for the last four years in Canada.'

'In Canada? How interesting.'

Ross had nothing to say to that.

The don put on his glasses. 'Well, now let's get to business.'

He bent down, pulled open one of the drawers of his desk, and took out a large, untidy portfolio. He put this on the desk before him and opened it; it was stuffed with a great mass of manuscript. He turned these papers over talking half to himself as he did so. 'There are several things here that I must show you presently. But this—no, this—and where is the other one? Where can it be? Here we are. These two will do to start with.'

He thrust two large photographs across the desk to Ross. 'Now, what do you make of those?'

The pilot took them in silence. One was an air view of a field, taken vertically downwards from about two thousand feet, with a bit of a wood across one corner of the area. There was nothing on the photograph to show where it was. The other was an oblique downwards view taken from a lower altitude, possibly from a hill-top, of a barren-looking stretch of land running into the sea at a little promontory. Again there was no information on the print.

The pilot looked at these two photographs in silence, and his heart sank. It was clear that he was expected to say something intelligent, and at first glance he could think of nothing to say. They were just photographs. He was no good at puzzle pictures, but he couldn't say that. He scrutinised them in silence; there must be something in the prints to connect them with each other, or they would not have been given to him together. Presently he remarked:

'I don't know what these are of course, I see there seems to be a similar pattern here. The lumps and ridges in this field make a sort of cross in double lines with a circular thing in the middle. And in this other one there seems to be the same pattern, in a kind of way. Is that what you mean?'

Lockwood smiled gently, and took the photographs from him, scrutinising them himself. 'You have remarkably sharp eyes, Mr. Ross. But I suppose you must be very well accustomed to air photography?'

Ross hesitated. 'I've done about a hundred hours of survey flying. But I'm not a skilled photographer—I only did the flying. I've seen a good bit of it, of course.'

The other nodded. 'You must have done. Very few people see the connection between these photographs at first sight.'

He raised his head, and stared at the pilot over the top of his glasses. He held up one of the photographs. 'This one of the field is the remains of the Celtic monastery of Imchuin,

15

near Galway, in Ireland.' He held up the other. 'This one is a part of Brattalid.'

Ross asked: 'Where is that?'

'It was the original centre of the Eastern Settlement of the Norwegians, in Greenland.'

He mused over the photographs. 'Imchuin was completed in the year 932,' he said. 'According to the Landnamabok the Norwegians went to Greenland fifty years later.'

There was a silence. Ross hesitated to break it, afraid of speaking foolishly. He had never heard of the Landnamabok. He sat in his chair trying to work out what the don was driving at; presently he ventured:

'Do you mean that there is a connection between Galway and Greenland? Is that what these photographs show?'

The don stared at him over his glasses. 'It may be so. But what sort of connection?'

The pilot shook his head. 'I don't know anything about these things. But I suppose these marks in the field in the one print, and on the moor in the other—I suppose those are the walls of ruined buildings, aren't they?'

'So I think.'

'I don't know if I'm speaking out of turn. But if the buildings are the same design, I suppose the same folks might have built the one as built the other.'

Lockwood eyed him keenly. 'In a very few words, Mr. Ross, that is the suspicion.' He took up the Brattalid photograph and thrust it across the desk. 'There's nothing Nordic about that. Pure Celtic, every line of it. Look at it for yourself.'

The pilot took it diffidently. 'I suppose that is so.'

The other leaned his arms upon the desk. 'The early Irish, Mr. Ross, were very much greater travellers than is generally supposed. They had a civilisation, forms of religion, and a culture far in advance of this country at that time. Their literature—they had a great literature—is full of references to the Happy Lands. Airchthech, the beautiful place, which lay far out over the Atlantic to the west. The Elysian Fields, Mr. Ross—the land beyond the sunset, where everything was clean and good, and happy. It was a cardinal part of their beliefs that such a place existed. They were always trying to find it, always sailing out into the sea in search of it.'

He was silent for a moment; when he spoke again it was in a softer tone. 'They never found it, Mr. Ross. They found Iceland. That was not the place they were looking for, but they built towns there, and monasteries, Mr. Ross—monasteries.' He paused. 'Did they go further, and find Greenland? There's our problem.'

He picked up the Brattalid print again. 'And now we have this photograph. One little piece of evidence, taken almost by chance. It was by the merest chance it came to me. But there it is. It's like a little chink of light in a dark room, seen through the crack of a door.' He eyed the pilot steadily. 'I'm going to pull that door a little wider open, Mr. Ross. There's something waiting here to be found out.'

There was a silence in the study after that. Absently the pilot took a cigarette packet from his pocket, pulled one out, and lit it mechanically. Suddenly he was confused. 'I'm so sorry,' he said awkwardly. 'Do you mind if I smoke?'

'By all means.' The older man picked up a battered half-smoked pipe himself and lit it.

Ross said: 'What do you want to do?'

The don blew out his match, and puffed a cloud of smoke from his foul pipe. Presently he said: 'Archæology today depends upon air photographs. I want an air survey made of the entire Brattalid district—say, forty miles long by fifteen miles wide. While that is going on I want to spend a month upon the site myself.'

'I see. Where is this place Brattalid?'

'About seventy miles north-west of Julianehaab. Not far from Cape Desolation.'

'Oh.' There was a momentary silence. 'That's on the south-west coast, isn't it?'

'That is so.'

They sat and smoked in silence for a time; the pilot stared at the books upon the wall in front of him. It was not the job that he had thought it would be. There would be none of the good young fellowship that he had looked forward to, nor would there even be the comradeship of a commercial company. It would be a lone-hand expedition; he would be a sort of private pilot, engaged for a relatively short job. But what a job! Already he could see that the whole work of the expedition would inevitably fall on him. He would have to do everything—organisation, flying, photography—every single thing except the archæology. He knew from his experience that the work would be immensely hard, the responsibility enormous, and the danger to life quite considerable. He had too long an experience of the north to undertake this lightly.

His mind went off at a tangent, and he said: 'Didn't you say this was the Eastern Settlement?'

'Yes.'

'Cape Desolation's on the west side of Greenland.'

'I know. But the early Norwegians called it the Eastern Settlement, all the same. There was another up the coast to the north-west, by Godthaab—they called that the Western Settlement.'

'I see.'

There was another silence. Presently Ross said: 'When do you want to go?'

'This summer. I am told that August is the best month for weather. I want to be there for the whole of August.'

The pilot raised his eyebrows. 'You've left mighty little time for preparation. It's the middle of May now.'

'Is that so short a time? I should have thought that it was ample.'

The pilot shook his head. 'It's very short.' He thought about it for a minute. 'How do you propose to get the machine out there? Put it on a boat, or fly it out?'

The don looked at him uncertainly. 'I'm afraid I really hadn't thought about it. The boats are so very irregular— I had assumed that we should fly out in the machine.'

Ross thought of the pack ice off the Greenland coast, and thought grimly to himself that this was going to be a lot of fun. He nodded slowly, and said aloud: 'How many of us will there be?'

Lockwood hesitated. 'I should like to take an assistant, but he isn't really essential. The basic points are—I must go myself, and we must get a good set of photographs. Then, during the winter I can study the air photographs, in preparation for a digging party next year.' He paused. 'This air survey is really a preliminary to the main work, which will be next year.'

Ross nodded. 'I see.'

Presently he said: 'Have you considered at all what a survey like this is going to cost?'

The archæologist shook his head. 'I really have very little idea. How much would it cost?'

Ross had to think quickly. He liked Lockwood, in spite of the fact that the don was grossly ignorant of what he was proposing. The pilot could see a mass of difficulties ahead already. Still, he liked the man and he liked the idea of the expedition; in spite of all the difficulties and dangers, he would like to have a crack at it. He did not want to kill the proposition at this stage by giving an inflated cost. What would it run out to, now? He would have to have a single-engined cabin seaplane. He could pick up a Bellanca or a Cosmos second-hand in Canada for five or six thousand dollars in that time of slump—not much to look at, but sound enough, petrol, oil, shipping the seaplane and erecting it, moorings to be laid at all the harbours they would visit—the camera, and all the photographic gear; the making up of the mosaic from a couple of thousand photographs. He calculated quickly in his head.

'I think you'd have to reckon on at least four thousand pounds,' he said.

To his relief Lockwood smiled. 'These expeditions always cost more than one thinks,' he observed. 'You'll have to talk it over with my brother.'

'Oh!'

The pilot ground his cigarette out in an ash-tray. 'You won't mind if I speak plainly?'

The other looked surprised. 'Not at all, Mr. Ross.'

Ross said: 'I'm not sure that you quite realise what it is that you're proposing.'

The don nodded slowly. 'Would the flight be so difficult?'

The pilot said: 'It's not impossible, but it's very unusual. Only four or five aeroplanes have ever been to Greenland, and those have met with difficulties and troubles that you don't get normally. Maintenance is difficult, because there's literally nothing there at all. The ice is a devil, I believe. The machines that have been there have been taken by powerful and wealthy expeditions after six months of preparatory work. And even then they had difficulties, and crashes. You want to go without the backing of a ground expedition, and with only six or seven weeks from now before we have to start.'

Lockwood took off his glasses and polished them on his handkerchief. 'There seem to be more difficulties than I had supposed,' he said mildly.

Ross smiled. 'I think that is so. Don't think I'm saying that the flight can't be done, or that we can't get your photographs. I think we probably can. But you'll have to realise from the start that there's a good bit of risk about it.'

The don said: 'I suppose you mean—danger to life?'

The pilot shrugged his shoulders. 'Well, of course, there's that as well. It won't be as safe as sitting in this chair. But I wasn't thinking about that. I was thinking of the money risk. You may spend thousands of pounds, and still get no results. We may get out there, and lose the ship at her moorings in a gale of wind. We may crash her. Anything could happen on a flight like that, with any pilot that you like to give the job to. Then you'll have spent your money, but you won't have any photographs to show for it.'

There was a momentary silence.

'But is there any other way to get these photographs?'

The pilot laughed shortly. 'No, there's not. To get a survey of that district, somebody's got to take a machine there and do the job.'

'Well, that's what I want to do.' The don looked curiously at the pilot.

The pilot looked with equal curiosity at the don. 'If that's your angle on it,' he said, 'it suits me. I'd like a job like that.'

'Would you say that there is a reasonably good chance of success?'

Ross sat silent for a minute or two, weighing up the conditions. At last: 'I think so,' he said slowly. 'August is the best month for a trip like that. We may make it very easily, or we may have a rough time. You want to stay there for a month and get the photographs. I should say it's better than a fifty per cent chance.'

He turned to the older man. 'When did you want to start?'

'I must keep it all within the Long Vacation. I could leave here at the end of July, and I must be back here at the end of September.'

The pilot smiled slowly: 'It's lucky your Long Vacation isn't in the winter.'

The older man looked at him mildly. 'I suppose that would make it more difficult.'

The pilot said: 'Yes.' There seemed to be nothing else to say.

Lockwood got up and walked over to the french windows. He stood there looking out into the garden, eye-glasses in hand, deep in thought. At last he said: 'You've given me a good deal to think about, Mr. Ross. What are your movements? You'll stay here for the night?'

'I will if you want me to.'

'Good. I have to dine in Hall—you might care to come

20

along. Then, perhaps, we can talk about it again in the morning.'

Ross said: 'There's just one thing about it. If we're going to go this summer, we've got to make a snap decision—now. Tomorrow at the latest.' He turned to the older man. 'Don't think I'm trying to rush you into this, but time is really very short indeed. I'll tell you what we've got to do, if you like.'

The other said: 'I don't suppose that I should understand you. But I see what you mean. I will make up my mind tomorrow, Mr. Ross. Then if I decide to go, you must go and talk the details over with my brother.'

'Where is that?'

The don looked at him curiously. 'In Coventry. You've heard of the Lockwood Tube and Wire Company?'

The pilot blinked. 'Is that the same?'

'Certainly it is. Sir David Lockwood is my elder brother.'

For the second time that afternoon Ross had to rearrange his ideas. He knew that Lockwoods were the largest makers of high-grade steel tube in the kingdom; they had an enormous business in aviation. He knew a good deal about the tubes. He knew a little about Coventry, too; they were hard nuts up there. Instinctively he knew that they would scrutinise his record and his competence. They would make enquiries at the Air Ministry; the pilot for Sir David Lockwood's brother would have to know his stuff. Well, he was not afraid of that. Much more important was the money side. While he had been talking to the don he had been desperately afraid of that. The flight would be a difficult and an exacting one; to enter into it without sufficient money would be a nightmare. But with Lockwood Tubes in the background the flight became a different proposition altogether. Immediately it seemed to him to be considerably safer.

They talked for a little longer about archæology, of which Ross knew nothing; then Lockwood showed the pilot to his room. It was a large and comfortable bedroom on the first floor, furnished in Victorian style with heavy dark mahogany chairs and wardrobes. The linen on the bed was very soft to the touch and smelt of lavender; there were little lavender sacks in the empty drawers. The old parlourmaid carried up his bag; presently she brought him hot water in a polished brass can. Ross changed into his dinner jacket, moody and a little depressed. It seemed to him that there was nothing

21

in that house in keeping with a Greenland expedition.

He went down to the study; the deep carpet on the stairs made no sound. Lockwood was there before him; on a side table there was a decanter with glasses.

'A glass of sherry, Mr. Ross?'

'I should like one.'

The older man poured out the sherry. 'My daughter is dining out,' he said, conversationally. 'It's the Bach Choir tonight.'

Ross said: 'Oh, really?'

For the first time he wondered what the family consisted of. It was a curious un-lived-in house, apart from the study. Probably, he thought, the wife was dead, and this girl kept house for her father.

'Are you interested in music, Mr. Ross?'

The pilot shook his head. 'I'm afraid I don't know anything about it.'

'My daughter is a great musician. They're doing Beethoven tonight—the Fifth Symphony.'

Ross said again: 'Oh, really?' and drank his sherry. He felt awkward and tongue-tied, out of his depth. He was powerless to keep his end up in this sort of conversation, and he looked forward apprehensively to dinner in college.

However, the evening passed off better than he had expected. They walked down to the college in the mellow evening sunshine, and drank another glass of sherry with the dons in the Senior Common Room. Presently Ross found himself seated at dinner at the high table in Hall above a crowd of two or three hundred undergraduates. On his right hand was a young don much the same age as he was himself, who was an officer in the Royal Air Force Reserve, and who talked of the games system in Canadian high schools. Ross got on all right with him, and appreciated Lockwood's tact in making the arrangement. On his left was an elderly man whose subject seemed to be wood. The pilot was able to maintain a short discussion on the trees of Northern Canada. He got on better than he had expected, but it was a relief to him when it was over.

He walked back in the twilight with Lockwood to the house in Norham Gardens. The streets were very quiet; the whole town seemed to be at peace. On the way the don said: 'I have been thinking about our talk this afternoon. It's evidently more of an undertaking than I had supposed. But I see no reason why we should not go.'

Ross said: 'Apart from the money side of it, there is no reason. We should be able to do what we want. If we fail, I think it will be because of something that we can't provide against—blizzards, or a bad season for the ice or something like that.'

They walked on in silence for a time. 'We'll talk about it again tomorrow morning after breakfast,' said Lockwood. 'I shall have made up my mind by then.'

They went into the house; a light showed beneath the study door. 'My daughter is home before us,' said the older man. They passed through the hall into the lit room.

'Alix,' said Lockwood. 'This is Mr. Ross, who has come to talk to me about Greenland.'

The girl got up, and held out her hand. 'Good evening Mr. Ross.'

She was a girl of medium height with grey eyes and pale yellow hair, worn long and arranged in two coils at the sides of her head. She had a high forehead accentuated by the style of her hair, and a long serious face with rather a determined chin. She had a good figure concealed and stultified by an unpleasing purple dress with a little frill of lace arranged around the throat. She had slender legs encased in grey cotton stockings; on her feet she wore black buckled shoes, plain, sensible, clumsy and very ugly. She had been sitting in a deep armchair and drinking Ovaltine; a violin case lay on the floor beside her.

Lockwood said: 'Whisky and soda, Mr. Ross?'

'Thanks.'

The don crossed to a side table and began manipulating the decanter and siphon. Over his shoulder he said to the girl: 'How did the Symphony go?'

She said: 'Oh—all right, but for the third movement, I wish he'd do something about the 'cellos.' She brushed the hair back from her forehead. 'We did the Sibelius thing afterwards.'

'Was the Master there?'

'I didn't see him.'

She turned to Ross, faintly hostile. 'Do you play any instrument, Mr. Ross?'

He had once played drums, cymbals, and triangle in the jazz band of his Wing in Iraq, but he did not dare to say so. Instead he felt awkward and said: 'I'm afraid I don't.'

She smiled, a little frigidly. 'We're both very keen on music. My father finds it a great relaxation.'

The pilot took the glass handed to him and held it tight. There at least was something that he understood. 'I'm sure it must be.'

Lockwood said: 'Mr. Ross is a flying man, my dear. We've had a very interesting talk this afternoon.'

She said coldly: 'I hope you aren't going to fly over Oxford, Mr. Ross. There was a wretched aeroplane this evening—right in the middle of the second movement. We were all furious.'

She hated aeroplanes and motor bicycles. She could remember a time, when she had been a little girl after the war, when you hardly ever heard an aeroplane, and motor bicycles were few and far between. Then you could really listen to music, lose yourself in it, become submerged in it entirely. Now, that was hardly possible. You were roused from the dream sharply, irritatingly, by the infernal clamour of an engine in the air or on the road. In summer-time, by day or night, it was now impossible to listen to music without interruption from the skies. Only in winter, in the windy rainy nights, when even the big bombers stayed on the ground, was it possible to lose yourself in music, as it had been when she was a child.

Ross said: 'It must be a frightful nuisance in a place like this.'

Lockwood asked: 'Isn't it possible to silence aeroplanes like motor cars?'

The pilot shook his head. 'It's the prop that makes the noise—the thin sections buzzing round. It's like a siren. It's not easy to see how you can deal with that. Nobody would like to see them silenced more than the pilots.'

The girl said irritably: 'If they can't keep them quiet, they might at least keep them away from civilised places.'

She got to her feet and picked up her violin case. 'I think I'm going up,' she said. 'It's been a bit tiring.' She went over and kissed her father; then she turned to Ross. 'Breakfast at nine, Mr. Ross. Daddy will show you your bathroom.'

She turned away. 'Good night. Don't sit up too late, Daddy.'

Lockwood said: 'Good night, my dear.'

She closed the door behind her. A feeling of constraint was lifted from the men; to Ross her departure was a conscious relief. 'Keeping the aeroplane away from civilised places comes rather appropriately,' he said, smiling. 'There's not much civilisation where you think of going.'

The other shook his head. 'I imagine not.'

The pilot considered for a moment. 'That's another aspect of it,' he said. 'I don't suppose we should find any buildings out at this place Brat—Brat——'

'Brattalid.'

'Brattalid. We should have to make a camp and live in tents. I'd hope to be able to get natives—Eskimos to come and do the work for us, but it may be that we should have to depend upon ourselves. Are you prepared for that?'

'Oh, I think so. I did a good deal of field work when I was younger, in Arabia, and in Crete.'

They went upstairs to bed. Ross lay in bed between the lavender-scented sheets for a long time before putting out his reading light, staring over to the far side of the room. There would be a most terrific lot of work in this thing, if it ever came off. The few words that they had exchanged about the camp had opened up a whole new vista. Apart from all the work of flying and maintaining the seaplane he would have to see to all the camping gear, the clothing of his passenger, the food supplies. Most of this stuff would have to come with them in the machine, unless he could arrange to get it shipped to Julianehaab or Ivigtut in time for their arrival. Then there were the petrol and the oil supplies—arrangements must be made for shipping those. And then a mooring for the seaplane must be laid at every place they were to go to.

What was really needed was a small supporting expedition to go on ahead of them by ship, to meet the machine at Julianehaab, to make the camp for them and help him with the seaplane. If he could get a really good photographer, one who was used to seaplanes, he would be a godsend to them.

He wondered what sort of place Julianehaab would prove to be.

He supposed they all spoke Danish there.

He slept.

He woke early, slept again for a few minutes, and woke finally at about a quarter past seven. Breakfast was not till nine, but he could not remain in bed till then. He got up, had a bath, shaved and dressed, and was downstairs by about twenty minutes past eight. The aged parlourmaid was doing out the study; she gave him a black look. To escape her he went out into the garden.

For a time he walked up and down the lawn in the sun, looking at the flowers, and enjoying the cool freshness of the morning. He reflected that these Oxford people knew how to make themselves comfortable. But then, of course, with Lockwood Tubes in the background a man could make himself comfortable anywhere.

He wondered what sort of a reception he would get at Coventry.

From her bedroom window Alix saw him walking up and down the lawn, and her lips tightened a little. There was a difficult little matter that she had to deal with; she might as well take this opportunity and get it over. Indeed it looked a good one. She finished dressing quickly, gave a final pat to the heavy coils over her ears, and went down to the garden.

He saw her coming, dressed in a black serge skirt and a black-and-white-striped blouse that made her look middle-aged. He wondered absently if anyone had ever told her what a frump she looked. Those stockings, and those shoes. He supposed that that was what they did at Oxford. He wondered how old she was—somewhere between twenty and twenty-five probably, but she looked older. He did not care much about her, but he went to meet her with a smile.

'Good morning,' he said. 'It certainly is a lovely day. I've been admiring your garden.'

Her attention was diverted from her object; she was very fond of flowers. 'The polyanthus are nice, aren't they?' she said. 'Did you sleep all right, Mr. Ross?'

'Very well indeed, thank you.'

She stooped and picked up a golf-ball that was lying on the lawn. Then she turned, and walked beside him up the garden. 'I've been wanting to have a talk, Mr. Ross,' she said.

He raised his eyebrows. 'Surely, Miss Lockwood.'

She said: 'I know what my father asked you to come down about. It's about this idea he has of going in an aeroplane to Greenland, isn't it?'

Ross nodded. 'We were discussing it yesterday afternoon.'

She said: 'It's a tremendous undertaking, isn't it?'

The pilot considered for a minute. 'I wouldn't put it quite like that,' he said at last. 'It's an unusual sort of flight, but with proper organisation, and in summer weather, I don't think it's so bad. It means a lot of hard work of course.'

26

She said eagerly: 'I know it does—it means a frightful lot of hard work. It's a job for a young man to do.' She hesitated, and then said: 'My father gets so wrapped up in his archæological work that he overlooks the practical considerations, Mr. Ross. But he could never make a journey of that sort at his age. He'll be fifty-nine next October, nearly sixty. It's difficult to speak about his age in front of him, because he's so sensitive about it. So I thought if I could have a talk with you, I could tell you how the matter stands.'

The pilot rubbed his chin. 'I didn't mean there'd be much work in it for him,' he said. 'I was thinking of myself, I'm afraid.'

'But in a trip like that there'd be great hardships for my father. His health would never stand it, Mr. Ross.'

The pilot's heart sank. He might have known that it was too good a job to be true. He said quietly: 'I see. His health's pretty bad, is it?'

The girl was silent for a minute. Then she said: 'I can't say that he's in bad health. But when you're nearly sixty it's time to start to take care of yourself.'

Ross became aware that he disliked this girl very much indeed. He asked directly: 'Has he got a weak heart?'

She hesitated. 'No—I don't think he's actually got that. But at his age he can't expect to do the things he used to do as a young man. There comes a time when one has to sit back, and leave the more strenuous work to younger men. You do understand, don't you, Mr. Ross?'

The pilot said nothing.

The girl said: 'I thought if I explained to you how matters stand, perhaps you could avoid encouraging him in this thing. I'd hate him to go to a lot of trouble and then be disappointed later on. With your experience of flying you can put it to him in the proper light, and he'll be quite content to give it up.'

The pilot still said nothing.

The girl looked up at him doubtfully. 'You see what I mean, don't you, Mr. Ross? It's just that you should avoid encouraging him in this thing.'

There was a long silence. The girl could feel the antagonism of the pilot, and it puzzled and annoyed her. She did not understand why he should not have met her willingly in what seemed to her to be a very reasonable request. A word from him would have put the matter right.

27

They walked the length of the garden in silence. At last the pilot smiled at her and said: 'You put me in a very difficult position, Miss Alice.'

The girl said: 'Alix is the name, Mr. Ross. But perhaps Miss Lockwood would be better.'

The pilot flushed hotly; whatever compromise he may have had in mind went with the winds. But outwardly he smiled again, and said:

'Your father asked me last night if I could do the flight, if he decided to go. I told him I thought it could be done, and if he wanted me, I'd like to work for him.'

She turned to him impulsively. 'But, Mr. Ross, a man of my father's age can't possibly go flying off to Greenland in an aeroplane! Surely you see that?'

He shrugged his shoulders. 'I took a man of seventy-eight from the Mackenzie to Quebec, two years ago. And that was in winter, too.'

The names meant nothing to her; the distance might have been from Holland Park to Kensington. She was irritated at his denseness, and she said:

'I'm trying to get you to help me, Mr. Ross. My father's much too old to go on such an expedition.'

The pilot said shortly: 'That seems to be your father's business, not mine. I can't go diving into that.'

Her lips tightened, and she said: 'I had hoped to get more help from you than this.'

They walked on for a minute or two in silence. Presently he stopped, and turned to face her. 'You must understand the way I'm fixed, Miss Lockwood,' he said. 'I fly aeroplanes and seaplanes for a living. That's what I do. At present I'm out of a job. Your father seems to want to offer me a job to do what I'm specially fitted for—that flying in the north. If I get the offer of that job, I'll have to take it—if I don't, that's just too bad. But you can't expect me to evade a good job when it's offered to me.'

She had never had to earn her living. In her outlook she was very far from the pilot. She stood looking up at him, the quick anger mounting in her. 'I see what you mean, Mr. Ross.' she said evenly. 'You're going to do all you can to encourage my father to go on this trip, in order that you can make money out of him. It doesn't mean a thing to you that he's an old man, that his health won't stand the sort of life that you and your sort can put up with. So long as you get your wages, that's the only thing you care about.'

He was as angry as she was. He thrust his hands deep in his pockets, and stared down at her. 'You can put it that way if it pleases you,' he said. 'It's not true but if it pleases you to think like that, it's O.K. by me. And, anyway, you've made my mind up for me.'

The quick colour mounted in her cheeks; she had very seldom argued with an angry man. 'What do you mean by that?'

He eyed her steadily. 'I mean just this, Miss Lockwood. I think your father is as fit as I am. If he wants me to fly him to Greenland, I'll fly him to Greenland if it snows ink, and neither you nor anybody else is going to stop me.'

There was a silence after that. They stood for some moments staring hotly at each other on the lawn. Presently Ross relaxed, smiled and said:

'I'm sorry that we can't agree, Miss Lockwood. Let's forget about it. He may decide not to go.'

She shrugged her shoulders. 'For his sake I very much hope he does.'

They turned and walked towards the house without another word spoken. Lockwood was in the study looking through *The Times*; they went together to the dining-room for breakfast. During the meal the girl hardly spoke at all.

At the end of it, Lockwood said: 'We might go through into the study if you've finished, Mr. Ross.'

In the study, with the door closed, he stood before the window filling his pipe.

'Well, Mr. Ross,' he said, 'I've thought about this matter a good deal. I don't think the difficulties are insuperable, although there seems to be more in it than I had supposed. I've decided to go on with it.'

Ross said: 'All right. If you want to give me the job I should be very glad to do it for you.'

The don smiled. 'You must go to Coventry and see my brother. I'll give you a note to him. If he approves of you, come back here and we'll start making plans. I realise there's not much time to lose.'

Ross went down to the station, and took the next train up to Coventry. He got there early in the afternoon, left his bag at the cloak-room, and walked up through the town to the offices of Lockwood Tube and Wire Company. He told his business to the uniformed commissionaire; then he waited for some time in an oak-panelled waiting-room, reading the trade papers on the table. Finally, he was led down a long panelled corridor and shown into an office.

A thin, middle-aged man, slightly bald, got up to meet him. 'My name is Hanson,' he said. 'I am Sir David's secretary. I understand you have a note to Sir David from his brother?'

Ross showed the note. The secretary took it from him, opened it, and read it through. Then he laid it carefully upon his desk. 'Ah, yes . . . I see. You are Mr. Ross?'

'Sir David is busy at the moment. I think he may wish to see you in a few minutes. In the meantime, would you give me a few details of your experience in aviation, Mr. Ross?'

The few details proved to be a comprehensive survey of his life to that date, with cross-references to people who could vouch for him, with their telephone numbers where he knew them. The secretary took this down in shorthand very rapidly. It took about twenty minutes; at the end of that time Mr. Hanson scanned his notes through quickly, and then said:

'Have you prepared any estimate of the cost of the journey that Mr. Cyril Lockwood proposes?'

Ross shook his head. 'I'm afraid not. I only heard about it for the first time yesterday afternoon. I could give you a few very rough figures now, if you like.'

Hanson turned to a fresh page of his notebook.

'Perhaps that would be a good thing. Then I can give the whole picture to Sir David in a very few minutes.'

Ross sat in silence for a minute. Then he said: 'Well, the most expensive single item is the aeroplane, of course. Sea-plane, I should say—it's a job for a float machine. And I don't think we shall find it possible to get insurance for it.'

The secretary made a note. 'Is that because of the great risk?'

'Not entirely. Flights of that sort are done so seldom that there's no experience for underwriters to base a rate on.'

'I understand.' He made another note.

The pilot said: 'We should have to have a six- or seven-seater cabin seaplane for the job. You won't want to spend more money than you need, of course. I could pick up one that had done five or six hundred hours in Canada for about six thousand dollars. Probably less.'

The secretary laid down his pencil, and stared at Ross. 'Do you mean a second-hand aeroplane, Mr. Ross?'

'Yes.'

There was a long pause. Then Hanson picked up his pencil again, and made another note. 'I doubt if Sir David would consider a second-hand machine for Mr. Cyril's expedition,' he said patiently. 'Still, I've made a note of the figure. What would a new one cost?'

'About twenty-five thousand dollars, for a Cosmos with a Wasp engine, on floats. A good second-hand one would be quite all right, and you can pick them up very cheaply now.'

The secretary shook his head. 'I think Sir David would be very much against it.'

'All right. I'd rather have a new machine, of course; the work of maintenance will be much less. But I wouldn't let that kill the expedition at the start.'

Hanson looked down his nose. 'I do not think that that will be the case, Mr. Ross.'

The pilot was silent for a minute, revising his ideas. 'If you decide to have a new machine, we'll have to cable an order to the Cosmos people right away, because our time is getting very short indeed. They're in Detroit. Or, better still, let me have five minutes on the telephone with Johnnie Finck, their sales manager.'

The secretary made another note. 'Sir David would very much prefer to use a British aeroplane,' he said. 'Isn't that possible?'

The pilot shook his head. 'If you want the best machine for flying in the North, you must go to the States for it,' he said. 'The British manufacturer hasn't gone for that market.'

'Sir David will be disappointed.'

Ross shrugged his shoulders. 'I've got to tell him what machine is best for the job. I only wish he'd start in building aeroplanes himself to suit Canadian conditions.'

The secretary gave him a long look. 'He may want to talk that over with you,' he said discreetly. 'In the meantime, we must take it that it's an American machine?'

'That's right.'

They proceeded with the budget, and came presently to the pilot's remuneration.

'I should like some form of payment by results,' said Ross. 'There's about five months' work in this thing, as I see it. You can pay me monthly at the rate of eight hundred a year, starting now, with a bonus of five hundred pounds if the job is done all right. We can define what that means with Mr. Cyril Lockwood later on. But I can tell you this—the job's worth that amount of money.'

Hanson made his note. 'I have no doubt of it,' he said drily. 'I am quite prepared to put that to Sir David. In principle, it seems a very fair proposal.'

In half an hour they had covered all the ground; the secretary totted up the figures on his pad. 'Including your estimate for photography, nine thousand seven hundred and eighty pounds,' he said. 'Call it ten thousand.' He eyed Ross keenly. 'Sir David very much dislikes increasing estimates. Once a figure has been given, it has to be adhered to. If we said twelve thousand pounds to cover every contingency—should we be safe at that?'

Ross said: 'Absolutely, I should think.'

The secretary made his note.

He looked over the pages of his notes. 'I think that covers everything,' he said at last. He got up from his desk. 'Now I'm going to ask you to excuse me for a minute or two.'

He went out through a side door into the next office, and closed it softly behind him. Ross was left waiting for a time; in the next room there was a low murmur of voices. Ten minutes later the secretary reappeared.

'Would you come in?' he said. 'Sir David would like to see you.'

Ross went through into the next room, a large office furnished with rather shabby chairs, and a large desk. A thick-set, heavy man in a black coat was sitting at the desk. He was going bald; he had a firm, determined face with much the same features as the don. The relationship was evident. The face was vaguely familiar to Ross from the illustrated papers; Sir David Lockwood was not a Lord Nuffield, but he was a very wealthy man.

He raised his head, gave Ross a long, appraising look,

and motioned to a chair with the end of the fountain pen in his hand. 'Sit down.'

Ross obeyed in silence.

'You've been in Canada?'

'I was there for about four years.'

'What sort of a car did you drive out there?'

'A Packard.'

'Like it?'

'Yes.'

'Why?'

This, Ross felt, was not what he had come to talk about at all, but he began to talk diffidently about motor cars to the man who had forgotten more than Ross had ever known. Sir David kept him talking upon varied subjects for ten minutes by the clock. At the end of that time he had satisfied himself that the pilot talked good sense, that he was modest, probably competent to maintain things mechanical, probably honest and hardworking.

He turned to the letter that Hanson had laid before him. 'You spent last night with my brother, I see. He tells me that he's decided to go on this Greenland trip. He wants you to take him.'

'Yes, sir.' The pilot hesitated. 'There's one thing that I'm a bit worried about.'

The grey eyes of the manufacturer fixed his own. 'Well, what's that?'

Ross said: 'His daughter seems to be very much against the flight. She had a talk with me about it this morning.'

'Alix? What's it got to do with her? What's she got against it?'

'She thinks her father is too old to go off on a trip like that.' The pilot hesitated. 'I thought you'd better know the way she feels.'

The manufacturer gave a snort. 'Too old? I never heard such nonsense in my life. That girl wants a good whipping —that's what she wants. Too old! Has she said that to my brother?'

'I really couldn't say.'

'You don't want to pay any attention to that. Is there any reason, in your view of it, why my brother shouldn't go?'

Ross considered before answering. 'I don't think so,' he said at last. 'There's a certain risk in flying so far over the open sea, of course. I should go by Reykjavik; that splits it up

33

into two hops of about six hundred miles each over sea. But flying down the coast of Greenland ought to be all right if we wait and pick a decent day for it, and when we get to this place Brattalid we make a camp and operate from there quite normally. At least, that's how I see it at the moment.'

Sir David nodded. 'My brother has had good health all his life. He's fifty-eight years old. Are you afraid of trouble if you take him with you?'

'Not in the least.'

'Of course not. Too old!' He sat brooding at his desk for a moment. Then he shot a sidelong glance at Ross. 'He's three years younger than I am.'

The pilot could not think of anything to say to that.

The manufacturer turned to the secretary. 'Twelve thousand, Hanson?'

'Yes, Sir David. That was the outside figure—it includes the whole cost of the machine. It should come out a good deal less.'

The older man scrutinised the list of figures for a moment, then turned back to Ross. 'It's a lot of money. You'll have to show results for that amount of money.'

The pilot shook his head. 'I wouldn't take this job if I had to guarantee results, sir. It's too unusual. I'll do my best, and in my judgment we can get the photographs Mr. Lockwood wants without much difficulty. But we may run into sheer bad luck.'

'I don't want you to take more risks than are essential to the job. Especially if my brother's going with you.'

Ross nodded. 'It should be quite all right. But if it's not, I shall play for safety first. In that case, we may spend the money and show no results—this year, at any rate.'

The manufacturer looked at him closely, weighing him up. At last he said: 'Well, we'll let it go at that. Mr. Hanson's going to check up on your references. If those are satisfactory, he'll write you a letter of engagement on the terms you want. You'll have to fix up with Hanson and my brother the conditions for your bonus.'

He got up from his desk. 'All right. I shall be seeing more of you, I expect.'

Ross said: 'I'll do my best to get this through all right, sir.'

'You'd better. Don't pay any attention to that silly girl. I'll sort her out at the weekend.'

34

He paused, standing erect behind his desk. 'I offered Cyril twenty-five thousand for his research six years ago,' he said. 'He hasn't taken a thousand yet. I hope this means he's come to realise that money's meant to be used.'

Ross left the room with Hanson. In the outer office he turned to the secretary, and said:

'We shall have to hop around now, Mr. Hanson, if we're going to get through in time. How soon can we start and order the machine?'

The secretary looked down his nose. 'Today is Friday. If all goes right, we should be able to engage you definitely on Monday, Mr. Ross. After that, you can make a start.'

'All right. I'm going back to Oxford now to see Mr. Lockwood. Over the week-end I'll make out a programme of what we've got to do. Unless I hear from you to the contrary, I'll be back here on Monday morning.'

The secretary smiled. 'I should be ready for you by that time. But you've got six weeks, or more. A day or two won't make much difference.'

The pilot said: 'That's just where you go wrong, Mr. Hanson. If we get that machine delivered, shipped and erected in this country, ready to start, six weeks from now, we shall do damn well. I don't believe it can be done that quickly. But that's when we've got to have it. If we don't get that order placed on Monday you can call the whole thing off.'

The secretary nodded. 'I see what you mean. I'll talk it over with Sir David.'

Ross left the works, and was carried swiftly in the works car to the station. He caught the next train back to Oxford. He got there at about nine o'clock at night, and rang up Lockwood from a telephone booth at the station.

The don said: 'I have had a long talk with my brother on the telephone, Mr. Ross. Would you care to come and spend the night again? That's fine. Come along now.'

Ross took a taxi to the house in Norham Gardens; the job seemed sufficiently secure for that expenditure. He was very tired; before meeting Lockwood he made an excuse to the parlourmaid and went and washed his face. Then he went to the study; the don was there with his daughter. Lockwood got up from his desk and came to meet him; the girl remained in her deep chair, reading her book.

Lockwood said: 'You seem to have made a good impression on my brother, Mr. Ross.'

35

The pilot smiled. 'I'm very glad to hear it. I had a long talk with his secretary before I saw Sir David.'

'You mean Mr. Hanson? He's been with my brother a long time. He helps me a great deal with my income-tax.'

They talked about the expedition generally for a time.

'I'll have a look at the route over the week-end,' said Ross. 'The machine will have to be shipped to Southampton. I'll get it erected somewhere on Southampton Water. Then we'll have to go to one of the places in the north—Scotland —Oban, or somewhere like that. From there to Reykjavik in Iceland must be eight or nine hundred miles—we'll have to make that in one hop. From Reykjavik to Angmagsalik is five or six hundred, I believe, and about the same from Angmagsalik to Julianehaab. But I'll have to look it all up— I'm only speaking from memory. We'll have to have radio for a trip like that. That's another thing.'

'I suppose so,' said Lockwood vaguely. 'Tell me, are there any hotels at these places, do you think?'

The pilot shook his head. 'There won't be anything at Angmagsalik or Julianehaab.'

'Where should we sleep?'

'Oh, there's bound to be a Danish family who'll take us in. I don't think we shall have to camp until we get to this place Brattalid.'

He glanced at Lockwood. 'Does anybody live at Brattalid?'

'I really couldn't say. I believe it's quite deserted.'

Ross nodded slowly. 'It looks as though we'll have to depend entirely on ourselves.' He thought about it for a minute or two. Seventy miles from anything, right up near the Arctic Circle. He would have to be very thorough in his plans for camp equipment and provisions.

He said: 'Sir David seemed very anxious that everything should be done properly. It's rather a relief, that.'

Lockwood asked: 'Done properly—in what way?'

'I mean, he realises that the trip is going to cost a good bit of money. He wouldn't hear of buying a second-hand ship.'

The don frowned a little. 'How much is it going to cost, Mr. Ross?'

Ross said: 'It's a bit difficult to say, at this stage. Your brother gave me a limit of twelve thousand pounds.'

In the far corner of the room, in her deep chair by the fire, the girl dropped the book that she had been pretending to read. She turned and stared at the two men.

'Twelve thousand pounds!' she cried.

The pilot turned and looked at her. 'Sir David gave me that as the outside figure that he was prepared to spend,' he said. 'Actually, it won't come to anything like that unless we get some real bad luck. If everything goes well, by the time we've sold the machine second-hand and cleaned it all up, I daresay it will have cost six or seven thousand.'

'But that's a small fortune! It can't possibly cost anything like that amount!'

The pilot's lips tightened; he was very tired. 'I'm afraid it can, Miss Lockwood. We shall probably drop three thousand selling the machine second-hand, as a start. Shipping it from Detroit to Southampton will cost about three hundred. Fuel and oil may cost another four hundred, by the time we've got it shipped to Greenland. I'm not quite sure about the cost of the photography—something between a thousand and fifteen hundred pounds by the time that the mosaic is made up. We shan't be far off the figure that I said.'

The girl said: 'It's perfectly fantastic!'

Ross sighed. 'I'm sorry, but that's what aircraft cost to run, Miss Lockwood.'

The girl got up from her chair and came over to the desk. There was an air about her that reminded Ross immediately of Sir David. 'Daddy,' she said, 'this wants looking into a bit more. Isobel told me that she flew to Rome the other day for fifteen pounds, and I believe that's further. It can't possibly cost this amount of money. Don't make any decision tonight.'

The don glanced at Ross. 'It seems to have gone up a good deal,' he said mildly. 'You told me four thousand yesterday.'

In his fatigue, depression closed down on the pilot. 'That was reckoning on a second-hand aeroplane,' he said. 'But your brother won't hear of that. If he's got the money to spend, I think he's quite right.'

Lockwood said: 'Ah—yes, I had forgotten that. I suppose you lose more money when you're selling a new machine than when you're selling a second-hand one.'

'Certainly. It's like a motor-car.' He paused. 'With the slump that's on in Canada, the price of a second-hand ship is very low. It makes a lot of difference.'

Lockwood nodded. 'I quite understand.'

The girl burst out: 'But, Daddy, Uncle David can't possibly go spending thousands of pounds in this way. Think what that money would mean to them down at the Mission!'

37

The pilot came to the conclusion that he had had about as much as he could stand. He got up from his chair. 'I'm a bit tired,' he said. 'Would you mind if I went to bed now? We can go on with this in the morning.'

Lockwood looked with irritation at his daughter. He wished that she had kept out of it. He knew instinctively that the pilot was in the right in this contention, that Alix was making a fool of herself. He wanted to spend the rest of the evening with Ross making plans for the expedition; at the same time, he could hardly discipline his daughter in front of this young man. Besides, the pilot might be really tired. He said:

'By all means, Mr. Ross. You know the way to your room. We'll go on with our arrangements after breakfast.'

The pilot nodded. 'We shall be fresher then. After that, I must get back to London if we're going on with this. Good night, Mr. Lockwood—don't get up.' He passed the girl and nodded to her coldly. 'Good night, Miss Lockwood.'

He went up to his room, undressed moodily, and got into bed. The job did not appear to be so very safe, after all. It was all right except for that infernal girl. He hoped that she'd marry a commercial traveller, and have triplets. Keep her quiet. But no commercial traveller would look at her. A little bitch, with ugly clothes and with an ugly mind. To hell with her.

He slept.

In the study below Alix faced her father. 'I know you're cross with me, Daddy,' she said quietly, 'but I can't help it. I'm quite sure there's something wrong here. It can't possibly be necessary to spend all those thousands of pounds.'

Lockwood said irritably: 'My dear, your uncle has built up a very big business, and he's got a very good business man as his secretary. Don't you think we might leave the money side to him? After all, it's their money. If you're afraid that Mr. Ross is trying to cheat them, you can set your mind at rest. He'll be a clever man if he gets anything past Hanson.'

The girl said: 'I know, Daddy. But the whole thing is being so rushed. Don't go any further with it tonight. Is Uncle David coming down tomorrow?'

'Yes. He'll be here in the evening.'

Daddy, how much is Mr. Ross going to make out of this expedition? How much are you paying him?'

Her father said: 'I really don't know. David said that

they'd fixed up terms with him, but he didn't say what they were.'

She stuck her chin out. 'Well, I'd like to know.'

'My dear, he's got to earn his living, like everybody else.'

'I know, Daddy. But he's in such a hurry to rush us into this, and there's really no hurry at all. It's over ten weeks before you want to be there, on the first of August. I know you've got to get there, but Isobel flew further than that in one day when she went to Rome. It all makes one smell a rat.'

Lockwood faced his daughter. 'Do you think he's a rogue?' he asked directly.

She hesitated. 'No . . . I don't quite think that. But I think he wants this job very badly, and he's trying to rush you into it.'

There was a long silence after she said that. Lockwood, for all his years, was still the victim of an inferiority complex. He knew himself to be a good lecturer, a useful member of his college, a fine classical scholar and a brilliant archæologist. With these accomplishments, he was a child in business and in money matters, and he knew it. He knew it much too well. Various sad experiences as a younger man had shown him that he could be imposed upon, and he had accepted the position with docility.

He said doubtfully: 'I'm not sure that you're right, Alix. I like him very well.'

'I know, Daddy. But that doesn't alter the fact that he's hoping to get a job out of you.'

He said: 'All right, my dear. We'll wait and talk it over with David when he comes.'

She said, a little hesitantly: 'It's going to be a terribly difficult expedition, anyway. You couldn't go back to Crete, I suppose?'

'Crete!' He stared at her. 'Don't talk so foolishly. Nobody's going to Crete. The work is in Greenland.'

She said no more.

Ross got up in the morning worried and upset. It seemed to him that the Lockwoods had got to realise that flying aeroplanes to Greenland cost a lot of money. Unless they were prepared to face that fact he would do better to wash his hands of it, go back to his aunt at Guildford, and scratch about for something else to do. A flight like that could only be done at all if money were no object, particularly in the time.

39

He went down moodily to breakfast. After the meal he went with Lockwood to the study. The don said: 'David is coming here this evening, Mr. Ross. What are your movements?'

The pilot smiled. 'I see that you're not quite decided on this thing,' he said. 'I think I'd better get back to London. I can start to look up points about the route and the formalities, although it's Saturday. I've arranged to go to Coventry on Monday morning unless I hear from them to the contrary. We'd better stick to that arrangement. By that time you'll know more about it.'

Lockwood nodded. He was a little ashamed of his vacillation; in the cold light of morning he could not quite see why he had agreed to hesitate. Moreover, he liked the young man, and he realised that the uncertainty was making a bad start for the adventure, if it was to come off. Still, Alix was probably right; it would be better not to rush things.

He said: 'I think that's wise. My brother will be here this evening, and I'll have a talk with him. We shall be able to make a definite decision one way or the other then. Are you on the telephone, Mr. Ross?'

The pilot hesitated. 'I'm afraid I'm not. I'll give you my address at Guildford; a telegram will get to me.'

'That will do perfectly. I will wire you if there's any change in the arrangements.'

Ross went back to London, half convinced that the girl had killed his job stone dead. He went first to the Guild of Air Pilots; from there he went to the aeronautical department of the Automobile Association. He spent all afternoon there, plotting his route and examining the records of previous flights to Greenland. Later in the afternoon he tried to get in touch with a fuel company upon the telephone, but it was Saturday afternoon and he had no luck.

In the evening he went down to Guildford. He leaned against the kitchen wall, his hands thrust deep into his trouser pockets, and told Aunt Janet all about it. She heard him to the end in pawky silence.

'It's a terribly costly piece of research,' she said at last. 'The lassie's got the right idea of it, to my way of thinking.'

The pilot shrugged his shoulders. 'If they want survey made of that part of the world, that's what it will cost them,' he said. 'I can't tell you if they really want it done or not. I think they're drawing back a bit now.'

'And well they may,' said his aunt drily. 'It's a mighty lot of money to be spending at one go.'

She turned to him. 'If they dinna want you, Donald, what else would you do?'

He shook his head. 'I don't know. I'll have to find a job of some sort, soon.'

'Aye,' she said prosaically, 'that's a fact.' She got up and began moving about the kitchen. 'Come on and help me lay the supper. Ye'll do nae good with worrying.'

In Oxford the Bentley, driven by the well-disciplined, efficient young chauffeur in blue uniform, turned into Norham Gardens at about six o'clock and drew up at Lockwood's house. The chauffeur sprang from his seat and came round to the door; Sir David heaved his heavy body up and got out. 'You'd better wait a bit,' he grunted. 'Give my bag to the maid.' He went forward into the house.

Ten minutes later he was lighting a cigar, seated alone with his brother Cyril in the study. 'Well, how about the Arctic?' he said, heavily jocular. 'Got your fur coat yet? Made all your plans?'

Not for the first time, Cyril Lockwood felt a fool over this thing. 'As a matter of fact, I haven't yet,' he said. 'I thought we'd have another talk about it.'

'What's the matter? I thought you'd made up your mind to go. Been talking to Alix?'

The don stared at the manufacturer. 'How did you know about Alix?'

Sir David blew a long, aromatic cloud of smoke. 'That pilot told me she was dead against you going on the trip at all.'

'He told you that? I wonder how he knew.'

'She had one of her little talks with him.'

'Did she, though? Well, it was straight of him to tell you about it. I thought he was a good lad, David.'

'Oh, aye—he's all right. But there's plenty more where that one came from. You want a good pilot if you're going on a trip like that.'

'I suppose you do. Is he a good pilot?'

'I don't know. Hanson will know by Monday.' He turned to the don. 'Well, Cyril, are you going or not?'

The don hesitated. 'I don't know. It's going to cost far more than I ever thought, David. I was quite staggered when Ross came back last night and told me the figures.'

The manufacturer said: 'What's that got to do with you?'

'It's your money that you've put at my disposal, David—very generously. I've got to advise you how to spend it. I've got to be very sure that you spend it to the best advantage. And—well, I'm not sure. It seems to me that this Brattalid expedition may cost more than it's worth.'

'Suppose you stick to archæology and let me spend my money my own way.'

The don stared at him. 'My dear chap—I didn't mean to hurt you.'

'And you haven't. But look here, Cyril—you'll hurt me very much if you don't start and use that money that I put in your research account six years ago. In six years you've spent nine hundred and thirty-four pounds out of twenty-five thousand. If you tell me that in six years you couldn't have done more if you'd spent more money—I'll call you a bloody fool.'

The don nodded. 'You're perfectly right. But it seems such a lot to spend.'

'The tubes will make as much again when you've spent that.'

'I suppose so. How are the works going?'

'Can't grumble, things being as they are. I got Hanson to figure out last week's output if it was stretched out end to end. Forty-seven miles of drawn steel tubes we turned out—in one week. That's over and above the wire.'

'It's very wonderful, David.'

The other blew out a long cloud of smoke. 'Aye,' he said quietly, 'it's very wonderful. In twenty years' time I shall be dead, and all that tube will be just little smears of rust upon the ground. In thirty years Coventry folks won't know the name of Lockwood, unless they go and read the plate up at the Hospital. But in thirty years people will still be talking of your work. In a hundred and thirty years. That's what strikes me as wonderful.'

There was a short silence.

'That's what it is,' the manufacturer said at last. 'I make the money, and you make the name. I wish we could row together a bit more.'

The don shifted uneasily in his chair. 'I didn't know you felt like that,' he said. 'It's quite true. There is a lot that could be done . . .'

'Then, for God's sake, go ahead and do it,' said the other

42

testily. 'This Brattalid thing, Cyril. Is it a good one? Will you find out something—something that's worth knowing?'

The don leaned his arms upon the desk. 'It's a good one, David,' he said seriously. 'I *know* the Irish went to Greenland. I *know* they did, but I can't prove it yet. There's just the one link missing, still. That's the first thing that we've got to do—to establish definitely that they went there. After that there's the ethnological problem. What happened to the Irish that were there? What happened to the Norse settlers?'

He stared across the room. 'I never felt so certain in my life as I do about this thing,' he said quietly. 'There's something big there, David—waiting to be uncovered. I don't say that I shall get it. But someone will, one day.'

The other said: 'Go on and get it for yourself, and don't be a bloody fool.'

The don laughed, and relaxed. 'All right. I really had decided on it before I sent that young man up to see you. But then when he told me what it was all going to cost, it seemed too much to spend.'

'And Alix put her oar in, I suppose?'

'Alix thinks it's too dangerous.'

'If Alix were ten years younger I'd stretch her out across the couch and tan the pants off her.' The manufacturer threw the stub of cigar into the grate. 'When we get to thinking things are too dangerous—things that we want to do—we'll be no more good,' he said. 'That's right, Cyril. That makes a static business, when you get to thinking things are dangerous that you want to do. And a static business is a ruined business in a year or two.'

The don said mildly: 'Alix is a good girl.'

His brother said: 'She looks it. She dresses like hell, Cyril. Put her in among our Coventry girls and she'd look like a dead fish.'

Lockwood sighed. 'I suppose the truth of it is that she doesn't get about enough.'

'Too true. She'll be an old woman in a year or two unless she can snap out of it.'

He got up from his chair. 'It's settled that you're going, then?'

'I think so. I'd like to have that young man Ross for the pilot, David, if he's good enough. We get to know something about young men, here in Oxford. I'd have confidence in him, I think.'

'Aye. I daresay he could do the job as well as anyone. He's coming up to Coventry on Monday. He's in a great hurry to place the order for his aeroplane, because of the delivery.'

'I suppose that is very important,' said Lockwood vaguely.

'Well, you won't be able to fly to Greenland without it.' They walked in the garden till dinner-time, talking of other matters. After dinner Lockwood had business in his study with a couple of young men; Sir David went out into the garden with Alix in the still, warm, summer evening. The old parlourmaid brought them their coffee at the table under the beech-tree.

When she had gone the manufacturer said to the girl: 'I here you think your father's too old to go to Greenland.'

She looked up, startled. 'I never said that to him.'

'I should hope not. Pretty mean if you had. But you think it, just the same.'

She met his eyes. 'Who told you that, Uncle David?'

'That pilot chap who came to see me.'

'Oh . . . Well, I did say that to him. And I do think it.' She dropped her eyes. 'I don't want to be nasty. But Daddy's nearly sixty, and Greenland is a job for a young man. I wouldn't say that to him, because I wouldn't want to hurt him. But it's true, all the same.'

'Greenland's the job your father wants to do.'

'I know it is. But he could find something else that wouldn't be so strenuous.'

'You talk as if he were an invalid. Look at me. I'm three years older and three stone heavier. I wouldn't mind going to Greenland.'

She said doubtfully: 'You're different. I mean, you've done things—all your life, Uncle David. But Daddy's not like you. I'd be afraid of him getting wet and not changing or eating bad food and getting ill. And if he got ill upon a trip like that, with only the pilot and mechanics, it would be awful.'

She paused. 'It'd be almost as good if he left the field work to a younger man, and studied it back here.'

'Not quite as good. He knows more about this thing than anybody else. At least, that's how I understand it.'

She hesitated. 'I know. But one really must be practical.'

'Sometimes it's better to be kind, Alix.'

There was a long silence.

'I hate the idea of him going in an aeroplane. He's never done any flying.'

'Have you?'

'No.'

'I suppose that's why you're so afraid of it for him.'

'I suppose so.'

Sir David said: 'You'd better make the best of it and let him go. If you stick your toes in you can probably stop him, and you might be sorry all your life. Cyril's more set on this thing than anything I can remember in the last ten years. You'd better make the best of it, and be a sport.'

She said irritably: 'It's all that wretched pilot, I believe. He wasn't half so definite about it all before the pilot came. He just talked Daddy into it.'

Her uncle was doubtful. 'Your father was very set on it when last I talked to him. I don't think its anything new.'

There was a little pause.

'If only I could feel that he'd be well looked after if he did get ill . . .' she said.

'Well, that's a real point, I admit. Let's see now if we can't get over that.'

On Monday morning Ross left Guildford by an early train. He was depressed about the whole affair, but he had heard nothing from Lockwood and so his arrangement to go to Coventry held good. He got to the works at about half-past eleven and was shown into Mr. Hanson's office.

The secretary met him with a smile. 'I think you will be able to go straight ahead today, Mr. Ross,' he said. 'I have drafted this letter of engagement. If you would read it through now, I will have it re-typed for Sir David to sign.'

The pilot sat down with the letter. A flood of relief swept over him; it was quite all right. He had got the job. Now he had a straight run of well-paid, interesting work to get his teeth into—a hard job, maybe, but not more than he could manage. He would increase his reputation if he pulled this off successfully.

He read the letter carefully. 'That's quite in order,' he said. 'That covers everything.'

'All right. Sir David will sign it this afternoon.' The secretary put it with the other papers on his desk. 'Now you will want to get to work, I expect. I hear you're going to have another passenger.'

The pilot stared at him. 'Who's that?'

'Miss Lockwood. I understand she's going with her father.'

CHAPTER III

FOR a minute the pilot sat silent, stunned by this announcement. He had the good sense to say nothing till he had reflected a little. He did not want to lose a good job, but he couldn't possibly take that infernal girl in the machine with them. The flight would be difficult enough in any case; with her nagging at his elbow all the time it would become impossible.

He said quietly at last: 'I hadn't reckoned on that. That makes it very difficult.'

The secretary was genuinely surprised; he took off his eyeglasses. 'Why is that? I understand that the machine was to be a seven-seater.'

Ross was accustomed to dealing with the uninformed. He said patiently: 'It's designed to carry seven people on short hauls, when you don't have to lift much fuel. But this is different. I shall have to carry petrol for fifteen hundred miles on some of these hops, if we're going to be safe. There's going to be mighty little load to play about with when you're carrying that weight of fuel. An extra passenger means you can take less petrol.'

'I see. I hadn't realised that there would be that difficulty.'

The pilot bit his lip. 'It's not the only one.'

'What other difficulties are there, Mr. Ross?'

'There's the accommodation. I'd only reckoned to take one tent.'

'But you can take another tent?'

'Surely, but it all weighs more. There's her emergency rations, and her sleeping bag and luggage, and her seat. They all put up the weight, and that means less fuel still.'

He paused. 'I'd like to think this over, Mr. Hanson, before deciding one way or the other. It's a pretty serious thing to have to take a passenger upon a show like this who can't do anything to help. It's all adverse, if you understand me. You add to the risks without getting anything for it.'

46

The secretary said: 'I understand what you mean. Let me have a talk with Sir David, Mr. Ross. It may be that she could go out by boat.'

The pilot nodded. 'That would be much better, if she's got to go at all. The photographer will have to go by boat in any case, even if it means he's got to stay there all the winter till the next boat comes to fetch him home. After all, Mr. Lockwood is the only one who's really pressed for time.'

'I don't suppose Miss Lockwood could stay in Greenland all the winter, Mr. Ross.'

The pilot thought that that would be the best thing that could happen to her, but didn't care to say so.

Hanson picked up his papers and went through to the inner office to consult his chief; presently Ross was called in. Sir David looked him up and down. 'Mr. Hanson tells me that there's a difficulty about Alix,' he said.

Ross said: 'Taking her makes the flight a good deal more difficult, sir. It adds to the load, and so cuts down the fuel that I can take off with. And on this job I'll want all the range I can get.'

The manufacturer stared at him. 'Do you mean the aeroplane won't be big enough to do the job?'

The pilot hesitated. 'That's more or less what it comes to.'

'Well, get a bigger aeroplane.'

Ross was at a loss for a moment. Sir David saw his difficulty, and leaned forward on his desk. 'See here, Mr. Ross,' he said. 'You've just got to revise your plans, and that's all there is to it. There was one passenger—now there are two. I've decided that Alix is going with her father, and that's all about it. If the alteration means I've got to spend more money, work it out with Mr. Hanson and let me know how much more. But don't come up with any silly nonsense that it can't be done, or I'll get another pilot. I tell you that straight.'

The pilot met his eyes. 'It's making a difficult job more difficult,' he said. 'You'd better realise that, sir. It's not altogether a matter of the weights, nor the size of the machine.'

The secretary shifted slightly.

Sir David said: 'I see. You mean it's Alix herself.'

Ross nodded. 'I don't think Miss Lockwood is very well fitted to go on an Arctic expedition, sir.'

'In fact, you won't take her?'

'I'd like to think that over for a bit. It's going to add to my difficulties to take any girl on the trip. If you pile too much on me the flight may be a failure, and we'll all be sorry then.'

'She gave you a bit of the rough side of her tongue, I suppose?'

The pilot smiled. 'She did, but I wouldn't let that worry me. The trouble is, she doesn't believe in the flight at all. She thinks it's useless and extravagant. As a matter of fact, she thinks I'm doing all I can to swindle you. And I tell you straight, sir, I don't much fancy having that at my elbow all the way.'

'I see.' The manufacturer was silent for a minute. 'Why didn't you talk like this at first, instead of coming out with all that stuff about the aeroplane not being big enough?'

The pilot smiled. 'I didn't know how you'd take it,' he said simply.

The older man grunted. He eyed the pilot for a minute. 'I want Alix to go on this trip,' he said. 'My brother's not a young man, and the girl's offered to go with him. She's got a good heart, Mr. Ross.' The corners of his mouth twitched ever so slightly.

The pilot considered the position for a moment. He wanted to be reasonable. 'I've told you that I'd like to have a bit of time to think it over,' he said. 'Would you agree to leave it open for a week or so? I'll go ahead and make my plans upon the basis of two passengers. If I find it's really going to make things too difficult to take Miss Lockwood, I'll come and tell you so in good time. Then you can get another pilot, or send a man with Mr. Lockwood instead.'

Sir David thought about it for a minute. 'I'll give you this next week. You'll be seeing Alix again, Mr. Ross. Try and get alongside her. I want her to go, and I'd just as soon you had the job as anybody else.'

Ross nodded. 'I'll do my best, sir. I've only spoken to her twice, but each time we had a bloody row.'

'Well, see you don't have a third.'

Ross went back into Hanson's office and began upon the preparations for the flight. That afternoon they put in a transatlantic telephone call to Johnnie Finck, in Detroit. It came through at about four o'clock, clear and distinct.

'Hey, Johnnie,' said the pilot. 'This is Ross—Donald Ross, used to be with Cooper in Quebec. That's right. How are you keeping? How's Rosie? Fine. Look, Johnnie—I

48

want a ship, a new ship for delivery at once.'

The secretary listened on another receiver as they talked. 'I want the wings and the fuselage all chrome,' the pilot said. 'That's important. Tell Edo that I want the colonial-type pontoons, the strongest he can build for beaching. They've got to be able to take it, where I'm going to.'

They talked for a quarter of an hour. When he put down the telephone Ross had placed his order for delivery on the quayside in New York, crated and packed for shipment, in three weeks' time.

'It's the best I can do,' he said, a little ruefully. 'And that's better than I hoped for. Add a fortnight for the crossing— that means we'll have it in Southampton by June 25th. Then it's got to be erected and tested, and have the camera and wireless installed. We shan't get away before the first week in July.'

The secretary nodded. 'Still, that leaves three weeks before you want to be in Brattalid.'

'And that may not be too much, either. We may be later starting or we may get stopped by weather.'

They worked together till six o'clock upon the programme of arrangements for the flight. Then they got on the telephone to Lockwood in Oxford. Ross left Coventry shortly before seven, and was in the study in Lockwood's house by half-past nine. Alix was there; over a whisky and soda the pilot outlined to the don what had happened in Coventry. The girl sat quietly in a chair, saying nothing.

Presently Ross turned to her. 'Sir David told me that you had decided to come with us, Miss Lockwood,' he said pleasantly.

She said, a little primly: 'We decided that my father ought to have somebody with him.'

'Of course.' He turned again to the don. 'Have you got a map of Brattalid? I want to get an accurate idea of the area to be surveyed, so that we can get quotations for the job.'

Lockwood raised his eyes. 'Quotations?'

The pilot explained. 'I talked this over with Mr. Hanson. If you agree, we thought it would be best to put the photographic work with a firm of repute who are used to this sort of thing. You couldn't go to better people than Photowork— they do this all over the world. I'm going to see them to-morrow. I was going to try and fix that they should sent out a photographer ahead of us by one of the boats from Denmark, to meet us in Julianehaab. He'll probably have to start within the next fortnight to get there in time.'

'That seems to be a very good arrangement, Mr. Ross.'

'I think it will be, if I can get them to take the job upon those lines. I can get a man who's used to aero engines, too —most of their photographers are ground engineers as well. He'll be able to give me a hand with the maintenance of the machine.'

'Is that a very big job?'

'There's a lot of work in it—more than I'd care to tackle single-handed for any length of time. You must have help with a machine like that.'

The don got up and poured him out another whisky and soda. 'Have you made out a route yet, Mr. Ross?'

Ross took the glass. 'We'll have to go by Reykjavik and Angmagsalik,' he said. 'I'd really rather have started from the other side—from Halifax in Nova Scotia, or Quebec. I believe it would be easier that way. But it wouldn't be practical. Hanson or somebody would have to come over there with me right away, and you'd have to join us over there later. I'm afraid that's all too difficult. It's not practical to organise a flight over here and start it from America. Not in the time.'

'I suppose not.'

'I decided against that. In July we should be quite all right, going from here through Iceland. There's really only the pack ice at Angmagsalik—that's going to be a worry, but we'll have to take our chance of that.'

'Do you mean that there won't be water for the seaplane to land on?'

The pilot shook his head. 'There should be plenty of water at that time of the year. But as I understand it, the sea's never quite free from little bits of floating ice at Angmagsalik, even in the middle of the summer. If we hit one of those and rip a float up taking off, that finishes the expedition for this year.'

The don nodded without speaking.

Ross hesitated. 'I wish we hadn't got to go so far up north, but I can't see any way out of it. There's one thing, though. If you agree, I'd like to lay down fuel supplies for us to come back home the other way. Over to Hopedale in Labrador, down to Halifax, and finish up at New York.'

'By all means, if you prefer it. Why do you want to do that?'

'I think it might be easier. The middle of September;

that's the equinox. It's three months after mid-summer—getting a bit wintry up in those parts, Mr. Lockwood. I don't much like the thought of going up so far as Angmagsalik and Reykjavik so late in the season. We might run into trouble, and we don't want that.'

He paused. 'There's another thing. We'd sell the machine second-hand more easily on that side than on this.'

Lockwood opened an atlas on his desk. The pilot crossed the room and bent over his shoulder. 'There you are,' he said. He traced the route with his finger. 'Over to Hopedale—after that we're practically back in civilised parts. He stared at the map reflectively. 'Battle Harbour might be better.'

The don smiled. 'Hopedale,' he said thoughtfully. 'I like your idea of civilised parts.'

The pilot nodded. 'It's only about 600 miles from there down to Halifax. They've got everything you want there.'

From the atlas they turned to a study of the land round Brattalid. The only map they had was a very sketchy one forming part of an archæological paper, which was at pains to indicate that it was not guaranteed. 'I'll have to see if they can help me at the Danish Legation,' said Ross. 'But very probably there is no map. They may come and ask for the loan of our photographs when we get back, to make a map from. I've known that happen before now.'

They talked far on into the night. The pilot went to bed a very tired man.

Again he woke up early, and went down into the garden before breakfast. The girl was there before him; he approached her cordially. 'I'm glad you're coming with your father, Miss Lockwood,' he said. He must try and make the best of it. 'It's going to be quite a strenuous trip, and it'll help him to have you there.'

She nodded. 'It wouldn't be possible for him to go alone,' she said a little coldly. 'There's one thing, Mr. Ross. Most people say "Sir" when they speak to my father. Now that he's engaged you, I think you ought to do the same.'

The pilot did not answer for a moment. He must keep his temper at all costs, retain his sense of humour. He forced a smile.

'Surely,' he said. 'Would you like me to call you Madam?'

She flushed hotly. 'I don't think that will be necessary,' she said icily. 'You can go on calling me Miss Lockwood.'

The ringing of the breakfast gong relieved the situation.

He left Oxford after breakfast, and went by train to London. He spent the rest of the morning, lunch, and the early afternoon in a conference with Photowork, the first of many. In the late afternoon he went to the Danish Legation; the air attaché was out, and he made an appointment for the morning. He went to the Royal Aero Club and rang up Hanson in Coventry to report progress, and went home to Guildford for the night.

Over supper he told Aunt Janet all about it. 'I'm glad, for your sake, that you've got the job, Donald,' she said, 'though it's a terrible part of the world to be flying to. And so the lassie's gaeing with her father. Weel, I'd say that's no' a bad thing. She'll keep a check on you. You were always terrible wild with the money, Donald.'

He laughed. 'She'll keep a check on me all right,' he said ruefully.

There followed three weeks of intense restless work. He was wise enough to have the telephone installed in his aunt's house; but for that he could not have completed his arrangements in the time. He concluded his deal with Photowork in the first week, spent an afternoon with Jameson the engineer-photographer selected for the trip, and took the contract up to Coventry to be signed. He discovered that Greenland was a closed country to the casual tourist. First of all the Home Office required assurances that the expedition served a useful scientific purpose. They would then put it to the Foreign Office, who would approach the Danish Government through diplomatic channels for permission for the flight. If this were granted, five hundred pounds must be deposited in Copenhagen to pay for the expenses of a search if the machine were lost.

Sir David said: 'I'm beginning to understand why people don't go there for the week-end.'

It meant a lot of work for Ross. He visited the Home Office and the Foreign Office and the Danish Legation, not once but many times. He made two hurried trips to Oxford, while Lockwood negotiated with the Vice-Chancellor the formal request from the University to the Home Office that permission for the expedition should be applied for.

He made arrangements with Photowork, and with a small firm that built large cameras for the installation of the photographic gear in the machine. He made arrangements for the supply and installation of the wireless. He had several talks with the Canadian liaison officer at the Air Ministry; he found that the Dominion Government quite rightly insisted that he should carry a hundred pounds of emergency rations and a rifle and ammunition if he flew to Canada. He made arrangements with the police for a permit to buy a rifle.

Sir David went to Oxford each week-end during this time. On the first of these visits he had a serious talk with Alix.

'Well, Alix,' he said cheerfully, 'I fixed things up with Mr. Ross. He wasn't very pleased when he heard he'd got to take another passenger, but he came round all right.'

'I suppose you mean he wasn't very pleased when he heard he'd got to take me, Uncle David.'

The manufacturer said diplomatically: 'Only because you're a girl.'

'What's that got to do with it?'

'Now don't take that attitude. I won't have it, Alix. There's a lot of good sense in what he said.'

'What did he say?'

Sir David cocked an eye at her. 'He told Hanson that taking you was adverse—all debit and no credit, if you understand. He meant you weigh more, and your luggage weighs more, and your tent weighs more, and all that. That means he won't be able to lift so much petrol in the aeroplane, and so he won't get the flying range he would have had if you weren't going. That's true, of course. To balance that, he doesn't think that you can help him very much.'

'He'll find himself very glad of my help if Daddy gets ill.'

Her uncle looked at her doubtfully. 'Yes . . . if he does.'

She shrugged her shoulders. 'I know he doesn't want to take me.'

'Now, put that out of your head, Alix. He wants to do his job, and I've made it very plain to him that his job is to take you and your father to Greenland. But I see what he means. You'll have to do everything you can to help him on the flight, and not add to his work.'

'I shan't do that.'

He looked at her uncertainly. 'Have you ever done any camping?'

'Of course I have, Uncle David. I ran a troop of Guides up to two years ago.'

He looked dubious. 'I should think this would be a bit different to camping with the Girl Guides, Alix. Still, I suppose that's something. What about languages? I suppose you don't speak any Danish?'

She shook her head. 'If that's what you want, I could learn a good bit in six weeks.'

'Well, that's something on the credit side if you do that.'

He stared at her reflectively. 'Try and get alongside him,' he said at last. 'The biggest danger on a trip like this is when people are fighting each other all the time. He as good as told me that.'

'That's nice of him.'

He was suddenly irritated. 'Well, Alix, when it comes to the point, I'm going to leave it in his hands whether you go or not. If he thinks it's going to make his job too difficult to take a girl, you don't go and that's that. We'll find a young research lad to go with your father.'

She touched his arm. 'I'm sorry, Uncle David. I didn't mean to be a beast. Of course I'll do everything I can to help him with the trip.'

He glanced at her. 'What's the matter with him, Alix?'

She laughed shortly. 'I don't know—he's such a stupid man. And he thinks he knows everything. He doesn't seem to have an idea in his head beyond the number of gallons of petrol and the number of tins of bully beef.'

'Well, that's his job. And that's the job you've got to help in, if you're going on this trip.' He paused. 'You can't help him with your violin.'

She laughed. 'Don't be silly. But really I will do what I can.'

'That's better.' He looked her up and down. 'Are you going with all that hair on your head?'

She was genuinely surprised. 'Why not?'

'Get the nits in it, likely as not.'

She laughed again: 'Oh don't be so absurd!'

In the first few days of June Ross made a quick trip to Copenhagen with Jameson, the engineer-photographer. A ship was leaving Copenhagen for Iceland and Greenland; travelling slowly through the pack ice and calling at many settlements Jameson should reach Julianehaab shortly before they got there at the beginning of August. He took with him all the photographic equipment and most of their camping gear, food, equipment, and supplies.

In all they had nearly a ton of baggage. They visited the Gronlands Styrelse, and made a number of last-minute purchases. Then they went to the boat and saw the stuff on board; Ross said good-bye to Jameson, and stood watching as the vessel left the quay. Then he started back for London, travelling by night and day.

He was tired when he got back, but there was not time for rest. The seaplane left New York upon the day that he got back to England, on a ship bound for Southampton. He travelled down to Southampton, visited two aircraft works, and made arrangements with a firm at Hythe to erect the machine and house it for him during the test flights. He went back to Southampton, and made arrangements for the transport of the crated aeroplane by lighter from the ship to the works at Hythe. He interviewed the Customs both in London and Southampton, and entered into a long negotiation regarding the admission of the machine into the country in bond.

In London, the Royal Geographical Society told him where to get the concentrated foods, the pemmican and so forth, that he was compelled to carry as emergency rations in the machine. He visited each firm in turn arranging the lightest form of packing for the food; already he was desperately worried about weight. He bought a rifle and ammunition. Weight became his constant pre-occupation; he had certain limits that he must not overstep or he would carry insufficient fuel for safety. His worry over weight began to break his sleep; frequently he would wake at two in the morning and stay awake for hours.

In his researches into weight he weighed himself, and found that since he started on the job he had lost seven pounds. The fact cheered him; there were seven pounds in reserve that he had not known about.

He went down to Oxford and saw Lockwood and the girl. He weighed them both; the don was twelve stone six and the girl a little under nine stone. 'I'm getting flying suits, helmets, and boots for both of you,' he said. 'You'll be more comfortable that way, especially up North.' He figured quickly on a pad. 'In those suits, that makes you about two hundred and two pounds, sir, and you a hundred and forty-seven, Miss Lockwood.'

The girl asked: 'How much petrol weighs a hundred and forty-seven pounds, Mr. Ross?'

He raised his eyebrows. 'Enough for about ninety-five miles.'

She smiled. 'I see. You'll expect me to do a lot of work to be worth that amount of petrol.'

He was embarrassed, and said awkwardly: 'I wouldn't put it quite like that, Miss Lockwood. We shall be all right with the petrol we've got now, so long as we can keep the weight from creeping up on us.'

He turned to the don. 'I've made a note of thirty-five pounds for your technical equipment, sir. Now, about your personal luggage. I'm getting linen kitbags made up for you both—they'll save the weight of suitcases. I'm afraid you'll have to limit yourselves to fifteen pounds each.'

Alix said impulsively: 'But that's impossible! We can't go half across the world with only fifteen pounds for clothes and everything!'

The pilot turned and faced her. 'I'm afraid you've got to, Miss Lockwood,' he said firmly. 'I shall be taking nine pounds myself. I think if you start weighing out your things you'll find that you can get a great deal into fifteen pounds.'

She said: 'Daddy can't possibly take his dinner jacket in that.'

'He won't need it in Greenland, Miss Lockwood.'

'But what about the boat on the way back? We must change for dinner on the boat.'

The pilot sighed. 'He'll have to buy a dinner jacket in America. Or—how about this? If you like to pack a trunk with things I'll have it shipped to New York.'

The don said: 'Mr. Ross is right, Alix. I think the trunk is a very good idea. I'm quite sure you'll find that you can manage on fifteen pounds while we're travelling.'

The girl looked very doubtful, but said nothing more.

Lockwood said: 'How is the load looking now, Mr. Ross? How much petrol will we be able to take?'

The pilot lit a cigarette. 'It's rather indefinite,' he said. 'I arranged for the machine to have tanks for fifteen hundred miles. Some of that's in the fuselage, by the way—we shan't be able to smoke. But now that there are three of us, I shan't be able to get her off the water with that weight of fuel. Fourteen hundred miles brings her back to a thousand pounds overload—she should get off with that in good conditions.' He hesitated. 'You might say that we'll have thirteen hundred safe.'

'I see. How far is the longest flight we have to do?'

'Invergordon to Reykjavik—just on eight hundred miles.'

'You seem to have a good margin in hand.'

'And we may need it, Mr. Lockwood. If we don't I'll buy you a drink when we get to New York.'

He went back to London to unravel an appalling complication in the petrol shipments to Labrador.

Three days later the machine arrived at Southampton Docks. Ross was there to meet it, saw it unloaded, and travelled with it on the lighter to the works at Hythe, across Southampton Water. He stayed with it while it was erected, with the exception of one quick trip to London to expedite the delivery of the wireless apparatus. Then he was back with the machine, watching it come together. He was pleased with his judgment. It was a fine, robust, workmanlike seaplane, most suitable for the job it had to do.

When it was finished and ready for flight he had it put upon the scales. It was a hundred and four pounds over weight.

Desperately worried, he had it weighed again upon a different pair of scales. This time it was a hundred and ten pounds over weight. He did not have it weighed a third time for fear it might go higher still.

With two mechanics to help him he set to work to get the weight down. They tore out the light roofing and upholstery of the cabin, weighing each fragment as they took it out. They stripped the three seats of their upholstered backs, reducing them to bare steel frames; the sleeping-bags would serve to pad them a bit more. They ripped out the safety glass windows of the cabin and substituted cellon, that was lighter and would last the trip. They ripped out a luggage locker in the tail. They removed a few fittings for the land undercarriage, and scrapped a little ladder that made it easy to get into the cabin.

He weighed her again. She was still twenty-seven pounds over weight, but he let it go at that.

Then for three days he laboured with the wireless mechanics to install the radio. The worked eighteen hours a day, far on into each night. When it was finished they made a ground test of the wireless in the middle of the night. An unexpected fault developed in the set; it had to go back to the works next morning in a car.

Ross was on the telephone to the technical director of the wireless company early next morning, speaking his mind. Then he had the seaplane fuelled, and took it out for a short

57

test flight. He took off down Southampton Water after a short run and climbed to about two thousand feet; he stayed up for about an hour, pleased with the machine.

He landed with three pages of his pad covered with notes of minor adjustments and modifications to be done. Work started on those in the afternoon. Late that evening the wireless set came back again; they worked far on into the night refitting it to the machine. A ground test carried out at three in the morning was satisfactory; in the grey dawn Ross went to bed and slept for a few hours.

He was in the air again by ten o'clock, with two engineers of the wireless company with him. Transmission from the set seemed to be good. Reception was nil; the only thing that could be heard in the headphones was the rattle of sparks from the ignition systems of the engine. The homing indicator did not work at all.

Ross landed without delay, and taxied into the slipway in a black temper. Again he spoke his mind upon the telephone. Two officials started hurriedly from London; that afternoon there was a conference in the hangar and another short test flight to rub the experts' noses in the mess. By the late afternoon the fault was diagnosed. The magnetos and ignition wiring of the engine were electrically screened; the sparking plugs were not. The sensitivity of the receiver made screened plugs a necessity.

The telephone came into play again. One plug manufacturer could deliver a set of screened plugs in three months' time, another had plugs in stock but unsuitable for an American engine. The representative of the engine manufacturer, when appealed to, thought that he might get a set in Amsterdam.

Ross reported his difficulties by telephone to Hanson in Coventry and to Lockwood in Oxford, left Hythe, and went to London. He got there late at night, turned into a hotel, and slept very badly; early next morning he was with the engine representative. Together they rang up Amsterdam and talked for a quarter of an hour. Finally they had the satisfaction of arranging that a parcel of screened plugs, a set and a spare set, would be upon the afternoon plane from Amsterdam to Croydon.

Ross reported again to Coventry, and went down to Croydon. He met the air liner, claimed his parcel, travelled back to London, and went down to Hythe. He got to the hangar late at night; an engineer was waiting there to help him. Together they changed the eighteen sparking plugs, refitted the cowling of the engine, and saw the machine all ready for flight before they went to bed at about two o'clock in the morning.

That night he hardly slept at all. He was down at the hangar by eight o'clock and in the air by half-past eight with the wireless experts in the machine with him. The wireless troubles were now over. He stayed up for an hour and a half operating the set himself on all wave-lengths, transmitting in morse, homing on various stations. Finally he was satisfied, and landed with a lighter heart than he had had for some time.

He rang up Lockwood at Oxford. 'We're all set now, sir,' he said. 'I'd like to get away to Invergordon as soon as we can.'

'Is everything ready?'

The pilot said: 'The machine is all ready to start now. So far as I know, the only thing we've got left to do is to get your personal flying kit, sir, and Miss Lockwood's. If you could both meet me in London tomorrow morning we could get that, and then come on down here. Then we could have a short flight in the afternoon, sleep in the hotel here, and get away in the morning.'

He arranged that with them.

He went back to Guildford to his aunt, to spend the night with her. He had not been there for a week; she raised her eyebrows when she saw him.

'My! Donald,' she exclaimed, 'you're looking awfu' tired. Whatever ails you?'

He said irritably: 'I'm all right.'

'You're not all right—you're looking thin and peaked. What have you been doing with yourself?'

He said: 'It's been hard work getting this thing ready in the time. But the back of the job's broken now. Now there's only the flying to be done, and there's no real work in that.'

'Is there not?' There was a pawky sarcasm in her voice.

He sighed. 'Well, anyway, it'll be easier than the last month has been.'

'It will need to be.' She took him into her little sitting-room. 'Sit ye down, now, Donald, and stay quiet a bit while I get the supper. I got some meat and vegetables in when I got your telegram, so we could have a nice drop of Scots broth. And then there's the rice pudding with the golden syrup that you like. Go on, and sit ye down.'

He sank into a chair, and lit a cigarette. She came back from the kitchen in a minute. 'There's your evening paper.'

He did not open it, but sat smoking cigarettes quickly and restlessly, lighting one from the stub of the last. His mind kept running over the arrangements for his flight, searching for points that he had forgotten. Once or twice he made a note in pencil on the back of an envelope; in the last few days he had discovered that he could not altogether trust his memory.

When his aunt came into the sitting-room an hour later to call him to his supper she found him asleep in the chair, the paper unopened on his knee. She stood looking at him grimly for a minute, pursed her lips, and woke him up.

They went through to supper in her tiny kitchen.

Over the meal she said: 'I have over the half of a bottle of Phosferine left, that I was taking last winter when I was poorly. If I give it to you, Donald, will you mind and take it?' She paused. 'You're looking terribly run down.'

He was touched. 'I'm really quite all right, Aunt Janet.'

'Ye'll be better for the Phosferine.'

He said: 'I won't take yours. I'll get another bottle.'

'There's no call for you to go to that expense. I'll put it in your bedroom, and mind you take it.'

'It's awfully good of you. It might make me sleep a bit better.'

He began to tell her all his plans for the flight. She was not well versed in the geography of the North; he sketched a map for her on the back of a calendar that the grocer had sent her at the New Year. She watched intently as he traced the outlines of Greenland, Iceland, and Labrador; then she took it and hung it upon its nail in the wall, the back outwards so that she could see the map.

'I'll be keeping it by me,' she said. 'Will they pay for you to send a telegram now and again, Donald, the way I'll know where you are?'

He smiled. 'I'll be able to do that, Aunt Janet.'

'Only if they pay for it on your expense account, Donald. Now that you're making good money again you don't want to be throwing it away on telegrams, or any other way. Ye want to put it by.'

'All right, Aunt Janet. I think I can manage to squeeze in a telegram for you from time to time.'

She sighed. 'I'd like fine to have come and see you off, Donald. But with the examinations coming on next week I canna get away.'

'Never mind,' he said. 'It's just a seaplane taking off. There's nothing much to see.'

'All the same, I'd like fine to have come.'

He went to bed early that night; in the bed that he had slept in when he was a boy he had a good night, and awoke refreshed. He had to get up early in order to meet Lockwood and his daughter in London; he left the house at Guildford at about eight o'clock.

His aunt came with him to the gate. 'Mind and take the Phosferine, Donald,' she said.

He smiled: 'All right. I won't forget. I'll be back about the end of September, Aunt Janet.'

'I'll have the room all ready for you. Guid luck, Donald.'

'Good luck, Aunt Janet.'

He travelled up to London, and met Lockwood and Alix at their hotel. The sole luggage that they had was the linen kitbags with fifteen pounds of their personal luggage in them; Ross gathered that the hotel had looked askance at them. 'They didn't seem to think that this was luggage at all,' said Lockwood, smiling; 'they made us pay for the rooms in advance.'

The girl seemed to take it personally. 'It's perfectly absurd,' she said. 'We'll never come here again.'

She was wearing a grey coat and skirt and a grey felt hat with a brim. There was something in her appearance that Ross could not place. She seemed different, younger. It was not until they reached the outfitters to try on flying clothing that the mystery was solved.

She took off her hat to try on a black leather helmet. The yellow hair clustered round her head in a clipped shingled mass.

Ross stared at it, caught unawares: 'Why—you've had your hair cut!'

'I know. I thought it would be less trouble.' She did not repeat the rather coarse remark that Uncle David had made, but turned to the glass.

The pilot fitted them both with helmets; then he had padded combination flying suits brought out. He said to

Lockwood: 'Would you mind slipping this one on, sir? It looks about right in length.' To the girl he said: 'You'll have to get rid of your skirt for this, Miss Lockwood.'

She gave him a freezing look, and said nothing. He turned to the man. 'You've got a dressing-room?'

'Certainly. If madam would step this way?'

She went with him; Ross sighed, and turned back to her father. Things were going to be very difficult in the intimacy of camp life. He ought to have been firmer, and refused to take a girl at all.

She came back presently, dressed in the flying suit, and laughed shortly when she saw her father. 'I don't know what you look like, Daddy.'

He said maliciously: 'I know what you look like, Alix. You look as if you'd just come off the pillion of a motor bicycle.'

'Oh . . .'

Ross fitted them with soft sheepskin boots with the fur inside. It was a very hot July day; within a minute or two Lockwood was sweating and the girl was red in the face. 'It's all very comfortable, Mr. Ross,' she said. 'May I go and get out of it now?'

He looked at her critically. 'You're quite sure the boots aren't tight?'

'There's heaps of room. I shall die if I have to stay in this thing any longer.'

She went back to the dressing-room. Presently she reappeared, normally dressed and carrying the suit over her arm. 'Mr. Ross,' she said, 'I'm sure this is going to be lovely when we get up North, but I shan't have to wear it in this weather, when we start, shall I?'

He shook his head. 'Not unless you want to, Miss Lockwood. Up to Invergordon you'll be quite all right as you are. You may want to wear it after that.'

He had their flying clothes packed up, and they took the parcels with them in the taxi to Waterloo. They had lunch in the train on their way down to Southampton. Over lunch Ross learned that Sir David was coming down from Coventry late in the afternoon to stay with them for the night and see them off.

They took a taxi to Hythe; Ross took them into the hangar and showed them the machine, standing upon its beaching wheels before the open doors, ready for flight. 'There she is,' he said. 'If you'll excuse me for a minute, I'll get her pushed out to the slipway.'

He went off to find the foreman. The girl stared at the seaplane, the first she had ever seen. It was certainly an arresting sight. It was painted a vivid yellow colour all over, wings and fuselage, relieved only by the dead-black registration letters. It was so bright it almost hurt the eyes to look at it.

Alix turned to her father. 'Daddy,' she said, 'it's awful! Whatever made you have it that appalling colour?'

'I never said a word about the colour,' he replied. He hesitated uncomfortably. 'It certainly is very bright.'

'It's simply terrible. I suppose that's his idea of what looks nice—he probably thought we'd like it. Do you think we can get it changed? We can't go round looking like a circus.'

A squad of men began to push the seaplane out; Ross came back to them. 'Like it?' he asked cheerfully.

The don said mildly: 'It's rather a conspicuous colour.'

The pilot nodded, still cheerful. 'The most conspicuous one there is, on any background. You'd see that ten miles away.'

The girl said irritably: 'I don't know that we want to be quite so conspicuous as that, Mr. Ross.'

The pilot said patiently: 'I had it that colour on purpose, Miss Lockwood. It's the best colour of all for a job like this. If anything happens to us and we have to land, they'll send out a search party for us—either by land or in another aeroplane. That colour shows up like a flame, on any background —snow, or trees, or grass, or water. It's saved dozens of lives, that colour has.'

Lockwood looked at it with new interest. 'That's very sensible,' he said. 'I should never have thought of that.'

Alix said nothing. In theory, she had known what she was in for; she had known that there were elements of danger in the flight, and she was not afraid of them. What was good enough for her father was good enough for her. At the same time, it was a new idea to her that the colour of the paint might mean for her the difference between living and enjoying life, and dying in the wilderness. It made her thoughtful. It was in a milder tone that she said to Ross:

'It's only got one wing. Is that as good as having two?'

The pilot nodded. 'It's a monoplane,' he said. 'As aircraft

go, it's a very good machine. Your uncle insisted on your having the best I could get.'

'I know. I suppose that's why it's costing such a lot of money.'

'That's right,' he said. 'You can't get something for nothing.'

He helped them up into the cabin and showed them the rather cramped accommodation. A good deal of the space was occupied by a large petrol tank; with the tank and the three seats there was only just room for their sleeping-bags, emergency rations, mooring and refuelling gear. The welded tubes of the structure stood bare and stark to the interior of the cabin, innocent of any trimming or upholstery.

'It all looks very workmanlike,' said Lockwood at last. He stared at the array of instruments before the pilot, at the grey boxes of the wireless by his elbow.

'It's a good machine,' said Ross. 'I never saw a better one for the job.'

The girl stared round the cabin, and said nothing. It seemed to her like sitting in the engine-room of a ship, or on the footplate of a locomotive. So far as she had thought about it at all, she had imagined that the aeroplane would be like a saloon car, or like a first-class carriage in a railway train. She had never travelled on an air line, but she knew that they were like that. This was very different. She would have to sit upon a little air cushion with a bare metal tank containing a hundred and fifty gallons of petrol at her elbow, already smelling strongly, filling the cabin with its tang. Everything she touched was bare metal, new and shining, slightly oily, and rather smelly. Clustered around the pilot's seat immediately in front of her there was a vast array of dials and little handles, forty or fifty little things, perhaps. She did not know the name, or the function, or the purpose of one of them.

For the first time she began to realise what this expedition meant to her. She was stepping from the world she knew into a world of different values. For the first time she appreciated the weight of what her uncle had said to her in Oxford. On this trip she would be adverse to its success; she knew nothing of what had to be done, or how it could be achieved.

'It all looks very nice,' she said at last, a little weakly.

Ross settled them in their seats, and saw that they were comfortable. Then he had the machine pushed to the head of the slipway. She started with a hand inertia starter; he had chosen that method rather than risk exhaustion of the batteries by electric starting. With run-down batteries they would have inefficient wireless; with inefficient wireless they might be in danger.

He knelt upon the pilot's seat awkwardly in the confined space, fitted the crank and began grinding away at the flywheel. By the time it was spinning sweat was pouring off him, that hot summer afternoon. The girl sat and watched him labouring at the crank, almost on top of her; she had not imagined it would be like this. The hum of the flywheel rose to a high whine; the pilot stopped cranking suddenly, pulled a little handle on the instrument board. The propeller in front of her started to revolve, the engine burst into life, and the airscrew was lost to sight. The pilot took out the crank and stowed it behind his seat, wiping his forehead.

He smiled at her. 'I shan't be sorry when we get up North,' he said.

'It looks terribly hot work.'

Lockwood said: 'You must teach me how to do that. I could give you a hand turning that thing, anyway.'

'It's not so bad,' said Ross. 'Take it easily, and it goes all right.'

He slipped into his seat, and sat for a few minutes warming up his engine. He showed them the oil pressure and temperature gauges, and explained what he was doing. The don was able to follow what he said; the girl sat watching the little needles move under the glasses without understanding. She sat silent, feeling rather lost.

The pilot signalled to the ground crew and the seaplane was eased down the slipway. She took the water and floated for a few minutes while the men in waders cleared the beaching trolley; then Ross opened his throttle a little and moved out over the water. Lockwood was in the seat beside him, watching his movements with interest, asking a question now and then. Behind him the girl sat stiff and rigid, worried and alert.

Presently Ross turned the machine into the wind pointing down Southampton Water, and peered around in all directions. Then he glanced back over his shoulder at the girl. 'All right, Miss Lockwood?'

She moistened her lips. 'I'm quite ready.'

He smiled. 'I'm going to take her off now. Just sit relaxed in your seat—there won't be any motion.'

65

The engine opened out with a roar; she saw him press his wheel forward, felt the machine rise and trim forward on the floats. Then they were running over the surface of the water; from her seat she could watch the port float, watch the feathery spray as it flew sideways from its midship section. The feather grew smaller; quite suddenly it was not there at all. She looked up, wondering; to her surprise the trees upon the bank were level now with the machine, falling below her. they were fifty feet up.

In front of her, the pilot was playing a complicated fantasia upon his controls. He throttled back, and the harsh note of the engine sank to a lower tone. He wound a little handle in the roof above his head, felt the wheel, and wound the handle half a turn further. He wound another little handle on the floor between his feet; the machine yawed from side to side till he was satisfied. Then he turned to a thing like a gigantic fishing reel low down beside his feet; it started to rotate and the copper wire upon it rapidly grew less.

Presently, to her alarm, the New Forest got up vertically beside the wing tip and began to revolve. In a moment it settled down again, and she found that they were heading westwards down the Solent.

The pilot was delicately adjusting the condenser of his wireless receiver. He took the headphones from his head and passed them over to the don. 'Radio Normandie,' he said. 'It's quite clear now.'

Lockwood took the headphones diffidently and put them on as the Isle of Wight passed by below them. He heard the closing bars of a dance tune, the silvery notes of a bell. Then he heard a clear woman's voice. 'Mrs. Jones—I must tell you about my Elsie, three years old last March. Her tongue was dreadfully coated yesterday morning, and she was ever so listless and fretful. Mrs. Johnson advised me to give her Candy-Iax, the delicious children's laxative that tastes just like Edinburgh Rock. My dear—it was marvellous. You really ought to——'

The don removed the headphones from his ears. The pilot said: 'There's none of that ignition noise there now, is there?'

Lockwood shook his head. 'It's very clear.' He did not know what ignition noise would sound like, but the wireless seemed to work all right. He handed back the headpiece.

'I'll just try the transmission again.' For a time the pilot busied himself with the tapping key, head down, intent upon

66

the wireless. Uncontrolled, the aeroplane held a straight course, climbing slowly and heading out to sea. For a quarter of an hour they went on like that, the coast-line gradually receding behind them. Lockwood and the girl gradually relaxed in their seats. In this noisy, motionless ascent over the sea there was nothing to disturb them; they found themselves capable of looking round, appreciating their situation. They noticed that it had grown considerably colder.

Presently the pilot took the headphones off and hung them on a hook beside him. 'It's quite O.K.,' he said. 'I was working Croydon and Bristol then.'

Lockwood asked: 'How high up are we?'

'Seven thousand.' Ross showed him the altimeter.

He glanced at the far line of the shore, fifteen miles away on his right hand, and swung the machine round. He throttled a little to prevent her climbing higher, took his hands from the wheel, and half turned in his seat. 'Are you quite comfortable, Miss Lockwood?' he asked.

She nodded. 'It's a bit cold.'

'I know. I'll bring her down in a minute. Does the noise worry you?'

'Not now. It did at first.'

'If you'll remind me, I'll get some cotton-wool for your ears before we start. Are there any draughts round that seat?'

'There's one by my legs.'

He nodded. 'I'll see if I can fix it when we get down. See if you can see where it's coming in.'

He turned again to his wheel and throttled down. The engine noise died away and a whispering rush of air succeeded it; the nose fell below the horizon and they sank down towards the sea. At two thousand feet, with the Isle of Wight before them, the pilot opened up again; he turned to the don beside him.

'I think she's quite all right, sir. Would you like to stay up a bit longer, or shall we go home now?'

Lockwood said: 'I'm quite comfortable here. But I should go back if you've got anything to do.'

The pilot nodded his agreement, and began reeling in the aerial.

They passed swiftly over the Solent, over the New Forest between Lymington and Beaulieu, and round over Hythe at about five hundred feet. He throttled back and sank towards the water, flattened his glide, lifted her to the stall, and rubbed the heels of his floats gently into the surface. The seaplane sank forward on to the body of the floats, bit down into the water, and came to rest. Ross turned her, and taxied in towards the slip.

The floats grated gently on the concrete, Ross switched off, and the men in waders busied themselves with the beaching wheels. Ross turned to Lockwood, and indicated two figures on the shore. 'There's your brother, sir, with Mr. Hanson.'

The cable was attached, and the machine was pulled up to the hangar at the head of the slipway. Ross got out first, helped his passengers down on to the float, and so to the ground. Sir David came to meet them. 'Well, Cyril—how do you like flying!'

The don said: 'I think it's very plesant. We seemed to go a long way in a short time.'

'That's what you do it for.' Sir David turned to the pilot. 'I saw you make a very perfect landing.'

Ross said: 'She's a very nice seaplane, sir. She's very stable, but the control's there when you want it. They're really very easy to fly, these things.'

Her uncle turned to Alix. 'What about you, Alix? Feel like going to Greenland in it?'

She nodded. 'It's all right. But my feet got very cold.'

Ross turned to her. 'If you'll show me where that draught comes in, Miss Lockwood, I'll see if we can do something about it.' They got back into the cabin and bent over her seat. 'Oh, I see—where the petrol pipe goes through. I'll get a bit of soft leather put over that.'

The Lockwoods went off together to the hotel; the pilot stood by the door of the hangar with Hanson. Wearily he pulled his cigarette case out, and offered one to the secretary. 'Well, that's the first part of the job done,' he said, and blew a long cloud of smoke. 'I never thought we'd get the bloody thing through in the time.'

Hanson said: 'Is everything going all right now, Mr. Ross?'

The pilot nodded. 'I'm quite happy about her now. I'll stay on and see her filled up tonight, and then we'll be all ready to start in the morning.'

The secretary looked at him keenly. 'I'm afraid you've had a hard time over this thing, Mr. Ross. I never would have believed that there'd be so much work in it.'

Ross nodded. 'That's so,' he said. 'The hard work in a show like this is before you start.'

'You're feeling all right, yourself?'

'Oh, I'm all right. I'll go to bed early and get a good night's sleep to-night, now that the machine's ready. Then off we go in the morning.'

The secretary made no comment. Presently he went up to the hotel, after the others. 'I'll see you up there, later on,' said the pilot.

He turned back to the machine. With the ground engineer to help him he changed the engine oil, and cleaned the fuel and oil filters. They took off the engine cowling, opened the valve covers, and checked the tappet clearances of eighteen valves with a feeler. Then they replaced the cowling, had the machine pushed beneath the petrol hose, and filled in fuel for twelve hundred miles. They drained the sump of each petrol tank in turn.

Finally they rested against the float. 'That's the lot then,' said the ground engineer. 'She's all ready for you in the morning, now.'

The pilot nodded; he was very tired. 'I wish we were starting next week,' he said. 'There's always too much bloody rush about these jobs.'

'That's so,' the man said. 'Still, you got her through in time, and that's the main thing. I don't think you'll have much trouble with her.' He stroked the float, almost affectionately.

'She'll be all right,' said Ross. He went back to the hotel, got out of his overalls and had a wash, and went down to the lounge. He found Sir David there alone. 'Have a drink, Mr. Ross.'

The pilot said: 'I'll have a tomato juice, sir.'

He lit a cigarette with quick, nervous movements and sipped his strange, unsatisfying drink. They talked for a short time about the expedition. The manufacturer said: 'I'm sorry that you aren't taking an engineer with you. It would have made things easier. I see that now.'

Ross shook his head. 'I shan't need one. There'll only be three stops before we get to Julianehaab—at Invergordon, Reykjavik, and Angmagsalik. I can manage alone for that length of time. Then when we pick up Jameson I shall have all the help I want.'

Sir David eyed him keenly. 'Now, are you really sure

about that? I'm quite prepared to cut out Alix now and send an engineer instead, if you think that would be safer.'

'I wouldn't do that, sir. We shall be quite all right as we are.'

'Is Alix behaving herself?'

The pilot smiled slowly. 'She didn't much like it when I told her to take off her skirt.' He added a few details of the incident.

Her uncle smiled with him. 'It's going to be good for her, this trip. I hope you won't find her a difficult passenger.'

The pilot yawned, and stretched himself. 'There's no such thing in transport,' he said drily. 'The passenger is always right, like the customer. One time I took a goat in the machine from Churchill to Eastmain—and did he stink! But we got along all right.'

Sir David eyed the pilot with new interest.

They dined together in a party, talking about the route; the pilot would drink nothing but water. At the conclusion of the meal he turned to Lockwood.

'I think I'll leave you now, and go to bed. I'd like to have breakfast tomorrow at half-past seven and get away from here soon after eight, if that suits you, sir. If we do that we should be up at Invergordon easily by tea-time.'

Lockwood said: 'Make whatever arrangements for us you think best, Mr. Ross. We'll do whatever you say.'

The pilot smiled. 'All right—I'll tell them about the breakfast in the office. Good night, sir. Good night, Miss Lockwood.'

'Good night, Mr. Ross.'

He left them, and went upstairs. Alix followed him a little later. Sir David went out with his brother and walked a little way down the road with him as they finished their cigars.

'I should keep an eye on that young chap, Cyril,' he said presently. 'See that he doesn't do all the work.'

The don nodded. 'I'm afraid he's had rather a hard time in the last few days.'

'Hanson was talking to me about that before dinner. None of us realised how much he'd have to do before the flight began.'

'That's very true. Do you think he ought to have a few days' rest before we start?'

Sir David shook his head. 'He wouldn't take it. He wants to get on. No, just keep an eye on him—and see that Alix makes things easy for him, too. He's looking very different now to when we saw him first.'

'He's thinner, isn't he?'

The other nodded. 'I keep on thinking that we should have sent an engineer with him. Still, it's too late to make an alteration now.'

CHAPTER IV

In the warm morning sunlight the machine moved down the slipway to the water. Knee-deep in water, the men removed her beaching wheels for the last time, and she taxied out slowly from the shore. At the water's edge Sir David and his secretary stood in city clothes waving to them with their umbrellas; from the cramped cabin of the seaplane Alix and her father waved in reply. The pilot opened his throttle a little and took the seaplane over to the far shore.

The day was already hot; at that slow speed the heat was stifling in the cabin. None of them were wearing flying clothes. Lockwood and Ross wore tweed coats and grey flannel trousers; the girl wore her grey coat and skirt and a silk blouse. The back of the cabin was piled high with their sleeping-bags, luggage, and emergency rations; the flying suits were on top, ready if they were wanted on the way. It would be possible for Lockwood and his daughter to get out of their seats and put on flying suits in the air; the pilot would have to stay as he was till they landed.

The take-off, with twelve hundred miles of fuel on board, went moderately well. There was a light south-easterly breeze blowing up Southampton Water; the pilot headed into this and opened his throttle full. Then as she gathered speed slowly he worked with his elevators to rock her forward on to the step of the floats; she ploughed ahead, leaving a deep wash. Half a mile from the start he got her up on to the step; thereafter she gained speed quickly and finally left the surface after about a mile. For a few moments he nursed her upwards from the water, tense and alert; then as she gained speed he put her into a normal climb, and relaxed.

Lockwood said: 'We seemed to go a long way on the water.'

'I know. She's got fuel for twelve hundred miles on board.

71

If we get her off with thirteen fifty, it's all she'll ever do. Of course, there's not a lot of wind.'

'How far is it to Invergordon?'

'About seven hundred and fifty miles, the way we go. We've got to keep round the coast. Say six and a half hours. We ought to get there at about four o'clock, if all goes well.'

He turned, and began flying eastwards down the coast of England, past Portsmouth and Brighton, on to Dungeness.

It was about nine o'clock in the morning. Ross climbed the machine slowly to about four thousand feet; the temperature up there was moderate. He reeled out his aerial and tested his wireless again, then settled down to the flight. The weather was perfect. The south coast of England, flat and uninteresting from the air, passed slowly by them. For the first half-hour Lockwood and the girl were interested and asked many questions about the towns they passed, the speed of the machine, and the height. Then they fell silent; the seaplane droned monotonously on.

The end of the first hour found them a little way past Dungeness, nearing Dover. He left the coast at Folkestone and cut across the end of Kent on a course for the Norfolk coast. They passed near Margate, and headed out over the Thames estuary.

By eleven o'clock they were near Yarmouth, cutting across a corner of the land again on their way to the coast of Lincolnshire.

The pilot sat motionless at the wheel. He wore a flying helmet fitted with headphones; he had turned on the radio to one of the continental stations and was listening to dance music. From time to time he made a small adjustment to the tail control above his head; as fuel was consumed the trim of the machine altered very slightly. Now and again he pulled a map from beneath his leg and compared it with some feature on the ground; from time to time he did a little sum upon a slide rule to check his ground speed. Every twenty minutes he re-set the directional gyro in agreement with the compass. These little occupations lessened the monotony for him; between them he listened to the dance band.

In the seat beside him, Lockwood had fallen asleep.

Behind the pilot Alix sat motionless, staring at the slowly moving countryside. She had not expected that a flight would be like this. She had expected that to fly would be thrilling, or at least interesting. In fact, she found that it was neither. Her head felt sick and woolly from the clamour of the engine. A patch of sunlight lay across her lap; that part of her in the sun was unbearably hot, out of the sun she was a little cold. She could not move to any other seat; there was no blind to be pulled down.

They had been two hours in the machine; already she was tired, bored, and cross. The pilot said there were another five hours to go.

Her seat was getting very hard. She shifted her position uneasily.

At twelve o'clock they passed the mouth of the Humber, and Spurn Head. There were clouds in the sky now, and more ahead; the day was gradually becoming overcast as they got further north. Lockwood was awake again and studying the map, comparing it with the coast. Behind them the girl was falling into an uneasy coma of fatigue.

Presently Ross suggested lunch. They had brought sandwiches with them from the hotel at Hythe; they ate these off Sunderland, proceeding steadily towards Scotland. The food woke them up, and refreshed them. The weather here was almost wholly overcast and rather cold; they came down to fifteen hundred feet and felt better.

At two o'clock they were off the Firth of Forth; away to the west they saw the smoke of Leith and Edinburgh. They crossed the mouth of the firth and met the coast again at Arbroath; then for nearly an hour they followed it to Aberdeen. At Aberdeen they took a cut across the land, and came to Banff at about three o'clock.

Up there the day was bright again, and the sun warm. Ross turned north-west by compass for Cromarty; presently he was able to show his passengers an indentation in the heather-covered cliffs ahead, and an appearance of water behind.

'Cromarty Firth,' he said. 'Invergordon's on the north side somewhere.'

Lockwood smiled. 'I shan't be sorry to get there.'

'I know. It's very boring, isn't it?'

He turned and spoke to Alix: 'Are you very tired, Miss Lockwood?'

She shook her head. 'No—I'm not tired. But I shall be very glad to get out.'

Ross brought the machine down to a thousand feet and

flew into Cromarty from the sea. He had never been there before, but he found Invergordon without difficulty and circled low over the water to find the red buoy that he had arranged should be prepared for him to moor the seaplane to. He saw it in the position that he had arranged, a little to the west of the main jetty. There were no ships in the firth, and no sign of any boat to meet him at the buoy. He went up to a thousand feet again and turned to Lockwood.

'When we land,' he said, 'we've got to make fast to that red buoy. I can taxi up to it on the water; can you get down on the the float and catch it?'

'Of course I can. Tell me what I'm to do.'

The mooring gear was very simple. A bridle of steel cable joined two stout bollards, one in the nose of each float. From the centre of this bridle a cable was led down the outside of the port float to a point near the cabin door, and was held in clips from which it could be readily pulled out. At the aft end this cable carried a large spring hook, exactly like a dog-leash clip on an enormous scale.

To moor the seaplane, somebody had to get down from the cabin and stand upon the curved top of the float as the seaplane taxied up to the buoy. The top of the float was only a few inches from the water; if there were waves they would wet his feet. He had to pull the cable from its clips along the float and have the spring hook ready in one hand. Then the machine would manœuvre to bring the buoy to his feet; he would catch it with a little boathook that they carried in the cabin, clip the hook on to it, and let it go. The seaplane would then ride to the buoy, attached to it by the cable and the bridle to the floats.

Ross explained this to Lockwood as they cruised around over Invergordon; the don had no difficulty in understanding what he had to do. But the girl interposed.

'You'd better not do that, Daddy,' she said. 'I can get down there much better. You stay here.'

She turned to Ross 'I've just got to catch the buoy with the boathook, and clip the spring hook on to it?'

He nodded. He was glad that she had volunteered. It seemed to him that there was nothing difficult about it, but perhaps it was a job better for youth than for age. 'That's all you've got to do,' he said. 'Keep a good hold on something —the float may be slippery. Try not to lose the boathook. There's a little leather loop on it—put that over your wrist.

And look, don't try and hold on to the buoy if you can't manage. Let it go, and I'll bring her round to it again.'

'I suppose there's something on the buoy for the spring hook to clip on to?'

'There ought to be a metal ring.'

'That's quite clear, Mr. Ross.'

'All right. I'll put her down now. Don't open the cabin door until I tell you.'

He made a wide sweep into wind and sank to the surface of the water. He touched down gently; the machine sank forward on the floats and pulled up quickly. Ross opened the side window at his elbow to its full extent, swung the machine round, and taxied towards the buoy. When he was near it he slowed the machine down to a walking pace and turned to the girl.

'All right now, Miss Lockwood. Be careful how you get down on the float.'

She got up from her seat and opened the door. The float below was practically awash; she did not like the look of it at all. Still, she had said that she could do it. In any case, it had to be either her or her father, since the pilot could not leave his seat. She was suddenly angry that he should expect her to do such a thing. It was absurd that she should have to do this. It was an error in the organisation, and inefficiency for which he was responsible. Still, there was nothing for it.

She crawled backwards out of the open door and, lying on her stomach on the sill, felt for the float with her toes. She levered herself out further, and touched it. Her skirt was rucked up to her waist, making her angrier still; mercifully there was nobody there to see.

She found her foothold on the float and stood erect. He had warned her that it might be slippery; it was. She was wearing her normal walking shoes, with leather soles and medium high heels. She ought to have had rubbers on for this. He should have told her.

She clutched the wing strut and turned forward; from his window he was watching her intently. 'Are you all right?' he asked.

She said shortly and acidly: 'I'm quite all right, thank you, Mr. Ross.'

She turned gingerly and took the boathook from the floor of the cabin; then she stooped down and unfastened the spring hook from the float. The pilot opened a chink of throttle very gently, keeping one eye upon the girl standing behind his shoulder on the float; the machine crept forward to the buoy.

There was a strong tidal current running past the buoy. The wind was light; he made a circuit and approached up the tide. He knew from much experience in the past that the only real danger in this sort of thing lay in allowing the machine to become held by the mooring with the floats broadside to the tide. Then, if the tide were strong enough, the seaplane might be capsized, it was a real danger, that. In a way the tide made it easier, however; he could keep steerage way and yet come very slowly to the buoy. The girl should have no difficulty, he thought.

A wave slopped over the float and over the girl's feet, filling her shoes with water. She became suddenly furious, but said nothing.

The buoy appeared beside the float. Ross nursed the machine gently up to it. Alix stooped as it came to her, caught it easily with the boathook, and slipped the cable to the ring. From the window ahead of her the pilot said:

'Good show. Let it go now.'

She did not hear him very well. She stood there with the buoy held in her hand, looking forward at him. 'Do you mean put it in the water?'

He sat screwed round in his seat, looking backwards at her. 'Just throw it all in.'

She shuffled a little, and threw the buoy back into the sea with the cable attached to it. 'Do you mean like that?'

'That's fine.'

The pilot swung round in his seat. In the short time that he had taken his eyes from the forward view the seaplane had been blown round, and she now lay well across the tide, drifting rapidly down-stream as the slack of the cable took up. There was no time to be lost.

He said: 'Bloody hell!' and thrust the throttle wide open, treading hard upon the rudder to get her straight again. The engine opened out with a roar and a blast of air from the propeller; at the same moment there was a considerable jerk from the floats as the machine was brought up sharply on the mooring. There was a scuffling noise behind him as the seaplane swung back to the stream, and then a splash. The machine swung straight, he pulled the throttle back, and turned in his seat, aghast. The girl had fallen in.

Ross jumped from his seat, pushed past Lockwood, and was at the cabin door in a moment. She was swimming strongly a yard or two away from the float; the swing had carried the machine a little way from her. He was down on the float in an instant, caught her hand, and pulled her up beside him; she still held the boathook.

Her wet silk blouse clung to her like a bathing dress. For the fraction of an instant the pilot's eyes rested on her figure in subconscious surprise. She could be beautiful. Then he was full of stammering apologies.

'I say Miss Lockwood—I'm terribly sorry. Did you hurt yourself?'

In the cabin door her father stooped, looking down at her, and he was laughing.

She had swung round on the pilot. She was streaming with water, and she had lost one shoe; she balanced precariously on the other upon the slippery float.

'You did that on purpose!' she said furiously. 'You meant me to fall off!'

Her father had stopped laughing. 'Don't talk such non-sense, Alix,' he said sharply. 'It was an accident.'

'It wasn't an accident at all! He put on his engine, and the rush of air pushed me off the float!'

Ross said: 'I'm really most awfully sorry. I had to open her up and get her straight, or I'd have had her over. She was all across the tide.'

She said: 'I don't believe a word of it.' The pilot said nothing; in stony silence she got back into the cabin, helped by her father.

Over her shoulder Lockwood glanced at the pilot expres-sively; Ross smiled, and shrugged his shoulders. He followed her into the cabin, squeezed past them, and stopped the engine. Through the windscreen he saw a motor-boat approaching them from the shore.

He got down on to the float again and held the boat off as it came alongside, fearful of damage to the machine. The boatman knew his job, however; it was not the first time he had had to deal with seaplanes. In silence the girl and her father got down into the boat. Ross went back into the cabin, closed the windows, and handed down their personal luggage; he passed her flying boots down to the girl.

'I should put these on, Miss Lockwood,' he said impas-sively. She could not walk up to the hotel without a shoe.

She took them without a word.

The pilot joined them in the boat, and in the golden summer afternoon they were carried to the shore in silence. Ross spoke a few words to the boatman to arrange for him to be available in half an hour to refuel the seaplane; then they were at the jetty and he was helping the Lockwoods from the boat. They walked up through the little town to the hotel with hardly a word spoken.

The hotel was a good one, situated in the middle of the one street of the little town; it was owned and run by the British Government. There were no warships in the firth, and the hotel was practically empty. Ross made arrangements for their rooms, and they went to them at once.

Lockwood came into the pilot's room with him. 'I'm sorry my daughter said what she did,' he said directly. 'I saw the whole thing. It was a pure accident.'

Ross smiled. 'Don't think any more about it, sir. She's probably a bit tired. Anyway, I ought never to have let her get down on the float in shoes like that. She'll be all right in the morning.'

The don bit his lip. 'I shall have to have a talk with her,' he said at last.

'I wouldn't do that, sir. Let it blow over. I'll see if I can think up some other way of picking up the moorings.'

'I don't see how you can do the whole thing. You must have somebody to help you.'

He walked over to the window and stood looking out over the sunlit blue water of the firth, the purple, heather-covered hills. The air was fresh and sweet. He turned back to Ross. 'I know you would rather have had a young man on this trip, in place of Alix,' he said. 'I'm beginning to see what you meant.'

The pilot lit a cigarette. 'I've no quarrel with Miss Alix, sir,' he said. 'I should be quite prepared to carry on as we are. But you've got to understand what we're in for. I reckoned Invergordon as an easy landing, and it was. From now onwards we're going to have a whole lot of difficulties that we haven't had yet. This is a tough trip, Mr. Lockwood. I've said so all along, and nobody believed me. We can make it all right if we all pull together. But the sort of little accident we had today is going to happen every day, in one form or another. We'll have to get out of the way of slanging at each other, or we shan't get very far.'

'That's very true.'

Ross said: 'I expect she's tired. After all, it's the first flight she's ever made, except the short one we had yesterday. You have a cup of tea with her alone, sir. Then we'll meet for dinner, and I'll see if I can make things right with her this evening.'

The older man looked at him. 'What are you going to do?'

'I've got to see to the refuelling, and look over the engine. Don't worry about me.'

'How long will that take?'

'Two or three hours.'

'I'll come and give you a hand.'

Ross shook his head. 'You stay with Miss Alix, sir. The boatman can give me all the help I want. I'll meet you for dinner.'

'You must have a cup of tea yourself before you go.'

The pilot smiled. 'I'll get something. Then this evening I'll ring up the Air Ministry for a weather forecast. If it's any good, I'll get another one at four o'clock in the morning. If that's all right, we'll make a start for Reykjavik. If not, we'll have to wait until it is all right. I want decent weather for the big crossing.'

The don left him and went to his own room. Ross undid his personal kit, sponged his face, and went down to the jetty again to meet the boatman and commence refuelling.

A quarter of an hour later Lockwood tapped at the door of his daughter's room. She opened it to him, clad in a kimono and very little else. He could see that she was still very angry; her clothes were in a wet heap on the floor. 'How are you getting on?' he asked. 'Put on some things, and come down and have tea.'

'I can't come down. I haven't got anything to change into.'

'But you've got other clothes?'

'I've got everything except a skirt. I thought that one would do.'

He said: 'There are shops here. I'll go out and get you one. What size waist?'

She sniffed despondently. 'I don't suppose there'll be a thing that I can wear.'

He was suddenly cross with her. 'You'll wear what I get you,' he said sharply. 'What size waist?'

'Twenty-five inches, Daddy.'

He went out and down into the wide, straight street. The

only draper's shop could make a skirt in half a day, but had nothing in stock. They directed him to the ironmonger's, a comprehensive establishment that sold everything from sheepskin rugs to sporting cartridges and salmon rods. Here he got a tweed skirt of the right waist measurement from a dusty package labelled July 1923.

'There's not a great demand for these goods,' the man told him. 'Just once and again.'

It was a bright green tweed. He knew she would not like it, but he bought it and took it back to the hotel with him. He took it up and gave it to her in her room; she took it meekly and without a word. He told her to come down to tea.

She joined him a quarter of an hour later, silent and subdued. She was wearing a pale blue roll-neck sweater with her vivid green skirt, a combination which was impressive but not pleasing. The tea refreshed the girl; by the end of the meal she was venturing a little conversation with her father.

When it was over, Lockwood suggested that they went out to explore the little town. In the warm summer evening they found their way down to the jetty, built out on piles into the firth. From there they could see the seaplane at her moorings with the boat alongside. Ross was in the cabin engaged in the endless, wearisome task of filling the contents of seventy petrol cans into the big tank, stopping from time to time to pump fuel from the big tank into the service tanks up in the wings. From the shore the Lockwoods could not see exactly what was going on. They saw enough to make it clear to them that the pilot, as tired as they were, was still working.

Lockwood said gently: 'You'll have to take back what you said to him this afternoon, Alix.'

She did not speak.

'It was a pure accident, you know.'

'I'm not so sure about that.'

'Now you're being silly. He couldn't possibly have done anything else.' In a few words he told her what had happened. 'He's very worried that you should have thought he did it on purpose.'

She said in a low tone. 'He never wanted me to come upon this trip at all.'

Her father smiled. 'Well, that's perfectly true. He said that if another person was to come, it ought to be a young man, who could help him. And all you've done so far has gone to prove him right.'

The evening sun beat down upon the timbers of the jetty, bringing out the scent of tar and creosote from the wood. Beneath their feet the calm water lapped, and shoals of grey fish moved unmolested. Presently the girl said quietly:

'Does this mean you want me to go home, Daddy?'

He considered before speaking, and her heart sank. 'I can't have you quarrelling with Mr. Ross like this, Alix,' he said at last. 'It's not fair to him. On a difficult trip like this, it may even be dangerous to all of us unless we can be good friends. I want you to come on with us. But if you feel that you can't hit it off with him, then you must say so before you leave here and I'll get an undergraduate to come up and join me. Collins would come, and be glad to get the chance.'

'I see.'

He laid his hand upon her shoulder. 'Have a talk with him' he said gently. 'He wants to be friends.'

She stared out over the firth to where the pilot was still working on the seaplane. 'He's such a queer sort of man— all machinery and stuff. And half the time he talks American. I don't know what he thinks about, or likes.'

'You've got to make your mind up by tonight, Alix. I can't have any more rows like we had today.'

The girl nodded. 'I see that, Daddy. If I go home, you'd wait till someone else could join you? You wouldn't go alone?'

He hesitated. 'I don't think so. I think there's enough time to wait a day or so.'

She said: 'Will it do if I think it over, and tell you tonight?'

He nodded: 'Think it over.'

They went back to the hotel. Lockwood turned into the lounge; the girl went thoughtfully to her room and gave her wet clothes to the maid to be dried. When Ross returned, a little after seven o'clock, she was waiting for him on the wide veranda facing on the street.

He was very tired and hot and dirty. He said: 'Good evening, Miss Lockwood.'

She said hesitantly: 'Good evening, Mr. Ross. Did you get all your jobs done?'

He paused on the steps. 'She's all O.K. now—filled right up. If it's like this when we take off we'll have to dump some of it, I expect.' She did not understand him in the least. 'I got the filters cleaned, too, and the sumps checked. So she's all ready to go.'

She knew, vaguely, that this meant he had been doing a good deal of work; she wanted to say something about it, but she didn't know quite what to say. At last she said: 'If I'd known, I'd have come with you.'

He smiled. 'That's very good of you, Miss Lockwood. But that boatman knows his stuff all right. He gave me a hand.'

'Oh?' She hesitated for a moment, and then said: 'My father has been explaining to me what happened when we landed. I didn't understand.'

He nodded; this was hopeful. 'I've been wanting to speak to you about that, Miss Lockwood. I'm afraid I was very much to blame. We ought to have practised it at Hythe. And I should never have let you go down on the float in those shoes, and without a lifebelt on.'

She laughed: 'I can swim all right.'

He smiled slowly. 'I saw that.' He hesitated in turn and then said: 'Would you like a glass of sherry before dinner?'

'If you're having one.'

'I'll have a tomato drink. Look, I'll order them and go and have a wash. I'll be right back.'

He came back in about five minutes; the drinks were standing on a table by her side. He lifted his tomato cocktail. 'Here's luck.'

She drank with him. 'What sort of shoes ought I to wear, Mr. Ross, for getting down on to the float?'

He did not answer her directly. 'I've been trying to scheme out ways of doing it myself,' he said. 'I think it could be done, if we brought the cable up the front strut to the fuselage and I had a Grabit boathook.'

The last part of that was Greek to her. She said: 'But that isn't necessary. I can do it all right. We did the actual mooring all right today.'

He glanced at her in surprise. 'That's so. Are you sure you wouldn't mind doing it again?'

'Not if I had proper shoes. Would sand-shoes be all right?'

He thought about it for a minute. 'I think that would be best—sand-shoes and no stockings. Then it wouldn't matter if your feet did get wet a bit. Of course, you could wear gumboots and keep dry, but then if you did happen to fall in again they wouldn't be so good to swim in.'

She smiled a little. 'I'm not going to make a habit of falling in, Mr. Ross.'

'Of course not.'

'I'd rather it was sand-shoes than gum-boots.'

'Well, we could get those up the street here, after dinner.'

He lit a cigarette; she refused one. They sat in silence for a time. Presently she said: 'It's not only my shoes.'

'I know. I ought to have seen you had a lifebelt on. They're stowed in the rack at the back of the cabin.'

She shook her head. 'I didn't mean that. It's all my clothes —I feel I'm not dressed right for this sort of expedition.' She glanced down. 'Daddy got me this awful skirt, because mine was wet.'

He eyed her for a moment. 'Would you consider wearing an overall suit, Miss Lockwood?'

'You mean without a skirt at all?'

'That's right. A boiler suit, like mechanics wear.'

'It'd look awfully funny in the hotel.'

'You could wear your ordinary clothes in the hotel, except when you're going backwards and forwards to the machine. Besides, there won't be many more hotels, you know. There's one at Reykjavik, and that's the lot.'

She stared at him in wonder; they were getting very near to the unknown. 'I suppose that's so.'

He nodded.

'It would be more practical, wouldn't it?'

He nodded again. 'We might be able to get a white one. They look very nice.'

They finished their drinks and went to look for Lockwood; they found him in the lounge, and went in to dinner. The don was relieved to see that they had come to some kind of understanding; he did not want to lose his daughter and have to wait till he could get an undergraduate to join him. Besides, the whole thing was absurd. Alix had got to learn to get along with people.

Ross left them sitting over their coffee, and went and stood for an interminable half-hour in the telephone box in the hall. He had arranged for a special series of weather reports for the crossing to Iceland. In the end he got through to the Air Ministry; they told him:

'Invergordon at dawn: wind north-east, fifteen to twenty-five miles an hour, falling and backing. At noon,

83

light variable winds over the whole route, cloudy to one thousand feet. Considerable fog patches in Iceland.'

He scribbled this down upon the back of an envelope, and rang off. He took it to Lockwood in the lounge; the girl had gone upstairs.

'I don't know that I'm so struck on this, sir,' he said. 'The wind at dawn—that's fine. Just what we want to get us off with a good load of fuel. But the cloudy to one thousand feet and the fog patches aren't so good.'

'I'll leave it to you, ·Mr. Ross. If you'd like to wait for better weather, we've got plenty of time in hand.'

The pilot stared at the envelope. 'Considerable fog patches . . .' He shook his head. 'I think I'd wait a day, sir. It's over five hundred miles of open sea from the Hebrides to Vik. We don't want to run into trouble at the end of that.'

The don nodded. 'I think that's very wise. We'll wait here for a day or two.'

The pilot left him, and went out and down the street to the cottage of the boatman. He was a little worried about the wind of twenty-five miles an hour that was coming to them. He got the man out, and they went down to the jetty, got the motor-boat, and went out to the machine again in the dusk. They worked for nearly an hour, passing a stronger bridle from the bollards on the floats direct to the mooring chain, in order to eliminate the risk of the light aviation cables parting in a strong blow.

In the hotel the girl came down to the lounge: her father showed her the weather report. 'We've decided to stay here tomorrow, anyway,' he said.

She nodded. 'I think that's a good thing, from every point of view. I want to go to Inverness and get some more clothes.'

'Have you made up your mind, then?'

'I want to come on, if you'll let me, Daddy.'

'All right.' He did not refer to the subject again.

Presently she asked: 'What's happened to Mr. Ross?'

Her father said: 'He went out with the boatman to do something to the moorings of the seaplane.'

'He's out there again? It's very nearly dark.'

He glanced at her. 'He's a very responsible young man, Alix. I think he's taking his work very seriously.'

She stared out of the window. 'He's certainly working very hard.'

84

'A day's rest won't do any of us any harm,' said her father.

Ross came back to the hotel at about eleven o'clock and went to bed. He had an alarm clock with him which he set for half-past three in the morning; by a quarter to four he was walking down to the jetty in the darkness. He rowed out to the seaplane in a little dinghy belonging to the boatman; the wind was fresh and the machine was pitching in the waves. He had a good look at the mooring and the machine generally, but there was nothing to be done; she was coming to no harm. He rowed back to the jetty, returned to the hotel, and went to bed again in the grey light of dawn.

He got up late, and went down to breakfast tired and stale. The Lockwoods had nearly finished the meal.

'What are you going to do today?' he asked. 'I'm afraid Invergordon isn't a very exciting place to have to wait about in.'

Alix said: 'I want to go to Inverness—I've got to get another pair of shoes. And I'll see if I can get an overall. Will you come with us, Mr. Ross?'

The pilot shook his head. 'I'd rather stick around here with the seaplane till the wind goes down,' he said. 'I've got one or two little jobs I want to do on her, too.'

Lockwood said: 'Is there anything I can do to help you, Mr. Ross?'

'No, thanks, sir. I'll only just be pottering about.'

He spent the morning out on the machine, moving the pilot's seat a little and fashioning a pocket for his maps. He came back to the hotel to lunch alone; in the afternoon he took a newspaper upstairs and stretched himself on his bed to read it for a few minutes.

When next he opened his eyes it was five minutes to seven. He got up dazed with sleep, washed his face, and went downstairs. He found the Lockwoods in the lounge.

He ordered sherry for them, and a tomato cocktail for himself. Alix said: 'I got myself an overall, Mr. Ross.'

He smiled. 'Good enough. A white one?'

'Yes, and a pair of sand-shoes.'

'That's fine. I'm sorry to say I've been asleep all the afternoon.'

She eyed him seriously. 'I'm very glad to hear it.'

'I'm not—it makes one feel like death to sleep in the day-time.' His sleep had not refreshed him; he was feeling stale and ill. He did not eat much dinner.

He rang up the Air Ministry again while the Lockwoods took their coffee in the lounge, standing about for half an hour and waiting for his call. When the report came he scribbled it down hurriedly.

'Wind south-west ten to twenty miles an hour, clouds five tenths at three thousand feet. Visibility good. Iceland at noon, wind light and northerly, visibility good.'

'O.K.,' he said. 'I'll ring again at 04 hours to check that before I take off.'

He put up the receiver and went through to the lounge, envelope in hand. He showed the report to Lockwood. 'We'll never get a better one than this, sir,' he said. 'We'd better reckon that we'll go.'

'Very good, Mr. Ross.'

Alix got up from her chair. 'I'd better tell them to cut us some sandwiches tonight, hadn't I?'

The pilot turned to her in surprise. 'Why—yes, if you would. It's a good long way. We ought to have something with us.'

'What time ought we to have breakfast?'

He hesitated. 'I want to make a very early start. Could you manage breakfast at half-past four, do you think?'

'Of course we can. I'll tell them that. I'd better pay the bills tonight, hadn't I?'

'Don't bother. I can see to that.'

She eyed him for a minute. 'I think you'd be much better in bed, Mr. Ross. You're going to have a long day tomorrow. You'd better let me do the little things I can do.'

He smiled. 'All right—if that's the way you feel about it.'

She nodded. 'That's how I feel about it, Mr. Ross. Have you got anything else to do?'

He hesitated. 'I've just got to go down and tell the boat-man that we'll want him in the morning. That's all.'

'What time do you want him?'

'Five o'clock at the jetty.'

'I'll go and tell him. You go up to bed.'

'All right.'

He went up to his room and undressed slowly, wondering at the turn that things had taken. It was going to make an enormous difference to him if the girl carried on like this.

When they reached Julianehaab and connected up with Jameson his work would be much relieved; until that time he wanted all the help he could get. He was grateful to her.

He put on his pyjamas, turned out the light, and got into his bed. She had a lovely figure, when her things were wet. If only she'd wear decent clothes she could be really beautiful.

He slept.

Alix paid the bills for all of them, arranged for them to be called, for their breakfast, and for their sandwiches. Then her father joined her, and they strolled together down the wide main street of the little town to the boatman's cottage, and gave him his instructions. They sauntered back to the hotel in the warm evening.

Lockwood said: 'Well, we're off on the big hop tomorrow. Six or seven hundred miles over the sea to Iceland. Are you still glad you decided to come?'

'I think so, Daddy.'

They walked on in meditative silence. 'So am I,' the don said at last. 'But there's much more in this trip than I thought there would be.'

'I know. I thought it would be just like going somewhere in a train.'

'I didn't think it would be quite like that . . .' He glanced down at the girl. 'We're absolutely in the pilot's hands. If he makes a mistake, we'll be done for, Alix. How do you feel about that? Have you got confidence in him?'

She met his eyes. 'I have. He's so wrapped up in his work, I don't believe he could make a mistake.'

Her father said: 'I feel like that myself. I think we're going to be all right.'

They went back to the hotel and to their rooms.

Next morning before dawn Ross was standing in the chilly, deserted hall in his pyjamas, talking to the Air Ministry from the telephone box. The weather report was unchanged. He went back to his room and dressed, and brought his slim kit-bag down to the hall again. Alix was there before him.

She was wearing the white overall and her fur-lined flying boots; she was bareheaded. He met her with a smile. 'Good morning,' he said. 'We've got a decent day for it, I think. Is your father getting up?'

'He's just coming.' She hesitated. 'Do you think this is all right?'

He looked her up and down. 'It's very serviceable. You'll be able to get your flying suit on over it all right.' He felt the texture of the material on her arm. 'It's good stuff, too. How much did they stick you for it?'

'Nineteen and six.'

'It ought to be a good one for that.' He smiled. 'It looks nice, too.' The girl was unreasonably pleased.

Lockwood joined them, and they breakfasted. Then, carrying their small personal luggage, they left the hotel and went down to the jetty. The boatman was waiting for them, and in the clear light of the dawn they were carried swiftly to the seaplane. The sun was just rising at the entrance to the firth; the sky was clear, the water a deep indigo blue between the heather-covered hills. The air was fresh, and crisp, and invigorating.

The Lockwoods got up into the cabin, and for twenty minutes Ross busied himself about the machine. Finally they signalled to the boatman to cast off. A light wind was blowing down the firth from the west; the pilot turned and taxied down towards Cromarty till he had a run of several miles before him. Then he swung round into the wind and opened up his engine. The heavily laden floats were sunk deep in the water; the seaplane ploughed along with a great wash, gathering speed very slowly. After nearly a mile she rose on to the steps of the floats and gained speed more rapidly till she was skimming from wave-top to wave-top, cracking down heavily on each. In the seat the pilot sat tense and anxious, trying everything he knew to get her off. Once she was bumped up by a lucky wave and made a long hop in the air, but she sank back again; he could not keep her flying. Finally he throttled back.

'We'll have to dump ten gallons of our fuel,' he said. 'She'll never make it with this load.'

He taxied over to the motor boat and stopped his engine; they passed a light line to the boat. Ross got down on to the floats and busied himself at the sump of the big tank beneath the fuselage; presently a stream of petrol poured away into the sea. He made the cock secure and got back into the cabin; with Lockwood to help him he started up the engine again, and cast off from the motor-boat.

This time he chose a run slightly more under the lee of the land where the waves were not so high. Again she ploughed along a long way before getting up on to the step,

but after that it went better. She left the water after a run
of about a mile and a half, touched again lightly; then she
was clear and climbing slowly from the firth, her floats
dripping and drying quickly in the rush of air. The pilot
let her climb straight ahead for a time; at three hundred feet
he put her in a wide turn and relaxed.

He flew back over Invergordon and crossed the neck of
the land to Tain, running out his aerial as he did so. Scotland
lay spread out before them, purple with heather, cut with
deep blue lochs, and very beautiful. The pilot turned and
flew north-west to Lairg; then he followed the length of
Loch Shin to the west coast. As soon as the aerial was out
he began transmitting on his wireless, and was soon in touch
with the Fleet Air Arm station at Evanton. He reported his
position, course and speed; then he changed his wave and
tried to get in touch with Reykjavik. To his surprise he got
them straight away, and tapped out a message to them in
morse.

It was about a quarter to seven when he left the water at
Invergordon. They were over the west coast of Scotland at
a quarter to eight, flying at three thousand feet. They headed
straight out to sea from the coast, passing the Butt of Lewis
on their port hand at a quarter-past eight. That dropped
astern. Then there was nothing to be seen except the wide
disc of the sea, a grey and corrugated sea, blotched here and
there with cloud shadows.

Ross abandoned the English stations and concentrated
upon Reykjavik, transmitting his estimated position each
half-hour. Between transmissions he peered through his drift
sight at the slowly moving waves below, did little sums upon
the slide rule, plotted their position on the map. He was
continuously busy. Lockwood sat beside him watching these
activities, bored and a little uneasy. They were so far from
land, so far from any possibility of help if they should need
it. In the whole crossing they only saw one ship, a trawler
soon after they left Scotland.

Alix sat behind the pilot, wondering from time to time
what he was doing. The tapping of the little key, she knew,
meant that he was sending out a message on the wireless;
she did not know to whom he was sending, and he was too
preoccupied to explain. She did not know what he was looking at when he stared downwards through a hole cut in the
floor, fiddling with some instrument. She did not know the

purpose of the little handle above his head that he adjusted delicately from time to time, or what calculations he was doing on the slide rule. Yet it was clear to her that he knew just what he was doing, and that everything was going well. There was no uncertainty about his movements, no fumbling or hesitation. They were in good hands. Presently she relaxed and dozed a little.

They went on like that, hour after hour.

The clouds came lower as they went on, forcing them down to fifteen hundred feet. The weather remained good, however, and the sky was never wholly overcast. At twelve o'clock Ross said to Lockwood:

'We might see land ahead any time now, sir. By my reckoning we're about sixty miles off.'

The don peered forward, but the horizon was hazy; there was nothing to be seen. Presently the clouds came lower still; Ross took the machine down to about eight hundred feet. From that height they could see the waves; there was a long swell running, difficult to land in if they had to. The girl looked at the grey rollers pensively; she felt that she hated the sea. Any sort of land would be better than this grey stuff, with its little streaks of foam.

Suddenly she leaned forward and said: 'Mr. Ross!'

He swung round in his seat. 'Yes?'

'What's the matter with the sea? It's gone a different colour.'

He looked down quickly. The dark grey had changed to a dirty, milky hue. He said: 'Good enough—that means we're very near. Quick of you to spot that.'

'Does the sea change colour near land?'

'It does here, according to the books. It's the glaciers or something.'

They peered into the haze ahead. In a minute or two the pilot said:

'There it is. See? Over there.'

They followed his direction. A dark lava rock was standing in the sea, ringed with white foam; then there was another, and a little island. Suddenly a rocky and forbidding coast was plain before them; the pilot pulled the seaplane up a little higher. Lockwood stared forward. 'What a horrible-looking place!'

The pilot smiled. 'I've heard of people coming to Iceland for their summer holiday.'

Freed from the strain of the last hours, Alix laughed, a little shrilly. The pilot turned in his seat. 'Let's have those sandwiches,' he said. 'It'll be an hour before we get to Reykjavik.'

The little occupation of unwrapping the sandwiches steadied the girl; the food itself refreshed them and removed their fatigue. The presence of the land raised their spirits; they began to study the countryside with interest and to comment on it cheerfully as they had their lunch. It was a land of little barren farms along by the sea-shore, with hills rising sharply to the north, lined with white streaks of glaciers running down from the ice-cap. Ross flew a little way inland from the coast, homing with his wireless upon the broadcasting station. Presently they crossed a ridge of high land by a lake; in front of them lay Faxa Fjord, and Reykjavik.

Ross circled over the town, studying the port. 'I think I'll land outside in the fjord and taxi into the harbour,' he said. 'There ought to be a red buoy for us, straight opposite the jetty.' He turned to the girl, smiling, 'Can you possibly do your stuff again, Miss Lockwood?'

'Of course.'

'Good enough. Look, put on one of those life-belts before you get out.'

He made a wide circuit, throttled back and brought the machine down to the surface by the harbour wall. She touched gently, sank down into the water, and came to rest. In the cabin the girl took off her stockings and put on her sand-shoes and her life jacket; the pilot turned and taxied into the made harbour.

This time the mooring went off without an incident. The pilot saw his buoy some distance off and taxied over to it; fifty yards away he slowed down to a walking pace and the girl got down on to the float, boathook in hand. He brought the buoy up to her feet; she caught it with the boathook, clipped the spring hook on to it, and threw it back at once.

She stood on the float looking up at the pilot, leaning sideways out of his window. 'How's that, Mr. Ross?'

The seaplane drifted back and lay quietly at the mooring. 'Money for jam,' he said. 'It's too easy.'

She laughed. 'I didn't even get my feet wet that time.'

He stopped the engine and turned off the petrol. A motor-boat came out to them from the shore and drew up near to them; the man in it hailed to them.

'Hvor kommer De fra? Fra Skotland?'

Ross shook his head. He called out to the man, 'Are you Mr. Sorensen?'

The boatman smiled at them. 'Not speak Engelsk,' he said. He added an incomprehensible sentence.

Alix, still standing on the float, said: 'Er De Herr Sorensen?'

The man addressed himself to her. Presently she turned to Ross, a little doubtfully. 'I think he's saying that Mr. Sorensen has had to go away, and he'll be back tonight. He's Sorensen's man, all right.'

The pilot stared at her. 'Do you speak Danish?'

'Not properly. I did a month at the Berlitz school before we started.'

They beckoned to the boat to come alongside. The girl spoke to the boatman for a time, slowly and haltingly, fumbling for her words. Then she turned back to Ross. 'He says, Mr. Sorensen told him to look out for us. We can use the boat. He knows where the petrol is, if you want it.'

The pilot nodded. 'We'd better get our things up to the hotel, and then I'll come back and fill her up. If this fine weather lasts I want to go to Angmagsalik tomorrow. Get along while the going's good.'

They collected their personal luggage from the machine and got into the boat. As they went towards the shore the boatman began explaining something to Alix. She listened with strained attention to his many repetitions. Then she turned to Ross.

'He says he knows a good place where you can get the seaplane on shore, right out of the water, if you want to. It's something to do with trawlers, I think. I couldn't quite make out what it is.'

'Probably a slipway.' The pilot looked around him at the sky. 'It all seems pretty settled. Tell him I want to get a weather report. If it's a good one, we'll leave her where she is, I think, and go on in the morning.' He smiled at her. 'Can you put that over?'

'I'll try.'

She made arrangements for the man to meet him again in an hour's time for the refuelling; then they landed at the jetty and walked up to the hotel through a small crowd of spectators. The girl felt conspicuous in her overalls, and was glad to get into her room to change. From the hotel, the pilot went alone to the Meteorological Office in the broadcasting building.

He was welcomed warmly by the meteorologist, who had been responsible for the Reykjavik end of their wireless messages in the morning as they crossed from Scotland. He told Ross at once that the weather between Reykjavik and Angmagsalik was fine that day, but liable to sudden changes. However, they expected it to last for the next day or two.

Ross talked his programme over with the meteorologist and made arrangements with him for a forecast at six o'clock next morning. A true isobaric forecast would not be available; the best that they could do would be to get a message from Angmagsalik to say what it was like there. If it was good at both ends, he decided, he would start.

He asked: 'Is there much ice in the fjord at Angmagsalik?'

He was told: 'It has been a good season. The pack broke early, and the ice has been not much at Angmagsalik. There has been fog this year—plenty, plenty.'

Of the two, he would rather have had ice. Both were bad enough.

He went back to the hotel, and told Lockwood what he had decided. 'If you're game for it, sir, I'd like to get along tomorrow—the weather seems as good as it ever is in these parts. If we did that I wouldn't mind how long we take to do the rest of it.'

The don nodded. 'You're quite happy about the machine? You wouldn't like to have a day here to look her over?'

The pilot shook his head. 'She's all right. I'm just going down to fill her up, with the boatman; then she'll be all ready for us in the morning.'

He went out through the hall of the hotel. Alix was there, dressed in her blue jersey with rather a sad-looking grey skirt. She said: 'Are you going to fill up, Mr. Ross?'

He nodded. 'I'm just going down now. I want to get that done right away.'

'I'll come with you.'

He smiled. 'Don't bother about that, Miss Lockwood. I can manage all right with the boatman.'

'I'd like to come, if I won't be in the way.'

He shook his head. 'You won't be in the way. As a matter of fact, you'll be able to talk to him for me.'

They found the man down at the jetty. The petrol was in

cans in the fuel store three hundred yards from the boat; Ross and the boatman set to work to carry it down, helped by a little boy. The girl stood and watched their work, can after can, journey after journey, from the store to the boat. At the end of three-quarters of an hour of heavy work they were ready to go out to the seaplane.

The refuelling commenced. The girl squatted in the rear part of the cabin, translating now and again for Ross. Apart from that, there was little she could do to help him. Sitting there and watching, she was amazed and a little shocked at the hard physical work the pilot had to do. First, the contents of the big tank had to be pumped into the service tanks in the wings. The pump was a small double-acting cylinder beside the pilot's seat, worked by an oscillating handle that could be operated only with one hand. About a hundred and ten gallons had to be pumped from the big tank to the service tanks, five feet higher in the wing. For half an hour the pilot worked the handle; then the boatman took a turn and Ross came aft to Alix, streaming with sweat, mopping his face with a handkerchief.

She said: 'That's a terrible job, Mr. Ross. Isn't there any better way of doing it?'

He said: 'It's not so bad, really. In the air that amount of fuel would last about six hours. You'd have that time to get it up. It's no work then; the pumping gives you something to do. It's only when you're filling up that it's a bit of trouble.'

He sat down by her on the sleeping-bags, dazed and fatigued. The strain of the morning's flight was coming out; he felt sleepy, sick, and muddled in the head. It was impossible to smoke a cigarette because of the petrol fumes. He yawned. 'Get to bed early tonight,' he said. 'I want to go on early tomorrow morning, if we can.'

'Wouldn't you rather wait a day, Mr. Ross? We've got plenty of time in hand.'

'I don't think we'd better, unless you're anxious to, Miss Lockwood. We've got good weather now. Once it breaks, up in these latitudes, it may be bad for a long time. We might get stuck here for a fortnight.'

'I suppose so,' Alix said. 'Shall we be starting very early?'

He smiled slowly. 'I won't make you get up at half-past four again. We'll have an easy day. Breakfast at half-past five.'

She laughed. 'I don't mind getting up at half-past four, if you want to start then.'

He shook his head. 'There's no point in it. I must have the weather report before we go, and I can't get that till six.' He considered for a moment. 'Besides, we aren't going so far. It's only four hundred and eighty miles to Angmagsalik.'

The pump sucked. The boatman got down into the motor boat and began passing up petrol cans to Ross. The petrol was in two-gallon cans. The pilot stood in the cabin emptying these cans into a very large duralumin funnel lined with chamois leather; from long experience of the North he was insistent on straining every drop of petrol that went into the machine.

In all, they put in about a hundred and forty-five gallons: seventy-three cans. Very soon they found the routine. The boatman handed up a can to Alix at the cabin door, who passed it up to Ross at the petrol tank, receiving from him an empty one in exchange. She passed that down to the boatman and took another full one; it went on interminably. The cockpit windows and the cabin door were open, but the cabin was filled with petrol fumes. Before long the girl was faint and dizzy; she had to force herself to go on with the work. The pilot, stooping above the petrol funnel in the close, hot little cabin, worked on doggedly. It took them rather over two hours to put in the petrol.

After that there was the oil tank to be filled, the filters to be cleaned, and the sumps to be checked.

The girl sat in the boat while this was going on, recovering herself in the clean air, watching the pilot as he stood upon the floats at his work. It was nearly seven o'clock; they had been working for three and a half hours, and she was very tired. The sun was getting towards the horizon; the mountains and the little town were bathed in the warm glow of evening. The seaplane and the motor-boat rocked quietly together on the calm, dappled water of the harbour. The pilot worked on steadily, methodically. For the first time Alix began to understand long-distance flying. It was not courage, or resourcefulness, or ability that counted in this game, though they were necessary subsidiary qualities. It was the capacity to work efficiently at tiring, menial tasks upon the ground that made great flights a success.

At last Ross was finished. He locked the cabin door and got down into the boat, hot and dirty. As they were carried

95

to the shore she made arrangements with the boatman for Ross to be able to get at the boat if wind should get up in the night, and for the boat to meet them at the jetty at a quarter-past six in the morning. Then they landed, and walked slowly up to the hotel.

'It's been very good of you to come and help, Miss Lockwood,' said the pilot wearily. 'It's got us through much quicker.'

'I never knew that there was so much work in it.'

'It's not so bad really. Takes a bit of time. Your Danish came in very handy.' He glanced at her curiously. 'Did you go and learn it specially for this trip?'

She nodded. 'Uncle David said it would be useful.'

'Uncle David knows his stuff.' They reached the hotel. 'Would you like a drink when we've had a wash, Miss Lockwood?'

'I should think we've earned it.'

He nodded. 'Sherry? I'll order it when I get down.'

He met Lockwood in the lounge as he came down from his room; the don ordered the drinks. 'Sherry for Miss Lockwood,' said the pilot. 'I'll have a tomato cocktail.'

Alix came in as he spoke. 'Break your rule and have a whisky and soda,' she said. 'It'll give you an appetite.'

He shook his head. 'I'm all right,' he said smiling. 'I'd rather stick to something soft, if you don't mind.'

Lockwood said: 'Do you make a point of that?'

The pilot looked uncomfortable. 'Well—in a way. I'll drink a bucket with you when we get down to New York.'

Presently they went in to dinner. The Lockwoods made a good meal; the pilot was too tired and too sick from the petrol fumes to eat very much. At the end they got up and went to take coffee in the lounge. Ross stretched himself in his armchair and relaxed. 'I'd like to take a little walk along by the harbour presently,' he said. 'Not very far, and then a spot of bed.'

Lockwood said: 'That's a good idea: I'll come out with you. You've had a heavy day, Mr. Ross.'

'Oh, not so bad. But I'll be glad to get to bed.'

A stout Icelandic gentleman came bustling into the lounge and asked a question at the desk. Then he crossed the room to them, irradiating bonhomie, and bowed to them stiffly from the waist.

'Sorensen,' he said. 'I am very sorry that I was not here

to meet you when you arrived. Just now I have come back from Thorlakshavn.' He explained. 'Just now. Directly.'

The pilot got to his feet; the others followed him. Introductions were made and they all shook hands; Alix got a specially low bow. Ross said: 'You left us in very good hands, Mr. Sorensen. Your boatman did everything most efficiently.'

The stout man beamed. 'I am happy. He has said that you are now full up with gas.'

The corners of the don's mouth twitched ever so slightly. They talked for a few minutes about the seaplane and about the flight. Ross knew something about the agent; he was a member of the Government and an important man in Reykjavik.

He said: 'You have already eaten? I feel very bad. I have not been in Reykjavik to meet you, and to entertain. In Reykjavik we have great interest in the sciences, and in archæology. Have you yet seen our Cathedral? There is much interesting there.'

Ross shook his head. 'I'm afraid we haven't had time to see anything of Reykjavik. We've been refuelling the machine all the afternoon, and we're going on in the morning. I want to make an early start to get to Angmagsalik while this good weather lasts.'

'So! Then we have very little time. We will go now, and I will show you the Cathedral, and the Town Hall, and the Fishing Docks. In my auto we will go—yes. And then we go to my house to meet some members of our Government, who wish to welcome you to Iceland.'

The pilot's heart sank. He was resolved to make an early start next morning, and he was longing for his bed. At the same time, it was clear that he could not refuse this invitation without giving offence. Some sixth sense warned him that he had better not do that; he might have need of Mr. Sorensen.

He said: 'It really is most kind of you. I want to get back early, though. We've got to make a very early start tomorrow morning.'

Lockwood said diffidently: 'You do us more honour than we deserve, Herr Sorensen.' He, too, was thinking of his bed.

The agent bowed stiffly from the waist. 'On the contrary, it is Iceland that is honoured.'

Alix said boldly: 'Would you feel it rude of me if I let the men go alone, Herr Sorensen? I'm not really accustomed to flying, and I'm very tired.'

He excused her and she went to bed at once; Lockwood and Ross went with him to the car. For an hour they drove around the town, still bathed in evening light in those high latitudes, maintaining a flow of polite admiration for the buildings and the harbour works that he showed them with such local pride, in which they could feel little interest. Finally they drew up at a large, well-built house a little way outside the town.

They went in, and were presented with some ceremony to Fru Sorensen. Then they were presented to six or seven Icelandic business men, sombre in dark clothes, wooden and courteous, and speaking very little English. In this atmosphere of formal hospitality it was impossible for the pilot to refuse a glass of schnapps.

'It is very healthy to drink Bols in Iceland,' said Fru Sorensen solemnly. 'It is necessary for the cold and damp. In Iceland, those who do not drink Bols become ill.'

Almost immediately the double doors of the salon were thrown open, and supper was announced. They went through to a heavy meal prepared in their honour in the next room. Ross was unable to refuse another Bols; the hot, stinging liquor gave him an appetite, and he ate a good meal. Coffee came, with more Bols, and they settled to the serious business of the evening. Lockwood, on his part, had to give a little lecture on the scientific objects of the flight. He found he had a well-read and attentive audience, who started a discussion upon Celtic influence in Iceland that went on interminably, in very difficult English. Then it was the pilot's turn, and for half an hour he had to tell them all about the flight.

It was after midnight when they got back to the hotel, tired, overeaten, and stupefied with liquor. They parted from Sorensen in the lounge; on the stairs Lockwood said ruefully: 'They certainly are most hospitable.'

Ross said: 'That's the curse of trips like this. They can't do enough for you.'

He turned into his room, set his alarm clock for five o'clock, and sank into a drugged insensibility. Four and a half hours later the clamour of the bell woke him; he got up feeling tired and unwell. He had a bath and felt much better; then he dressed and went down to the lounge.

Alix was there. 'I had a lovely night,' she said. 'What time did you get to bed?'

The pilot smiled. 'We weren't so late. I think we've got a good day for our crossing.'

Lockwood joined them, and they went in to breakfast. Then, while Alix paid their bill, Ross walked up to the Meteorological Office.

He was told: 'There is a little wind at Angmagsalik, and it is fine. Yesterday there was fog in the afternoon, but it is clear now. Today there may be fog later.'

Ross said: 'It's only five hours' flight. If I take off now I ought to be all right.'

'So. I have told Angmagsalik to listen for your messages, and to tell you of the weather as you go.'

'That's very kind of you. If it looks bad, we'll come back.'

'That will be safe. I think there will be wind here later, but not to stop you landing.'

Ross left, and went down to the harbour. The Lockwoods were waiting for him at the boat, talking to Sorensen. He came out with them to the seaplane. Ross took him into the cabin and explained the machine and the controls to him; then he got down into the boat again, and they were ready to start.

CHAPTER V

THE machine took off after a long run, with fuel for about thirteen hundred miles on board. Ross turned on to the course for Angmagsalik, a little to the north of west, four hundred and eighty miles away. He let the machine climb slowly as she went, till they got up to about three thousand feet.

The day was bright and sunny; there was no cloud in the sky. In spite of the sun it was much colder than in lower latitudes; they were all wearing flying clothing, and glad of it. The machine droned on over a steel-coloured sea; they settled to the familiar routine of a flight. Away to the north they could see a mountain with a white snow-cap, Snaefell, nearly seventy miles away on the north side of Faxa Fjord. Presently this was left behind, and they went on into the blue.

99

They had left the water at about seven o'clock. At half-past nine Lockwood nudged the pilot and pointed to the sea ahead of them, now flecked with white. 'What is all that?' he asked. 'Is that ice?'

Ross nodded. 'It's the pack ice just beginning. It'll probably get thicker as we get towards the coast.'

It may have done, but they were not to see it. As they crossed the beginning of the pack a mist formed low down on the water; as they went on this turned into a bank of cloud below them. Ross had spoken to Angmagsalik half an hour before; he now sent out another message asking what the weather was like there.

The reply was to the effect that the sky was clouding over. Visibility was still good, but likely to get worse.

Ross scribbled down the letters as they came upon the pad strapped to his knee; the message ended, he switched off the receiver, and considered the scrawled message. It would be over two hours before they could reach Angmagsalik; the question that he had to solve was whether visibility would be too bad to land when he got there. He showed the pad to Lockwood, and explained the position to him.

'I think we'll be all right,' he said. 'It's getting worse, but we ought to be there before it's really bad.'

The don nodded. 'Do just as you think fit,' he said. 'If you think we should turn back, do so.'

The pilot shook his head. 'We've got plenty of fuel on board. I think we'll carry on for a bit, and see how it goes. We'll never get there if we wait for perfect weather in these latitudes.'

An hour later the clouds had risen close beneath them and they were climbing slowly to keep in the clear air. Angmagsalik reported a cloud ceiling at fifteen hundred feet, and visibility five kilometres. The pilot's lips tightened; it was getting worse, but they were little more than an hour's flight away. He decided to go on.

Presently they were flying at five thousand feet just above the cloud, which stretched as a white, level plain upon each side of them, and rose to greater heights ahead beneath the clear blue sky. Ross was busy with the wireless, homing upon Angmagsalik. After a time he turned to Lockwood.

'We must be just about on top of it now,' he said.

The time was about noon. At five thousand feet the cloud plain was uninterrupted, brilliant in the sun. The pilot put the seaplane into a wide turn and peered around. 'I don't want to go down blind through all this muck,' he said. 'It's very mountainous around here. We've got to find a hole, or we may land before we want to.'

Behind him the girl shivered a little.

For a quarter of an hour they flew in circles, looking for a gap in the clouds. In one wide sweep the machine went further to the west than hitherto; the cloud plain in that direction rose considerably higher. The white surface approached the floats; the pilot, looking vainly for a hole, absently pulled the machine a little higher to clear the cloud.

Quite suddenly, he knew that something was not right. He jammed the throttle open with a swift reflex action before he stopped to think, pulled on the wheel; the seaplane soared upwards in a steep climb. The sudden changes startled Alix and Lockwood; they grabbed hold of their seats and stared at the pilot. He was leaning his shoulder to the open window at his side, staring down intently. Presently he relaxed, and throttled down again.

He turned to the don, his tanned face a little paler than usual.

'Just look at that!'

Lockwood could see nothing unusual. 'The cloud?'

Ross exclaimed: 'It's not a cloud. It's snow! That's the bloody ice-cap!'

They stared down at the surface, fascinated. It merged into the cloud plain behind them, barely distinguishable at the junction. Presently Lockwood said mildly: 'It's a good thing you noticed it. I should never have known the difference.'

The pilot smiled wryly. 'We'd have known the difference quick enough if we'd tried to fly through it.'

He turned again to the wireless; his face was set and anxious. From the strength of the signals Angmagsalik was evidently very close. They told him that the clouds had come down to a thousand feet, and visibility was not more than two kilometres. It had begun to rain. Up there, in the bright sunlight, with the blue sky and the brilliant clouds, it seemed incredible that it should be raining.

Ross swung the seaplane round on to an easterly course and tried his petrol gauges very carefully. Then he turned to Lockwood; he had made up his mind.

'It's no good sir,' he said. 'I'm going back to Reykjavik.'

The don said quietly: 'Have we got enough petrol?'

The pilot nodded. 'I think we'll be all right. I wouldn't have taken off without enough to get back with if this happened to us. I'm sorry, but it's the only thing to do. We'll break our bloody necks if we try going down in this.'

Lockwood said: 'Well, let's have lunch.'

Alix unpacked the sandwiches and passed them round. As she did so, Ross tapped out a message to Reykjavik to say he was returning. They acknowledged it, and gave him the weather report:

'Wind here thirty kilos north-east probably going to east.'

The pilot read this on his pad; his face was a mask. A twenty-mile-an-hour head wind meant that they would be the best part of six hours in getting back. He tried his petrol gauges again carefully; in theory, and if the gauges were correct, they should be just all right. He ate a couple of sandwiches and took the machine slowly up to seven thousand feet; there he weakened the mixture to the utmost that he dared, and set his course accurately for Reykjavik.

Already they had been in the air for well over five hours. He turned in his seat and spoke to the girl. 'I'm afraid this is going to be a long business,' he said. 'Are you very tired?'

'I'm all right, thanks, Mr. Ross. One gets a bit sore, sitting in the one position all the time.'

'Why don't you change places with Mr. Lockwood?' he suggested. 'It makes it a bit less boring to move round now and again.'

The don said: 'That's a very good idea.'

They changed places. The movement made a diversion and the change of seat refreshed them for a time. The seaplane droned steadily across the sky. An hour or so later the clouds fell away beneath them and grew thinner; presently they saw a rough grey sea, thickly spattered with pack ice. The pilot sent another message to Reykjavik reporting his estimated position and asking for the wind strength; it was much the same.

The steady, even droning of the engine, the high altitude, the warm sunlight, were all infinitely soothing. They had been in the air for about seven hours; the pilot's eyes dropped from the gyro compass, lost their focus. Slowly the eyelids fell over his eyes, his chin sank slowly to his chest. For an instant he slept. Then, with a violent start, he was awake again.

He shot a glance furtively at the girl beside him. She did not seem to have noticed anything. In a few minutes his eyelids dropped again. He jerked himself awake, moved in his seat, and stretched himself. He studied the clock, flogging his tired mind to concentrate. Cruising at his most economical speed, his ground speed was not more than eighty-five against this wind. That meant four hours more, at least.

He turned to the girl, dozing beside him. 'Miss Lockwood,' he said quietly. 'would you mind talking to me? I'm afraid of going to sleep.'

She roused, and realised the significance of what he had said. 'Of course I will. I was nearly asleep myself. Are you very tired?'

He shook his head. 'Not tired. But it's like driving a car on a hot afternoon.'

She said: 'I know. Look, tell me what some of these things are. What's that?' She pointed to the directional gyro on the instrument board.

'It's the gyro. You use it to steer by. You see these figures on it? They're degrees.'

'Is it a compass?'

'Not exactly. You set it by the compass.'

'Why don't you use the compass then?'

Behind them Lockwood was sound asleep. The girl would have liked to sleep herself; she had sufficient wit to realise the danger. If she slept, Ross would sleep; then they would all sleep for ever in the Arctic Ocean. She opened the window at her side and let in a cold draught. She shifted in her seat, and forced herself to try to understand the instruments; on his side Ross exerted himself to explain to her in simple language how the things worked. Presently the craving for sleep left him.

The instrument board and the controls, explained and demonstrated in every detail, lasted them for an hour. The seaplane droned on over the sea; for a short time they were silent. Alix glanced at the pilot, saw his gaze become vacant, and nudged him with her elbow.

He turned to her. 'It's all right,' he said, smiling. 'I wasn't asleep.'

'You'd have been asleep in a minute. Come on, let's go on talking.'

'All right. What shall we talk about?'

'Tell me how you came to take up flying.'

'I just went into the Air Force from school.'

'Where did you go to school?'

'At Guildford. I was a day boy.' She was absolutely right; they must keep talking. He began to tell her about his life as a boy. It didn't matter what he said; the main thing was to keep talking. He told her about the little house in Guildford where he had been brought up. He told her about Aunt Janet who taught mathematics at the girls' school for two hundred pounds a year, and how she had spent a good part of that upon his education. As they talked, the Arctic Ocean flowed slowly past beneath their windows. He told her how Aunt Janet had wanted him to go to Oxford, but there was no money. He told her how she had sent him into the Air Force as the next best thing. Alix said: 'It may have been a better thing for you, Mr. Ross. Oxford isn't the right place for everybody, you know.'

The pilot said: 'I suppose not. But I'd have like to have gone there.'

The girl said: 'I think Aunt Janet sounds a dear. She must be very fond of you.'

Ross frowned a little. The idea of Aunt Janet being fond of anyone had never really crossed his mind. He said slowly: 'Yes, I suppose she must be. She'd never show it, though.'

The girl laughed. 'I'd like to meet her. Go on, Mr. Ross. What happened to you when you got into the Air Force?'

He told her about his training time in England, and about his service years in Egypt and in Iraq. Then for half an hour he told her about Canada, about the Company and all they did up in the North. Presently she stopped him for a moment, and pointed to the far horizon.

'What's that over there?'

He followed her direction, and saw a very faint white peak. 'Must be Snaefell. It can't be anything else.'

'It's nice to see a bit of land again.'

Ross swung the machine for a moment and took a bearing of it; then, working awkwardly with map and protractor on his knee, he laid off their position. 'About a hundred and ten miles still to go.'

He took another reading of the petrol gauges, and his lips

tightened. There was nothing else to do. He throttled back a little more, and slowly opened the altitude control to its extreme limit. The engine immediately began to run very rough; the indicator of the cylinder-head temperatures went up fifty degrees. The pilot sat watching his instruments intently for the first sign of real trouble. He might be ruining his engine with the weak mixture; on the other hand, it should last them for an hour or so. The alternative was to come down in the sea before they got to land, a rough sea in which the seaplane could not hope to live for very long.

He sent out another message to Reykjavik telling them his estimated time of arrival and asking for facilities to get the seaplane up on shore. He thought ruefully that there would be a lot of work to do upon the engine before the seaplane flew again.

Still, it was no good worrying about that. He turned back to Alix by his side. 'Tell me about yourself, Miss Lockwood. We may as well keep talking.'

She said: 'There's nothing to tell, Mr. Ross. I was born in our house—the one you know—and I went to school near Oxford.'

'Have you lived in Oxford all your life?'

She nodded. 'Yes—except for holidays. I've been to Switzerland for winter sports. And I went to Crete with Daddy once. I didn't like it, much.'

She paused, and then she said: 'This is the biggest thing that ever happened to me.'

The pilot smiled. 'It's the biggest thing that ever happened to me, too.'

They talked on for a time about her school, and about her time at Somerville. On the horizon Snaefell grew rapidly larger. Lockwood woke up, and they showed him the mountain and the distant line of coast, clear in the evening sunlight.

He said: 'Isn't the engine running differently, Mr. Ross?'

The pilot turned in his seat. 'I've had to put her on weak mixture, sir, to make the fuel last out. I think we've got enough to get us into Reykjavik, but I'll have to have a good look round the engine after this. I've told them that I want to get her up on shore, so that I can get the cowling off and have a good look round.'

In the end the town loomed up before them. The sea in the outer harbour was running fairly high; Ross decided to land in the confined space of the inner harbour. He rubbed a hand across his tired eyes, brought the seaplane low, rumbled in just above the breakwater, and put her down into an open lane between the trawlers. The quick reaction that made him a good pilot was killed by fatigue; the machine bounced heavily upon the dirty water of the harbour, and rose into the air again. He caught her with a little burst of engine; she bounced down heavily again in a great shower of spray, lurched forward on the floats, and came to rest. Slowly she pivoted round into the wind.

It was seven o'clock. They had been in the air for exactly twelve hours. There were five gallons of petrol left in the tanks, enough for about twenty minutes' flying.

The pilot sighed. He turned round in his seat and spoke to Lockwood. 'Home again,' he said wearily. 'I'm sorry about this, sir, but it really wasn't fit to go down at Angmagsalik. It's all in between the mountains—we must have decent weather to land there.'

'I'm sure you did the right thing, Mr. Ross. What is the next move?'

There was a fresh wind blowing in the harbour; the machine pitched slightly on the little waves, heading into the wind.

'We'll have to get the seaplane up on shore before tonight, sir. It may be going to blow hard.'

A motor-boat, the same that they had had before, came to them from the jetty; in it were Sorensen and a couple of dock hands. It drew up beneath the yellow wing. Sorensen beamed at them. 'So—you have returned? The weather was not good at Angmagsalik?'

The pilot shook his head. 'I want to get the seaplane up on to the slipway for the night,' he shouted. 'Can we do that?'

'All is quite prepared. We have heard your radio. There is a slipway for the trawlers, which is good.' He held up a rope. 'We will pull with the boat.'

They nosed the boat up gently to the floats from behind; Ross stopped his engine, and they took the seaplane in tow. The pilot sat slumped down in his seat, tired to death; the silence closed in upon them strangely.

Alix said quietly: 'You'll have to get to bed directly after dinner, Mr. Ross. No roistering with Sorensen tonight.'

The pilot passed a hand across his eyes, and turned to her. 'I should think we'd all be glad to get to bed. It makes a long day, when you're flying for this length of time. I'm sorry I made such a rotten landing.'

Lockwood said: 'It was bumpy, but you had very little room.'

'I know. I didn't like the look of the swell outside the harbour.'

They came slowly to the slipway. Men in waders were waiting to receive them; the machine was pulled up to the water's edge. One by one they got down on the float and so to shore. The ground felt heavy to their feet, their knees were weak.

Ross turned to the Lockwoods. 'Would you go on up to the hotel and get our rooms?' he said. 'I'll be along as soon as I've seen everything all right here.'

The don hesitated. 'Isn't there anything that we can do to help?'

'I don't think so, thanks. There seem to be heaps of people here, and Mr. Sorensen speaks English. If you'd go up and tell them to keep some dinner hot for us . . . I'll be along in about half an hour.'

It was much longer than that. The general opinion was that it was going to blow hard during the night. Ross could not leave till he had seen that the machine was pulled up well clear of the high tide, and firmly lashed down on the travelling cradle. There was no shelter available to house the seaplane. He spent a long time supervising the arrangements, till finally he was satisfied that she was safe.

It was between half-past eight and nine when he got back to the hotel. The Lockwoods were waiting for him in the lounge; they had not dined. He went and had a hurried wash, then joined them in the dining-room. Lockwood said: 'What are you drinking, Mr. Ross?'

'I think I'll just have water.'

Alix said unexpectedly: 'Are we going on tomorrow, Mr. Ross?'

'I'm afraid we can't, Miss Lockwood. After all that weak running, I must have a look at the engine. I'll have to take a couple of the pots off, I expect.'

She nodded. 'If we're not going to fly, you can have a whisky and soda. It'll do you good.'

'All right.'

Lockwood ordered him a double whisky; he drank it, and felt better. In the relaxation following the strain of the flight, the meal passed in a dream of fatigue. Over the coffee the eyelids dropped slowly down over his eyes, his head sagged. Alix, sitting beside him, nudged him with her elbow; he straightened up again.

She said: 'You'd better go to bed, Mr. Ross.'

He passed a hand across his eyes, and smiled. 'I'm so sorry. I was half asleep.'

The don said: 'I should go on up to bed. I'm going in a minute. So is Alix.'

'I believe I will—before old Sorensen come in and catches me.' He got to his feet, steadying himself by the table. 'Good night, Miss Lockwood. Good night, sir.'

He went out through the lounge and up the staircase. They watched him as he went. Lockwood said: 'I think our pilot's had about as much as he can stand.'

His daughter said: 'It was the party last night, Daddy. It was cruel, that. He can't have had nearly enough sleep.'

The don nodded. 'It would have been very difficult to get out of,' he said mildly. 'Still, I'm very glad to hear his engine needs attention. It won't do us any harm to wait here quietly for a day or two, and rest a bit.'

She laughed shortly. 'Do you think you'll get him to rest if his engine needs attention?'

Ross was in bed by ten. He slept immediately, a sleep of stunned insensibility. But by two o'clock he was awake again. In Reykjavik in summer there is no real darkness; his room was full of a half-light. He lay in bed, half sleeping and half waking, with a restless mind. He'd made a proper muck of things. Lord knew what sort of state he would find the engine in. The exhaust valves must be burnt out—probably the seatings, too. True, he had a set of new valves with him, just for this contingency. But if the seatings were destroyed, as they must be, the cylinders would have to go back to Detroit before the flight could continue. The pistons might be burnt as well. He rolled over on his pillow, sick at heart. He'd made a frightful mess of it! This flight was the big chance of his life to make a reputation—and he'd thrown it all away. He ought to have gone down at the first sight of clouds and crept in at five hundred feet between the pack ice and the cloud ceiling. He'd have got to Angmagsalik all right that way. He ought to have turned back earlier, at the first sign of doubtful weather. He ought never to have started. He ought to have done anything but what he had done.

He rolled over again, and the memory of the ice-cap came to him. Gross, unpardonable carelessness! He could still see the snow-slopes close beneath his floats—to think that anyone could be so reckless as to take them for a cloud. He had put them all within an ace of a crash—and such a crash! He lay in bed and felt the splintering impact, the violence of the pressure on his seat as the machine turned over, the hot blood welling out over his eyes, the snow cold on his hands. He might have killed them all. If they had lived through the crash they would have been there now, lying in the snowfield far from any help, freezing to death. Lockwood, who had given him the job because he had believed in him. Alix, who had helped him all she could, and talked to him to help him keep awake, who had a lovely figure when her things were wet . . .

Alix . . .

He roused himself, got out of bed, and had a drink of water.

He got back into bed and lay there wide awake, his active, restless mind at full pressure. He wouldn't have to send the cylinders to Detroit. They could be done at Amsterdam. If he got one off first thing in the morning for inspection . . . he could get the lot off before night. When he knew the worst, he could cable Amsterdam and make arrangements. If only there were a boat—a trawler, anything leaving Iceland. If he could get to the north of Scotland and get on the air line, he could fly to Amsterdam. Say five days—six days—from Reykjavik to Amsterdam, two days to replace the burnt seatings, six days back. Three days to reassemble the engine and test the machine. Three weeks' delay in all. The season would be far gone, but not irretrievably. They would get going again in the first week in August.

That was, if Lockwood was prepared to trust him again after a mess like this . . .

He dozed and lay awake intermittently for the rest of the night, restless and distracted. At six o'clock he got up, washed his face and dressed, and went downstairs. The porter of the hotel made him a cup of coffee; he drank it, and felt better. He went out into the town and found the boatman, and made him understand that he required a table. They got one from the boatman's house and carried it through the streets to the trawler slipway. Ross set it up beside the engine, tied a blanket down on it, got a bucket of paraffin, and began his work.

At half-past nine Lockwood rapped on his daughter's door. 'I'm getting up, Daddy,' she said. 'I'll be down in about ten minutes.'

She met him in the lounge. 'Where's Mr. Ross? Is he still in bed?'

Her father shook his head. 'He seems to be down with the seaplane. The porter says he had a cup of coffee and went out at about a quarter-past six.'

'But that's quite absurd! He can't possibly have had enough sleep!'

'He'll have had seven or eight hours.'

'Has he had any breakfast?'

'The porter said he had a cup of coffee.'

Alix said impulsively: 'We can't let him go on like this. I'm going down to fetch him up to breakfast.'

Her father stopped her. 'Let him do his work in his own way,' he said. 'Come on and eat your own breakfast. Then we'll go down and see what he's doing.'

She went through with him into the dining-room and ate a hurried meal.

Down on the slipway Ross was standing upon a trestle, carefully drawing the master cylinder off its piston. He carried it down to the ground and laid it on the table, then went up on to the trestle again and wrapped clean rags around the piston and the hole. He got down, and began to dismantle the valve mechanism on the cylinder.

A quarter of an hour later he was lighting a cigarette smeared with paraffin, and staring in wonder at the bits and pieces laid out on the table, still dripping from their wash.

There was no damage to that cylinder, at any rate. The piston was unharmed, the seatings were as bright as when they left the factory. The exhaust valve was a little red in colour but quite good; it would not even need re-facing. So far as he could see, in fact, that cylinder was in good condition.

There was a movement behind him; he turned, and there was Lockwood and the girl. He smiled at them. ''Morning,' he said, 'I've just been having a look at this.'

To Lockwood, he was looking drawn and tired. The don said: 'Is there much damage to the engine?'

The pilot blew a cloud of smoke and laughed, a little awkwardly. 'Nothing at all to this cylinder. I want to take another one off as a check, but it looks as if it's all a mare's nest, sir.'

Alix said: 'Have you had any breakfast, Mr. Ross?'

'Not yet. I wanted to see how matters stood down here.'

'Won't you leave it now, and come and have your breakfast?'

He shook his head. 'I'm quite all right, Miss Lockwood. I'd rather take another pot off right away, and make sure. I'll be through by lunch time. Then if everything's all right, I can start reassembling this afternoon.'

Lockwood said: 'Can we help you at all, Mr. Ross?'

'I really don't think there's anything that you could do, sir. I may want a hand this afternoon, but I can get a chap from the garage.'

Alix said: 'You won't be able to talk to him.'

He smiled. 'You'll have to come and translate for me again.'

They went away after a little time, and he went on with his work. An hour later another cylinder lay dismantled on the table; it was in similar condition to the first. There was no damage to the engine at all.

The pilot lit another cigarette. With the relief from the tension of anxiety he now felt curiously tired; it was as if all energy had been drained from him. He now felt that he had been foolish. He had been worrying himself unnecessarily, scaring himself with the bogies that did not exist. He should have been able to set his mind at rest and have a good night's sleep, instead of worrying himself crazy all that time he was in bed. It was no good going on like that. Great flights were made by men who kept their heads.

He reassembled the valve gear of both cylinders and put the cylinders and the tools carefully on the floor of the cabin. It was nearly time for lunch; he locked the cabin door and went up in to the town. He found a chemist's shop without much difficulty, and asked for aspirin.

The man shook his head. 'I have not aspirin. I have others, better. But not aspirin. You have pain?'

Ross said: 'I wanted it to help me sleep.'

'Ah, you cannot sleep! I have here what is good.' He went to a drawer and produced a little bottle of tablets. 'This good for you if you cannot sleep.'

Ross took it doubtfully, and examined it. It was the product of a German firm at Hanover, and was called Troxigin. 'It is like aspirin,' the chemist said. 'For sleep it is better.'

'All right,' said Ross. 'I'll take some of these.' The bottle held twenty-five tablets. 'But I shall want more than this. Have you got a bigger bottle?'

The man looked at him doubtfully. 'One only,' he said. He held up one finger. 'One each night. It is not good to take more.' He took the bottle and showed Ross the instructions, printed in German. 'One only.'

The pilot nodded. 'I understand. But I'd better have some more. There are two other people with me, and we are going on to Greenland.'

'Ah—to Greenland.' The words explained everything to the chemist; he made no further demur. He sold Ross a bottle of a hundred tablets; the pilot slipped it in his pocket and went back to the hotel for lunch.

He met the Lockwoods in the lounge and had a tomato cocktail with them. Alix said to him:

'At half-past four there is a meal called tea, Mr. Ross. I'd like you to remember it.'

He smiled: 'All right. I'm a good deal happier now than I was this morning.'

'It's all right, is it?'

He nodded. 'Quite all right. I'll get those pots put back this afternoon and finish off tomorrow morning. Then we can take her up for a short test flight tomorrow afternoon, fill her up, and get away next day if the weather's decent. Have another crack at it.'

They lunched; he had a good appetite, and ate well. He was not surprised to feel sleepy as he left the dining-room; he had to force himself to go and work.

Alix said: 'I'll come along this afternoon, Mr. Ross, if I may.'

He said: 'That would be very nice, Miss Alix. But don't if you've got anything else to do. I'll have to get a man from the garage.'

'What sort of help do you want?'

'Oh, only somebody to hold things for me. I wouldn't let a garage hand do any work upon the engine.'

'Well, I can hold things.'

He looked doubtful. 'I'm afraid you'll get very dirty.'

'I don't mind.'

She went down with him, and they worked together all afternoon upon the engine. Each cylinder in turn was cleaned with loving care and smeared internally with oil. Then Ross got up upon the trestle, undid the rags, cleaned and oiled the piston. Then Alix handed up the heavy cylinder to him: he held it while she got up on to the trestle by him. Then she held it while he delicately persuaded the piston to enter it, and slid it down gently on to its seating on the crank-case. Bolts were put on finger-tight; then the whole process was repeated with the other cylinder. Finally the engine was turned over with the propeller, and the bolts were tightened down and locked.

In the end, Ross got down and offered her a dirty cigarette. She took it with dirty fingers. 'I don't smoke much,' she said. 'But then, I don't do this much, either.'

He lit it for her. 'Do you know what time it is?'

She blew a cloud of smoke, and shook her head.

'Five o'clock. We're late for that tea you were talking about.'

'It doesn't matter. Daddy's gone to the Cathedral with Herr Sorensen.'

The pilot stretched himself. 'I don't feel like doing any more tonight. I'll finish off in the morning. Let's pack up.'

'All right. Have you written to Aunt Janet?'

He looked at her, startled. 'How did you know about Aunt Janet?'

'You told me about her.' She was amused. 'Yesterday, when we were flying back.'

'So I did. I had such a lot to think about yesterday, I'd quite forgotten that. I told you all about her, didn't I?'

She nodded. 'I think you might write and let her know how we've got on.'

He said: 'I'll send her a cable tonight.'

'Write her a letter, too. She'll like to have that, and there won't be any opportunity in Greenland.'

'All right.'

He locked up the machine and saw that everything was snug for the night. They walked back to the hotel, tired and dirty. Lockwood had not returned; presently they were sitting together in the lounge for tea.

The girl got up presently and went and fetched a pad of cable forms. 'Here you are,' she said. 'Write it out now, and we'll walk out and send it off.'

He smiled, and took the forms. 'Anyone would think she was your aunt, not mine.'

'Well, if it wasn't for me she wouldn't be getting a cable tonight, Mr. Ross.'

'Shall I tell her that?'

She laughed. 'If you like.'

Two hours later the messenger delivered a telegram at the little house in Guildford. Aunt Janet took it into the kitchen put on her spectacles, and opened the buff envelope. The message read:

ARRIVED REYKJAVIK WEDNESDAY GOING TO ANGMAGSALIK TOMORROW ALL WELL MISS LOCKWOOD SENDS REGARDS.

DONALD.

She read this in silence with pursed lips. It was good news that all was well, and they had got to Iceland safely. But why did the lassie send her regards, and above all why did Donald waste good money in saying so in a cable at seven-pence or eightpence a word, maybe more? It seemed a wicked waste. She put the cable on the mantelpiece, and set about making a little milk pudding for her supper. Presently she picked the cable up again, and stood it up so that she could see it.

'He never was one for saving money,' she muttered to herself presently. 'I doot he's getting fond of her.'

That night Ross went to bed early, soon after dinner, having posted a short letter to Aunt Janet. He opened the bottle of Troxigin in his room and took one of the tablets with a glass of water. He got into bed, not feeling very sleepy, but within ten minutes he was sound asleep. He slept quietly and well the whole night through, and did not wake until the morning call.

He lay awake for a few minutes before getting up, luxuri-ating in the feeling of freshness that he had gained by his sleep. He really had had a wonderful night, the best night's sleep that he had had for months. He realised that it was wholly due to the Troxigin, and was grateful to the drug. These German chemists knew their stuff all right...

That day was not a hard one. He was down at the machine by half-past eight; by eleven o'clock he had finished his assembly work, put in a hundred gallons of fuel, and sponged out the bilge-water that had leaked into the floats. Then he started up the engine with the seaplane still lashed down upon the slipway, ran it for twenty minutes, stopped it, and made a careful inspection. Finally he put on the engine cowling and made all ready for flight. Then he went back to the hotel for lunch.

'I'll take her up for a short test this afternoon, sir,' he said to Lockwood. 'Then I'll put her back on the mooring and fill her up with petrol. Would you like to come up with me?'

'I think Mr. Sorensen has something that he wants to show me at a place called Keflavik.'

Alix said: 'I'd like to come with you, Mr. Ross. I don't want to go to Keflavik.'

'All right.'

They got the seaplane down into the water at about half-past two, and took off shortly after that. Ross did a short test of the wireless with the Reykjavik station, then reeled in his aerial again.

Alix asked: 'That lever that you've got your hand on is the throttle, isn't it?'

'That's right. The little one is the mixture.'

'And then you steer it with the wheel?'

He shook his head and explained the rudder to her; for a time they flew erratically round the sky as she felt the controls. 'Beautifully balanced, isn't she?' he observed.

She did not know exactly what he meant. 'It must be rather fun flying her,' she said, relinquishing the wheel.

He glanced at her quizzically. 'Nasty, noisy things. Particularly when they're flying over Oxford.'

She flushed. 'They're beastly in Oxford. But it seems more suitable up here. I mean, they've got some purpose.'

He nodded.

They landed after about forty minutes' flight; the motor-boat met them and towed them to the mooring. They spent the rest of the afternoon filling up with fuel, hot and stifled by the fumes.

In the evening Ross went up alone to the broadcasting station. The report for the next day was good, with a light following wind and probably good visibility. He went back to the hotel and found Lockwood in the lounge, and told him about it.

The don looked at him keenly. 'How do you feel yourself, Mr. Ross? I know you haven't had a lot of sleep recently. If you'd like to stop another day and have a real rest, I think we've got plenty of time.'

The pilot smiled. 'That's very kind of you, sir. I appreciate it. But I'm quite all right now. I had a fine sleep last night—nearly twelve hours.' It was on the tip of his tongue to tell Lockwood about Troxigin, but he did not do so. 'I'd really rather get along, if that suits you. The weather's very chancy in these latitudes. I think we should go while the going's good.'

'You wouldn't make a final decision tonight?'

Ross shook his head. 'I'll go up to the wireless station in the morning, before we take off.'

'All right, then. We'll all go to bed directly after dinner.'

'That suits me.'

They did so. Ross was not particularly tired as he undressed; in fact, he was less tired than he had been for many days. That, he thought, was because they had had a relatively easy day, and because of the long sleep that he had had the night before. Tomorrow would not be so easy; it would be prudent to ensure another good night's sleep before they flew back to Angmagsalik. He took another tablet of his Troxigin, set his alarm clock for five, and got into his bed.

He slept beautifully, a quiet, dreamless sleep till the alarm woke him in the morning. He got out of bed at once, feeling well and strong; as he shaved in the morning sunlight he was humming a little tune. He dressed and went down to the dining-room, and began his breakfast.

He had nearly finished by the time the Lockwoods joined him, the girl in her white overall. 'I made a start,' he said. 'I thought I'd just nip up to the wireless station while you're eating your breakfast, and get the weather report. It's a grand morning for us, here. If it's like this at Angmagsalik we'll be all right.'

Alix said: 'You're very full of beans this morning, Mr. Ross. Did you sleep well?'

'Never better in my life.'

Lockwood said: 'It's fine here, but we may run into cloud again in Greenland, like we did before.'

The pilot nodded. 'I'll get off with every pound of fuel we can lift. But it's going to be all right this time, sir—you see.'

He got up and left the room confidently. Lockwood turned to his daughter. 'He seems a different man,' he said mildly.

'I know. I believe he was terribly worried about his engine; although he didn't say so.'

Her father said: 'Of course, it's a very anxious time for him.'

The weather report was still good. They took off at about half-past seven from the outer harbour, having drained off fifteen gallons of fuel after an unsuccessful run. There was a thin layer of nimbus cloud at a great height; the day was cold but visibility was good.

Again they climbed to about three thousand feet, and went droning over a grey, unpleasant sea. After a time Snaefell sank below the horizon; an hour later they came to the first pack ice. Ross had been in touch with Angmagsalik on the wireless since the take-off; the weather report there was clear weather and little wind.

There was a cloud over the pack, a thick mist that went right down to the water. In spite of his previous experience, Ross chose to fly above it, depending on his wireless reports of clear weather ahead. For an hour they flew on at about four thousand feet over a sea of cloud; then suddenly the clouds came to an end. Before them, a great distance off, they saw a long line of jagged mountains running down into the sea, with glaciers winding down the coast in furrows, and a mass of pack ice at the foot.

Ross caught his breath. 'Well, there it is, sir. It looks a pretty ghastly place.'

Lockwood said: 'It's very inhospitable.'

In that clear air they could see well over a hundred miles. Above the jagged mountains the white line of the ice-cap was distinct. The sea was thick with pack ice for as far as they could see. The coastline was evidently rocky and in-dented; along its edge there seemed to be a wild mix-up of icebergs and rocky islands. They looked at it with awe.

'I believe the south-west coast, at Brattalid, is very dif-ferent,' said Lockwood. 'There is no pack ice there.'

Ross nodded. 'It's a different sort of place altogether. They have pastures there, and cattle—so they told me in Copenhagen.'

Alix stared ahead. 'It doesn't look as if there's anything of that sort here.'

Homing upon the Angmagsalik wireless signals, in three quarters of an hour they were over the estuary. Ross switched off his receiver and stared down intently, glanced at his map, and stared down again. 'There we are,' he said. 'That's it. See the wireless masts? Along by the water, where the river runs into the sea. There.'

The Lockwoods followed his direction. 'I see them,' said

the don. 'There's a little house there with a spire, like a church.'

Alix stared down incredulously. 'But is this all of it?' she asked. 'Seven or eight tiny wooden houses, like that?'

The pilot nodded. 'That's it all right.'

'But it's not even as big as a village!'

Her father said: 'It's the biggest place in East Greenland. You'd have to go five or six hundred miles to find a bigger one.'

The girl said nothing.

Ross wound in the aerial, and circled low for a landing. The inner harbour was dotted with moored rowing-boats; in the outer harbour the pack was thicker than he cared about at all. When they had told him that there was little ice at Angmagsalik the term must have been purely relative; there was plenty there to impede the landing of his seaplane. For a time he flew in circles at about a hundred feet, choosing the lane between the icebergs in which he would land. Then he went up a little, and turned to the Lockwoods.

'I'm going to put her down in that lane—there,' he said. He showed it to them. 'I'm going to fly over it first, about ten feet up. Would you keep an eye open for floating lumps of ice on your side, sir—and you on your side, Miss Lockwood? Especially the little black ones in the water, that don't show up much. I don't want to rip a float up in this place.'

The seaplane swept down towards the lane and flew along at slow speed close above the surface; they scanned the water carefully. Then she went up again and circled round as they exchanged impressions.

'Right you are,' said the pilot cheerfully. 'Down we go.'

He rumbled in very slowly over a floating berg, throttled, and let the machine sink down to the water. Then a quick, short burst of engine, the floats touched and sank down in the water, and the machine pulled up with a short run. Ross swung her round and taxied in towards the settlement, threading his way between the lumps of floating ice.

He turned to the girl beside him. 'I'll go straight to the mooring. It ought to be a red buoy, like the others. Would you mind hooking on?'

'Of course.'

She got into the back of the cabin and took off her flying suit and sheepskin boots; then she took off her stockings and put on rubber shoes. Finally she put on the lifebelt over her white overalls. As she was doing this, Ross taxied round the island at the harbour mouth and saw the red buoy on the water. On shore, some men were getting into a boat.

He turned round. 'Right you are. There's the buoy straight ahead.'

The girl opened the cabin door and got down on to the float with the boathook; a wave washed suddenly across her feet. For a moment she gasped, stunned by the cold of it. Then as the seaplane moved forward the buoy came to the float, she reached out and grabbed it, pulled it up, and snapped the cable hook into the ring. Ross, watching her from the side window, cut his switches and the engine came to rest.

Alix turned forward to him, catching her breath and laughing. 'This water's simply freezing, Mr. Ross.'

'I'm sorry—did you get wet?'

'My feet did.'

'Give them a rub, quickly. I wouldn't fail in here, if I were you.'

'I won't.'

She got back into the cabin, pulled off her wet shoes, and began massaging her feet. The boat pulled from the shore with three men in it, Eskimos, with merry Mongolian faces. It came alongside the float; Ross jumped down quickly on to the float, and held it off from bumping. One of the men shipped his oar, stood up, and said: 'Me Thomas.'

He wore a very old seaman's hat, a dirty white jumper of sailcloth, serge trousers, and home-made sealskin knee-boots; his face was copper-coloured and dirty, with a cheerful smile. The pilot said: 'My name is Ross. Is the Shell representative here?'

The Eskimo beamed at him. 'Me Thomas. Me Shell representative.'

The pilot said gravely: 'I'm glad to meet you. Have you got my petrol here?'

The man nodded emphatically. 'Plenty petrol. Plenty gasoline. Plenty oil. Plenty in store.' He pointed to the shore.

'That's fine. We'll come on shore with you and have a look at it.'

They collected their luggage, left the machine, and got into the boat. As they approached the shore a man came down to meet them, a white man dressed in a seaman's jersey and top-boots like the rest.

'Good morning,' he said, speaking in English with a strong accent. 'I am the governor. Have you had good flying?'

They went up to his house and trading post. He called his wife, an Eskimo, who greeted them shyly and took them upstairs to the attics. There were two rooms. In one there was a bare camp-bed with no mattress or bedding; the only other furniture was a couple of dead ducks hanging by their feet from the roof. In the other there was no bedstead, but a miscellaneous heap of pelts and woollen trade goods. The woman pointed to these hospitably. 'Bed,' she said.

Ross said quickly: 'It's very good of you to let us stay here.'

She grinned and shook her head. Alix produced a laborious sentence in Danish; the woman grinned again, and made a deprecatory gesture. Then she said: 'Vi vill spise snart,' and went down the steep ladder staircase to the room below.

Lockwood asked: 'What did she say then?'

Alix said: 'Dinner before long, Daddy,' She stared around her at the attics.

Ross turned to her: 'I'm afraid it's very rough,' he said. 'I'll get our sleeping-bags up from the seaplane after dinner, and we'll be able to fix up something comfortable. But it's not just like the Savoy, is it?'

Lockwood said: 'Don't worry about us, Mr. Ross. It's very kind of them to take us in at all, in a small place like this.'

The girl said slowly: 'I believe it's going to be fun.'

'I'm glad you think so,' said the pilot. 'Which room will you have?'

'I think I'd like to have the bed.'

'All right. After we've got the fuel on board we'll bring the bags up here, and see what we can make of it. It'll only be for one night, I expect.'

Alix asked: 'Is Julianehaab like this?'

The pilot shook his head. 'It's a much bigger place. There are over twenty white people living there.'

They went down to a meal of pickled vegetables, bread and butter, and home-brewed beer. They found the governor to be a cheerful, hospitable man, much looking forward to his retirement in Denmark. His English was not so good as they had first supposed, and they very soon found that a combination of English with Alix's Danish dictionary served them best.

The meal over, they went with Thomas to the fuel store. Ross was surprised at the amount of aviation fuel and oil of various brands that was in store at Angmagsalik. It seemed that every Greenland expedition using aeroplanes habitually left a quantity of petrol behind, having brought with them fuel for flights that never came off, for aircraft that were quickly crashed. In this way a great quantity of petrol had accumulated in the store and, what was even more important to Ross, one or two pumps of highly efficient design for putting the fuel into aeroplanes.

They found refuelling at Angmagsalik absurdly easy. With two or three men to assist they rolled down two drums to a large row-boat, got them on board, and rowed out to the seaplane. With a length of hose and one of the expedition pumps from the store they put a hundred gallons into the machine in half an hour. Ross checked the filters and the sumps, and passed down the sleeping-bags into the boat. In very little more than an hour they were on shore again, with the machine ready to start off in the morning.

They went up to the wireless station. The pastor was there with the wireless operator; they had then met the entire non-Eskimo population of Angmagsalik. Ross asked the operator for the weather reports from Julianehaab.

They were not very encouraging. There had been a fog at Julianehaab the day before. That morning had been clear, but there was fog there now. The weather was settled; to-morrow it would probably be clear in the morning and foggy in the afternoon.

'There has been much fog in Greenland this year,' the man told him. 'The ice broke early, but there has been much fog.'

It proved to be impossible to get a morning weather report before seven o'clock, and that only by a concession on the part of the operators, who had regular hours of watch. As they left the wireless station Ross discussed it with the don.

'We've got to watch our step here, sir,' he said. 'It's a bit over five hundred miles. It'll be some time before we can get into the air after getting the weather report, especially if the ice is like it was today. If we don't get off the water before eight o'clock it will be one by the time we get to

Julianehaab, and by that time there may be fog down there.'

Lockwood nodded. 'We've got plenty of time in hand. If the governor can put up with us, we can afford to wait for a decent day.'

The pilot nodded. 'Still, I think we should get on with it,' he said. 'Jameson should have got to Julianehaab yesterday. There's nothing to prevent us going straight to Brattalid as soon as we arrive.'

The don said: 'Of course, the more time we can have upon the site the better.'

Ross thought for a minute. 'I wonder why the operator at Julianehaab didn't have any message for us from Jameson? He must be there by now.'

'That's rather curious.' They discussed it for a minute or two, and decided that it was not worth a special message. 'We'll probably be there tomorrow morning.'

In the evening they took a short walk up the hill above the settlement. The little harbour lay below them with the yellow seaplane moored in the middle, bright and conspicuous. Beyond the harbour lay the coast, mountainous, rocky, and desolate, rising up out of a sea thick with ice.

Lockwood said: 'My goodness, it's a terrible country.'

Alix shivered. 'I'll be glad to get away from here. It's uncanny.'

Ross glanced at her. 'Why do you say that?'

She shook her head. 'I don't know. But I wouldn't like to stay here long.'

He nodded. 'Neither should I. But the people are nice—what there are of them.'

She stared around. 'I know—but the country's horrible. It's so absolutely barren. Just these tiny plants among the rocks.' She indicated them with her foot.

Her father said: 'It's really not a habitable land.'

'I should think not.'

They went back to the governor's house and had an evening meal of porridge and dried fish and coffee. Then, at about nine o'clock, they went up to the attics. Ross carried up the sleeping-bags, and put one on the bed.

'They're all the same size, Miss Lockwood,' he said. 'It'll be too big for you, but that's a fault on the right side.'

With the coming of the night the room was bitterly cold. The windows were sealed tight, nor did they want to open them especially. She asked him: 'What do you do with it, Mr. Ross?'

He showed her how it opened. 'Get into it and go to sleep. Look, I'll get you some of this stuff from our room to make a mattress to put it on.'

She looked at him, amused. 'Are you supposed to undress properly and wear pyjamas in it?'

He smiled. 'That's nobody's business but yours, Miss Lockwood. I'm not going to take off much myself. It's too damn cold.'

He went into the next room and attacked an opened bale of blue serge cloth; he carried a large quantity of this back into the girl's attic, and arranged it in many layers over the skeleton of the bed. 'There's your mattress,' said the pilot. 'Now the sleeping-bag on top of that.' He arranged it for her. 'Now if you don't take off too much, you should be really comfortable.'

She turned and faced him. The wavering light of the one candle in the room threw moving shadows in the corners. The two dead eider ducks hung from the beam, their wings outstretched and throwing a grotesque shadow on the wall.

The girl said gently: 'Thank you, Mr. Ross. It's been good of you to take so much trouble. You've made me a lovely bed.'

The pilot said: 'I hope you have a decent night. Good night, Miss Lockwood.'

'Good night.'

He went out, closing the door behind him. In the attic the girl stood deep in thought, looking after him. Then she roused herself, took off her overalls, and got into her sleeping-bag in her underclothes.

In the other attic Ross found the don laying out his bed upon the floor, methodically and efficiently. Ross joined him; they contrived to made good beds upon the trade goods. They took off their outer clothes, wriggled into their bags, and lay for a time before sleeping.

Lockwood said: 'I suppose this represents the most difficult part of the flight, Mr. Ross?'

'That's so,' said the pilot. 'After this, we shouldn't get any more ice. Julianehaab's a bigger place than this, too. And at Brattalid we'll have a proper camp. No, this is the really tricky bit. Taking off tomorrow in all that ice is going to take a bit of doing. I may have to dump a good deal of fuel to get her off the water in the space we've got.'

'I suppose you must have done a lot of flying in this sort of ice?'

'Not more than I could help.' The pilot yawned. 'Hudson Bay gets a bit like this at the break-up. But there it's all in slabs—you don't get bergs like these.'

The don nodded sleepily. 'Because there are no glaciers.'

'I suppose so.'

They lay silent; presently the even breathing from the other bag told Ross that Lockwood was asleep. He lay wakeful, with an active mind. It was odd that Jameson had not been in touch with them. With wireless communication all along the coast, he must surely know where they were. But it was probably all right.

He thought of the take-off in the morning. It would need the greatest care. Any damage to the seaplane here would end the trip, and mean the charter of a special ship from Reykjavik to get them home that year. Otherwise they would spend a year of their lives in that attic. He'd have to play very, very safe. He must balance the safety factors. It would be safer to make sure of the take-off even if it meant starting with fuel for only eight or nine hundred miles.

He thought of Alix in the next room, wondered if she was asleep. She was helping him enormously with her Danish, and in the refuelling. It was panning out much better than he thought it would when he first met her in Oxford. Far, far better . . .

Alix, Jameson, the ice-pack, the fuel, the fog, Alix . . . His mind ran slowly round in circles as he dozed in the bag.

Presently he stirred and looked at his watch. He had been in bed an hour, and was no nearer sleep. This wouldn't do at all—at all costs he must have a decent night. He reached out for his pack and took a tablet of Troxigin. Soon he was sleeping quietly, his steady, even breathing joined with Lockwood's.

He slept till his alarm clock went off; yet, on awaking, it seemed to him that he had not slept very well. He had been dreaming. He could remember nothing of his dreams, but he knew that they had been very vivid. The fact impressed itself upon his memory because he seldom dreamt at all. Still, he awoke refreshed and rolled over and wriggled out of his bag. He went over to the window and wiped the condensation from the glass.

Lockwood asked: 'What's the day like?'

'Fine. There must be a fearful fog in here.'

There was a stir of movement in the lower parts of the house, showing that the governor and his wife were about. Lockwood called to Alix, and got a sleepy reply that she was getting up. Presently they were all downstairs, eating a meal of porridge and jam washed down with hot coffee.

Outside, the day was bright. They walked up to the wireless station; the operator was receiving and they waited till he had finished. Presently he came out to them.

He told them that the weather was good at Julianehaab, but there was fog about. It would probably stay clear till noon.

Ross thought about it for a minute. 'It's another of these touch-and-go ones,' he said irritably. He turned to the operator. 'Is that a good report? Do you ever get a report of settled, clear weather in these parts?'

The man shrugged his shoulders. 'This year there has been fog part of all the days. It has been very calm.'

The pilot hesitated, irresolute. 'What's it going to do here?'

The wireless operator looked around. 'I do not know. It is calm. I think it will remain calm. If I were sending a forecast, I should say there would be fog here later.'

'Will it be better tomorrow, or the next day, do you think?'

The man said: 'For Greenland, this is good weather. There is no storm. Sometimes here the wind blows two hundred, two hundred and fifty kilometres an hour. The weather now is very good.'

The pilot turned to Lockwood. 'I think we'll go, sir. I'll keep in touch with Julianehaab on the wireless; if it gets thick there while we're on the way we shall have to come back. You've got to take a bit of a chance in this sort of place, or you'd never get anywhere.'

They went and said good-bye to the governor and his native wife; then they went with Thomas to the seaplane in a boat. They took an empty petrol drum with them; Ross worked for some time down on the floats draining off forty gallons from the big tank in the cabin, to lighten their load for the take-off. Then they dropped the mooring, and the boat took the machine in tow towards the entrance of the inner harbour.

Presently they cast off, started the engine, waved good-bye to Thomas, and taxied out towards the ice-pack.

It took them a quarter of an hour of taxi-ing among the ice to find a suitable lane. At last they found one about three-quarters of a mile long. Ross cruised over it at a slow speed on the water, keeping a sharp look-out for floating ice, and returned to the leeward end. He swung round into the wind, and opened the throttle.

The take-off was an anxious time for them all. The sea-plane was nearly half-way down the run before she was riding smoothly on the step; the floating ice raced by them on each side at a great speed. The pilot sat tense and motion-less, waiting for the last moment to try to pull her off the water. With a hundred and fifty yards of their clear water left ahead of him he eased the wheel back firmly, prepared to throttle down at once if she did not respond. She left the water, however, touched again lightly; then she was two feet up and gaining speed. He slewed her gently to avoid a peak of ice ahead of them; white ice flashed past immediately beneath the floats. Then they were clear and climbing slowly out over the pack. Ross sighed a little, and relaxed.

At five hundred feet he turned, and began to fly west-wards, following the coast. Soon the coast turned south and they turned with it, flying at about three thousand feet above sheer desolation. The coastline stretched rocky and in-dented for as far as they could see. Inshore, the white line of the ice-cap bordered the sky; from it the glaciers ran down between rocky outcrops to the fjords running deep into the land. There was no sign of habitation or of life of any kind.

The pilot reeled out his aerial, and sent a message to Julianehaab asking for the weather. The reply was much as it had been before. The weather at Julianehaab was fine, but there was fog about and it was expected to be foggy later on.

They droned on steadily down the appalling coast, making good about a hundred miles an hour. At the end of the first hour Ross again spoke to Julianehaab. He was told that there were banks of fog out at sea.

He showed this message to Lockwood. 'It's one of those bloody tip-and-run days,' he said discontentedly. 'We can't land if it's foggy there. Would you like to play safe, and go back to Angmagsalik?'

'How much petrol have we got?'

'We took off with enough for ten hours. Say nine hours more.'

'Suppose we go on for another hour, and make our decision then?'

The pilot thought about it for a minute; the weather all around them was quite clear. If the worst came to the worst they could land anywhere upon the coast, beach the machine, and spend a cold night in the cabin. 'All right,' he said at last. 'We shall be nearly half-way by that time.'

They flew on steadily along the coast. Three-quarters of an hour later the don said: 'There's a little house down there, Mr. Ross.'

Alix and Ross leaned over to look. It took them a little time to see what Lockwood meant. Then they saw a long hut, built of rough blocks of the local stone and roofed with turf, merging in colour with the hillside. It was near the edge of the water. Drawn up on the beach in front of it were one or two skin-boats, and a few kayaks. Several people were outside it, staring up at the yellow seaplane.

Immediately Ross throttled down, and made a note upon his pad. The machine sank towards the hut in a great circle. 'It's an Eskimo house,' he said. 'Let's have a look at it.'

They flew past at about three hundred feet. There was a beach there, free from ice; on it they seemed to be skinning a seal. There were windows to the hut, glass windows in frames roughly chocked into the piled stone work. There were about fifteen or twenty people, some of them children. They saw all this as they passed; then it was left behind and they rose slowly on their course to three thousand feet again.

At the hour, Ross sent another message for the weather report. Julianehaab replied:

> For coming in from sea expect visibility less than five hundred metres in an hour.

Ross passed his pad across to Lockwood with a shrug, and swung the machine round till they were heading back for Angmagsalik. 'That's no good to us,' he said. 'We must go back.'

The don said: 'It seems the only thing to do.'

The pilot set the course and busied himself upon the wireless again, transmitting to Angmagsalik. Then he switched over, and wrote down the letters of the reply as they came to him.

> Visibility three kilometres getting worse do not advise you return here.

He passed it to Lockwood without a word. Then he began transmitting again to Julianehaab.

Fog at Angmag present position 220 miles south Angmag request governor's permission to land Eskimo settlement here.

The reply came at once.

Permission granted do not give natives firearms or intoxicants.

He transmitted again.

Can make safe landing no need search or relief party will fly tomorrow weather permitting and communicate you by radio.

He got an acknowledgment, reeled in his aerial, and turned to Lockwood. 'It's the only thing to do, sir,' he said. 'We've just got to park here and wait for the weather.'

Alix asked: 'Isn't there anywhere else to go?'

He smiled at her over his shoulder. 'I've got enough petrol to get back to Reykjavik.'

She laughed. 'I don't want to spend my life flying in circles round the Arctic, Mr. Ross. I think I'd rather go down here.'

They reached the little house and made a wide turn over it, staring down pensively. 'It'll be a funny sort of night,' the pilot said. 'But they're quite all right; they're friendly people. You'll just have to look after your things, that's all. They've got so little—they'll probably pinch everything they can get hold of. That's if they're anything like the ones in Hudson Bay.'

He throttled, brought the machine down to the water, and landed near the beach. The seaplane swung round into the wind and came to rest.

They stared at the shore. A little crowd of people had assembled on the beach; one or two men were getting into kayaks. Lockwood said: 'I don't think they're afraid of us.'

The pilot said. 'I don't think they are. Look, I'm going to go right in and beach the machine straight away, sir. If we let them come around us we shall have to stop the prop or we'll be cutting their heads off, and I don't want to do that.

We'll go straight in. Keep an eye open on your side for shoals.'

He opened his throttle, swung the seaplane round, and taxied in towards the beach. Twenty yards out he throttled down and let the seaplane carry her own way; as they approached the kayaks he cut the switches and the engine stopped. The machine slid in between the boats and grounded gently on the sand.

The natives surged around the bows of the floats upon the beach. 'Better stay here a minute,' said Ross. 'I'll get hold of the chief.' He slipped out of his seat, pressed past Alix, opened the door, and got down on to the float. He made his way along the float, taking the mooring cable with him, and jumped ashore. A horde of dogs immediately set up a violent barking; the natives surged around him, chattering and fingering his clothes. From the cabin window Alix watched him apprehensively.

He smiled, and raised his hand above his head. There was a silence, but for the children and the dogs. He said: 'Chief. Bestyrer. Governor.'

A man pressed forward; the others drew aside. He pointed to himself. 'Luki,' he said.

Gravely the pilot pointed to himself. 'Ross,' he said. The dirty, copper-coloured face beamed with pleasure. 'Rogg,' he repeated. Then they shook hands.

The pilot said: 'Do you speak any English, Luki?'

The man thought for a moment, and said something. Ross shook his head.

Alix leaned from the window of the machine. 'I think that's Danish, Mr. Ross.' The crowd stared at her; there was a busy chattering from the women.

The pilot turned to the machine. 'It's quite all right for you to come down now, sir—and you too, Miss Alix. If he speaks Danish we're in luck.'

He helped the don down from the float on to the shore, and then the girl. She had taken off her flying suit, and was wearing the white overall. 'Look, Miss Alix,' he said. 'They'll want to know about your clothes—the women will. Be decent to them, but don't let them maul you about. Give them a slap if they get too inquisitive. They understand that.'

'All right. Don't get too far away from me, Mr. Ross.'

They turned and faced the chief. The girl said: 'Taler De Dansk—eller Engelsk?'

The man answered with a few single, isolated words. Alix turned to Ross.

'It might be Danish,' she said hesitantly. 'I don't know that it's going to get us very far.'

'Never mind. Can you ask him if the tide is going out or coming in?'

This was important, with the seaplane on the beach. From the look of the shore it seemed to be about half-tide. Alix looked very doubtful, thought for a time, and spoke a sentence laboriously to the chief. It had no effect at all.

The pilot smiled. 'Never mind. I believe I can get it through to him with signs. Hey, Luki!' He led the man down to the water, and went through a pantomime. The Lockwoods watched his gestures, quick and expert. The copper-coloured face brightened with intelligence, a few more gestures, and the pilot stood erect.

'Going out,' he said. 'She's all right where she is. It's nice soft sand for her to rest on.'

Indeed, the sea had already receded a little since they landed. Ross got up on to the float and locked the cabin door; then he came back to the little crowd upon the beach. 'Luki,' he said.

He pointed to the sun and traced its passage down to the horizon, made gestures of sleeping and gestures of awakening. Then he pointed to the seaplane, and up into the sky. The man smiled and nodded, and said: 'Sove her inat.'

Alix said quickly: 'That's Danish all right, Mr. Ross. He said: "Sleep here tonight."' She repeated the Danish words to him; the man nodded emphatically and said them again, beaming with pleasure.

Ross went back to the machine, and fetched a light coil of rope to moor her with when the tide rose again. Returning, he saw the girl surrounded by a crowd of women. They were fingering her white overall, touching her hair, examining her fur-lined flying boots. Then they discovered the zip fastener upon her chest. A dirty hand give it a little downwards tug; there was a squeal of delight.

Ross said sharply: 'Luki!', pointed to the girl, and frowned. The man said something and the women drew back, still staring avidly. Alix laughed breathlessly. 'I don't mind a bit, Mr. Ross, but let them look one at a time.'

'Ask him which one is his wife.'

The girl spoke to the chief in Danish, and a brawny

copper-coloured matron came forward shyly. She wore a chequered jumper of rough cloth, a dirty cloth skirt, and sealskin boots; her hair was piled up curiously upon her head in a great ornamental curl. Ross said: 'Be nice to her, Miss Alix. Then she'll keep the rest of them away.'

'All right.' The girl patted the woman's arm, and they began examining each other's clothes.

Luki smiled broadly and said something interrogative. Ross turned to Alix. 'I didn't get that one.'

She said, a little shortly: 'Nor did I.'

Luki repeated his question. Alix hesitated, and then shook her head.

Her father asked: 'What was that?'

She forced a laugh. 'He was asking if I was married to Mr. Ross.'

The pilot said: 'Of course he would ask that.' He turned to the man and smiled. 'No,' he said, shaking his head.

Luki did not seem to think this very satisfactory, and was inclined to pursue the subject, but abandoned it after a time. Instead, he led them into the house, crawling through the narrow stone tunnel which served as a door.

Inside the hut, the smell hit them like a blow in the face, a mixed smell of rotten meat, urine, dogs and babies. For a moment or two it was nauseating; Alix drew back in disgust. Ross touched her arm.

'It's pretty foul,' he said quietly. 'Stick it out if you can. These people are very sensitive, and I don't want to seem rude.'

She stuck it out, and after a time ceased to notice the odour. The house was quite a long building, of one single room. Half a dozen posts standing in the middle of the floor supported the roof; from these posts hide-thongs were stretched to the walls and hung with garments, making the place crowded and untidy and providing a small measure of privacy for the different families of the community. The floor was divided by a raised platform two feet high that ran for the whole length of the house. This was the sleeping bench, and on it the entire life of the community was carried on. The lower portion of the floor was used for dogs, cutting up meat, and repairing the hunting gear and sledges. Upon the edge of the sleeping bench two or three soapstone blubber-oil lamps burned with a wide, low flame under blackened cooking-pots. There was soot everywhere.

The natives thronged into the hut after them, and over-whelmed them with attentions. Their flying suits and boots were removed and placed carefully together on Luki's portion of the sleeping bench. Then an unappetising plateful of boiled meat and liver was brought to them.

Ross said quietly: 'We'd better make a show of this. Eat what you can.' He made Luki sit down with them to eat; Alix tried to induce the wife to eat with them, without success.

'She won't eat with her man,' the pilot said. 'She'll have hers afterwards. You see.' There were no implements; eating was with the fingers.

Lockwood said presently: 'It's delicious meat, anyway—whatever it looks like. What do you think it is?'

The pilot said: 'I should think it's seal, sir. I've never had it before, but I guess that's what it is.'

Alix got out her Danish dictionary, looked in it, and spoke a word interrogatively. Luki beamed and nodded. 'That's it,' she said.

After a little time they could eat no more. They lay back against the furs and sleeping-bags, conducting a desultory conversation with Luki with the aid of the Danish dictionary. It was not easy. Most of the words they found were unknown to him; he only knew a few of the most common Danish words. Presently Lockwood said:

'I've been looking round to see if we could do anything for them in the medical way. We've got the first-aid box. But I can't see much wrong with them.'

Alix said: 'They could all do with a wash. Apart from that, they look very healthy, all the lot of them. Especially the children.'

Ross nodded. 'They're very healthy people. I tell you what they will like, though. We've got the emergency rations. We can give them some of those tonight—the coffee and the oatmeal. They'll like that.'

They got up and went outside; the air seemed fresh and clean after the stench inside the house. The seaplane was high and dry upon the beach. Ross got some pieces of drift-wood and put them under the floats; then he carefully instructed half a dozen men where they were to heave, and the machine was pulled up above high-water mark. He passed lashings from the pegging-down points on the wings to boulders on the ground, securing the seaplane as well as possible against a gale.

Finally, he was satisfied. There were banks of fog to sea-ward; it did not look like wind. He unlocked the cabin door and got up into the machine with Alix, and passed down their sleeping-bags. They left all their luggage in the cabin; they did not want to show too many of their possessions in the communal atmosphere of the house.

'We've got little enough as it is,' said Alix. 'I'd hate to have to give away my only change of clothes.'

They opened the emergency ration box in the cabin with the door shut, screened from the natives' gaze.

'I think we'll give them about a third of this stuff,' said Ross. 'We must keep some in hand in case we land again be-tween here and Julianehaab.'

'I suppose it's not much good giving them money,' said the girl.

Ross shook his head. 'They'll like this better.'

They separated out a quantity of Bovril, pemmican, margarine, biscuits, oatmeal, sugar, cocoa powder and chocolate, and got out of the machine with these in their arms. They gave them to Luki while the others crowded round; he accepted with delight. Immediately he divided the chocolate into equal portions, one for each family; within five minutes it was gone. He carried the rest of the food into the house and put it in a corner covered over with his fur sleeping-bag.

They spent the rest of the day examining the life of these people. There was no agriculture at all, nor any attempt to grow anything in that barren soil. There were a good num-ber of sledge-dogs running loose, scavenging from the de-caying seal carcasses on the beach; there were no other animals at all, no poultry. The whole life of the community seemed to be centred round the seal-hunting. They seemed to have no other food but seal, though from the bones and feathers it appeared that they would eat gulls and other sea-birds on occasion. But the seal was obviously their mainstay. Seals provided their food, a good part of their clothing, their sleeping-bags, the covering of their kayaks and their women's boats, the bone tips to their harpoons, their fuel, and their light.

Two or three of the young men got into their kayaks and gave a pantomime display of seal-hunting, sheltering behind a small white sail erected on the bow of the kayak to hide the man and simulate an iceberg. Presently they began to roll the kayaks, till one of them stuck upside down and had to be helped up by the others. This was a great joke to them; they came on shore convulsed with laughter, shaking the water from their hooded sealskin jumpers.

In the evening Ross walked with the Lockwoods a little way up a barren hill behind the house. Inland the white snow of the ice-cap rose to a level skyline penetrated here and there by peaks of rock; to the seaward the rocky black, indented coast was lost in mist. Ross said: 'It's coming on much thicker now. I expect it will be clear again in the morning.'

The don nodded. 'It was rather like this yesterday, at Angmagsalik.'

The sun dropped behind the ice-cap to the north-west; in the half-light of the night it quickly became very cold. They went down to the settlement and went into the house, stifled by the atmosphere at first. Lockwood said: 'It's going to be difficult to sleep in this.'

The girl said: 'It's simply terrible. I suppose there isn't anything else that we could do?'

The pilot shook his head. 'I'm afraid it's got to be,' he said. 'The only other thing would be to sit up in the machine, and that would be frightfully cold.'

'I know,' said Lockwood. 'It froze hard at Angmagsalik.'

Alix said: 'I suppose we'll get accustomed to it in a minute . . .'

They settled down upon the sleeping bench with Luki. His wife and several other women were preparing a communal stew of their oatmeal, margarine and pemmican, all in a large pot. It was soon evident that all foodstuffs were shared equally in this community. Luki was chief, but it was quite beyond his philosophy that he should keep food to himself. Even the cocoa powder was put out in mathematically equal portions, poured into each grubby palm, and sucked off it. The donors of the feast were included; Alix turned to Ross with cocoa smeared across her face.

'I haven't done this since I was ten years old,' she said.

Presently the stew was ready, and was attacked with a variety of tin mugs, plates and bowls. Finally the biscuit and the sugar was distributed in microscopically equal portions. Half an hour later the tribe were laying out their sleeping-bags, undressing with a complete absence of false modesty, and getting into them.

Luki showed them where to put their bags. The pilot said

to the don: 'Miss Lockwood had better go between us, sir. I think they're quite all right, but that might be the best way.'

Alix said decidedly: 'I'm quite sure it would.'

He helped her to lay out her sleeping-bag. 'You'd better take your things off inside it,' he said. 'I'm afraid they're bound to take a certain amount of interest in you.'

She smiled at him. 'I can manage all right, thanks,' she said. 'Besides, I really am quite decent underneath.'

Lockwood and Ross slipped off their outer clothes and got into their sleeping-bags. Alix took off her shoes and got into the bag, struggled and heaved inside it for a time, and threw out her white overall and a jersey. Then they settled down to sleep.

Sleep was not easy. The atmosphere, though they had ceased to notice it particularly, was heavy and oppressive. The Eskimos twitched and whimpered in their sleep in chorus with the dogs upon the lower part of the floor; it was rather hot. Ross lay awake, considering their position. It was not so bad. There was every indication that the next day would be like the last, with clear weather in the morning and fog in the afternoon. They had about two hundred and fifty miles to go to get to Julianehaab. If they got off soon after dawn they could be in the air with several hours of clear weather ahead of them. Julianehaab wireless station came on watch at seven o'clock; if they started then they could make contact on the radio before they left the neighbourhood of the settlement, and get the weather report. It was about two and a half hours' flight. He had set his alarm clock for half-past five. With any luck they should be there by ten.

Presently he dozed, turned over restlessly, and dozed again. He could not get to sleep properly.

Soon after midnight there was a dog-fight on the lower portion of the floor. Luki roused and threw a tin mug at the fighters; it bounced and rattled on the rough stone floor, and the dogs settled down again. Ross turned restlessly around.

Beside him Alix said quietly: 'Are you awake, Mr. Ross?'

He turned towards her. 'I've been awake most of the time. Can't you sleep?'

'No. It's so hot.'

He leaned up on one elbow. 'Look, you've got your bag all buttoned up. Undo that top part, and turn it back.'

She sat up, and leaned forward to undo the flap. She was wearing a light vest; in the half-light he saw her slim white arms, her bare shoulders, the firm lines of her breast. He thought that he had not seen anything more beautiful.

She threw back the heavy outer cover of the bag. 'That's ever so much better.' She looked at her father and turned back to Ross. 'Daddy slept all through that.'

'I wish I could,' he said. He was careful not to look at her too hard; he did not want to make an awkwardness.

'Haven't you been to sleep at all?'

'Just in bits and snatches. I've a good mind to take one of my tablets.'

'What are those?'

'Some stuff I got in Reykjavik because I couldn't sleep. They're very good.'

'Let me see.'

He reached over to his clothes and got the bottle; she stretched out a bare arm, and he handed it to her. She could read the label in the dim light. 'Are they good?' she asked.

'Rather. They make you sleep like fun. Would you like to have one?'

She shook her head. 'I don't think I will. It doesn't matter if I feel a bit washed out in the morning. But you'd better take one, Mr. Ross.'

'I think I will.'

She watched him while he took it, slightly uneasy, although she had just recommended him to do so. 'That's better,' he said cheerfully. 'Now for a real sleep.'

She slipped down on to her pillow, and said: 'Good night. Thanks ever so much for showing me about the bag.'

He turned on his side. 'Good night, Miss Alix.'

'Good night.'

She lay and watched him till his even breathing told her that he was asleep. Then she, too, slept.

CHAPTER VI

Ross slept very heavily. He did not wake with the first stirring of the tribe; he did not wake when the girl by his side wriggled from her sleeping-bag and put on her overall, nor when she roused her father. It was not until the alarm clock went off in his ear that he stirred and rolled over, rubbed his eyes, and sat erect.

The whole tribe was awake. Beside him Alix was fully dressed and putting on her flying boots. She smiled at him. 'How did you sleep?'

He did not answer for a moment. Then he said: 'I had an awful lot of dreams.'

'About aeroplanes?'

He shook his head. 'I was running somewhere . . . over a sort of moor. Miles and miles of it . . .'

She laughed. 'I'm not surprised you dreamed in a stuffy place like this. Running to get away from it, I should think.'

The pilot got up and put his clothes on. He went out with the Lockwoods into the clean, cold air outside; they drew deep, satisfying breaths. Lockwood said thoughtfully: 'Well, it's been an experience. But I hope we don't have to have another night of it.'

Ross said: 'I think we'll get away today, all right. It's good enough to make a start, anyway.'

They went down to the water's edge and sluiced their faces in the ice-cold sea. Refreshed, they went back into the house. Luki pressed a plate of cold boiled seal meat on them by way of breakfast; they ate what they could of it. Then they carried their sleeping-bags down to the seaplane.

They had little else that they could give the tribe. They would have liked to have left clothes behind, since that was evidently what was needed most, but they did not dare to part with any of their wardrobe. They gave Luki two more tins of pemmican and some more oatmeal and cocoa. Then, with the help of the tribe, they launched the seaplane down the driftwood rollers laid upon the beach, and turned her round in the shallows till the nose pointed out to sea.

They shook hands all round and got into the cabin. Lockwood and Ross started up the engine; the pilot slipped into his seat. He waved to the Eskimos to let go, opened the throttle a little, and the machine moved from the shore.

They found a lane for the take-off without much difficulty; by seven o'clock they were in the air. Ross reeled out his aerial and got in touch at once with Julianehaab. The report was that there was clear weather there, likely to continue for some hours. They circled and swept low before the Eskimos, then rose to three thousand feet and followed the black jagged coastline to the south.

The flight gave them little difficulty. They followed the coast southwards for an hour and a half. Then, homing upon the occasional transmission of the wireless station, they struck inland a little over the lower end of the ice-cap. Very soon they could see the sea upon the far side of the land; by half-past nine they had identified Julianehaab and were circling above it.

It was a much bigger place than Angmagsalik, covering about fifty acres with scattered red-and-white wooden houses. There were roads between the houses, and a little white bridge across a stream. They saw their red buoy lying on the water of the harbour as they flew around; finally they landed near the harbour mouth. They taxied in towards the buoy; Alix got down on to the float, and they hooked on without difficulty. Ross cut the switches and the engine came to rest; Alix got back into the cabin and dried her feet.

Ross turned to Lockwood. 'Well, we've got here, anyway,' he said. 'That's the first part of the job done.'

The don nodded. 'You've done very well, Mr. Ross,' he said quietly. 'It's only July the eighteenth, now.'

The pilot rested his hands upon the wheel, relaxed. 'I know,' he said. 'We've got time to spare. But that's because we've had such good luck with the weather—we haven't had to use the allowance that I had in hand. We might have been held up for days at Angmagsalik.' He paused. 'I hope I haven't rushed you along too quickly, sir.'

Lockwood shook his head. 'The more time we have here the better, from my point of view. But I feel that it has been a great strain upon you.'

'Oh, I'm all right. Besides, now we shall be linking up with Jameson and he'll take a lot of the work off my shoulders.'

A boat approached them from the shore. It was rowed by two Eskimos, but very different Eskimos from the east coast tribe with whom they had slept. These men were taller and had longer, more European faces; moreover, both of them spoke English fairly well.

They drew up alongside the float. After the first greetings Ross said:

'Is there another Englishman here waiting for us? A man called Jameson? He should have come here on the boat two or three days ago.'

The men consulted together in their own language. Then one of them said: 'He is not here. He has gone on in the ship to Godthaab.'

138

'But that's impossible!'

Lockwood said: 'They must be talking about someone else.'

The native said: 'No, your man. He cannot walk. His leg is hurt. The boat returns in three days; then you will see.'

Half an hour later, in the governor's house, they had the whole story. Jameson had broken his thigh. It had happened about a week before, in a rough sea; he had been thrown heavily against a hatch and had fallen awkwardly. The leg had been stretched and set in his bunk, and there he was. The governor had refused point-blank to allow him to be landed.

'It is not suitable here to nurse an injured man,' he said. 'If I give permission that he land, he stays in my hospital two months, and then remains here all the winter. That I will not allow. The hospital is for Greenlanders. He is well cared for and comfortable on board ship, and they will take him back to Copenhagen.'

Nothing that they could say would shake him from that decision; indeed, they did not try very hard. There was good sense in what he said. Jameson with a broken thigh would be no use to them as a photographer or as an engineer; they could not take him into camp at Brattalid in that condition.

Ross turned aside and spoke to Lockwood. 'We'll just have to get on without him, sir.'

'Is that possible?'

'Lord, yes.'

The don glanced at him keenly. 'I'm afraid I know very little about photography, and nothing at all about air survey work.'

The pilot said: 'Well, we've got to learn. The only other thing to do would be for me to fly back to England and get another photographer.'

Lockwood hesitated, the memory of their own flight fresh in his mind. 'That sounds like a tremendous undertaking.'

Ross nodded. 'I don't know that I fancy it myself. We might get held up by the weather, or we might get into trouble with the ice.' He eyed the don seriously. 'I'm not so keen on going back to Angmagsalik, sir. We got away with it all right this time, but I don't say that we'd be so lucky again. And if we were to have an accident with the machine up there, this expedition will be over—for this year, at any rate. We'd never get repairs done in time to go on this summer.'

Alix said: 'Apart from the actual work of doing it, is there anything in the photography that we can't learn?'

Ross shook his head. 'No. I've done plenty of survey flying in my time. I've never done the photography, but I know what the camera looks like, and I know more or less how it works.'

Lockwood said: 'You mean we can tackle the job by ourselves?'

The pilot said cautiously. 'I'd like to answer that this evening, sir.'

It seemed that Jameson had had some such idea in his mind. He had caused the whole of the expedition gear to be unloaded from the ship; it had been put into an empty two-roomed house. The governor suggested that they should rent this little wooden shack and make it their headquarters in Julianehaab; he could provide an Eskimo woman to cook for them, and look after it while they were away. Lockwood agreed to this arrangement on the spot.

They left the governor, and went to look at their new dwelling. It was a simple wooden building built with double walls and windows; it was painted white with a roof of red wooden tiles. Inside it was divided into two unequal portions. by a matchboarding partition that ran most of the way across the hut; there was no door to cut off one room from the other. There was a cooking stove in the larger room, and a great pile of the photographic gear and camping kit that Ross had shipped from Copenhagen.

Lockwood looked around. 'I should think this will do.'

Ross turned to the girl. 'I'm afraid it's a bit matey,' he said. 'You'd better have this inside room, and I'll rig up something for a curtain.'

She smiled. 'I'll be all right.'

They decided to stay there till the ship returned in three days' time, and spent the remainder of the morning settling in. Ross went out to the seaplane again, moored her more securely, and came back with their luggage and their sleeping-bags. Lockwood spent the morning unpacking and sorting out their camping gear and food supplies. The Eskimo woman turned up and announced herself as Gertrud; she spoke a little Danish and one or two words of English. Alix made her light the stove, and set to work to organise a meal.

They lunched on bully stew and biscuits. Then Ross opened the packing-case that contained the camera, and spent some time studying it and the mass of photographic gear. He was fortunate enough to find a little book of maintenance instructions with the camera; he settled down to read this carefully. By tea-time he was ready to report to Lockwood.

'The way I see it is like this, sir,' he said. 'There's no doubt that we can take photographs of a sort. But they may not be very good ones. I'm not much worried about getting the strips lined up right. I've done that often enough before —I don't think there'll be many gaps when we come to make up the mosaic. I can teach Miss Lockwood how to change the film chargers on the camera. We can do the actual photography all right, I think.'

'I see. But the quality may be rather poor?'

The pilot nodded. 'There's that risk. I don't say that they'll necessarily be bad, because we shall all do our level best to make them good. But, frankly, sir, I know very little about the exposures and the apertures to give. Then there's the developing—we must do a percentage of check developments to see that we aren't wasting all our time and film. I don't know a thing about that. Jameson can tell us a good bit when he comes through on his way home. It's just a question if he can tell us enough.'

Alix said doubtfully: 'I used to develop my own Kodak films, in the holidays.'

Ross said: 'So did I. But this is a bit different to that.'

The girl stared at the mass of equipment. 'I don't see why we shouldn't have a go at it,' she said. 'After all, it can't be so very different. Mr. Jameson ought to be able to tell us about the developing. And as for the exposures, we'll just have to learn how much to give. There seems to be plenty of film.'

The pilot looked at the heaped piles of aluminium canisters. 'There surely is. I should think he's brought three times what was needed.'

'Well, that's a good thing in itself,' said Lockwood.

The pilot sat for a few minutes, deep in thought. 'Jameson will be back in three days' time,' he said. 'If we're going to have a crack at this I'd like to make a flight tomorrow. I'd like to take a trial set of photographs with different exposures and apertures, and get them developed before the ship arrives.'

The don said: 'Why not wait till he comes?'

'The ship only stays for a few hours. I think we'd better have a trial first to find out the difficulties. Then he can tell us where we've gone wrong. We don't want to find our difficulties when he's gone for good.'

Lockwood nodded. 'That's good sense. Would you like to get the camera on board and do a flight tomorrow?'

'I think so. We can make a flight out over Brattalid, and perhaps pick out a decent site to camp.' He looked at his watch. 'Six o'clock. If we're going to do that, I'd better get the machine fuelled up this evening.'

Alix said: 'Can't that wait till the morning?'

The pilot got to his feet. 'I think I'd better get on with it tonight. Tomorrow morning we'll have all that we can do to get the camera rigged up and make the flight before the fog comes down. We don't seem to be able to count on flying after noon, these days.'

'I'll come along and help.'

He smiled at her. 'Don't do that. You stay and get the place cleared up and make up beds of some kind for us. I'll get a couple of the Eskimos to help. I may be a couple of hours.'

'All right. I'll have something hot for you when you get back.'

He went out to find the boatman, and to locate the petrol store. In the hut the girl turned to her father. 'He won't rest,' she said.

Lockwood frowned. 'I don't think he's looking very well. It's bad luck about this fellow Jameson.'

The girl stood at the window, staring at the figure of the pilot going down the hill. 'The work all falls upon his shoulders,' she said quietly. 'There's so very little we can do to help.'

Her father said: 'We're definitely ahead of time. Do you think I ought to make him take a rest? Do nothing for the next three days?'

She rubbed her finger on the window-sill. 'It's so difficult, because he's always right. It's obviously sensible to have this try-out of the photographic stuff, Daddy, before the ship arrives.'

The don nodded. 'There's the weather, too. I think he'd take it badly if we tried to make him rest while the good weather runs to waste.'

'I'm quite sure he would.'

In the end they decided to do nothing.

Ross went and found the Danish trading manager, and opened up the petrol store. It was three hundred yards from the jetty; he got a couple of Eskimos to help and carried a hundred and twenty gallons of petrol in two-gallon cans down to the boat. They rowed out to the seaplane and began to put it into the big tank.

It was nine o'clock when he got back to the hut, tired, sick and dizzy with the petrol fumes. Alix had hot soup waiting for him; while he was eating that in the dim light of a paraffin lamp she cooked him bacon and eggs, with fried potatoes and coffee. Presently he leaned back and lit a cigarette, rested and refreshed.

'Well,' he said, 'I got her filled up. Tomorrow we'll get up early and take the camera on board, and fix that up. Who's going to work it?'

He explained. 'It goes in the cabin, at the aft end. There's a round patch in the floor that comes away, and it goes vertically over that, with the lens looking out downwards. It's semi-automatic, but it needs attention all the time. Would you do that, sir—or Miss Alix?'

The girl said: 'I'd better do that, Mr. Ross. Daddy wants all the time that he can get upon the ground at Brattalid.'

Ross nodded. 'That suits me all right.' He turned to the girl. 'Look, we'll just wash up these dishes. Then I'll run over the camera with you, and show you what you'll have to do.'

Half an hour later he settled down with Alix and the camera, and began to explain the rather complicated mechanism to her. He found that she had little mechanical aptitude. She was immensely willing to be taught, but she found it very difficult to grasp the principles involved.

After half an hour she said despairingly: 'I see why it has to make a record of the time and height and the serial number on the edge of each negative. But I can't see what the spirit levels are for, Mr. Ross.'

He went back and explained to her again the rectification for tilt. Then he glanced at his watch. 'It's nearly half-past eleven. We'd better go to bed if we're going to be up early in the morning. I think you'll manage it all right now.'

She looked very doubtful. 'I hope so.'

Lockwood asked: 'What time do you want to start, Mr. Ross?'

'I want to get off the water by nine at the latest, so that we can fly the seventy miles or so to this place Brattalid and start photography by ten. I want to be back here by twelve, on account of the fog.'

'What time ought we to get up?'

The pilot said: 'There's no reason for you to get up early, sir. I told the boatman to meet me down at the slip at six o'clock. That gives me about two hours to get the camera installed before breakfast. Let's have breakfast at eight o'clock, sharp.'

Alix said: 'I'd like to come with you and see you fit the camera, Mr. Ross. I don't feel that I know it properly yet.'

He smiled. 'I'm setting the alarm for half-past five. If we get up then we'll have heaps of time.'

The girl made a few arrangements with her father about breakfast; then they went to bed. She had made her own bed behind the matchboarding partition, where she had some privacy in spite of the absence of a door. The men slept in the living room, at the far end.

Ross did not sleep very well that night. He had taken his sleeping tablets for four nights in succession; he thought that it was likely that he would have to take a lot of them in camp. The day that was now over had been quite an easy one; the next day would not be very strenuous. He felt that he could sleep without a tablet; after all, he was quite tired.

But he did not sleep. His restless active mind kept running over the new problems that were thrust upon him by the removal of Jameson. They would camp with a couple of Eskimos with them to do the heavy work, but the responsibility for the smooth running of the camp would fall on him; Lockwood had no experience of camping in the North. Clearly, he would have to adjust his work to the bare minimum of effort in order to get through what he would have to do. He would have to run the camp, do the flying, do the refuelling, maintain the engine and the airframe, superintend the photography, do most of the test developing, and stand watch over the machine in case of trouble. It was the last aspect of his duties that worried him most. They would have to take an anchor with them to Brattalid to make a mooring; the Eskimos could bring that with them in a motor-boat. But what would happen if the wind got up, and the seaplane began to drag its anchor?

He tossed restlessly from side to side. If only he had someone with him who knew seaplanes, who knew when trouble was likely to arise; someone who could keep a watch on the machine for him while he got some sleep.

In any case, they would be too shorthanded to cope with the machine if it began to drag its anchor. That must not happen. They must get it off the mooring and bring it up on shore if the wind were likely to get up.

It might be better not to have a mooring at all. The other way would be to pick a sheltered, sandy little cove and beach the seaplane after every flight. If she were half-way up the beach on a receding tide she would be safe on shore for six hours while the tide went out and rose again, and he could sleep with a quiet mind. He had operated like that once or twice before when he had been shorthanded, and it had worked all right. True, it meant that you never got more than a few hours' sleep at a time, and that time came at odd periods of the day. But the seaplane was quite safe like that, and you could sleep in peace. That was the main thing, after all.

He lay revolving all these matters in his tired mind, while the others slept quietly. After a time he fell into a doze, and slept for about three hours till the alarm clock woke him.

He called to Alix as he got up; she joined him in a few minutes. Lockwood was awake; he lay in his bag and watched them as they went out, carrying the camera in its wooden case between them. When they were gone he dozed again in his sleeping-bag. He was fit and well, but for the last day or two he had begun to realise that he was nearly sixty years of age. The hard pace of the expedition was telling on him, as it was upon them all.

Ross and Alix found the boatman, went out to the sea-plane, and unpacked the camera in the cabin. They fitted it into the emplacement that had been prepared for it, and spent some time adjusting it and making the connections to the power supply in the machine. Then Ross settled down upon the floor with Alix to coach her in the job she had to do in the air. They went at it quietly and patiently; at the end of an hour it seemed to the pilot that she knew her duties perfectly.

'It's really not so very difficult,' she said in the end. 'I think I'm beginning to see what it's all about.'

He nodded. 'We'll see how it pans out today. I think you've got it, now.'

They went back to the house for breakfast. The pilot did not eat much; he was feeling tired and stale. He drank a cup of coffee and smoked several cigarettes; then they went down to the machine again. Shortly afterwards they took off for Brattalid.

In contrast to the east coast, the sea here was practically free from ice. They flew for a short time towards the north; the coast consisted of a succession of long fjords running deep into the land between considerable hills. There was not a great deal of flat country. Between the fjords the hills were covered with short pasture grass and a low scrub; there were no trees of any size. From the air it seemed to be a barren, desolate expanse of country, habitable, perhaps, for a short time in summer, but not, in fact, inhabited.

Lockwood was studying his map, culled from the pages of an archæological review. 'This must be it,' he said. 'Fly up that fjord there.' He pointed to the east.

They were cruising at about two thousand feet. Ross leaned across, and looked at the map. 'That's it,' he said. 'Tunug-something.'

The don said: 'Tunugdliarfik is the name of the fjord. The mountain over there—the big one—must be Igdlerfigsalik.'

The fjord was about twenty miles long. It ran north-eastwards into the land; at places it was two or three miles wide. They flew on up it at two thousand feet; near the end it split in two by the mountain of Igdlerfigsalik towering above them, apparently a good six thousand feet in altitude. On Lockwood's instructions they took the fork that trended to the north. A couple of miles further on he said:

'This is it. Brattalid was on the west shore, here.'

The pilot put the seaplane into a wide turn. The place the don had indicated was a neck of land between two fjords, fairly flat, but rocky, barren ground. They stared down at it, circling around. It was clear that there had been some habitation there in the far past; the ground was seamed with lines and little rectangles that must once have been stone houses. 'That's it, all right,' said Lockwood.

They circled round that district for a quarter of an hour. On the other side of the neck of land, in Sermilik Fjord, the pilot saw two little coves, either of which might do for sheltering the seaplane. Both were about two miles from the centre of the Brattalid site. They were so far up the fjord that there could be no swell, and one of them at any rate had a sandy beach. Ross explained what he wanted to Lockwood and showed him the coves. 'I don't want to land today,' he said, 'I'd rather wait till we get a party out here with a boat. But I'd like to go and have a look at them.'

They swept low over the site, and circled round the little coves at about two hundred feet. The one with the sandy beach had a stream running down into it. 'That one would do us fine,' the pilot said. 'We can make our camp there by the stream and get the seaplane up on shore any time we like.'

They went up to five thousand feet and began the photography. Ross had arranged with Alix to take a trial strip of the coast, varying the shutter speeds and apertures according to a programme which he had written down for her upon a pad. She got out of her seat and crouched down beside the camera, troubled and apprehensive. She took the shield from the cabin floor, exposing the lens; a strong draught whistled up around her. The clamour of the engine and the cold rush of air confused her mind; she could remember very little of what she had known perfectly that morning.

Ross turned in his seat and shouted back at her: 'I'm just coming on the line now. Are you all ready?'

She was not, but she nodded her head.

'O.K. Start her up now.'

She switched on the current to the camera and hoped for the best. The pilot flew a steady course, his eyes sighting a corner of the windscreen on a far mountain peak. He could not turn his head without spoiling his line, but he said to Lockwood, 'How is she getting on?'

The don screwed round in his seat and shouted to the girl: 'All right?'

She looked up unhappily. 'Yes . . . no. It isn't working properly. The film doesn't seem to be going on.'

Lockwood repeated this to Ross. The pilot turned in his seat, and saw her in distress. 'I can't make it work at all,' she shouted. 'The film won't go—it's stuck, or something.'

He could do nothing to help her while they were in the air; he could not leave his seat. He said: 'All right. Switch it off, and put the cover back over the hole. We'll land now and have a look at it.'

He brought the machine low, circled once above the water

147

of the fjord, and landed about a quarter of a mile from the shore. The machine pivoted round into the light wind and lay there rocking gently, with the engine ticking over. The pilot got out of his seat, went aft in the cabin, and bent over the camera with the girl.

He smiled. 'Look, you've got it set for manual working. This little catch wants to be over this way.'

She stared at it miserably. 'I am a fool. Of course it ought to be.'

'Cheer up. It'll go all right next time. Let's just run through your programme again.'

He went over the exposures and apertures with her, told her exactly what she had to do, and settled her down comfortably beside the camera. Then he got back into his seat and took off. She removed the cover from the floor and waited till he had got to his altitude and till he shouted that he was coming on the line again. Then she went religiously through the exact motions of starting the camera.

She watched it apprehensively. The indicator of the exposures suddenly flicked to a fresh number. It seemed to be working; apparently it had taken a photograph. She was surprised. She consulted her pad hurriedly, and re-set the aperture.

Ten minutes later she shouted to him: 'That's all, Mr. Ross.'

He swung round. 'All right. Switch it off, and put back the cover.'

She did so, and came forward to him. He asked her: 'How did it go that time?'

'I believe it was working all right. The numbers on the cyclometer thing kept changing.'

He nodded: 'Good show. We'll nip along back home and get these developed.'

He turned to the don. 'Is there anything else that you would like to do, sir, while we're here?'

Lockwood shook his head.

An hour later they landed again at Julianehaab and picked up their mooring. The boatman came out to meet them. Ross carefully detached the film charger from the camera, and they all went ashore.

Alix set to work to get the lunch ready. Gertrud, the Eskimo woman, produced a lump of beef which had been boiling on the stove most of the morning, and a loaf of home-made bread. The girl set to work to open tins of vegetables,

Ross put the film charger carefully aside and turned to the developing materials.

He puzzled over them all the time that he was eating his lunch. There were instructions on the various bottled powders that would have been comprehensible to a photographer; they were not comprehensible to him. The meal finished, Alix came and leaned over his shoulder and read them with him. The chemical descriptions meant nothing to them at all.

Alix said despondently: 'When I used to do my Kodak ones there was a powder in a blue paper and one in a white paper, and it told you what to do with them.'

Ross nodded. 'I remember those. The trouble is, we haven't got a book of words.'

Lockwood said: 'Does that mean we're stuck?'

The pilot shook his head slowly. 'It's not looking quite so good at the moment.'

He lit a cigarette, got up, and walked to the window. A sea-gull outside wheeled, and banked past the window with a sharp cry. Ross started and turned back to the Lockwoods. 'Is the governor a photographer?'

The don stared at him. 'I haven't an idea.'

'His house was full of photographs—enlargements, on the walls. Sea-gulls, and things like that. Don't you remember?'

Alix said: 'Of course there were. Like somebody who's had a Leica given to them as a present.'

Ten minutes later they were with the governor. He beamed at them over his spectacles, a little puzzled. 'Yes, I am enthusiast,' he said. 'It is good in winter here, in the long night, to make enlargements. That is very interesting, I think. I will show you.'

They explained their predicament to him. 'Come,' he said, 'we will go and see. This morning, I have come to see you because I wished you to show your big camera. I am much interested in the photographic apparatus. But already you had flown.'

They went back to the shack; on the way Ross explained to him what they had been doing. The chemicals presented no difficulty to him at all. 'With this,' he said, 'the emulsion is developed, and with this made hard. With this it is fixed. This, and this, are for the printing.'

He glanced at them. 'I will show you. In my house I can make a dark room—you understand?'

They left Lockwood to his own devices, and Alix went with Ross to the governor's house. They spent the remainder of the afternoon in and out of his dark room. Finally the governor held up the developed strip of negative to the light, still dripping from the wash, thirty exposures each five inches square. It lay in a bucket in a great coil, fifteen feet in length; he passed it rapidly through his hands. 'All have too much light,' he said. 'These are best, but still too much light.' He showed them the last negatives.

Ross showed him the list of apertures and exposures; they compared it with the strip of negative.

'With this light, as today, one hundredth second instead of seventy-fifth, and stop just a leetle smaller. That would be good.'

Ross nodded. 'We'll fly again tomorrow and have another shot at it.'

They sent for Lockwood to join them, and the governor entertained them to coffee and cakes. Over the little meal they discussed their plans for the camp in the sandy cove near Brattalid.

The governor heard them to the end. 'I will introduce you to two good men, natives,' he said, 'that you may engage for your camp. Each can speak Danish a little, and one of them, Ajago, has a good motor-boat.'

Lockwood arranged to meet the governor in the morning to engage these men, while Ross and Alix did another photographic flight. Presently they thanked the governor for all his help, and went back to the shack. Refuelling the seaplane was not necessary; she had plenty in her for the next day's flight.

A feeling of utter weariness, almost of collapse, came over Ross when they got back to the hut. For the first time in weeks he had an evening free, with nothing on his mind to worry him and nothing urgent to be done. He went and sat on his bed and smoked a cigarette, held between fingers that trembled a little. With the relaxation from the tension of his worries, fatigue came soaking out of him in great waves.

Lockwood had gone out to pay a formal visit to the pastor. Alix busied herself with the Eskimo woman about the stove; after a time she noticed the pilot, sitting inert and listless on his bed. 'Tired?' she said.

He did not hear her. He was far away, sunk in an abyss of

fatigue and depression. She glanced at him again, then went and opened a bottle of whisky. She poured out a stiff peg, added a little water, and brought the tumbler over to him.

'Come on,' she said. 'Drink this.'

He started and raised his eyes. 'Sorry,' he said. 'I was just thinking. What's that?'

'A whisky. Go on and drink it.'

He smiled. 'I don't want that, Miss Alix.'

'Go on and drink it. It'll do you good.'

'All right.' Obediently he took the glass from her. 'But I'm quite all right. I'll go to bed early tonight.'

She sat down with him on the edge of his bed. 'How did you sleep?'

'Not so well. I was thinking about this photography. But I believe we've got that buttoned up now.'

'Did you take one of your tablets?'

'No. I don't think it's good to take those things every night.'

She nodded. She could not help agreeing with that. The fact remained, though, that she had never seen him look so utterly worn out. 'I should take one tonight, if I were you,' she said gently. 'Have a really good night. Then tomorrow we'll make time for some exercise.'

He glanced at her gratefully, tumbler in hand. 'You've hit the right nail on the head,' he said. 'It's getting no exercise that makes it difficult upon a job like this. What I want is a ten-mile walk.'

She nodded. 'We'll do that tomorrow afternoon.'

'There'll be that film to be developed.'

'We can do that any time. It's more important to keep fit.'

He raised his eyes to hers. 'We could walk up towards the head of the fjord. It looked rather pretty up there, I thought.'

'I'd love to do that, Mr. Ross.'

The whisky and the little talk had killed his fatigue; he got up and helped her with the meal. Lockwood came back and they sat down to supper; as they ate they talked about the survey. Afterwards they got out the only map they had, spread it out upon the table, and continued the discussion. Presently the pilot straightened up.

'All right, sir,' he said. 'We'll do the big one first. Forty miles long and fifteen miles wide, with each photograph as nearly half a mile square as we can manage. He considered for a minute or two, and did a calculation with a stub of pencil.

'With wasted time, that might be about twenty hours' flying. Say six days' work.'

The don nodded. 'After that, if we've got time, we'll do the other one.'

Ross said: 'There's not much in that one. Say another two days. If this weather holds, we'll do that on our heads.'

They went to bed soon after supper. Ross took one of his tablets, and slept almost at once. He slept till about six o'clock in the morning, a restless and uneasy sleep. He woke up suddenly, in a great fright. It seemed to him that he had dreamed of something terrible, disastrous; he could not think of what. He was rather cold about the hands and feet, but the black hair upon his lean, tanned forehead was all damp with sweat. He lay awake until the others woke, gradually growing calmer, thinking with pleasure of the walk that they were going to take that afternoon.

He planned to take off at nine o'clock and to do his photography above Brattalid, as before. It would have been possible to make a local flight to try out the photography, but he preferred to fly to Brattalid to do it. That was what they had come to photograph, and it was always possible that the trial photographs he took would serve to fill a gap in the mosaic if he should leave one out by mistake.

Shortly before they were ready to leave the hut, the governor came to the door. He had with him the trading manager and the doctor and the pastor, a great part of the Danish population of Julianehaab. Lockwood greeted them warmly.

'We have come,' said the governor, 'to see the flying start. That is very interesting, I think.'

They all walked together to the shore, and went out to the seaplane in the motor-boat. Ross led the way into the cabin; the visitors crowded in after him, and he showed them the camera, the instruments, and the controls. For half an hour he answered their questions, explaining everything to them.

Then they got down into the boat, and watched with interest while Ross and Alix wound the heavy handle of the inertia starter. The engine fired, and Alix slipped down on to the float and cast off the mooring buoy. She got back into the cabin and closed the door. The seaplane turned with a burst of engine, taxied a little distance away, and headed into wind. Then she took off, swung round in a climbing turn to north, and dwindled in the distance.

The governor turned to Lockwood. 'Froken Lockwood has flown much, I think,' he said genially.

The don shook his head. 'She had never flown at all before we started on this trip.'

'So? She has managed the setting free of the machine very well, for so little experience. Herr Ross is a very reliable flyer.'

'I think he's very careful.'

The governor nodded. 'I think so too.'

The doctor stirred beside them. 'To fly to Greenland is a great strain.'

Lockwood nodded. 'That's very true. I never realised when we started how difficult everything was going to be.'

The doctor said: 'So? Then may I be permitted the word of a friend, Professor?'

'Of course.'

'As soon as your plans will permit, it will be wise that your pilot should rest and be quiet for some days, I think.'

The don nodded. 'I am very much obliged to you for the advice,' he said. 'I will do my best to arrange things in that way. But with a man like that, it's very difficult to make him rest until his work is done.'

The governor said: 'Jo. That I can well understand.'

The doctor protested: 'You understand, I do not know Herr Ross. But I see nervous movements, and large pupils to the eyes, and a tired face, and smoking very many cigarettes, Herr Professor. And I say to myself—I am a doctor, and these things are noticed—I say, there is a good man who works too hard.'

They went on shore, and the governor took Lockwood to interview the Eskimos for their camp. There were two of them recommended by the governor as reliable and experienced men; one of them was the owner of a motor-boat. This man was called Ajago, and had a long, lean face like a horse. The other was called Mayark and had a similarly European face; both, however, were pure Eskimo. Neither of them spoke any English, but both spoke a little Danish; with the help of the governor Lockwood settled down to explain the programme to them.

Ross and Alix had an uneventful flight. The girl flew to Brattalid in the front seat next to Ross; then she got into the back and they did their trial strip over a course closely parallel to the former one. Then they went up to twelve thousand feet, about as high as Ross could make the sea-plane go, and ran off another strip at that altitude to test the exposure at that height. They came down as soon as they could; it was bitterly cold up there.

There were no mistakes this time, nothing to be done again. Alix climbed back into the front seat next to Ross, and they flew back to Julianehaab. They landed at about twelve o'clock, taxied in, and made fast to the buoy.

They met Lockwood on his way back to the hut for lunch, and walked up with him. Alix said: 'Mr. Ross and I are going to take the afternoon off, and go for a walk. Will you come Daddy?'

Her father said: 'I don't think so. I said I'd go and see this motor-boat, this afternoon.'

The pilot said: 'Would you like me to come with you, sir?'

'You're taking me for a walk this afternoon, Mr. Ross,' the girl said firmly. 'It's no good worrying about the motor-boat, because it's the only one there is to hire. The governor said so.'

Lockwood told them about the men that he had engaged. 'I think they'll be all right,' he said. 'It's a pity that they don't speak English.'

Ross smiled. 'It's a damn good thing Miss Alix learned that Danish,' he remarked.

They had a light lunch, and started off inland. They crossed the little wooden bridge and went on through the settlement and out through the meadows of the sheep-breeding station. Presently all civilisation was behind them, and they were walking towards the ice-cap over rough screes and through meadows of rough sedgy grass and low scrub. They did not talk very much; the going was too strenuous for that.

Two hours later they stopped for a cigarette before turning homewards. Below them the fjords lay spread out in map-like form, almost as if they had been flying; behind them the ice-cap was very near, grey, dirty and forbidding. They leaned against an outcrop of a basalt rock and rested.

Alix said: 'What are you going to do after this, Mr. Ross? I mean, when this job is all over.'

He shrugged his shoulders. 'Things seem to be picking up a bit in Canada. What I'd like to do would be to get into Imperial Airways. But they're pretty particular who they take, these days.'

She was amazed. 'But surely they'd take you?'

He smiled down at her. 'I'm not such a wizard as all that, Miss Alix. You've got to be good to get into Imperials.'

'But you *are* good. I should have thought anyone who could fly out here like this was good enough for them. Doesn't a flight like this make any difference?'

He glanced at her, flicking the ash from his cigarette. 'It all helps. If we get through this job with the seaplane in one piece they might take notice. After all, not so many people come this way in aeroplanes.'

She nodded. 'I don't think Daddy ever knew what sort of trip it would turn out to be.'

The pilot said dourly: 'Well, he knows now.' And then he turned and smiled at her.

She said quietly: 'You must have thought us beastly people when you met us first of all.'

He glanced sideways at her. The sun shone on her fair, short hair, her lean serious face not quite unlike his own, her slim figure in white overalls. Quite suddenly he knew exactly what he wanted. And being Scotch, he let the moment go.

'Why, no, Miss Alix,' he said. His voice was a little unsteady; he was feeling tired and depressed again. 'I just thought you didn't know much about aeroplanes.'

He ground out the stub of the cigarette beneath his heel.

'Suppose we get on back,' he said. 'I want to do those spools of film before we go to bed.'

CHAPTER VII

NEXT day, at ten o'clock, the ship arrived and anchored off the settlement. She had come down from Godthaab and was only due to stay for a few hours before leaving for Reykjavik and Copenhagen. There was a great state of excitement in the settlement. All boats were launched and everybody crowded on board her as soon as the anchor dropped. The Lockwoods and Ross followed the first rush.

Jameson was lying in his berth with a weight hanging over a pulley to stretch his thigh. 'I can't say how bad I feel that this has happened,' he said. 'Letting you down and all. I wouldn't have had it happen for the world, Mr. Ross.'

The pilot said: 'Never mind—we'll talk about that later. Just take a look at these, because we haven't got a lot of them.'

The photographer took the spools and passed them quickly through both hands, stretching the film and looking through it at the light from the porthole. Ross told him briefly what they had been doing. 'Not bad,' he said. 'This is the first one—the over-exposed one, I see. These other two seem quite all right. But they've all been over-developed, Mr. Ross. You've got them much too dense.'

'Right,' said the pilot. 'Now you tell us how to do it properly.'

Alix settled down beside the bunk with a pencil and pad. Outside the winches clattered and groaned as bales of pelt were taken on the ship; all round the little cabin was a turmoil of shouted greetings and orders. Two hours later Alix stopped writing; she had covered seven or eight pages with her pencilled notes.

'Well,' said Jameson wearily, 'I think I've told you everything I can. Don't forget what I told you about the hardening. I wish I could stay with you, in the house. I could help with the processing, anyway.' He looked up wistfully. 'I suppose you couldn't get round the governor?'

Lockwood shook his head. 'I'm afraid he won't consider it.'

The man sighed and lay back. 'Well, I don't suppose I'd be much good to you, really. You've got the hang of it all right, now. Don't worry to do much developing out in the field—it's always a risk of spoiling stuff. Just do one from time to time, to satisfy yourself that it's all going on all right. Take all the duplicates you can . . .'

They made him comfortable, provided him with what small luxuries they could arrange, and saw that he had all the money that he needed. Then it was time for them to leave the ship; her loading was completed. They were bundled on shore with the crowd of Danes and Eskimos, and stood on the beach with them and watched her get up anchor, watched her steam away. The little crowd about them dispersed quietly, silent and morose. There would be no other ship at Julianehaab till the following June.

They spent the remainder of the day in making arrangements for their camp. Lockwood and Alix were to leave early next morning in the motor-boat, with Ajago and Mayark and all the camping gear. It was doubtful if they would be able to cover the seventy miles to Brattalid in one day; more probably they would camp somewhere for the night. It was arranged that Ross should stay at Julianehaab with the seaplane, and fly to Brattalid on the following day.

'That suits me,' he said. 'I don't want to get there before you do and have to beach the machine alone. There's always a risk of trouble in that sort of game. In fact, if I don't see you at Brattalid when I get there, I shall come back here and come along again the next day.'

Lockwood said: 'There's another thing, Mr. Ross. I want you to use this time to have a real rest. This gives you a day and a half free while we're getting there. I know this flight has been a strain on you. Take that time off and have a lazy day.'

The pilot smiled. 'I could use that,' he said. 'I'll just sit around and smoke.'

The girl said: 'Mind you do.'

It took them all the evening to get their stores packed and sorted, ready to be carried down to the boat in the morning. They planned to start at six o'clock. It was eleven o'clock at night before Ross was satisfied that everything was ready, before they got into their sleeping-bags. He lay for some time in his bag, awake. He knew that both Lockwood and Alix were inexperienced in camping, and he had no real confidence in the Eskimos. He ran over all the items of their camp equipment in his mind again, searching for items that he had forgotten. They ought to be all right. It was only for one night. It would be lonely in the shack without them, without Alix.

A day with nothing definite to do would be acceptable. It would give him a chance to get around all sorts of little odd jobs that should be done. He could get the seaplane beached at high tide and work on her for the rest of the day in comfort, clean the plugs and check the tappets. He'd feel happier when that was done, especially before going out into the blue . . .

Presently he looked at his watch. He had been in bed for an hour, and he was as wakeful as ever. For two nights now he had slept without his Troxigin, and he had slept very badly. There were only five hours of the night left before they must get up. He reached out and took a tablet; within ten minutes he was sleeping with the others.

He was up and about by five o'clock, feeling thick in the head and with a stale taste in his mouth. They had breakfast and carried the remainder of the camping gear down to the motor-boat. Ross said good-bye to the Lockwoods and helped them into the boat; by half-past six he was standing on the shore alone, watching the boat as it headed out from the harbour.

High tide that morning was at nine o'clock. He went and looked at the beach that he had selected for the seaplane and removed one or two large stones; then he hung about irritably till the tide rose. At high tide he went with the boatman to the seaplane and towed her in towards the beach. He put her carefully ashore at about ten o'clock; presently the water left her beached upon the sand and he could work on her in comfort and security.

He worked on her all day without a break. He took the covers off all the watertight compartments in the floats, sponged out the water that had entered, and sealed the covers up again with Bostick; this took him about two hours. He removed the engine cowling and took out the eighteen sparking plugs, carried them to the hut, took them to pieces and cleaned them, and put them back again. He removed the eighteen tappet covers, checked clearances, and adjusted one or two. He checked the contact-breakers on the magnetos. He drained the oil tank, and refilled it with fresh oil. He cleaned out all the filters and the sumps, reassembled everything, and ran the engine upon test. With an Eskimo to help him he carried a hundred and ten gallons of petrol a quarter of a mile from the store, and filled it, can by can, into the big tank. In the fading evening light, with water lapping round his feet as the tide rose, he went round all the flying control joints accessible by traps under the fuselage, grease-gun in hand.

At nine o'clock she floated, and with the help of the Eskimo boatman he towed her out to the mooring again. He made everything secure, and went back on shore; it was nearly ten o'clock when he got back to the hut.

That was his last day of rest. He had eaten nothing since the morning.

The hut was cold and deserted. He lit the Primus stove and made himself a cup of tea; he opened a tin of bully beef and ate that with some biscuits. It was lonely and desolate in the hut, and very cold. The pilot was depressed, and he knew it. He sat at the table alone, munching his cold, unappetising food, and he knew exactly what was wrong. He missed Alix very much. He had come to depend on her as an alleviation to fatigue; it didn't seem to matter being tired when she was

158

there. He knew quite well that he was coming to be very much in love with her.

Still, that was by the way. The work came first. He had a job to do. He had to carry out this survey and get photographs that could be used; then he had to get the seaplane down into the States, where she could be sold. That was the job he had engaged himself to do; it would take every ounce of energy that he had in him. He knew that very well by now. Everything else must be subordinate to that. Later, perhaps . . .

Presently, he got into his sleeping-bag and lay awake for a considerable time, worried and confused by his reflections. Then he took a tablet of his Troxigin, and before long he was sleeping heavily.

He slept late next morning, and awoke from a heavy sleep that left him unrefreshed. There was no reason to hurry; he lay in his sleeping-bag for a time, and got up at about nine o'clock. He made himself some breakfast but ate little; he waited till about eleven before going to the seaplane.

By noon he was flying about Brattalid. The motor-boat was beached in one of the little coves he had selected as a camping site; he swept low over it and saw Lockwood and Alix with the Eskimos. He turned and landed in the fjord; the boat came out to meet him and took him in tow.

The Eskimos in the boat towed him to a little sandy cove, sheltered from the north and east. Presently the floats grounded gently on the sand; he stepped on shore to meet the Lockwoods, leaving the machine to strand upon the falling tide.

The others had not been there very long. 'We camped about ten miles away last night,' said the don. 'Oh—very comfortable, thanks. Ajago looked after us very well. As a matter of fact, we could have come on here quite easily, but the men didn't want to.'

Ross wrinkled his brows. 'Have they been being difficult?'

'Not a bit. They've been very good. But I couldn't make out why they wanted to camp so early.'

Alix said: 'Ajago said they wanted to get here while the sun was up. I couldn't understand why, because it's quite light all night through up here.'

The pilot turned and looked about him. To the east the rough, tussocky grass mounted into a low hill strewn with basalt rocks; more to the south there was a little stream running down into the cove. The cove itself was sandy and protected from all winds except the west. 'Well,' he said, 'we couldn't have picked a better spot for a camp. The machine will be as safe here as she could be anywhere, and we can put our tents up by the water.'

The don nodded. 'We can made a good camp here. We aren't the first, either.'

Ross looked at him enquiringly.

Lockwood explained. 'You see that stony line in the turf there? And that other one at right angles? There.'

The pilot followed his direction. 'I see what you mean.'

'Well, there's been a house there.'

'How long ago?'

The don shrugged his shoulders. 'I haven't really looked at it. Back in the Brattalid time, I daresay.'

'Well, they picked the best place. We'd better put our camp there, too.'

He turned to the men. He knew a few odd words of Eskimo, sufficient to make his meaning clear. He now told them to get the baggage up from the beach and start to make the camp beside the stream.

There was a hitch. The men consulted with each other for a minute; then Ajago came forward and said something painstakingly and clearly in Danish. Ross did not understand the words, but the objection was very clear.

He turned to Alix. 'Did you understand him?'

She shook her head. 'Not properly. I don't think he wants to stop here. It's funny, because they've been so nice all the time.'

Ross took the man by the arm and led him up to the flat, level site beside the stream, seamed with old walls. He made motions of putting up tents. 'Camp here,' he said.

The Eskimo shook his head, and said something. Alix broke in quickly: 'He said, it's not good here.'

The pilot said patiently: 'We'll have to get down to this, Miss Alix. Ask him why it isn't good.'

The girl reflected for a minute, and then spoke a slow sentence to the Eskimo. The man answered her in Danish. She turned back to the two men. 'He says it's not good at night. At least, I think that's what he means.'

Lockwood said quietly: 'Are they superstitious?'

Ross nodded. 'Terrifically. I hope to God that isn't at the back of it. Ask him why it isn't good at night.'

The girl did so. 'He says, because of the old people.'

The pilot sighed inwardly. As if the job wasn't difficult enough, without this one. He forced a laugh and a bright smile. 'Tell him that the old people have no power over them while they are with us. Say that we are great and strong, that we can fly in the sky, and we will throw our power over them, and protect them.'

Alix looked dubious. 'I'll have to get the dictionary for that, Mr. Ross.'

A few minutes later the reply came through. 'He says, that may be all right for us, for not for them. At least, that's what he means. He wants to make camp over on the other side of the hill.'

The pilot said patiently: 'Well, let's get up on to the hill and have a look at it.'

From the top of the hill they looked around. The tide had fallen a good way, and the seaplane now stood high and dry upon the sand. The second cove that they had seen from the air, in which the Eskimos would have liked to make camp, was now seen to have a rocky bottom quite unsuitable for the machine. Moreover, the stream that ran down to the sandy cove was the only water in sight.

Ross and Alix settled down patiently with the dictionary to talk to the men. The Eskimos were friendly and reasonable, but utterly unwilling to sleep in the sandy cove. After half an hour a basis of arrangement was made. The main camp would be in the sandy cove near the machine, but the Eskimos would take one tent and make a sleeping camp for themselves in the rocky cove, a mile away. They would take all their food at the main cove, coming there each day at sunrise and leaving at sunset.

Ross shrugged his shoulders. 'It's a perfect curse, but it's the best that we can do. I must stay by the machine, myself. I think they'll get fed up with it in a day or two, when they see that we get along all right.'

They went back down the hill, and on that basis they set up the camp beside the stream, among the ruins of the ancient houses. They had three tents; they pitched two by the stream and gave one to the Eskimos to put up later for themselves. They built a fireplace of loose stones and got a fire going of the low, thin scrub that grew in patches on the moor. The biggest tree they found was a stunted birch, less than fifteen feet in height.

They lunched upon cold meat and biscuits. Lockwood went off for a short walk in the direction of Brattalid; Ross set the men to work bringing up the stores from the shore and stacking them by the tents. Then he set them to cut brushwood; presently he turned to Alix.

'If you've got time to spare now, let's have a look at the survey.'

They got out the drawing board, and pinned the rough map of the district down on it. They worked for an hour together, planning the strips of photographs that would cover the whole area. Presently Ross said:

'We'll have to chuck this now. I'll have to go and get the ropes on to that seaplane.'

She looked at him. 'What are you going to do with the machine? I mean, there's no mooring to put it on.'

He nodded. 'We'll run her from the beach,' he said. 'It's high tide at about ten o'clock today. I'll leave her on the beach all night. We ought to be in the air by nine o'clock tomorrow morning. Low water at four . . . If we let her ground upon the beach at midnight she'll be safe all night, and she'll float again at eight in the morning, when we want her.'

It took the girl a little time to realise this way of operation. Then she said: 'Does that mean that you've got to sit up till midnight, to see she grounds at the right time?'

The pilot smiled. 'I think I'd better. I wouldn't like to go to sleep unless I knew that she was safe. But she'll be safe enough on the beach.'

Alix looked very doubtful. 'It means another late night for you.'

He turned away. 'Don't worry about that, Miss Alix. I'll be all right.'

They went down to the machine, now sitting on the sandy beach far from the water. Ross and Mayark set to work with stakes and ropes. They drove a stake into the ground on each side of the little cove near the mouth and led a rope from that to the bow of each float; they led two ropes from the tail of the machine to stakes driven into the ground at the head of the cove. Then they had her located in the middle of the little cove, secure against a moderate wind, and so arranged that they could move her up and down the cove on the high tide to ground her when they wished.

Lockwood came back, and watched them at their work.

'You're making very certain of her, Mr. Ross,' he said.

The pilot nodded. 'She'll be all right like this while the fine weather lasts. If the wind pipes up we'll have to get her up on shore and fold the wings.'

It was dusk by the time that he was satisfied. The Eskimos had departed an hour previously with their tent; now their fire shone across the water from the other cove, a mile away. Ross felt for a cigarette and lit it wearily, looking across the water in the fading light. 'I wonder what it is they're scared about,' he said quietly.

They all stood silent for a minute, looking round about. The wind had dropped to a light air that drifted from the ice-cap, cold and desolate. It was very quiet.

Lockwood stirred. 'They're frightened by their own tradition.'

The pilot glanced at him. 'Tradition?'

They turned and walked towards the camp. The don said: 'This colony was Norwegian. Norse settlers from Iceland started it, about the year 980. It died out in the fourteenth century.'

Alix said: 'Is this the place that went native, Daddy?'

Lockwood nodded. 'The colony that died of neglect.'

'How did that happen?' asked the pilot.

'The Norwegians used to send a ship here every year, to trade, to sell the colonists axes, weapons, things of that sort in exchange for their furs. I don't suppose the trade was worth much to Norway. Under the Hanseatic League they began to send the ships less frequently. In the end, there was an interval of eighty years when no ship came here. When they did come at the end of that, there were no Norsemen here at all. Only Eskimos.'

The pilot asked: 'What happened to them?'

The don said: 'They became absorbed. You've only got to look at Ajago.'

Alix nodded. 'I was noticing him. He's got a much longer face than the Eskimos at Angmagsalik, and that place where we spent the night. More European.'

Her father nodded. 'They're like that here. He's got a Norse ancestry all right, although I don't suppose he knows it.'

Ross said: 'You mean the Norsemen intermarried with the Eskimos?'

'They had to. You see, while the ships kept coming here,

163

and they had iron weapons, timber, corn, and all the culture of their homeland, the colonists were better men than the Eskimos. When the ships stopped coming, the Eskimos became the better men, because they could live on the country. The colonists would have had to take lessons from the Eskimos in hunting, building houses, making clothes . . . All their superiority must have vanished very soon. In the end, it probably became an honour for a colonist to marry with an Eskimo.'

'And the result,' said Ross reflectively, 'is Ajago and Mayark.'

Lockwood smiled. 'Descendants of the Viking kings.'

They reached the camp, and began to make arrangements for their supper. 'This place is full of ruins,' said Lockwood, opening the tin that Alix put into his hand. 'I went practically as far as Brattalid. There are the stone walls of homesteads all over the country.'

His daughter said: 'In fact, we're sitting on one now. Don't spill that juice, Daddy—I want it for the stew.'

Ross said: 'We took some of the stones from that wall to build the fireplace. It's useful having them to hand like that.'

The don looked round him at the lines of the stone walls upon the moor. 'I'll have a look at this one in the morning, before you have to build another fireplace.' He studied it with an expert eye. 'It's been a farm—a large farm, I should say. You see that raised bit—there? That would have been the midden. If you dug there you'd probably find bits of broken pottery, and stuff like that.'

The pilot looked at their camp with a new interest: 'Are you going to have a crack at it?'

'It's not worth the time. I want to have a go at that church, over on the other side. But it's the Celtic influence that I'm really interested in. That means coming here again next year, after we've had the winter to digest what's in the photographs.'

Ross said: 'When we've done the survey you'd better come up with me, sir, and have a good look at it all by eye.'

The don nodded. 'I'll do that. But the main thing I want to do is to start digging on that church site, the one you saw in the air photograph at Oxford. That's about three miles from here.'

They supped off a meat stew cooked over the wood fire, with biscuits and jam. Around them the dusk fell. There was no real night in that latitude; the clear sky turned to a deep blue against which the hills made undulating black silhouettes. To the west of them two glaciers ran down from the ice-cap, which itself could be seen between the hills, a dark grey shadow under the indigo sky. It grew bitterly cold. From time to time Ross left the fire and went down to the beach to adjust the mooring ropes of the seaplane to the rising tide.

Presently the tide was full and it was necessary for him to stay down on the beach to fend the seaplane off and prevent her from grounding too soon. At last, at midnight, he pulled in the tail ropes and let her touch upon the sand. He waited for a time as the tide fell till he was satisfied that she was sitting evenly on both floats and coming to no harm. Then he went back to the tents.

Alix was already in her tent and in her sleeping-bag, laid out upon a bed of birch twigs gathered by the Eskimos.

Ross joined Lockwood in the other tent, undressed, and got into his sleeping-bag. It had been an easy day, but he had much to occupy his mind. He reached out and took a tablet of his Troxigin, and slept.

He woke in broad daylight, with Lockwood shaking him by the shoulder and looking at him curiously. 'Time to get up,' said the don. 'It's after seven o'clock.'

The pilot sat up, still bemused with sleep. Lockwood noticed that he was trembling. 'Did you sleep all right?' he asked.

The pilot passed an unsteady hand across his eyes. 'I had the hell of a dream,' he muttered.

Lockwood asked quietly: 'What was it about?'

'I don't know. Yes I do—it was about a bear. It came up out of the ice, because of the seal. It wanted to get at the carcass, you see. All I had was one of those little short spears, for seals, and I fought it with that.'

He stared around him, and began to get out of his sleeping-bag. 'Bloody funny, the things one dreams.'

'What happened after that?'

'After what, sir?' Already the dream was fading from his memory.

'After you began fighting with the bear?'

The pilot laughed. 'Oh, I don't know. I woke up.'

He dressed, and went out of the tent. The machine was still safely aground, the sea was calm, the day was bright.

He passed a hand wearily across his eyes. He was unrefreshed by his sleep, as always seemed to be the case these days. He had a great feeling of relief that he was awake. There had been a dream . . . what was it about? He could not remember. Already it had sunk into the subconscious.

Alix came out of her tent. ' 'Morning, Miss Lockwood,' he said. 'How did you sleep?'

'Splendidly, thanks. How did you?'

'Not so bad.'

She glanced at him. 'Haggard' was the word that came into her mind; she thought that he was looking awfully tired. 'Really?' she asked.

'Well, I slept all the time. You can't do more than that.'

She said a little doubtfully: 'I suppose not.'

An hour later they were loading the machine with films, and a small quantity of provisions and camp gear in case of forced landing. They got on board and started up the engine; the Eskimos waded into the water and turned the seaplane towards the entrance to the cove, and she moved out into the fjord. Ross swung her round into the wind, and took off. Lockwood stood watching them for a few minutes; then he left for Brattalid with Mayark, leaving Ajago to mind the camp and help with the machine when it came back.

All morning the seaplane flew up and down, backwards and forwards over hill, mountain, and fjord in exactly parallel lines. Alix sat huddled by the camera at the rear of the cabin, alert and intent on her work; ahead of her the pilot sat hunched at the wheel, staring at the horizon ahead of him, glancing from time to time down through the drift sight. Once a film jammed in the camera and they landed in a fjord to clear it; then they took off again and went on with the job.

They landed opposite the camp at about half-past twelve, both strained and tired with the concentration. Ajago was standing waist-deep in the icy water of the cove as they taxied in; he caught the float as it came to him and the seaplane grounded gently on the sand.

Ross swung round in his seat. 'That went all right, didn't it?'

Alix got up stiffly; she was cold and very tired. 'I think it did. The films went through the camera, anyway.'

Ross nodded. 'They're probably all right. We'll get on shore and have a bit of lunch. Then we'll pick one of them at random and develop it.'

They got down on to the float, and so to shore. Alix went up to the camp; Ross stayed behind with Ajago to see the seaplane settled. Together they put her in position and let her ground at once upon the falling tide.

After lunch they began their preparations for developing. The smaller of the two tents, the one that Alix slept in, had been made of a specially lined fabric for conversion to a dark room. They turned out her bed and all her kit, set up a little table in the tent, drew a couple of buckets of water from the stream, unpacked the chemicals and dishes, and began their work.

They spent the afternoon huddled together in the dark tent. Each spool of film carried a hundred exposures and was about fifty feet long. Working in close, intimate contact with each other in the darkness they cut the last few feet off two spools taken at random, developed the pieces, and fixed them. After a couple of hours they emerged blinking from the tent and examined the results critically.

'Well,' said Ross, 'they're quite all right. A bit on the dark side perhaps.'

The girl said: 'That means a smaller stop, doesn't it?'

'That's right.' He scrutinised the detail carefully. 'I don't know that we've got sufficient overlap for safety. We'll have to do something about that.'

They put the films back into the bucket, carried it down to the stream, and washed them carefully. Then they packed up the photographic gear again and put the bed back into the tent. They were both tired. Ajago had a kettle boiling on the fire; they made themselves tea and sat down by the tent. Alix asked: 'How long will it take to do the whole thing, Mr. Ross?'

He yawned. 'Four or five days for the big survey, if we get along like this. And then two days for the little one.'

She thought for a minute. 'That means that we'd be finished about Thursday of next week.'

He shook his head. 'We shan't go on like this each day. The weather may break. But, anyway, there's the petrol to think about. We've got enough petrol to do a flight tomorrow, but then we've got to go to Julianehaab to fill up. That's going to waste a day. Two days survey and one day refuelling is about the best we'll do.'

He yawned again. She said: 'Why don't you lie down and have a rest?'

He smiled at her. 'I believe I will. She won't float for another couple of hours.'

'Don't bother about the seaplane, Mr. Ross. We can look after her—Ajago and I. Go on and get some sleep, and I'll call you in time for supper.'

He shook his head. 'I'd like to be about while she's afloat. She's not too safe where she is, and we don't want to stick a rock through a pontoon. But I could use a little sleep.'

He went and lay down on his bed, having set the alarm clock for seven o'clock. He went to sleep at once, and slept quietly, without dreaming. It seemed only an instant before the alarm went off in his ear. He roused, rolled over, and came out of the tent rubbing his eyes.

Lockwood was back in camp, after a day's digging on the church site with Mayark. They discussed the survey for a few minutes; then Ross went down to the seaplane, now just afloat, and spent some time adjusting the mooring ropes. He stayed there till they called him up to the camp for supper.

In the evening they strolled a little way up on to the hill and stood looking out over the wild and barren countryside. 'This was the hell of a place to come to for a colony,' said Ross.

The don nodded. 'It's not attractive. But Norway was overcrowded in those days—too many people for the land to support. They had to get out and go somewhere else. They had battle after battle with the English, trying to settle in our country. They didn't have much luck in Scotland, or in Ireland. They got quite a good colony going in Iceland, and then they came on here as an experiment.'

'Which didn't work,' said Alix.

'It worked for the first couple of hundred years. They had about two thousand people here.'

The pilot said: 'I suppose all they needed was a square deal from the mother country, and they didn't get it.'

The don said: 'But for that, they might have been here still.'

They went back to the camp, and strolled down to readjust the lines mooring the seaplane. High tide that night was at about eleven o'clock, and low water at five in the morning. If the machine were to be afloat at eight in readiness for an early start upon the survey, she must be kept afloat till two in the morning, and not allowed to ground before then. By this schedule Ross would get five hours' sleep at the most, if he stayed up to see the seaplane safely grounded.

Alix was very upset when she heard this proposal. 'That's not good enough, Mr. Ross,' she said. 'You've got to get a longer night than that.'

'That's all right,' the pilot said. 'I got a couple of hours' sleep this afternoon.'

The girl persisted: 'Even with that, it's not enough—and anyway, you weren't asleep much longer than an hour.' She turned to her father. 'Daddy, we'll have to do something different. We can't go on like this.'

Lockwood said mildly: 'I can stay up and see the seaplane safely grounded, Mr. Ross.'

Ross, said, a little shortly: 'It's awfully good of you, sir. But really, I'm quite all right, and I'd rather do it myself.'

Alix said: 'But, Mr. Ross, you've got to have a decent night. You can't stay up till after two and then fly all day tomorrow.'

The conflicting strain of the girl's presence, of her solicitude for him, and of his technical responsibilities made him burst out in irritation. 'I'm perfectly all right, Miss Alix,' he said sourly. 'I'm going to see that seaplane safely on the beach, and we'll take off tomorrow morning at nine o'clock. It's very good of you to bother about me and I'd much rather that you didn't. I've got my job to do, and that's to keep that seaplane in the air and working. And I'd like to do it in my own way, please.'

There was a pregnant silence.

The don said pleasantly: 'Mr. Ross is quite right, my dear. He knows what he's got to do, and we can't help him with advice. Now, you run off to bed and get some sleep yourself.'

She turned, and went into her tent without a word to either of them, worried and furious with both the men.

Ross smoked a pipe with Lockwood by the blazing fire; the older man kept the conversation carefully upon safe topics. Then he turned in at about eleven o'clock and the pilot sat on by the fire alone, tired and irritated. If only he could be left alone! He knew that he had hurt the girl and he hated himself for doing it . . . but they must, must let him alone. He'd never get through this job unless he could give his whole mind and energy to it. He must be left to work in his own way.

He sat crouched over the camp fire, brooding and unhappy. From time to time he went down to the water's edge and adjusted the mooring lines; then he returned to the fire and sat by it again.

The slow hours went by. At two o'clock he let the seaplane go aground, and stayed with her for half an hour to satisfy himself that the floats were resting evenly upon the sand. Then he went up to the tent, took a tablet of his Troxigin, and got into his sleeping-bag for a short night; by three o'clock he was asleep, restless and uneasy in his sleep.

By nine o'clock they were in the air again. Relations were a little strained; Alix was distant and aloof and the pilot was too tired to make any effort to put matters right. The photography that they had done the previous day had ironed out all initial difficulties and they had little need to talk except in monosyllables. For three hours they sat in the machine flying backwards and forwards on the survey, Ross sunk deep in the depression of fatigue, the girl still smarting at her rebuff.

They landed after that, and beached the seaplane. Lockwood was away at Brattalid with Mayark. Ross and Alix lunched and spent the afternoon in the dark-room tent, talking in occasional monosyllables as they developed part of a spool of film.

When that was over, the pilot went into his own tent, lay down, and sank into a heavy sleep at once. Alix cleared away the photographic gear and put her tent in order; then she began to prepare supper, with Ajago to help her. She was still working when Lockwood came back at about six o'clock.

He asked where Ross was; she motioned to the tent. 'He's in there, fast asleep. I wouldn't wake him, Daddy—let him sleep. I had a look at him just now.'

He nodded and sat down beside her. 'I wouldn't dream of waking him. Let him get all the sleep he can.'

She smiled, a little bitterly. 'That isn't very much. He's set his alarm clock for nine o'clock; I said I'd get him his supper then.' She paused, and then she said: 'I've got a good mind to chuck that clock into the fjord.'

Her father asked: 'What's happening about the machine tonight?'

She said: 'He's going to sit up till four in the morning, as far as I can make it out. Low tide is at half-past five, and he wants to take off at eight o'clock to go to Julianehaab to get filled up with petrol.'

'Can't he go later?'

170

'He's afraid of the fog coming down in the afternoon, like it does sometimes.'

The don nodded slowly. 'I see. That means the seaplane mustn't ground till after three in the morning.'

'I think that's it. I do wish he'd let us look after that. It's only just pushing her off, and making sure she doesn't ground before the right time.'

He shook his head. 'He'd never let anybody else do that.'

She said irritably: 'I know he wouldn't. But he's just wearing himself out over it. I think he's looking awful.'

There was a silence. Presently her father said: 'I really don't know what to do about it, while this good weather lasts. If only we could have a decent gale he'd have to get her up on shore and lash her down, and then he'd get a real rest. But I'm afraid we'll never get him to give up and rest while this good weather runs away to waste.'

She sighed. 'I know. It's awfully difficult.'

Lockwood began to tell her of his dig at Brattalid. He had unearthed a runic stone and made a rubbing of it, and he had cleared a good portion of the floor of the big church. The girl said: 'I'll come over with you tomorrow, Daddy. I'd like to see it, and Mr. Ross won't want me for the flight to Julianehaab.'

They strolled a little way up the hill, and got back to their camp at about eight o'clock. Ajago and Mayark were just leaving to go to their own camp for the night; a stew was ready to be put on the fire for cooking. Alix said in Danish:

'Do you still want to sleep over there? It is much better here.'

Ajago shook his head emphatically. 'It is very bad here at night. This is a bad place to sleep. One gets ill.'

The girl smiled patiently. 'Nobody is ill here, Ajago.'

The man said: 'One is ill. Rogg is ill. This is a very bad place to camp.'

The girl fixed her smile. 'All right, you go along to your own camp. Be over here early in the morning.'

She watched them pensively as they went away, then turned and told her father what Ajago had said. He stood for a minute looking after them. 'It's quite absurd, of course,' he said at last. 'But that's how superstitions grow up in a primitive community. If Ross *should* get ill now, in this camp, the reputation of the place would be enormously increased.'

She turned away, shivering a little. 'I think it's about time to start and cook the supper.'

An hour later the alarm went off; presently Ross joined them by the fire. He was refreshed by his sleep, and feeling well. 'It's funny about this place,' he said. 'I seem to sleep a damn sight better in the daytime than I do at night. Has anybody else noticed that?'

The others shook their heads.

The pilot said: 'I think the reason is, it's not so cold. I believe my head gets cold at night, or something. I always seem to wake up with a bit of a headache in the morning. I'll have to buy myself a woolly nightcap in Julianehaab.'

Alix laughed. 'You won't get that in Julianehaab.'

'Just the sort of place you would get it. The governor's got one, probably. I bet they all sleep in nightshirts, if they sleep in anything at all.'

They sat smoking round the fire for an hour after supper; then Lockwood and Alix went to bed. Ross went down to the shore and adjusted the moorings; the machine was just afloat. Then he settled down for his long watch; for the first hour or two he sat beside the fire, paying only occasional visits to the shore.

At half-past twelve the falling tide made it necessary for him to move down to the beach and keep on pushing off the seaplane. He sat there drowsily, cold and stiff, getting up every now and then to adjust the ropes. Presently, at about two o'clock, he heard a movement on the path down from the camp. It was Alix; in her hands she held a steaming mug.

'I made you some Bovril, Mr. Ross,' she said simply.

He got up stiffly. 'That's terribly good of you,' he said. 'Did you make any for yourself?'

She nodded. 'I left mine up by the fire. I'll go and get it.'

She joined him presently, and they sat down together on the sandy turf. Both were wearing flying suits and fur-lined boots; they sat together in the half-light warming their hands upon their mugs.

Presently he said: 'I'm afraid I was very rude to you last night, Miss Lockwood. I was a bit tired. I didn't think what I was saying.'

She said: 'Oh, that's all right—I knew you were tired. But, Mr. Ross, can't we do some of this work for you?'

He said: 'I'd rather see to it myself. It's no work, really, just sitting here and giving her a shove from time to time.'

She did not press the point; she was afraid of irritating him again. And presently he said:

'I suppose you think I'm terribly fussy, don't you?'

She shook her head. 'I'd never think of you like that. But I think you're working much too hard, Mr. Ross.'

'I'm not. But even if I were, I'd rather do that than have a flock of accidents.'

She was silent for a minute. Then she said gently: 'Nobody could hold it against you if anything happened to the seaplane on a trip like this. We ought to have had four or five men to help you—proper engineers. My father sees that now. As for accidents, a fragile thing like that is bound to have an accident from time to time.' She pointed to the seaplane, rocking gently on the dark water of the cove.

He said emphatically, almost viciously: 'All seaplanes don't have accidents. Mine don't. And mine aren't going to. Accidents don't just happen of themselves.'

'Why do they happen, then?'

He sat staring out over the dark water of the fjord to the dim mountains on the other side. The night was very still. He said quietly: 'Accidents happen because men are foolish, and reckless, and negligent, and lazy. Sometimes, because there isn't enough money for what they want to do. One crash in a hundred may have been because God willed it so. Not more than that.'

She was silent.

He said: 'Sir David has seen that we've got enough money for this trip. If God has set His mind on it, we shall have a crash. Apart from that, my job here is to see we don't, and we're not going to.'

She sat there with him for the remainder of his watch. At half-past three he let the seaplane go aground, and waited till he could see how she was lying. Then they went up together to the camp, taking their mugs with them.

In the half-light she stopped by her tent. 'Good night, Mr. Ross.'

He stood before her, broad in his flying clothes, a massive figure dimly seen. 'Good night, Miss Alix,' he said. 'It was good of you to come down and sit up with me. I am sorry I was short with you that time. Don't mind about that.'

'I don't mind,' she said softly.

'Good night, Miss Alix.'

'Good night, Mr. Ross.'

He went into the tent where Lockwood was asleep, took a tablet of his Troxigin, and fell asleep himself.

He slept for an hour and woke up with a violent start, in a great fright. He raised himself upon one elbow and stared round about him, sweating and rather cold. He was terrified of something; he did not know of what. He got up and went out of the tent to see if the machine was still all right; she stood beached upon the sand far from the receding tide. He went over to the girl's tent and put his ear to it; the steady, even breathing told him all was well. He stood for a few minutes recovering himself; it was a fine, starry night with an icy little draught straight from the ice-cap. Everything was quiet and serene. He had made a fool of himself.

He went back to his sleeping-bag, but he did not sleep again. He lay dozing, half awake, and watched the blue sky framed in the tent door grow lighter into grey, to broad daylight. Presently he heard Ajago and Mayark moving about the camp; he woke Lockwood and got up himself.

That day he flew to Julianehaab to refuel. The machine was practically empty; with the assistance of the Eskimo boatman and his son he put in about two hundred and forty gallons. It took all the morning to do that. In the early afternoon he went and had a short talk with the governor at his house; then he took off for Brattalid again. He got back to the camp at three o'clock as the fog was just beginning to close down.

A period of very perfect weather followed then, ideal for survey. They flew the next day and the day after that; on the third he went to Julianehaab again to refuel. Then they went on with the survey. The tides, forty minutes later every day, became high in the early morning, later and later as the days went on. The pilot took his sleep in bits and snatches, as and when he could. He could usually manage to get in two or three hours after the test development, and another two or three hours at some time in the night. After a day or two he found difficulty in sleeping in the daytime at irregular hours, and had to resort to his tablets to assist him in his day-time sleep. For that they worked all right, but they became less satisfactory for his night-time sleep. Once in the night, dead tired but wakeful, and with only two hours' sleep to come, he took two tablets and slept heavily and well. He did not need to take two tablets the next night, because that was a refuelling day and he could get a stretch of over five hours on end; when next he took two tablets they had little effect. The next night, in desperation, with the survey all but finished, he took three.

Two and a half hours later the alarm rang in his ear till it ran down, but he did not wake up. After ten minutes Lockwood shook him gently by the arm, and then more vigorously. Then he called Alix from her tent.

CHAPTER VIII

THE pilot lay on his back in his sleeping-bag, with eyes closed and his tanned face drained of colour. The girl kneeled by him with her father; they shook him by the shoulder, without effect. He was inert and limp; his respiration was regular, but low.

The girl said: 'It's a sort of a faint. Wait, and I'll get some water.'

They sponged his face with the cold water from the stream, and raised his head. But he did not come round.

Lockwood was utterly at sea. 'I've never seen anything like this before,' he muttered. 'I suppose it's just exhaustion.'

His daughter said: 'It's those wretched tablets he's been taking, I should think.'

The don said sharply: 'What tablets are those?'

'He got them at Reykjavik when he couldn't sleep. He showed them to me once.'

'I never knew he was taking anything of that sort. Do you know where he kept them?'

There were not very many private places in the tent. After a short search Lockwood found the bottle; it was half empty. He read the label with interest and slipped it in his pocket.

'Well, that's the end of that,' he said grimly.

Alix said: 'What do you think we'd better do, Daddy?' A hideous feeling of disaster was in the background of her mind.

Her father did not answer for a moment. He knelt there by the pilot staring down at him. They had laid him in what seemed a comfortable position with his head raised; his face was wet and dripping from the water. 'I don't know,' he said irresolutely. 'I suppose we'll have to wait till he comes round. How many of the damn things did he take?'

She shook her head. 'I don't know. I never liked to ask.'

They became aware of Ajago and Mayark peering in at them through the opening of the tent. Alix got up and went outside to them. Ajago said in Danish. 'Rogg is ill.'

The girl shook her head. 'He is only asleep. Very soon he will wake up.'

Mayark said something in an excited tone in Eskimo, evidently in disagreement. Ajago answered him sharply in the same language, and got a volley of words in reply. An incomprehensible argument or quarrel developed between the natives; both grew very much excited. Alix sighed irritably, and went back to the tent.

A quarter of an hour later she discovered Ajago squatting morose and alone beside the fire. She asked him: 'Where is Mayark?'

Without moving the native said: 'One is foolish, and has gone away.'

'Why has he gone away?'

He raked awkwardly among the ashes. 'One has been afraid.'

The girl said: 'You are not afraid, Ajago? There is nothing here to be afraid of?'

He raised his eyes to hers uneasily. 'I will stay here,' he said simply.

'Thank you, Ajago.' She touched his shoulder, and went back into the tent.

She told her father what the Eskimo had said. He bit his lip. 'It's most unlucky,' he said quietly. 'They said that someone would get ill if we camped here, and now it's happened. I suppose Mayark's gone away for good. Will Ajago stay with us tonight? We'll be done if they both go.'

'I think he's all right, Daddy. You'd better come and have a word with him.'

They left the pilot, and went out of the tent. The native was still squatting by the fire; he had some kind of amulet in his hands which he concealed hurriedly as they came towards him. Alix remembered that he was supposed to be a Christian. He got to his feet to meet them.

Lockwood asked: 'Where is Mayark, Ajago? Has he gone to the other camp?'

Alix interpreted: the man said something in reply. 'He says, Mayark's gone home.'

'Ask him if he will stay with us.'

The man burst into a torrent of nervous speech, mostly in his own language. Alix interrupted him gently, and told him to speak Danish. For ten minutes they wrestled with the language difficulty.

The girl turned to her father. 'What he's trying to say is that we're crazy to stay here. He doesn't want to leave us. But he thinks we're awful fools to have camped here at all. And of course, he's saying that he warned us this would happen.'

The don stood looking round him, deep in thought. He saw the low, bare hill, the stream, the beach, the low stone walls of the abandoned buildings. Quite suddenly, it was distasteful to him; he came to a decision. 'Tell him that as soon as Ross recovers we'll all move over to the other camp.'

She did so. The man said something to her very earnestly, and repeated it several times.

'What's that?' asked Lockwood.

She turned to him with a scared face. 'He says that if we keep Mr. Ross here he . . . he'll die tonight.'

'Oh!'

There was a long pause; Lockwood had to do some rapid thinking. If the native felt like that about it, it was most unlikely that he would stay with them; if Ross did not recover very soon, Ajago would desert. Without the Eskimo it would become impossible for them to carry on at all. If they were to retain him, they must make some compromise with his superstition.

'Ask him if he would like us to move over to the other camp today.'

The girl did so; there was very little doubt of Ajago's feelings on that matter.

The don returned to his daughter. 'What do you think, Alix?'

She stared around at the camp site. 'I don't know, Daddy,' she said slowly. 'It's much better here, of course—the water's good, and there's more level ground. But we could pull the seaplane right up at high tide, and leave her. There can't really be anything in what he says, can there?'

Her father hesitated. 'Of course there can't,' he said, a little uncertainly. 'Ross has taken too many of those tablets —he'd be just the same in Oxford. Still—I don't know.'

Alix said: 'Daddy, I'd just as soon that we went over there . . .'

'All right.' He turned to the native. 'We will wait here till midday,' he said. 'If Ross has recovered then, we will stay here. If not, we'll move him over to your camp this afternoon.'

The girl translated this, and Ajago received it with a smile. They turned back to the tent. The Eskimo came running after them, and said something to the girl.

'What's that?' asked Lockwood.

She frowned, and hesitated. 'Literally, I think he's saying that Mr. Ross has gone on a journey with the people who used to live here, Daddy,' she said. 'In case we didn't quite understand . . .'

They nodded and smiled at the man, and went back into the tent. The pilot was still lying as they had left him; it seemed to them that the respiration was not quite so strong. They made another effort to rouse him and sponged his face with the cold water again, with not the least success. His hands and feet were growing cold; they filled bottles with hot water and put them in his sleeping-bag. Then they had done all that they could do.

At high tide Lockwood went down with Ajago to the water's edge, and beached the seaplane at the top of the tide. They made her fast to stakes driven into the ground, securing her as firmly as they could. Then they went back to the camp, where Alix was still sitting by the pilot in the tent, immersed in her own thoughts. She had learned, that morning, what the pilot meant to her.

From time to time she sponged his face with the cold water, with absolutely no effect at all. By noon they could not deny that he was a good deal worse. The respiration was very low, and the pulse was feeble. Outside, Ajago was busy constructing a stretcher of birch boughs. Lockwood turned to Alix.

'It's absolutely crazy,' he said, 'but I believe I'd like to take him to the other camp. He's doing no good here.'

She inclined her head. 'It *is* crazy, Daddy,' she said seriously. 'There's absolutely nothing the matter with this place—we've only got the wind up because Ajago's been talking to us. But I agree with you. If we wait till this afternoon he may be so weak that we won't want to move him. If we're going, we'd better go now.'

'I think so, too.'

They went and told Ajago of their decision. He finished the stretcher and went down and brought the motor-boat to the beach; then they lifted the pilot in his sleeping-bag and laid him carefully upon the stretcher. They carried him down to the boat and, wading in the shallow water, laid the stretcher across the gunwales. The stretcher made access to the engine difficult; rather than bother with it for the short trip, Ajago took the oars and rowed the boat across the cove. In half an hour they were carrying him up from the boat to the Eskimos' tent in the new camp.

At the entrance to the tent Ajago made them lay the stretcher down. Alix asked him the reason in Danish, and the man replied.

She turned to her father. 'He says, we've got to wait,' she said.

They watched the Eskimo, a little irritably. He went into the tent and dragged his own sleeping-bag out on to the grass. Then he took down a bunch of vegetation that was hanging in the roof, and began to sprinkle little portions of it on the ground sheet. Satisfied with that, he crushed the remainder in his hands and rubbed it over the cloth entrance flaps. Lockwood watched him, keenly interested.

Alix asked: 'What is that stuff? What's he doing to the tent?'

He said quietly: 'It's wild garlic. He's making a protection against spirits. I've never seen this done before.'

Satisfied with his work upon the tent, the Eskimo came over to the stretcher, and kneeled down beside the pilot. He looked at him critically and laid a hand upon his forehead; then he said something to the girl. She turned to her father.

'He wants to put some of those weeds in his bag,' she said.

Her father said: 'I guessed as much. I don't think it can do him any harm—it's only wild garlic. If we're going to try mediaeval treatment we may as well go the whole hog.'

They nodded their assent to Ajago. The Eskimo undid his bag and put sprigs of garlic in beside the sleeping man, and laid a little on his chest. Then they carried him into the tent and made him comfortable upon the bed.

They had a hurried meal; then Ajago and Lockwood spent the afternoon transferring the camp with successive journeys in the motor-boat, while Alix stayed with Ross. By evening a definite improvement was noticeable. The pilot's breathing was much stronger and the pulse was better; moreover, he seemed to be keeping warmer.

Lockwood stood up from examining him. 'It's wearing

off,' he said, a little uncertainly. 'Drugs of that sort get absorbed into the system in time. It's only a matter of time . . .'

Alix agreed. 'Of course. I mean, it couldn't be anything else.'

Ajago looked in at the tent door, bent over the pilot critically, and got to his feet very pleased. He said something to the girl, beaming all over his face; she turned to her father.

'He's saying, "I told you so."'

'Of course, he would say that.'

The man said in Danish: 'It is good. Tomorrow one will wake up.' He went out of the tent; when Alix went out later she discovered that he had spread a circle of wild garlic on the grass right round the tent.

That night they took turns to sit with the pilot. Alix went to sleep after supper and Lockwood stayed with the sick man in the tent; at two in the morning the girl came to relieve him.

She bent over the pilot and looked at him in the dim light of the candle lantern. 'He's ever so much better, Daddy,' she said quietly. 'He's got more colour, and he's warmer. He's breathing much more strongly, too, than when I saw him last. Ought we to try and wake him?'

The don said: 'I don't think so. I should let him sleep it off.'

The girl nodded. 'All right, Daddy—he's got plenty to make up. You go along and get some sleep yourself. I'll be all right.'

She settled down beside the pilot in the tent; Lockwood went to the other tent to sleep. The man lay motionless, his head a little on one side, his breathing regular and even. The girl sat by him, deep in her own thoughts. From time to time she went out of the tent and threw some wood upon the fire; the night was fine, and still, and starry. Over the barren moors and the mountains, over the ice-cap and the fjord, a great peace reigned. From time to time she stood outside the tent and looked around; in spite of everything she was happy. The barren landscape seemed to be a friendly place to her. There was nothing bad here, nothing to be afraid of. It was only a little strange.

The half-light became dawn, and then full day. She stayed with the pilot until seven o'clock; then her father came to relieve her, and they breakfasted. She lay down and slept for a time after that; when she got up at noon and came to see how Ross was getting on she found that he was sleeping naturally and lightly. He had turned over in his sleep.

Alix said: 'What about trying to wake him again now, Daddy?'

Her father said: 'If you like. Perhaps it would be better, if he's going to sleep at all tonight.'

The girl knelt down by the bed, and took one of the pilot's hands in her own. Then she leaned across him, and with her other hand began to wipe his face with a cold sponge. In a few moments he stirred, and opened his eyes.

He raised himself upon one elbow, still holding her hand, and looked her full in the face. 'This is a good country,' he said earnestly, 'better than Greenland. I will ask Leif to let us stay here when the ship goes back, and you shall have your children here.'

There was a momentary silence.

The girl forced a laugh. 'Wake up, Mr. Ross,' she said, a little tremulously. 'You're still asleep.' She passed the sponge over his face again.

He turned his face away, and stared at the tent wall. 'Did you say I'd been asleep?' he said after a time.

Lockwood said: 'You certainly have.'

There was a long, pregnant silence. The man lay motionless and silent, raised upon one elbow. At last he said: 'You're Miss Alix, aren't you?' There was a world of disappointment in his voice.

The girl said in a low tone: 'I'm Alix, Mr. Ross.'

He glanced down at the hand that he was still holding in his own, and laughed shortly. 'I don't know why we're doing this, Miss Alix.'

She coloured a little, and withdrew her hand. The pilot rubbed his eyes. 'I'm sorry if I overslept, sir. What's the time?'

The don said: 'It's about twelve o'clock.'

Ross said quietly: 'I'm sorry. If you wouldn't mind, Miss Alix . . . I'll get up.'

She said: 'Don't do that, Mr. Ross. Not just yet. You've not been very well. It's twelve o'clock, but you've missed a day. You've been asleep for thirty-six hours.'

He stared at her. 'More like three weeks, you mean.'

The girl shot a swift glance at her father.

'Stay quiet in bed for a bit, anyway,' she said. 'You're not too fit.'

He rubbed a hand across his eyes again. 'I'm sorry,' he said quietly. 'I don't know what I meant by talking of three weeks. How long did you say I'd been asleep?'

'Thirty-six hours.'

They became aware of Ajago in the tent door, beaming all over his face. 'One is awake,' he said in Danish. 'I told you so.' The last part of his sentence was familiar to the don by that time, and needed no interpretation.

The Eskimo left them and began bustling about the fire; when Alix went out a few minutes later she found him warming up some soup. She took it into the tent and gave it to the pilot to drink. He took it obediently, but spoke very little; when he did speak he was evidently still confused. Presently Lockwood motioned to his daughter, and they moved a short way from the tents.

'I'm not going to stay here any longer,' he said directly. 'We'll go back to Julianehaab tomorrow—for a time, at any rate.'

The girl nodded. 'That's the best thing to do. We can get the doctor there, if we still want one.'

'Of course we do. We must get somebody to have a look at him, after a bout like this.'

The girl said: 'How are you going to get him to Juliane-haab, Daddy?'

'He'll have to come in the motor-boat with us.'

'Leaving the seaplane here?'

'Yes. He can come back and fetch it when he's well again.'

She looked very doubtful. 'I don't believe you'll get him to do that.'

'Well, he can't fly it in his present state.'

'He won't take kindly to the idea of leaving it behind. You know he won't.'

They discussed this for some time, and came to no conclusion beyond the bare decision to get back to Julianehaab as soon as possible. Presently Lockwood said: 'Of course, he may be better in the morning. He's bound to be a bit confused at first, I suppose.'

He mused for a moment. 'It was a very odd thing, what he said when he woke up. Did you notice that?'

She said very shortly: 'Yes, I did.' She had no intention whatever of discussing that matter with her father. She

182

thought he should have had more sense.

The don was immersed in his own trend of thought. 'I'm sure he said Leif. You heard that, too?'

She was a little surprised. 'Yes—he did say some name like Leif.'

Her father said: 'That's very curious, you know. It's not as if Leif was a common name.'

She did not answer him, being determined to change the subject and avoid discussion of what Ross had said. Instead, she suggested that they should walk over to the seaplane, which they could see standing upon the sand across the inlet.

They found the machine in good order; the rise of tide had not disturbed it. When they got back to the camp, an hour later, Ross was up and dressed. He was much more himself. Alix went over to the fire to make tea; Ross walked a little way aside with Lockwood.

'I don't know what to say about this, sir,' he said. 'I really am exceedingly sorry.'

The don smiled. 'There's nothing to be sorry about. You've been working a bit too hard.'

The pilot nodded. 'I suppose that's the truth of it. It's not been very easy to get all the sleep one wanted, this last fortnight.'

'I know—you've had a very heavy time. By the way, Mr. Ross, I've got those tablets you've been taking. I think I'll keep them for a bit.'

Ross smiled wryly. 'I was wondering what had become of them. All right, sir—I expect they're better with you than with me. I don't suppose they really do one any good.'

'I don't suppose they do. Look, Mr. Ross—I've decided to go back to Julianehaab. I'm going to stay there for a week at least. We're all tired out, and we all need rest. I'm going to stop all work now for a week, and then we'll see how fit we are to come back here again. As a matter of fact, the survey's practically finished. I should be quite content to go home now and study the air photographs, and come back next year with a digging party.'

The pilot thought about it for a minute. 'I see. You want to go back to Julianehaab right away?'

'That's quite definite, Mr. Ross.'

The pilot said: 'All right, sir. If you don't want to come back here, we can finish the survey in a couple of flights from Julianehaab. If we're going to do that, I'll fly the machine back tomorrow and you can go with Miss Lockwood in the motor-boat—unless you'd rather come with me. That would be better. There's no point in you sitting in the boat for all that time.'

The don hesitated. 'One of us should stay with Ajago. As a matter of fact, I want you to come back with us in the motor-boat, Mr. Ross. You can come over and fetch the machine later on.'

Ross stared at him. 'I can't do that, Mr. Lockwood. We can't leave the seaplane here.'

The other faced him. 'That's what I want to do, Mr. Ross.'

'But why, sir?'

'I don't want you to fly again until you've had a good long rest.'

The pilot's lips set mulishly. 'I'm quite all right. If you think I'm not, sir, then I'd rather stay on here for a few days. But I'm not going to leave that seaplane here and go away, when I'm responsible for it. We paid over twenty-five thousand dollars for that seaplane, sir. You can't leave that amount of money blowing round the wilderness.'

They argued the point for a few minutes; the don found the pilot courteous but entirely stubborn. 'With every respect, sir,' he said, 'I know when I'm fit to fly and when I'm not. I don't want to break my bloody neck any more than you want to see me break it. But I'm not going to leave that seaplane out here and go back to Julianehaab.'

They reached a complete deadlock, abandoned the discussion without quarrelling, and had tea. The meal finished, Ross insisted on walking over to the other cove to examine the machine himself; he took Ajago with him to assist in shoring up the floats, if that were necessary. Lockwood and Alix stayed behind in the camp; he told her the substance of their discussion.

She nodded. 'I knew he'd take it like that. What are you going to do, Daddy?'

'I don't know. He's in a very nervous state. If we did stay here for a few days doing nothing, I don't believe he'd rest. He'd always be fussing round his aeroplane.'

She fully agreed with her father. 'He'd be much better back at Julianehaab under the doctor's eye. You'll have to let him fly it back.'

'He might faint in the air, and kill himself. It's not a thing to be decided lightly.'

She bit her lip. 'I don't see what else we can do. If he stays here he'll only make himself ill again. Look how he's gone off now.'

They stared across the water to the other cove, where Ross and Ajago were busy with the seaplane.

'It's a devil,' said Lockwood. 'Whatever we decided to do may turn out wrong.'

An hour later the pilot returned. Alix went out to meet him on the hill.

'Good evening, Mr. Ross,' she said. 'How are you feeling now?'

In the calm evening light he stopped by her. 'I'm right enough, Miss Alix,' he said quietly. 'Still, I think it's a good idea for us to go back to Julianehaab for a bit. It'll give us time to sort things out.'

She nodded. 'Daddy wants to make a start early tomorrow morning. You're going to fly the seaplane back, aren't you?'

The pilot glanced at her. 'That's what I was planning to do. But Mr. Lockwood didn't seem to think that was a very good idea.'

She smiled. 'Don't worry, Mr. Ross—I've had a talk with him, and he's coming round. Let me have another word with him. It's the only thing to do, for you to fly it back. If you're going to do that, I'd like to come too.'

He said. 'Of course, Miss Alix. There's no point in you sitting in the boat for all those hours.'

They turned and walked back to the camp. Ross went into his tent; the girl went and found her father. 'I've been talking to Mr. Ross, Daddy,' she said. 'You'll have to let him fly the seaplane back tomorrow—he'll never agree to leave it here.'

The don said: 'I suppose he won't.'

'I told him I'd go back in it with him. You won't mind going alone with Ajago?'

He was silent for a minute. Then he said quietly: 'You're all I've got now, Alix. I want you to feel that your life is your own property. But—don't go and chuck it away.'

She nodded gravely. 'He must have someone with him,' she said. 'It's been our expedition, Daddy, and it's our fault that he's got into this state.'

They understood each other perfectly. 'You must do as you think best,' he said, a little heavily. 'If you want to go with him, I wouldn't stand in your way.'

They spent the evening packing up the stores and photographic gear, and loading them into the boat, in readiness for an early start. They went to bed early. From time to time throughout the night Lockwood woke and raised himself to look at the pilot; each time he found him awake, lying upon his back, staring at the tent cloth. When dawn came and they got up, he said:

'Did you sleep at all?'

Ross answered: 'I think I may have done. Anyway, I'm all right, sir.'

Conveniently, the tide was high at about eight o'clock. They struck their camp and loaded everything into the boat; then they motored over to the other cove. It took their united efforts to launch the seaplane down to the water again on greased timbers laid beneath the floats, but after an hour of heavy work she floated. Ross and Alix got into the cabin, and the motor-boat towed the machine from the cove out into the fjord. Then they started the engine, and cast off.

Lockwood stood tensely watching from the boat. The seaplane taxied a little way away and headed into wind. The engine roared out, the white feathery spray flew sideways from the floats and she made a perfect take-off, circled around, and took a direct line for Julianehaab.

The don relaxed. 'Get along now,' he said to Ajago. 'As quickly as you can.'

Three-quarters of an hour later the seaplane swept over Julianehaab in a wide gliding turn, flattened out close above the surface of the harbour, and made a good landing. She lost way upon the water and came to a standstill, with the engine ticking over slowly. The pilot dropped his hands from the wheel, and turned to the girl beside him with a faint smile.

'I know why you came on this trip, Miss Alix,' he said. 'I'd like to say "thank you" before it gets cold.'

She said. 'Don't be absurd.'

He leaned across and slapped the trouser pocket of her overall. His touch gave her an unreasonable thrill. 'What's that bottle in your pocket?'

She said: 'It's my smelling salts, Mr. Ross.' She pulled it out and showed it to him.

'I suppose you brought that along in case you felt a little faint.' He prodded the bulge in her other pocket. 'What's this one?' He pulled it out. 'Oh, I see—brandy. I suppose that was to pour over your plum pudding.'

She laughed. 'I always take that with me when I travel.'

'Surely,' he said. 'In case the engine-driver gets sick.'

There was a momentary silence.

'I hope I'll never be so foolish as to fly when I'm not fit to fly,' he said. 'But you couldn't know the ins and outs of that.'

He turned the seaplane and taxied in towards the beach where he had overhauled her before leaving for Brattalid. 'Tide's falling,' he said. 'If we're going to be here for a week I'll put her up on shore at once. Maybe we can get her right out, up above high-water mark.'

He stopped the engine, and the floats grounded on the sand. A few men came running down towards them; Alix and Ross got down on to the float and jumped on shore. An hour later the machine had been pulled safely above high-water mark and firmly pegged down.

They carried their sleeping-bags up to the house, unlocked it, and dumped them on the beds. Then Alix said:

'We're going to see the doctor now.'

Ross hesitated. 'I don't think that's necessary, Miss Alix.'

She said: 'I do. If my father arrives tonight and finds you haven't seen the doctor, I don't think he'll be very pleased. You can't pass out for thirty-six hours and do nothing about it. Be sensible.'

He said reluctantly: 'All right. When do you want to go?'

'Now.'

She walked with him to the doctor's house and made him wait outside while she told the doctor what had happened. He listened carefully to her story. 'So,' he said. 'Your father has the bottle of the Troxigin? Good. I think that is a very bad drug. I will take it from him when he comes. Now, I will make examination of Herr Ross.'

Twenty minutes later he said to Ross, putting on his shirt: 'For three days you stay in bed, not less. I will tell the Froken your food, but in bed you must stay. When you have learned to sleep again, we will allow you to get up.'

He called in Alix and gave her instructions about diet. Presently they were back again in the hut, Ross peevish and irritable.

'Pack of damn nonsense,' he muttered.

The strain of the work in the camp, and the strain of their relationship, had made its mark upon the girl as well as on the pilot. She said: 'It's no good going on like that, Mr. Ross. You've got to get to bed and stay there. I'm going up to the

187

farm now to fetch some milk. You'd better get to bed while I'm away.'

He said irritably: 'I'll lie down after lunch.'

She swung round on him angrily. 'Look, Mr. Ross. My father's come here at a great expense to do a job of work. That's all been knocked on the head now, because you've gone and got ill. It seems to me, the least you can do is to carry out the doctor's orders and get well, so that my father can go on with his work.' She picked up the milk-can. 'I'm going up to the farm now. While I'm away I hope you'll have the sense to get to bed.'

She walked out of the house and slammed the door. When she came back with the milk she found the pilot had arranged his sleeping-bag upon the bench and was lying in it in pyjamas, motionless and staring at the ceiling.

Relations were a little strained between them. She gave him bread and milk for lunch, following the doctor's orders; he ate a little of it, but soon lit a cigarette. Then, hoping that he would sleep if she left him alone, she went out and up to the governor's house to report. She stayed there all the afternoon with the governor and his wife; they gave her coffee and little cakes to eat. In the late afternoon she went back to the house.

Ross was still lying in his bag, in practically the same position as he had been when she left him. She crossed over and sat down on the bench by him. 'Sleep at all?' she asked.

He shook his head. 'I don't feel that I'll ever want to sleep again.' Now that the strain of the work was no longer on him he felt listless, drained of all energy and initiative, but he did not want to sleep.

The girl said comfortingly: 'You'll sleep all right tonight. You get a cup of Ovaltine now, and some bread and butter.'

'I don't want that, Miss Alix.'

She was silent for a moment. He sounded lonely and unhappy, quite different from his normal manner. It struck her then that there was more in his illness than mere physical fatigue; she was sorry that she had spoken sharply to him earlier in the day. And searching for a panacea, she said:

'When did you write to Aunt Janet last, Mr. Ross?'

He wrinkled his brows. 'Aunt Janet? I forget. Not since Reykjavik, I don't think.'

'What a shame! Would you like to write a cable to her

now? I could take it up to the wireless station, and get it off tonight.'

He roused himself. 'It's awfully good of you, Miss Alix. I'd better send her one. Could you pass me over that pad, and the pencil?'

She sat on his bed and watched him draft the cable. It read:

SURVEY NEARLY FINISHED STAYING FEW DAYS HERE BEFORE RETURNING. DONALD.

The girl expostulated with him. 'You can't just send it like that, Mr. Ross. Send her your love, at any rate.'

He smiled. 'She'd never forgive me if I spent money cabling that.'

'I'll never forgive you if you don't.' She took the pad from him, and added:

ALL MY LOVE AND BEST WISHES FROM LOCKWOODS WILL SEE YOU BEFORE LONG.

He laughed. 'She'll have a fit.'

'Probably do her good. Here's your Ovaltine, Mr. Ross. I'll take this up and send it off at once.'

She left the house and walked up to the wireless station; when she returned she found that he had drunk the Ovaltine and eaten all the bread and butter.

At Guildford, Aunt Janet had the novel experience of being rung up on the telephone that Donald had installed, to have her telegram read out to her at ten o'clock at night. It was too late that night for her to do more than ponder the matter, and set the new cable up on the kitchen mantelpiece beside the one from Reykjavik, now growing rather dirty. But at nine o'clock next morning she was at the post office inquiring the cost of a wireless message from a place called Julianehaab.

After a good deal of research they told her it was one and sevenpence a word.

'Land sakes alive,' she muttered to herself. 'Over a pound —a pound and sevenpence for that last sentence. Donald must be daft, or he's in love.' But she was very pleased. It was as if he had spent that much money on a present for her. The confirmation copy had arrived when she got home: she carried it with her in her bag for weeks.

Lockwood landed from the motor-boat at about eight o'clock, relieved to see the seaplane in one piece upon the beach. He left Ajago to get some help to bring the gear up to the house, and went on himself. Alix came to meet him from the house, and told him briefly what had happened.

They gave the pilot some more Ovaltine and a milk pudding when they had supper, and another bowl of bread and milk at half-past ten when they prepared for bed. The girl said cheerfully: 'You ought to sleep now, after all this milk.'

Ross said: 'I ought to, but I shan't.'

As before, Alix slept in the inner room, screened from the main part of the hut by a matchboarding partition without a door. The men slept at the other end of the main room. Lockwood laid out his sleeping-bag beside the pilot, undressed, and got into it. 'Give me a call if you want anything,' he said.

At one o'clock he woke, raised himself, and looked at the other in the dim light. Ross was lying wide awake upon his back. He turned his head and looked at the don.

Lockwood said: 'Have you been to sleep at all?'

'Not yet. Don't worry about me, sir. I'm all right.'

The don sat up. 'You'd better have another cup of Ovaltine.'

'I don't want that, sir.'

Lockwood got out of his bag and pulled on trousers over his pyjamas. 'You'd better have it. I'll have one myself. No —you stay where you are.'

He busied himself with cups, and lit the Primus stove. Alix, behind her matchboarding partition, woke at the noise of the stove, heard the men talking, and realised what was happening. There was no need for her to get up; she lay quiet in her bag, listening to their conversation.

Lockwood, busy with the stove, said carelessly: 'Do you know anyone called Leif, Mr. Ross?'

The pilot did not answer for a moment. Then he said quietly: 'Why do you ask that?'

The other said: 'It's not really a fair question. But you said something about Leif when you were ill, when you were waking up. I was wondering if he was somebody you knew.'

Ross did not answer. Presently Lockwood poured the hot milk into the mugs, stirred in the Ovaltine, and carried the mugs over to the sleeping-bench. He gave one to the pilot, and got back into bed himself with the other.

They sat waiting for the drink to cool. 'I had the hell of a dream,' the pilot said presently. 'A chap called Leif came into it.'

Lockwood nodded. 'Do you dream much?'

'I don't dream at all, in the ordinary way. I suppose it's all that stuff that I was taking.'

'Very likely. What sort of a man was this Leif?'

'Oh, he was a grand chap. A great big man, with yellow hair, very kind, and very straightforward. He could do everything better than anyone else.'

'Who was he?'

'I don't know who he was.'

'Can you remember anything else about him?'

The pilot said: 'I can remember everything. If I could draw I could do you his portrait—now.'

The don asked: 'Where did he live?'

Ross laughed shortly. 'That's the funny part about dreams. They all get mixed up with real things, that you've seen yourself. I thought he lived in that cove where we camped, beside the stream.'

'Did he live in a tent, like us?'

'No—there was a farm there, where the ruins are. A lot of little stone houses, with wooden thatched roofs. It was a pretty squalid sort of set-up, altogether.'

The don sipped his Ovaltine. 'What were the windows of the houses made of?' he asked, with apparent carelessness.

'Some part of the guts of a cow. A sort of membrane, stretched on a wooden frame. It let the light in fairly well.'

'Were all these houses dwelling-houses?'

The pilot shook his head. 'They were mostly out-buildings for the cattle. I suppose fifty or sixty people lived there. But they all slept about in the cow-houses or anywhere—there was only the one proper house. I had a corner in the hayloft. A lot of us slept up there.'

Lockwood asked: 'Do you remember who you were, or any other details?'

Ross said: 'I remember everything.'

He turned to the don. 'In my dreams, the ones that I can remember, silly things have always happened. Foolish things —you know. But nothing like that happened in this one. It was all so—so real.'

'Bad dreams are like that sometimes. Was it very distressing?'

The pilot said softly: 'Not until it came to an end.'

The older man sipped his Ovaltine again. 'If you can't sleep, tell me about it.'

Ross said: 'I can't sleep because of it. I can't stop thinking about it, all the time. If I tell it to you, do you think it will put it out of my mind for a bit?'

Lockwood said gently: 'It's worth trying.'

The pilot said: 'This man Leif, who lives in the house, I thought that I was one of his slaves. My name was Haki.'

Behind her matchboarding the girl lay listening, wide awake.

CHAPTER IX

HE thought that he had not always been a slave. In his dreams he could remember the hovel that he had lived in with his parents and his brothers, a rough shelter made of stones and turf upon the edge of a sea loch in a barren land of grey skies and heather. They had a few sheep, and they had a crazy boat made of skins stretched over a light wooden frame; they used this for fishing.

He did not know how old he was, or how long he had lived in that place before the ship came. It was an enormous double-ended ship, built like an open boat but over a hundred feet in length. It had a short mast with a square sail brailed up on a yard; it had oars to row with, and it was manned by about thirty huge men with fair hair, the biggest men that he had ever seen.

He was out fishing in the boat alone; as he came homewards round the point and opened up the bay in which they lived he saw the ship upon the beach before their house, and the men swarming over everything. He stopped rowing to watch, and saw his parents and his brothers flying up the hillside, far outdistancing the blond giants in pursuit of them. And then he saw another thing. The men were driving all their sheep down to the beach, picking them up, and heaving them on board the ship.

He dashed on shore in a blind fury, armed with a heavy stick. They must not be allowed to take the sheep. He struck at one of the men; with the greatest ease the giant twisted the stick from his grasp and pinned his hands. Then they bound his arms behind him with a leather thong, and put him on the ship with the sheep.

There were other people on the ship in similar condition to himself, and other sheep. Presently the ship was pushed off from the beach, the grey woollen sail was dropped down from the yard, and she began to cruise along the shore before the wind. His captors undid his arms and offered food and water, but he would not take either. He could not understand a word they said to him.

He could understand what the other captives said, but they spoke very little. He learned from them that the blond men had come in the ship from Norway. Most of them seemed to take their position philosophically; the younger they were, the more they fretted and refused food.

Amongst them there was a girl with fair hair, about sixteen years of age; her name was Hekja. She sat crouched down among the sheep, refusing everything, silent and alert; all day she watched the land. He did not speak to her, but he knew instinctively that she was ready for any chance to escape, however desperate.

When night came the blond men gave them skin rugs to put over them, to keep them warm.

He did not know how long they were in the boat—two or three days perhaps. There came a morning when the ship approached the shore, to cut grass for the sheep. Beneath the cover of the animals he stretched out his foot furtively, touched the girl's toe, and glanced towards the shore. As the keel grated on the sand they were over the side like lightning, and running up the beach pursued by the most agile of the Norsemen.

The girl was as nimble as he, and a better runner. They went up the cliff like a couple of monkeys and set off together in a steady lope over the hill. The Norsemen gave up the pursuit when they had covered a mile, gasping and panting in their rough grey woollen clothes. As they stood sweating they watched the fugitives far above on the hillside nearly two miles away.

'Bad luck to lose them,' one of them remarked. 'Runners like that would have been a good present for the King.'

Some time later the fugitives stopped running, hardly out of breath. They seemed to be safe from pursuit. Haki stared about him with a growing concern. He could not yet see what lay beyond the hill, but it began to look as though they were on an island, and an uninhabited and barren place at that.

They went on, and an hour later knew the worst. They were on an island without beasts, or people, or anything to eat except the grass. Far below them they could see the vessel on the beach and the men spread out on the hillside cutting grass; they saw the smoke of a camp fire from the beach.

They wandered about all day at a safe distance, finding no food except a few shellfish. They were desperately hungry, having eaten practically nothing since their capture. When night fell they found a little cave and huddled together in it for warmth; in spite of that they were numb and stiff with cold when morning came. They had no means of warming themselves or making a fire, nor any hope of anything to eat barring the mussels on the rocks.

Far below them they could see the ship still on the beach, and the smoke of the fire.

Haki said: 'This is a bad island, with no food. It is better in the ship.'

The girl said desperately: 'I will not go back.'

He said: 'If we do not go back, we shall die.'

Presently they were walking slowly down towards the ship. The Norsemen saw them, and a man came towards them alone, carrying a lump of cooked meat still savoury and warm from the fire. They took it from him and ate it ravenously.

Presently the ship put to sea again; they were content to go with it. The men were kind to them and gave them good food and a cup of ale to drink; their break-away had marked them out from the other captives as slaves who were of value for their spirit.

After a voyage lasting for two days they landed in Norway. Haki and Hekja were separated from the other slaves and put to work on a farm, where they served in some manner as sheep-dogs to the herds of cattle that strayed across the moors. With this occupation their powers of running developed remarkably. From time to time high-born people came to the farm from the town; then the runners would be brought out and put to the test. They rather liked these days. It was child's play to them to cover fifty miles in a day across a trackless countryside; they ran steadily and lightly side by side all the day through. They carried nothing, and wore a minimum of clothing for the latitude. On arrival in the country they had been given material for clothes, white woollen vadmal, white for slavery. This they had worked up into a single garment, a white trousered overall with a hood that could be thrown back on the shoulders, open down the sides beneath the arms. It was the only sort of garment they knew how to make; it interested the Norsemen very much. They wore nothing else. The long slits beneath the arm-holes made it well ventilated and cool for running; when at rest they could button up these slits.

Their hair had been cut short as a sign that they were slaves, and they ran in bare feet. When on a journey they ate nothing and drank very little. On one occasion they covered seventy miles between dawn and dusk of a summer day.

This went on for eight or nine months. Then they were taken into town, to the King's Hall. The throng of people and the magnificence of everything left them frightened and confused; in this state they came before the King Olaf. He was talking to the man they later came to know as Leif.

'Lord,' said the man who had brought them from the farm, 'these are the runners.'

The King looked them up and down with interest. 'So. What country are you from?'

They were too scared to answer him. Even if they had not been scared they could not have answered, for they did not know.

The man said: 'Lord, they are from Scotland.'

The King said: 'So—they are Scots. Can they speak our language?'

'They understand it, Lord, but they speak it with difficulty. When they are frightened they become dumb, and they are frightened now.'

The King said: 'You have nothing to fear from us.'

They did not believe him; he was too powerful.

The King turned to the man Leif. 'These are the runners,' he said. 'I give them to you. They can run further and faster than anybody in the world. Take them with you in your ship, and use them to explore your new colony. I have forgotten the name.'

Leif said: 'Lord, we want to call it Greenland.'

'Is it, then, so green and fertile?'

Leif hesitated. 'In summer, Lord, there are meadows in the south-west of the country where cattle may pasture. But most of the country is a field of ice.'

The King frowned. 'A bad name for such a place.'

The man said: 'Lord, Iceland was called by a true name and people are afraid to go there, because of the ice. My father Erik wants people to come to our country, and so he asks your grace to call it Greenland.'

For a moment the King pondered this; then he burst into a great bellow of laughter, with all his court. It seemed to them to be a very subtle joke. The runners stood bewildered, and more frightened than ever. They had understood a great deal of the conversation, and saw nothing funny in it. They could not understand these people at all. They shrank a little closer together as the laughter roared about them.

They were taken away and lodged in a stable in the town. The bustle and confusion, and the many people thronging round and looking at their clothes, upset them; they were unhappy and refused to eat. On the second day Leif came to look them over.

He spoke slowly to them, using simple words that they could understand. 'So,' he said kindly. 'You ate nothing yesterday. What is the matter? You have nothing to fear.'

Hekja crouched down and shrank away from the great bulk of the man. Haki plucked up courage. 'Lord,' he said in his uncouth dialect, 'the people come and laugh at us.'

This big man nodded with understanding; he had had much to do with animals. 'This is not a good place for you. In a month we go by ship to my colony in Greenland. Would you like to go back to the farm until we sail?'

Haki said: 'Lord, we were happy on the farm.'

Leif turned away. 'You shall go back until I send for you.'

They were taken back to the same farm and resumed their old life, herding the cattle. In a month they were taken to the ship. It was a larger ship than the one in which they had come from Scotland. It was double-ended and open like a huge ship's lifeboat; it had a beam of fully twenty feet, with massive sweeps for rowing in a calm. It had one great mast carrying a yard and a squaresail that could be trimmed to the wind, and reefed; at the bow the stem rose high above the sheer line of the hull, carved like a dragon's head. It drew about six feet of water. There were no decks, but amidships there was a pitched roof like a house which formed a shelter for the perishable goods. There was a leather sleeping-bag for everyone on board. The bottom of the ship was covered with flat slabs of stone carried as ballast; towards the stern these were heaped together for a fireplace.

In this ship they sailed from Norway. They touched at several islands, and were at sea for a long time. At last they came to pack ice and pressed through it, rowing the ship and forcing through the ice. Finally they sighted land, rounded a cape and coasted on a little way until they entered a fjord and came to the farmhouse in the cove.

Many people came down to meet them, made them welcome, and helped them to unload the ship. The ship itself was pulled up from the sea on rollers laid beneath the keel and a rough shelter was built over it.

Haki and Hekja were put to work with the cattle as they had in Norway, running with verbal messages from time to time between the settlements. They were always sent together, in case one had an accident remote from any help.

They lived there two years.

All this formed the background for the pilot's dream, his memory of what had happened to him. But at the beginning he thought that he had driven two young heifers from the meadow down to the byre at the farmhouse on the cove, and Tyrker had seen him, and had said that Leif wanted him in the house.

This Tyrker was a German. He had been a slave of Leif's father, Erik, and had brought up Leif as a boy. He was now an old man and had been freed by Erik a long time before. He worked as a sort of foreman on the farm. He was a ve. y small old man, with a prominent forehead, small features, and restless eyes, but Leif thought the world of him. He was supposed to be very wise.

Haki went into the house, following Tyrker. Inside, a sleeping-bench ran the whole length of the house dividing it in two, raised about two feet from the floor. Leif was sitting on a low stool, on the bench. Tyrker got up and stood behind him; the runner stood upon the floor beneath them, as was fitting. He had long lost his early fear of Leif; it had been succeeded by a dog-like devotion and respect.

Leif said: 'Haki. You have heard the story that Bjarni saw a country west from here, where there was timber?'

Haki said: 'Yes, Lord.' It had been common talk since

Bjarni's ship had arrived. Sailing from Iceland Bjarni had contrived to miss Greenland altogether and had sailed about for weeks, angry, bewildered, and suspecting sorcery. He had seen land several times but none of it was like Greenland; being a single-minded man he had forbidden his men to land, and had sailed back upon his course to look for Iceland again. He had thus reached his destination, south-west Greenland.

Leif said explosively: 'Well, Bjarni saw a new country with woods, with great tall trees. And if you please, he did not go on shore! He might have brought a cargo back with him, and he did not. I think he is a fool.'

Haki could understand his master's irritation. They were badly hampered by a shortage of timber. The only trees in Greenland were weak, stunted birches. They could build houses with stone walls of almost any height, but for the roof-beams they had to depend upon imported wood.

The runner understood this very well. He ventured: 'With big trees we could build a big cow-house.'

Leif nodded. 'That is right. We can build proper houses if we get the timber for the roofs. We can build small boats— ships, even. This summer I am going in a ship to find that timber in the lands that Bjarni saw, and bring a cargo of it back.'

Haki said: 'Lord, how will you ever find the lands that Bjarni saw? There are no landmarks on the sea.'

Leif smiled. 'I have bought Bjarni's ship,' he said. 'The ship will show me where the lands are, for it has been there before.'

The runner was amazed at this sagacity. These people thought of everything. Of course, the dragon on the ship would know.

The Norseman said: 'I want you to come in the ship with me, with Hekja. If there are new lands to be found I must send reports back to the King, and you can run across the land and tell me what it is like.'

'Lord, we can do that.'

Leif said: 'Think well, and talk it over with Hekja. This voyage will be difficult and dangerous; I do not even know where we are going. We may meet with hard times. I will take no one with me upon such a voyage who is not a willing volunteer. No man shall say to me, when hard times come, that I have forced him into it.'

The runner was silent. He did not fully understand this reasoning.

'So, Haki,' said the Norseman, 'I say this: You are one with Hekja; I will not take one of you alone. If you two want to stop here when the ship goes, you may do so. But if you wish to come with me, and if you do good work, then when we return here you shall be free people. I will set you free, and I will give you land to farm for yourselves, and beasts to start you off. I will do this for you if you decide to come with me, but you must talk to Hekja first.'

The runner's eyes gleamed. 'Lord, I would have come with you anyway, but for these gifts I would follow you through hell.'

The big man smiled. Behind him Tyrker stooped and whispered something in his ear. Presently Leif said: 'There is another thing. I will have no unattached maid in my ship, for when men are far distant from their wives they will quarrel over her, and fight. Are you and Hekja lovers? Do you sleep with her?'

The runner said: 'Lord, she does not think about such things yet. Besides, she sleeps with the women.'

The Norseman threw his head right back and roared with laughter, rocking with merriment upon his stool. Haki stood looking at him, utterly bewildered. He had grown to like and admire these men, but he could never understand what made them laugh.

Leif calmed himself, and said: 'So. Before we sail Hekja must be betrothed to you, and I shall be the witness. If anyone wants to break that betrothal he must fight with me, and I shall slay him, under our law. In that way I can keep my crew in order.'

'Yes, Lord.'

'Go along now, and have a talk with Hekja. Come back tonight and tell me whether you want to go with me, or to stay here as slaves.' He made a gesture of dismissal.

Haki went to find Hekja. She was on the haystack pitching hay down to the ground before she carried it into the cow-house; he called to her and she slipped down from the stack and came towards him, very lovely in his eyes. He told her what Leif had said.

'If we go with him and if we please him with our running, he will make us free, and he will give us our own land to farm, and cows of our own. We should be free people then, like everyone else.' He glanced at her, short-haired in the sunlight, in her single overall. 'You would be able to let your hair grow long, and wear fine clothes and ornaments like other free women.'

She said: 'All this is very good, Haki.'

He plunged awkwardly into the difficult part. 'If we go, Leif says that you must be betrothed to me, in case other men, far from their wives, come after you and fight with each other.' He hesitated, and then said: 'This is for order in the ship. We can break the betrothal when we get back, if you don't want to marry.'

Her eyes softened, and she said gently: 'I don't want to marry anyone yet, Haki. But we are the same people and we think the same way. I would rather marry you than any of these people.'

She had never become accustomed to the Norsemen as he had done. She had never settled down to her new life.

He knew how she felt. 'Perhaps if we please him, Leif will give us land right away on the outskirts where we can live in our own way.'

She said earnestly: 'That would be very, very good.'

Preparations for the voyage went ahead quickly. The shed over Bjarni's ship was pulled down, and the ship was overhauled and recaulked. Then it was launched down to the still water of the cove on rollers. Stones for the ballast were gathered from the hill above the cove. Provisioning did not take long. Leif picked a crew of thirty-one good men from the settlement, great husky fellows chosen principally for their skill in battle. He also arranged that Tyrker should go with them.

It was originally intended that the expedition should be led by Leif's father, Erik, the grand old man of the settlement who lived at Brattalid. Everybody was in agreement that success must come to any expedition which he led; the least enthusiastic of them all was Erik. In his youth he had been a wild berserker with bright red hair, invincible in battle and a danger to all sober, honest men, particularly if they had attractive wives. He had been outlawed on Iceland and kicked out, and had sailed away to find and to establish his new colony, Greenland. Now he was old and tired, and not at all inclined to face another expedition.

Fortune was kind to him. The day before the expedition was to start he rode over on a horse to see the ship; the horse threw him, and he sprained his ankle. It was good enough. He said to Leif: 'This is an omen. I am not meant to discover any more lands. You go, and lead in my place.' With that he got upon his horse and went back home.

They started one bright, sunny morning. The ship was on the beach with the tide rising; men swarmed about her, putting on the perishable stores. In the crowd Leif saw Haki and Hekja carrying their sleeping-bags on board, and stopped them with a sudden cry.

'You Scots, come over here.'

They dropped their bedding in the bows of the ship and came to him on the sand. There was a pause in the work; the men looked at them with interest.

Leif roared out: 'Hear, everyone!' Work stopped completely; the men turned to him. 'A betrothal!'

They looked on curiously. Slaves were not normally betrothed at all but bred like cattle, but then it was not usual to take slaves on voyages like this one. Leif was doing them an honour; probably he meant to set them free some day.

Leif said: 'Take her hand, Haki. Do you know what to say?'

He took her hand. 'No, Lord.'

'Well, say this after me, and shout it out so that everyone can hear you: "I name Leif as witness that you, Hekja, betroth yourself to me, Haki, in lawful betrothal, with hand-shaking, without fraud or tricks." '

He said the words aloud; Hekja said nothing. There was an interested murmur from the men.

Leif cried: 'Now listen to me, all of you. This woman belongs to this man, and I am witness to the lawful betrothal. If anyone thinks differently at any time, he can come and talk to me, and he knows what he will get. Now, get on with your work, all the lot of you.'

There was a laugh, and the men turned to their work again. Presently the ship was rowed out from the cove, the sail was hoisted, and she crept down the fjord to the sea.

They sailed northwards for a day or two along the coast; then they headed out to the west. They had no compass; they steered by the sun and stars when they could see them, by the colour of the water and the run of the waves, and by the feel of the wind. At midday each day, when it was calm and sunny, Leif and Tyrker made a curious ceremony, which Haki took to be a rite of their religion. They laid the ship carefully at right angles to the sun and measured the length of the shadow of the gunwale on the middle thwart. This thwart had marks carved upon it, made on Bjarni's previous voyage with runic letters carved against the marks. Sometimes when the shadow of the gunwale fell exactly on a certain mark, Leif seemed very pleased. Only Leif and Tyrker seemed to understand this ceremony; it was a very high and holy matter. The men said that the dragon told them which way to sail when they were doing this.

Presently they came to land. It was a bleak barren country with no trees and no grass, a land of flat rocks leading up to the ice mountains. They anchored off it and launched a small boat that they carried; Leif went on shore with Tyrker and a couple of men. They came back after an hour or two.

'It is a bad land and no use to us,' said Leif. 'We will not stay here any longer. But I think this is the place that Bjarni came to last of all. I shall call it Stoneland. At any rate, we've landed on it, which is more than Bjarni did.'

With a northerly wind they sailed southwards down the land for two days and nights, keeping well off the shore but with the land in sight on their right hand. On the morning of the third day they saw that the character of the country had changed; it was now covered with forest, and there were no more ice mountains. It was a level wooded land, with broad stretches of white sand.

The wind failed them, and they rowed in to the shore, stopping at noon for the midday ceremony of the shadow of the gunwale on the thwart. Leif and Tyrker discussed this for a long time. Then they rowed on and dropped anchor in a little bay with a beach; again Leif and Tyrker went on shore together.

They came back presently. 'This is a better place,' Leif said, 'and here is all the timber that we need. We will come back later and load up the cargo, and explore the country. But now, while this good weather lasts, we will go on and see what other new things we can find.'

They called that country Woodland, and sailed on. Before long they came to a cape, and followed the land around. After that they sailed on west or south-west, before a north-east wind.

For some days they were out of sight of land. There was little to be done except to steer the ship before the wind, which Leif did most of the time. The rest of them sat about busy with various crafts, or slept. One afternoon Tyrker produced a chisel and a mallet, and began chipping at one of the stones of the ballast.

Haki watched him with interest. Then he asked: 'What are you doing, Father?'

The old German told him: 'In Norway I learned how to put words upon a stone, so those that come afterwards may see what I have said.'

Haki thought about this for a time. Then he said: 'That is very wonderful, but not much good. To understand the words needs somebody as wise as you, and there is nobody like that upon the ship.'

Tyrker said: 'That is true. But Leif also knows this art, which I am practising to keep my hand in.'

Haki might have guessed as much. Leif could do everything.

The German chipped on industriously for a quarter of an hour. Then he laid his chisel down and blew the dust off the stone, rubbing his hand across the marks. 'There,' he said to the runner. 'Look at that. Those marks mean Haki. That is your name.'

The Scot looked at them, and touched them with his finger gingerly. They were cut deep and well.

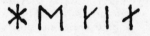

He smiled. 'This is a great wonder. A wise man coming afterwards would find my name.' He was very pleased.

The men crowded around, admiring the work and fingering the marks. Leif noticed them from his position at the helm; a faint frown crossed his brow. The leader must excel in everything. He gave the steering oar to a man that he could trust, and came down to the body of the ship. He stooped and felt the inscription. 'It is well cut, my foster father,' he said. 'Give me the mallet and the chisel, and let me see if I can still recall the craft.'

He squatted down beside the stone and hammered away industriously for a time. Then he rubbed the dust out of the grooves. 'There,' he said, and they all crowded round to look.

Someone asked: 'Lord, what does it mean?'

Tyrker said: 'I understand the meaning, Lord. It is Hekja.'

There was a murmur of applause; the stone was fingered and examined most minutely. Everyone could see that Leif's carvings were bigger and deeper than Tyrker's. Moreover, the word itself was longer. They had the right leader, no doubt about it.

Presently the men dispersed a little; Haki drew Hekja over to the stone and showed her the carvings. He explained it to her. 'These cuts mean my name, and those cuts mean yours. Leif has just done it.'

She fingered the marks, trying to understand the wonder. Crouching down by the stone, she raised her eyes to Leif. 'Lord, are these cuts our names?'

*ᛏᚱᛁ

*ᛗᚱᛁᛏ

He smiled down at her, towering over them. 'So, Haki and Hekja. Your names are now together, for as long as this stone shall endure.'

She stared up at him, and the pieces of the puzzle fell together in her mind. So that was what it meant! She turned to Haki. 'Are we married now?'

There was a great burst of laughter from the crew. She shrank down as the laughter roared and beat about her; her eyes filled with tears. 'Why are they laughing, Haki? What is this all about?'

He touched her hand, and spoke to her quietly in Gaelic. 'Don't let them see you crying—they'll only laugh more. I don't think they meant it as a marriage.'

The Norsemen were still laughing; jokes as rich and rare as this one did not often come their way on board a ship. Hekja said, angry and half crying: 'But that's what he said! He said our names would be together as long as the stone lasted. That means for ever. Stones don't rot away.'

Haki said doubtfully: 'I don't think they meant it like that. I don't believe that is the way they do a marriage.'

'It's as good a way as any other.' They were still speaking in Gaelic. 'Haki—I hate these people. I can't make out their customs, and they're always laughing at us. Can't we get away?'

He touched her hand again. 'Don't talk about that now —someone may understand. Besides, Leif is a good man, and he's promised that we shall be free.'

She said: 'I hate them when they laugh.'

For the rest of the day she was tearful and upset, but she would not leave the stone alone. She sat crouched down in the bottom of the ship with her eyes fixed on it; when it grew dark she crept over to it and laid out her sleeping-bag beside it, so that she could feel the indentation of the letters with her fingers in the night. It suddenly became her best thing, displacing all her few possessions in her preference. Her name and Haki's were together on that stone, for as long as the stone should last. That meant for ever. It was mystical, and wonderful, and comforting to her.

They sailed on for another day. Then in the morning they saw land quite close to them, a low-lying sandy point directly ahead. They sailed to the east of it and found that it stretched on ahead of them in the form of a continuous beach, uninterrupted for as far as they could see. At the head of the beach there was a sandy cliff a hundred feet or so in height that stretched along the shore indefinitely.

All day they sailed along this beach, mile after mile, hour after hour, marvelling at its continuity.

Leif said: 'I will not go much further. Here is another land, and there may be another, and another, to the far end of the world, but we will not go further now. These beaches are a very great wonder. We will sail them Wonderstrands.'

In the evening they came to a little sandy bay at a point where the beach seemed to divide, and anchored there for the night. In the morning they drove the ship on shore at half-tide, and all got out upon the sand to stretch their legs. They soon discovered that they were on a small, low-lying island; the mainland seemed to be across half a mile of shallow water to the west. It was a still, hot, summer day. And here they found a curious phenomenon. The dew upon the grass, when they tasted it, was as sweet as honey, very wonderful to them. The warm climate, the quiet and the shade upon the island, and the sweetness of the dew, induced in them a sort of awe. They had heard tales about the Islands of the Blest that lay beyond the sunset; was it possible that they had come to them? And if so, what would they meet next? Would earthly weapons be of any use to them?

It was a thoughtful party that embarked again when the tide rose.

They anchored for the night again a little way from the land, and sailed southwards when dawn came. Soon the land turned westwards and they followed it; to the south of them there were islands clearly to be seen. They coasted along them looking for a harbour; in the middle of the afternoon they found an entrance to the west of a low sandy spit that seemed to lead to an extensive stretch of inland water.

Leif said: 'This is as far as we will go. We will go in here and make a camp and rest, and find out all we can about the country.'

They sailed in past the sandy spit, lowered the sail, and got out the great oars. They found themselves in a long stretch of inland water running roughly north-east; on each side of them was a wooded land, with little beaches on the shores beneath the shade of the fir-trees. The water was calm and blue, the sun very warm.

None of them had ever been in such a place as that before. Essentially they were farmers, sailors only by necessity, and they were sick of the sea. They rowed on slowly into the heart of this magnificent new country, wondering, entranced. Presently the strait that they were in widened into a great bay; from this they saw a little channel leading northwards deep into the country, right away from the ocean. Leif steered his vessel into this. To the east of the little channel, hardly wider than a river, the land showed an open, park-like country of grass pastures and scattered trees; to the west low hills rose straight up from the channel, thickly clothed in firs.

They went on slowly, and in silence. Land birds swept around them; a herd of deer ran off across the pasture, startled by their approach. Presently the channel widened out again and they turned west, to find themselves in a still inland lagoon, half a mile long and a little less in width, entirely surrounded by the wooded hills. The trees cast perfect reflections in the still water; it was very quiet.

Leif sighed deeply, looking round about. 'Here we will rest,' he said.

They put the ship on to a sandy, shady beach beneath a little wooded knoll, and went on shore. Leif chose a site down by the beach to make a camp, and sent out parties to explore the country round about. Very soon they discovered that they were on a neck of land that ran roughly east and west, perhaps three or four miles broad from north to south. To the eastwards the land stretched out to the beaches they had known as Wonderstrands; to the west the country was unknown.

Leif said: 'Here is all the wood we want; we will unload the ship. These trees will make a good cargo for us. We will cut some of them down and trim them into roof-beams, so that we shall not have to carry useless weight back home with us.'

A party set to work upon the trees. Haki and Hekja were set to carry all the stores ashore up to the place selected for the camp. Suddenly Hekja dropped her load, caught Haki by the arm, and cried:

'Haki—look! They're throwing the stones overboard!'

True enough, a party of men were tipping the flat rocks of the ballast out into the shallow water round the ship, preparing to receive the lumber. Haki said: 'What about it?'

She cried: 'Our stone! Our stone, with our names on it!'

She set off running at top speed down to the ship. Haki followed at a more leisurely pace; as he drew near the ship he heard a burst of laughter. He clambered in over the side and saw Hekja struggling with the heavy stone, tears streaming down her cheeks, while the Norsemen stopped their work to enjoy the joke again.

She cried: 'Haki! Haki! come and help me with it.'

In the stern, old Tyrker turned to Leif. 'Lord,' he said quietly, 'is it your wish that there should be no fighting in this ship?'

The Norseman looked down at him in surprise. 'Surely, my foster father.'

The old German said: 'I think the men have laughed enough.'

Leif ripped out a sharp order and the laughter stopped; in silence the Norsemen stood watching the two runners as they struggled with the stone. They got it up to the bows of the ship and dropped it down on to the sand. Then they picked it up between them and staggered forward; sometimes carrying it and sometimes rolling it, they took it ashore with them.

Tyrker said: 'Their ways are not our ways, and they don't understand.'

Leif said: 'They are poor, simple people, but I like them very well.'

In the ship the work went on again; on shore Hekja pointed to a little rising knoll. 'I want to take it up there, Haki.'

With much trouble they got the stone up to the top of the little hill overlooking the lagoon. They arranged it with the utmost care on the exact summit; the letters showed up beautifully, and they were very pleased with it. They chocked it up with other little stones to make sure that it could never roll about.

The girl sighed happily. 'It will be quite safe there, Haki. Whoever comes up here will see our names together.'

The runner nodded. 'That is very good.'

They went back and worked till nightfall at the preparation of the camp. In the evening Leif called them to him.

'We are staying here for several days,' he said. 'Tomorrow morning, with the first light, I want you to set off and run to the west, to find out what sort of a country this is. You can be away for three days. Tomorrow you will run inland, and part of the next day, and on the third day you will come back by a different way, so that you give me an account of as much of the country as can be seen in the time. You understand what I want?'

Haki said: 'Lord, I understand very well. On the evening of the third day you shall have our story.'

'Good. Will you take food with you?'

The runner shook his head. 'Only a little tinder to make fire with, and a flint and steel. We will eat before we go.'

Leif gave him a long knife in a sheath. He strapped this round his waist; Hekja took flints and tinder in a little pouch. Then they ate a very large meal and lay down and slept at once before the fire. They were up before dawn, eating again; in the first light they trotted off together from the camp.

They travelled westwards. The first part of their journey was through a fairly thick forest of fir-trees: after a few miles the country grew more open with stretches of grassy meadow and a few beech-trees. They skirted a lovely circular lake with fir-trees all around and white, sandy beaches, and went on in a north-westerly direction. Presently they came to rising ground and went up to the top of it; from a height of about three hundred feet they were able to see the lie of the land.

They saw that they were on a cape. There was sea both to the north and to the south of them. Behind them, to the eastwards, the land stretched out into the ocean past their camp to Wonderstrands. Ahead of them there was a neck of land perhaps three miles across from north to south which joined the cape to what appeared to be the mainland; this stretched as far as they could see to north and south, and rose up to low hills on the horizon to the west.

They had been running for three hours, and had covered twelve or fifteen miles from the camp. They started off again and ran on to the west, passing on to the mainland from the cape.

After that, the character of the country began to change. The ground rose slowly, and the soil grew richer; the sea was now behind them and a considerable mass of land in front; how large they could not tell. The trees got larger. They knew pine-trees, and beeches, and silver-birches, but the cedars and the chestnut-trees were new to them, and strange. Presently Hekja dropped upon one knee.

'Look, Haki—cranberries.' They ate a few of them; they were larger and better than the ones they knew.

They went on westwards into what seemed to them to be a fairyland. Woods of tall trees alternated with meadows beside rippling streams; they saw several herds of small wild deer which fled away before them. They saw a great number of wild birds, bitterns, and geese, and mallard, and teal, and a great many more that were strange to them. One sort that flew with great long legs stretched out behind amused the runners very much.

As they went on, the fruits grew plentiful. They knew strawberries and raspberries and gooseberries by sight; they found all these growing wild, but larger and more luscious than any they had known before. They found a number of wild fruits that they had never seen before and they refrained from most of these, fearing poison.

But one new fruit intrigued them very much. It was a climbing plant and grew up trees, and carried large, soft purple berries massed together in a bunch. The soft, purple skin covered a juicy, pale green flesh with little seeds in it. They saw the birds eating these berries and coming to no harm: they tasted them gingerly and found them sweet and delicious. Soon they were eating them freely.

Presently they found a grassy seed-plant very like the wheat they knew.

As the afternoon progressed they went slower and slower; there was so much new to be seen. In the end they quite frankly stopped travelling altogether and wandered about in the warm sun in the meadows and the woods, marvelling at all the new things in this wonderful country. They had only covered a mere forty miles or so, but Leif would never know.

Hekja said: 'This is the best country I have ever seen, Haki. Better than Greenland or Norway, better even than our own country.'

Haki said: 'There is no limit to the cows that a farmer could keep here. There is grass for all the cows and sheep in the world.'

Hekja sighed happily. 'It is very good here, Haki. The land is beautiful, and it is very good to be alone together, and away from the Norsemen.'

Haki nodded. 'Leif is kind and just,' he said, 'but we have our ways and they have theirs, and the two are different.'

They may have been, but in many respects the ways of the Scots were not inferior. They found no difficulty at all in living in this fertile country. They could throw a stone with quite extraordinary accuracy and force, born of long practice at the quarters of the cattle that they herded. They gathered a few pebbles from a brook and wandered about until they saw a little deer; they stalked it carefully up-wind till they were close enough, and threw their stones together. At twenty-five yards range both hit it on the head. It staggered and fell down; they rushed up and despatched it with a knife. Very pleased with themselves, they carried it in turn till they reached a woody glade beside a stream; here they made a fire in a spot where bushes kept the draught from their backs.

As night fell, they cooked the meat on wooden skewers over a fire, and ate it with a quantity of the big purple berries. Presently, happy and amorous, they made a bed of twigs and leaves and grass beneath the bushes by the fire, and lay down and slept together.

They spent the next day wandering through that wonderful country, marvelling at everything they saw. They saw a scarlet tanager with brilliant red plumage; they both exclaimed at it, and tried various ways of catching it without success. They followed it for a long time; for them it was the high spot of the happiest day of their lives. They thought that they had never seen a bird so beautiful.

Presently Hekja had a wonderful idea. She said: 'Haki, don't let's go back to the ship. We can stay here, in this good land.'

The runner stared at her; new ideas came slowly to them both. 'Not go back?'

She said earnestly; 'We can stay here and be our own masters. They will never catch us again. We can go on into the country, away from the sea. They will not go far from their ship.'

He thought over her proposal. With anything abstract they had some difficulty, partly because their vocabulary was very small. But presently he said:

'Leif wants the story of this land. He is a good man, and we will go back.'

She sank down on the grass, and looked at him appealingly. 'Haki, I don't want to go back to Greenland with the Norsemen. They laugh at me, and this is a better land than any we have seen.'

He squatted down beside her, searching for the words that would express what he felt. 'Leif has been kind to us,' he said with difficulty. 'We have good news for him about this land. We must go back.'

She said a little piteously: 'I don't want to go back on the bitter sea with the Norsemen.'

He took her hand with awkward tenderness. 'We must go back to Leif,' he said again. She could not move him from that.

They spent the remainder of the day wandering southwards through the land. They spent the night together by their fireside in a grove of cedar trees; far off on the horizon they could see the sea.

Next day they ran eastwards till they came to the coast at what was evidently the west shore of a large strait, or bay, they could see land on either side. They followed the coast northwards, swimming across two fair-sized tidal rivers, and found at the head of the bay the neck of land that they had passed across two days before. They crossed it back on to the sandy, wooded cape and ran on steadily all day; at about seven o'clock in the evening they ran into camp.

Leif was waiting for them there, with Tyrker. They brought back with them a bunch of the great purple berries they had found so good, and a sheaf of the wild corn.

'Lord,' said Haki, 'this is a good country, better than Norway or my own land, better than Greenland. All the cattle in the world can pasture here, and there is food for everyone. It is the best land in the world.'

They took the berries and the corn from him, and examined them. Haki said: 'These fruits we found and they are good to eat. There are many other marvels.'

Tyrker smiled. 'Lord, I know these fruits. They grow in Germany where I was born. They are called grapes. You make wine out of them.'

Leif took them with interest, and tasted one. 'So these are grapes. I have heard of them, but never seen them before. I have drunk wine, and it is good.'

Tyrker said: 'Lord, if we get some more I will make wine, after the manner of my people.'

The Norseman said: 'So. We will call this good land Wineland, Wineland the Good.' He turned to the runners: 'You have done very well,' he said. 'You shall be free people when we get back home, living on your own farm, with cattle of your own.'

They flushed with pleasure. Then they went over to the fire and ate a heavy meal; they had had nothing since the previous night, and they had covered forty-five or fifty miles. Presently, when they could eat no more, Hekja said:

'Haki, let us go and see if our stone is still all right.'

In the evening light they climbed up to the summit of the knoll. The stone was just as they had left it, safe and firmly planted in the turf. They fingered the lettering and admired it for a little while; it was their own wonder, theirs alone. Presently they sat down on the short turf in the setting sun, and stared out across the quiet meadows to the east.

Hekja said happily: 'Our names are now together, Haki, for as long as the stone shall endure. Leif said so.'

He leaned towards her on one elbow, and took her hand in his. 'This is a good country,' he said earnestly, 'better than Greenland. I will ask Leif to let us stay here when the ship goes back and you shall have your children here.'

There was a momentary silence.

Alix forced a laugh. 'Wake up, Mr. Ross,' she said, a little tremulously. 'You're still asleep.'

He turned away and stared at the tent wall, bitterly disappointed.

CHAPTER X

TOWARDS dawn the pilot fell into a doze, and slept a little; in his turn, Lockwood lay awake till morning. He had an orderly mind that criticised all evidence, that made a stern distinction between fact and fiction. What Ross had told him was a dream, no more, a figment of a tired, drugged imagination—fiction. It was no more than that. As he rolled round in his sleeping-bag, he thought irritably that there was nothing in it to keep him awake.

For fiction, it was disturbingly concerned with fact. It could not be denied that there had been a man called Leif, the son of Erik, nor that he had discovered a new country on the mainland of America and called it Wineland the Good. The story occurred with variations in three separate sagas. The rational explanation was, of course, that Ross had read the sagas at some time; these memories had been fished up from the depths of his subconscious mind and joined to more recent memories to form a dream. Lockwood was not well versed in the vagaries of the subconscious mind, but he knew that such a combination formed the basis of a great many dreams. It was all quite easily explainable when you came to think of it.

Quite easily, if you discounted Ajago. He rolled around again, trying to put out of his mind the things the Eskimo had said. No reasonable man would give much weight to those, in any case.

He did not sleep at all.

At dawn he saw that the pilot was asleep. The don lay patiently in bed till eight o'clock to give the pilot sleep; then he got up and called Alix. Presently she appeared and began to get breakfast; with the slight noises that she made the pilot woke.

She crossed over to him. 'You've been asleep, Mr. Ross. Feel better for it?'

He yawned. His mind was quiet and at rest for the first

time for many days. He said: 'I feel fine. I suppose I'd better get up.'

She sat down on the end of his bed. 'You'd much better stay where you are this morning. I'll give you your breakfast in bed. The doctor said you were to have bread and milk again.'

He was disinclined to move; the nervous urge that had driven him since they left England had gone altogether. He smiled. 'All right. I'll probably go off to sleep again when I've had that.'

He ate his bread and milk while the other two breakfasted at the table. As soon as possible Alix and her father left the hut, hoping that in their absence Ross would go to sleep again. They walked down to inspect the seaplane on the beach.

It was a fresh sunny morning with a keen wind from the ice-cap; gulls wheeled about them with sharp cries, the blue water of the fjord broke in a tiny surf upon the sand. There was a feel of autumn in the air already. As they walked down towards the seaplane, Lockwood said:

'Our pilot told me a very odd story, last night.'

The girl said: 'I know, Daddy. You mean his dream.'

He looked at her in surprise. 'Did he tell you about it?'

She shook her head. 'No—I was awake last night. I heard him telling you.'

'Did you hear all of it?'

'I think so.'

He was silent for a moment. Then he said: 'What did you think of it?'

She did not answer immediately. They reached the seaplane and walked round it absently; then she sat down on the bow of one of the floats. He repeated his question.

She said slowly: 'I don't know what to think. What did you think of it, Daddy?'

He turned irritably aside. 'I don't know. One thing is clear. We've got to face the fact that he's been very ill, much worse than we realised.'

She said testily: 'I don't know what you realised. I thought at one time he was going to die.'

He turned back to her. 'I know,' he said more gently. 'I meant that, mentally, he's been through a great strain.'

She nodded slowly. 'That may be. If he has, he's come out of it all right. But anyway, that's no real explanation why he should start talking about Leif Erikson.'

Her father said: 'Well, that's quite easily explained. He must have read the sagas at some time or other. It's all in Hauk's Book and the Flatey Book.'

'All of it?'

He hesitated. 'Well, some of it.'

He turned to her. 'It's really rather interesting. He must have read the sagas at some time or other, or heard somebody lecturing on them. Those impressions sink down into the subconscious mind. In a time of great mental strain they come to the surface again, mixed up with a great mass of other memories, some recent, some far distant. The result is what we call a dream. Generally in a dream the story is an incoherent muddle. Sometimes by coincidence it makes a rational account. That's what this one is.'

She shook her head. 'He's not the sort of man who goes to lectures on Leif Erikson. You know he's not.'

He said doggedly: 'He's heard the story from the sagas in some way or other.'

She eyed him for a moment. 'Do you really think that?'

'It's the only possible explanation.'

She was silent. He filled and lit a pipe. 'It's possible to trace it all out,' he said meditatively. 'One must assume, to start with, that he has some knowledge of the sagas, buried deep down in the background of his mind. Next, in his dream he sees the cove where we were camping. Well, that's perfectly natural. A very recent memory. But he sees a house there, that isn't there in fact.'

The girl nodded. 'It's not so easy to explain away that one.'

The don smiled. 'It's not so difficult. A badly lit house, with a sleeping-bench running the length of it, dividing it in two. It's the Eskimo house—the one where we spent the night.'

Alix stared at him in wonder. 'I never thought of that.'

Her father smiled. 'That feature puzzled me at first. But you've got to put yourself in his shoes and try to sort back through his memories. It's quite clear to me now—that part of his dream was just a flash-back to the Eskimo house.'

The girl said slowly: 'What sort of houses did the Norsemen in Greenland live in, anyway?'

The don said: 'Stone houses, roofed with thatch or turf on wooden beams. There was generally a dais.'

She asked: 'Was a dais like a sleeping-bench?'

'I suppose so.'

The girl said: 'It seems to me that a Viking house was very like an Eskimo house. Do you think the Eskimos learned to build them from the Norsemen?'

'They may have done.' He turned to her. 'You mustn't try and stretch the evidence,' he said. 'A dream memory of the Eskimo house is the most likely explanation, and it's backed by so much else.'

She asked: 'What else?'

He smiled: 'For one thing, the sea voyage. While he was unconscious we put his stretcher on the boat and rowed across the cove. The motion of the boat and the sound of the oars penetrated into his sleeping mind, and he dreamed of a long voyage in an open boat.'

She was silent. Her father went on:

'Then there's the feature of the wonderful land he found, sunny and beautiful, and fertile. I think that's what psychologists would call a contrast-impression. In the last month he's been in barren lands, continually strained and anxious about ice, and storms, and fog. Subconsciously he must loathe all this sort of country. So when he dreams, he dreams about a perfect country, happy and wonderful. That's probably a country that he's seen before some time —perhaps in Canada.'

He paused, and then he said: 'Running—that's just the nervous urge of our journey, expressed in a different mental form, I think.'

The girl stirred and said: 'I see you can account for most of the incidents, Daddy. But one still has to explain his knowledge of the people, Leif Erikson and Tyrker, and the girl Hekja.'

'Leif Erikson and Tyrker come from his memory of the sagas. The girl has another explanation, of course.'

She stared at him. 'What's that?'

He smiled a little. 'A girl with short, fair hear, wearing a white overall, who was his companion in his work. You don't have to dig far into his memories to find somebody like that.'

She was silent for a moment. Then she said: 'You mean, that was me.'

He said gently: 'I think so. I imagine that's what they call wish-fulfilment.'

There was a long silence. The water lapped upon the

beach by their feet, the sea-birds cried around, beneath them the yellow seaplane quivered in the breeze like a live thing. At last Alix turned to her father, smiling a little. 'Well,' she said, 'I suppose one can take it as a compliment.'

'I suppose you can,' he said drily. 'The biggest one he has it in his power to pay you.'

She stood up suddenly, and changed the subject. 'What are your plans now, Daddy? Do you want to go back to Brattalid again?'

He shook his head. 'Not particularly. I can't do much out there alone, and it's really only working in the dark until we've studied the survey. I'm quite prepared to leave it till next summer, now, and come back with a digging party. What do you want to do?'

'It's your expedition, Daddy, and your work. I'll do whatever you decide.'

He eyed her for a moment. 'What do you want to do?' he repeated gently.

She turned away. 'I want to get away from here,' she said in a low tone, 'as soon as ever we can. I want to get back home.'

Presently they went up to the hut again and went in quietly; the pilot was asleep. They left without disturbing him and strolled back to the seaplane; deprived of the house and of the services of the pilot they were without occupation for the day. They walked up and spent an hour with the doctor, gossiping; then they went to see the pastor, who showed them his church. At lunch-time the pilot was still sleeping; they went and had lunch with the governor, who showed them his Leica enlargements of the seaplane.

He took them round the castle farms in the afternoon, and explained his scheme for raising good stock for the Eskimos. It was half-past six when they got back to the hut; the pilot woke as they went in.

Lockwood asked him how he felt. He said: 'Fine, sir. I must have slept all day. I'll get up tomorrow.'

'I should think you might, at this rate. Do you feel like sleeping tonight?'

'I think so.'

Alix was busy at the table with the evening meal; her father turned to her. 'What does he get for supper?'

'Bread and milk again, Daddy.' She did not come over to the bed, nor speak directly to the pilot.

The don said: 'I'm going to wind up the expedition now, Mr. Ross. I understand that there's a little more to be done upon the survey, but we'll do that from here.'

The other nodded. 'Two flights ought to finish it, I think. You don't want to go back to Brattalid yourself, sir?'

Lockwood shook his head. 'I've finished all that I can do there, for this year. As soon as the photography is done, we'll go back home.'

'I see.' The pilot thought about it for a minute. 'You aren't doing this for me, sir? I'll be perfectly fit to go on in a day or so.'

'I think you will be. But the work is done.'

'All right. We can probably finish off the survey in one good long flight.'

Lockwood smiled. 'Two comfortable, easy ones, I think.'

'All right.'

He lay silent for a minute, pondering his work. Then he said: 'I had a dump of fuel and a mooring put at Battle Harbour. If you agree, sir, I'd like to go back that way.'

'Over to Labrador and then down to New York?'

'That's right. I'd rather do that than go back to Angmagsalik. We might get into awful trouble in that ice.'

From the stove the girl said to her father: 'Would we fly straight to New York from Battle Harbour, Daddy?' It was a question that she might have asked the pilot.

None of them failed to notice the constraint. The don looked at Ross to answer. 'I don't think so, sir,' he said to the man beside him. 'It's too far for one hop. We'll have to spend a night at Halifax, or somewhere.'

Lockwood said smoothly: 'I'm quite in your hands, Mr. Ross.' Behind him the girl went on with her cooking. 'The only thing is this. I don't want to start from here till you feel perfectly fit, and able to tackle these long flights again. It's only the fourteenth of August now—we've plenty of time in hand.'

The pilot nodded. 'We'll run off these two little survey flights, and see how they go. But it's the ice that made the real worry on the trip out, sir. We shan't find this run down to New York very difficult.'

He thought about it for a minute. 'There's another thing. We'll have done with the seaplane when we get it to New York. As soon as we get there, I'll have a chat with Eddie Hanson on the telephone, down in Baltimore. We've got to sell her second-hand, and I believe he could shift her as well as anyone. If Sir David agrees to that, I'd fly her on to Baltimore and turn her over to him.'

The don asked: 'How far is it from here to Battle Harbour, Mr. Ross?'

The other shrugged his shoulders. 'Six-fifty—seven hundred miles, perhaps. I'll fix it with the operator here to keep transmitting, and we'll run down the bearing. We shan't have any difficulty, long as the motor keeps on turning.'

The girl brought a steaming bowl over to the bed. 'Here's your bread and milk, Mr. Ross.' She turned away.

Nothing happened during the evening to relieve the constraint. The pilot sat up in his sleeping-bag checking and re-checking his lists of film exposed against the canisters of the film itself, and against the map of the survey and his pencilled log, in order to assure himself that no gap in the survey had been left unphotographed. The girl washed some clothes and went to bed early, to try to read in bed by the flickering light of a candle. The don pondered his notes of his dig at Brattalid, and made pencil amendments. Presently they were all in bed, and the lights out.

The pilot was the only one who slept right through the night.

He got up in the morning, fit and well; when the girl put in an appearance she looked tired and jaded. She found that the pilot and her father had made the breakfast; there was nothing for her to do but sit down and eat it. They talked in monosyllables throughout the meal; the girl did not eat much.

As soon as possible Ross made his escape, and went down to the seaplane. He had his work to do, clean, practical and material work with metal parts and oil and grease, fit healers for a sick mind. He took the covers off the float compartments and sponged out the bilges; he took off the cowling ring and tappet covers and changed his eighteen sparking plugs for new ones, saved for the crossing of the open sea to Labrador. At one o'clock he went back to the shack for lunch, grimy and with a mind at rest.

Alix had spent the morning without proper occupation, restless and tired. At lunch she said casually: 'Do you want a hand this afternoon, Mr. Ross?'

He shied away from her proposal. He said: 'It's very good of you, Miss Lockwood, but there's really nothing much that you could do today. I'll let you know if you can help me at all.'

He went back to the seaplane directly he had finished eating, relieved to get away. In love, he felt, you cannot put the clock back; she was too much Hekja to him ever to be Alix again. He plunged back into his work, setting his tappets with a feeler gauge, cleaning the sumps, changing the oil. He did not know that for part of the afternoon the girl was sitting a quarter of a mile away upon the hillside, alone, watching him at work. Once a tear trickled irrationally down her cheek; she wiped it angrily away.

He worked till supper-time on the machine, and went on after supper refuelling till dusk, helped by Ajago and another Eskimo. In the twilight that passed for night, at about eleven o'clock, they launched the seaplane at the high tide and took her to the mooring. Ross got back to the hut at midnight, went to bed, and slept perfectly all night till eight o'clock.

They breakfasted, and were in the air by nine upon a survey flight. The girl was tired and listless; she had slept badly for the third night in succession. The pilot had reverted to 'Miss Lockwood' when he spoke to her; in turn she was stilted and polite to him in spite of herself, and hated herself for being so. At times she was unbearably like Hekja. Then the pilot felt something turning over deep inside him; he addressed himself woodenly to his work.

They flew all morning on the survey, Ross at the front end of the cabin and the girl crouched by the camera at the back. In the five hours of the flight they barely exchanged a dozen words. They landed back at Julianehaab at about two o'clock, tired and thick in the head. Ajago met them with the motor-boat; as they stood in the boat going towards the shore the pilot said:

'You're looking tired, Miss Lockwood. Five hours is a lot of flying at one time. Why don't you take a lie down after lunch?'

She said indifferently: 'I may do that.'

He had not finished with the seaplane. He went out to her again upon the mooring in the afternoon to grease and look over the controls, and to make a succession of small jobs that would keep him busy until evening, that would keep him with the machine and away from the girl. In the shack Alix went and lay down for a time; presently she fell asleep, and woke after an hour hot and muzzy, with a slight headache.

Lockwood was in the main room of the hut, the pilot was still out upon the seaplane. She made her father a cup of tea and had one herself; then they went for a short walk.

He asked her about the survey. 'It's practically done,' she said. 'In fact, I think it is done, but Mr. Ross thinks that we left a strip gap on the first day. He wants to go out again tomorrow morning and take some of it again, just to make sure.'

Her father nodded. 'He's very thorough.'

She said: 'I wish he wasn't. We could get away tomorrow, really.'

'To Battle Harbour?'

'That's where we're going, isn't it?'

'Yes.' He paused. 'You want to get away as soon as possible, don't you?'

She said quietly: 'Yes please, Daddy. I want to get back to Oxford. A Cunard boat leaves New York each Saturday. It's Wednesday the day after tomorrow. If we start then we could catch the one this week.'

'Don't you want to stop and see America?'

'Not this time, Daddy. I want to go home.'

He changed the subject, and they talked of other things. In the hut that evening he proposed to Ross that they should leave on the Wednesday morning.

'Suits me, sir,' said the pilot. 'Soon as the job's done I'll be glad to see the last of this place. It's been a miracle the weather's lasted like it has. Once we get over on the other side, to Labrador, I don't care if it snows ink. We can go home by boat. But if we pile her up in this place we might spend the winter here, likely as not.'

They flew again next day and finished off the survey, finally and without ambiguity. They were back at Julianehaab by half-past twelve. After lunch Ross made a check development of the two sets of exposures in the dark room at the governor's house; the girl did not offer to help him, but he found a willing assistant in the governor. The films were satisfactory; he returned to the machine and began refuelling for their departure, helped by Ajago.

Once as they rested, the Eskimo said: 'Go tomorrow?'

'That's right,' said the pilot.

The man pointed to the north-east. 'Angmagsalik?'

Ross shook his head, and pointed to the west. 'To Labrador.'

The man understood. 'Good.' He leaned over to the pilot. 'For you'—he leaned further and tapped Ross on the chest —'for *you*, Greenland not good place. For others, Greenland good. Not good for you.'

The pilot nodded slowly. 'Maybe you're right.' He eyed the Eskimo curiously. 'What's wrong with Brattalid?'

It is doubtful if the man understood him properly. He made a gesture of distaste. 'Brattalid no good,' he said. 'Alle ved det.'

They got up, and went on with the refuelling. In the hut Lockwood and his daughter were sorting out their stores. They packed the camera to be shipped back to England at the next opportunity, whenever that might be. They took with them in the seaplane only the sleeping-bags, the emergency provisions, and the films of the survey.

When Ross came back to the hut, they began an orgy of giving things away. They gave their surplus photographic supplies to the governor, most of the medicine chest to the doctor, and the surplus of tinned foods to Ajago. He received them with delight. 'It is too much,' he said in Danish. 'These foods cost many krone.'

Alix said: 'Take them all, Ajago. You've been so good to us.'

He went and got a sack and took them away.

Next day, early in the morning, they left Julianehaab. The governor and the doctor and the pastor all came down to see them off. For the last time Ajago took them to the seaplane in the motor-boat; they said good-bye to him, and got in. Ross and Lockwood swung the inertia starter together and the engine fired; Ajago cast off the mooring for them, and they taxied out into the fjord.

The first attempt to take off was unsuccessful. They had a very heavy load of fuel on board; the machine ran for two miles up the fjord, but failed to leave the water. They taxied back again and hung on to the motor-boat while Ross drained off some fuel into the sea; at the next attempt they left the water after a long run. Ross climbed the machine slowly to about three hundred feet; then he turned and passed over Julianehaab at about nine o'clock, letting out his aerial as he passed the settlement. He got on to his course, out over the sea.

Presently Julianehaab faded into the mists behind. There was a visibility of about fifteen miles; the sky was partly overcast at seven or eight thousand feet. They flew at about two thousand feet over a dappled leaden sea, transmitting on the wireless each half-hour. They sat in the machine, bored and motionless, for five hours. At two o'clock they saw the loom of land, very far ahead.

They held on the same course, and presently made out the entrance to Hamilton Inlet. Then they turned, having established their position, and flew southwards down the coast for another hour or so. Presently the pilot pointed to a few wooden houses scattered on a little island.

'That's Battle Harbour,' he said. Peering down, they saw the masts of the wireless station.

He throttled down and put the seaplane into a wide gliding turn above the little settlement; presently they saw the red buoy on the water. They landed near it and Ross taxied up to it; Alix standing on the float, hooked on. The pilot cut his switches and the engine came to rest. 'That's that,' he said, a little wearily.

They studied Battle Harbour from their seats, tired and reluctant to move. It looked very like Julianehaab, but not so big and not so well arranged. There were the same little wooden houses, a hospital, and a wireless station standing on the bleak, bare ground. 'What will you do about the fuel?' asked Lockwood. 'Will you fill up today?'

Ross said: 'I think we'd better, sir. The weather is good at the moment. I'd like to make the most of it, and get along tomorrow down to Halifax.' He stared at the shore. 'I don't suppose you want to hang about here any longer than we've got to.'

A motor-boat came out to them, and took them ashore. In half an hour Ross was back with the petrol, and was filling it into the machine with the assistance of a couple of men, trappers in the winter. By half-past six the work on the machine was done, and they were ready to go on next day.

The nurse in charge of the hospital provided a bed for Alix for the night; Ross and Lockwood slept in their bags in a loft over the Hudson Bay Company's store. They had little time to explore Battle Harbour. They took one short walk after supper and found the place alive with sledge dogs; then they returned and went to bed at nine o'clock, in preparation for an early start next day.

They were disappointed, for there was a morning mist. They were up at five to peer out into an iridescent, pearly fog with a pale sun above; they hung about disconsolately for hours. Shortly before ten o'clock a little breeze got up and blew the mist away; the pilot decided to make a start.

'We may have to come back again, if we don't like the look of it,' he said to Lockwood. 'But I think we'll have a stab at it!'

They thanked their hosts and said good-bye, and went out to the seaplane in the motor-boat. By half-past ten they were in the air and on a course for Halifax in Nova Scotia, flying above wreaths of the low mist that hung about the coast. Soon they came to the Straits of Belle Isle and crossed over them.

The northern part of Newfoundland was barren and low-lying, dotted with water lying on the land in lakes like puddles in a street. They followed down the western shore; slowly the land grew fertile, till it became thickly wooded. Presently Ross touched Lockwood on the elbow, and turned to draw the girl's attention. He pointed downwards; below them there was a winding track cut in the pine forest, and a puff of steam. Presently they saw the little engine and the trucks. 'This is the Bay of Islands,' he said, smiling. 'You can go home by train now, if you like.'

The girl said: 'I don't want to go by train—it's getting interesting now. Something to look at, instead of just sea. I never knew a forest looked so much like a game of spillikins.'

Her father said: 'I noticed that. There seem to be fallen trees everywhere you look.'

Ross nodded. 'It's always like that, but you only see it from the air. Any untouched, virgin forest looks like that.'

They followed the coast on down to Cape Ray, eating a lunch of bully beef and biscuits in their fingers. They crossed Cabot Strait and passed over the collieries and steelworks of Sidney; in the warm afternoon they followed down the east coast of Nova Scotia. At half-past five they came in sight of a large town upon the south shore of a wide, extensive harbour.

The pilot said: 'Halifax.' He put the seaplane into a wide turn above the town. 'That's where we land—that oil wharf —where the ferry's going in.'

Lockwood said: 'Do you know this place?'

Ross nodded. 'I came here several times, in the old days.'

The machine swept low beside an island opposite the docks and landed in front of the town; the pilot turned and taxied in towards the oil wharf. A flat-bottomed motor-dory with a couple of men in it came out to meet them and took them in tow; presently the seaplane was securely moored by bow and stern between two wharves, floating safely and sheltered in the bay between.

They got down into the dory for the few yards to the wharf; Alix stared around. She had never been in North America, and it had a foreign air to her. The piles that the wharves were built upon were just the rough-trimmed trunks of trees; in England the timber would have been squared off. Everything on the water-front was built of wood and corrugated iron, severely practical and rather shabby. The signs upon the buildings in themselves seemed strange, RAKWANA TEA and THE SCOTIA FLOUR AND FEED LTD. A little crowd of men upon the wharf contained three negro labourers.

One of the men in the dory turned to Ross.

'You come from Battle Harbour today?'

The pilot said: 'That's right.'

The man turned the chew in his cheek, spat into the water, and said: 'Why do them letters start with G? All the ones I ever seen begin with C.' He indicated the registration letters painted on the yellow fuselage.

Ross said: 'It's a British registration. G means England. C is for Canada.'

'Uh. Quite a ways from home, aren't you?'

The pilot said: 'That's so.'

They clambered up a rickety ladder on the oil wharf; the manager was at the top to meet them. ''Evening, Jimmie,' said the pilot. 'How've you been keeping? Guess you've put on weight since I was out here last.'

The manager said: 'Hi-ho, Donald—you don't alter much. Still going around in airplanes? Tell me, before the hands go home—what octane gas do you use in this thing?'

They talked about the details of the refuelling for a few minutes; the manager arranged to keep some men on over-time to fill the seaplane up for them. Ross turned to Lock-wood. 'We can leave it all to them, sir,' he said. 'They're used to handling ships here. I'll come down after dinner and just look her over; then we can get along tomorrow bright and early.'

They went up to the red stone Customs House carrying their tiny baggage. At the desk the officer looked at their passports deliberately, slowly, and with some interest. At last he said: 'You've come all the way from Southampton, then, by way of Iceland and Greenland?'

The pilot said: 'That's right.'

The man considered the position for a minute. Then he said: 'You made quite a flight.'

Ross said: 'Yes. We're not stopping in Canada. We're going on down into the States tomorrow—to New York.'

'Yah. I guess I'll have to see the boss. We don't get many Atlantic fliers in these parts.'

He took their passports off into an inner room; at the desk Alix turned to Ross in wonder. 'He said we were Atlantic fliers. Is that what we are?'

He smiled down at her. 'More or less, Miss Lockwood. We've flown it in a sort of way.'

The don said: 'I never realised that we were putting ourselves into that distinguished category.'

The pilot said: 'Well, sir, that's what you hired me for. And I remember showing you the map before we started, so you can't blame me.'

Lockwood said quietly: 'Yes, and you told me it was going to be a tough trip. You've done a very good job, Mr. Ross.'

The pilot said: 'It's been the weather. We've had awful luck with that.'

The girl said nothing. The reference to Atlantic fliers and the memory of the journey they had made were bringing home to her the magnitude of the task that the pilot had achieved. Each step of the journey, considered at the time, did not seem very difficult or very arduous; it was only when you came to look back upon it as a whole that you saw what a job it had been. Her father was right. They had never realised in Oxford what the journey would be like; if they had had the knowledge then that they had now, they might never have started at all. But the pilot, with his experience, had known all about it. He had known the difficulties that they would meet, and had not been afraid. She did not quite know if she was in love with Ross. She did know that she respected him enormously.

Presently the formalities were completed; they left the office and took a taxi up to the hotel. It was a fine, modern and luxurious hotel facing a park on the high ground behind the town. They marched in, carrying their little linen kit-bags, and registered at the desk.

In the spotless elevator, going up, Lockwood said diffidently: 'I'm not sure that we've got the clothes for a place like this, Mr. Ross.'

'We're quite all right, sir. Nobody changes for dinner here.'

Alix said: 'It will be nice to have a bath. I haven't had a bath since Reykjavik.'

Ross said: 'I'm afraid I had my last in Invergordon, Miss Lockwood.'

The memory of the hotels that they had stayed in came back to her. 'Shall we meet for a drink before dinner, Mr. Ross?'

The pilot smiled. 'Sure, Miss Lockwood. I'll slip down to the town and get a bottle. Shall I come to your room, or will you come to mine?'

She stared at him. 'Whatever are you talking about?'

He said: 'The licensing laws. You can't get a drink in the hotel here, like you would in England. You're allowed to buy one bottle a day in this province. You go and get it personally at the liquor store. You aren't allowed to drink it in a public place, or with your meals in the restaurant. So when you want to have a drink, you throw a party in a bedroom. It's the normal thing to do.'

He paused. Then he smiled slowly, and said: 'It kind of breaks the ice when you take a girl out for the evening.'

'I'm sure it does, Mr. Ross. But is this true? You're not pulling my leg?'

They reached the bedrooms; the bellboy opened the doors for them. The pilot shook his head. 'Sure I'm not. See, here's the bottle opener screwed on the window-sill, and here's the corkscrew. And here's the list of table waters, under the Bible.' He turned away. 'I'll only be able to get just one bottle, so you can't have a gin and Italian. Shall I get a bottle of Scotch?'

She said: 'All right. Daddy could drink a whisky and soda, I expect. Let's meet here, in my room, at seven o'clock.'

'Right you are. Would you telephone down for the soda, then?' He went down again in the elevator and took a taxi to the liquor store; then he came back and had a long, hot bath. At seven o'clock he tapped at her door, bottle in hand. Lockwood was there, they opened the bottle, poured out the drinks, and sat about the room drinking for a quarter of an hour before dinner.

'How much farther is it to New York from here?' asked Lockwood.

'Five or six hour's flight, sir. If we're in the air by eight o'clock it's plenty time enough. I told them at the oil wharf we'd be down there at half-past seven.'

'How do we go?'

'Follow the coast down to Cape Sable, sir, and then straight on a compass course. Then there's about a couple of hundred miles of sea to cross, and then we cut across a bit of Massachusetts. After that we go straight on down Long Island Sound.'

'Do you know the coast down there?'

The pilot shook his head. 'I've never been down in the States at all, except once to Detroit.'

They emptied their glasses and went down to dinner. Then they took a taxi and drove down to the wharf. Ross left them there, to go and check up the refuelling and to drain the sumps. The Lockwoods took the taxi on for a drive round Halifax in the warm evening.

They got back to the hotel at about ten o'clock. The pilot was before them; they found him sitting in the lounge. He got up as they came in; for a few minutes they discussed the town. Then he said:

'I'm going to turn in before very long, sir. Would you like another whisky and soda before going to bed?'

The don shook his head. 'I don't think I will; I think I'll go up now. You have one.'

Ross shook his head. 'I don't believe in solitary drinking.'

Alix laughed. 'What nonsense! I'm thirsty; I'll have a very little one with you, Mr. Ross.'

They went up in the elevator; Lockwood left them and went to bed. The pilot went with the girl to her room; the whisky and soda were still standing on her dressing-table among her personal articles, her brush and comb, her powder compact, her little bottle of scent. Most of these the pilot knew by sight already.

He poured out the drinks, a medium one for himself and a small one for her, and put in the soda. Then he took his glass and strolled over to the open window, and stood looking out over the harbour.

'It's not a bad place, this,' he said. 'I've had some good times here.'

She came and stood by him. 'It's a very shabby town.'

'I know. But there's something about it that I like. It's a man's town.'

'Have you been here a lot?'

'Half a dozen times, perhaps.' He turned to her. 'I'm glad we came here for the last night of our flight. Tomorrow we'll be in New York, and it'll all be over.'

She said slowly: 'I've been thinking of that, too. I've enjoyed this trip, every minute of it. I've never done anything like this before. It'll be something to look back on, all my life.'

He glanced down at her. The curl of the hair around her neck fascinated him; it was all he could do to prevent himself from touching it.

He stirred suddenly. 'It's the last lap tomorrow,' he said a little harshly. Then he smiled, and raised his glass. 'The last lap—may the luck still hold.'

She stood there looking up at him, more like Hekja than he had ever known her. Involuntarily he caught his breath. She raised her own glass. 'To our luck,' she said. 'No more dreams, Mr. Ross.'

He stared at her for a moment; she was Hekja to the life. 'No,' he said quietly, 'no more dreams.' He set his glass down, took her by the shoulders, and kissed her.

In a moment he released her, and they stood facing each other, breathing a little quickly. 'I'm sorry I did that,' he said unsteadily. 'But it's the last lap, and it's just as well that you should know.'

She said: 'I'm not sorry, if you wanted to, Mr. Ross. But please don't do it again.'

He turned back to the window. 'You needn't be afraid of that,' he said. 'I don't know why I did it then—something you said about my dream. But you know the way I feel about you.'

She smiled faintly. 'It was a pretty good demonstration.' She paused, and then she said: 'I've never been in love. Not since I was a schoolgirl, and in love with Leslie Howard. It doesn't happen easily to me.'

'I know,' he said. 'Nor very easily to me.' He turned back to her, and took her hand. 'Do you think that it would ever happen?'

She said in a low tone: 'I don't know, Donald. If it did, I'd let you know.'

They stood in silence for a minute; then he let her go. 'I

think I'd better say good night, Miss Alix,' he said heavily. 'It's a vicious law, this one that makes you drink in bedrooms. It puts ideas into one's head.'

She came with him to the door. 'Not a bit of it,' she said. 'They've been there for a long time. I know that.'

He smiled. 'Maybe you're right.' He turned to her. 'Good night.'

She said softly: 'Good night, Mr. Ross,' and shut the door on him. Both went to bed, and lay awake most of the night. Neither of them slept for more than an hour or so before the telephone bell rang to call them to get up.

They breakfasted in the deserted dining-room, the pilot taciturn, and Alix very attentive to the requirements of her father. Then they went down to the seaplane in a taxi. They went on board, the mooring lines were slipped, and the motor-dory towed them out into the harbour. By eight o'clock they were in the air, and turning to head southwards down the coast.

For the first hour they flew down the eastern side of Nova Scotia, past Chester and Liverpool. At a quarter-past nine they came to the end of the land; the pilot got upon his compass course and they went droning out south-westwards over a deep blue sea. It was warm in the cabin of the seaplane, though they were flying at three thousand feet. Lockwood dozed in his seat beside the pilot. Alix sat behind, watching Ross at his work, thinking about the episode of the night. She had become aware that she was very fond of him; it was inconceivable that after the flight was over she should never see him again. But it was everything or nothing, now. She must be fair to him.

The pilot busied himself with the navigation, and with transmitting messages upon the radio from time to time. For two hours the seaplane droned on over the sea.

Presently Alix leaned forward and touched the pilot on the shoulder. She pointed at a shadow on the far horizon, dead ahead of them. 'What's that? Is it land?'

He nodded, and turned in his seat to speak to her. 'It's Provincetown—the north end of Cape Cod. We're just about dead on our course.' He showed her the map.

Lockwood woke up and they all examined the map together; the pilot throttled a little and allowed the seaplane to lose height slowly as they approached the land. They sat back in their seats and waited as the end of the cape drew slowly near, as the machine sank gradually towards it. Fresh from his sleep, Lockwood looked around him and noticed the pilot's face; it was drawn and tired, and very intent on the land. His appearance worried the don slightly; it was just as well, he thought, that this was the last flight they had to make. Thinking it over, it seemed to him that Ross had not had nearly enough rest. They had come from Juliane-haab to Halifax in two long days of flying, and this was the third. It would be a good thing when they got down to New York, and there would be no more flying to be done.

The noise of the engine died suddenly to a whisper, and the nose of the machine dropped to a glide. The don glanced quickly at the pilot. He was still gazing intently at the spit of land now looming ahead of them dead on their gliding path, and growing larger every minute. Then he saw that Ross had his hand upon the throttle, and knew that he was gliding down on purpose.

The don said: 'What is it?'

The pilot never took his eyes from the low, sandy spit. 'It's all right, sir,' he said irritably. 'I throttled down.'

Lockwood said no more, but turned to look ahead. They were down nearly to a thousand feet, and the details of the land were clear. It was low and sandy; to the south of them it stretched on indefinitely. To the north it ended in the sea almost beneath them, curving away in a curious hook of sandbanks. There was a town of white wooden houses in the sandhills, Provincetown, and a very high square tower built of grey stone. There was a loop of arterial road around the town, with cars dotted about on it as it ran through the sandhills.

Then all this swung round to their left as the pilot turned away, still on the glide. They were now low enough to see the detail of the sea, a heavy swell that broke in white surf upon the sunlit, sandy beaches. For an agonising moment both Alix and her father thought that the pilot was going to land upon the sea; the experience that they had gained upon the flight told each of them that landing on that sea could only mean disaster. Both controlled their feelings, neither of them moved or spoke to Ross. Then the beach appeared again on their right. The pilot's hand moved slowly on the throttle, the engine came to life again, and they began to fly along the coast towards the south.

They flew only a hundred yards or so from the beach, and

barely twenty feet above a hideously rough sea. Both Lock-wood and his daughter had implicit confidence in Ross. He had never flown so low with them before and they did not like it; they knew that height meant safety in the air. Their confidence told them that he probably had some good reason for it and that it would be better not to worry him. They relaxed a little, and looked at the land.

It was extraordinarily similar. A sandy cliff seventy or a hundred feet in height seemed to be crowned with bushes and low scrub; as the top of it was above the seaplane most of the time they could only catch glimpses of the land behind. The foot of the cliff ran out in a short beach on which the white surf rolled and beat in breakers. Ahead of them, as far as they could see, this beach and cliff stretched on contin-uously, evenly, uninterrupted. They flew on low beside it for minute after minute, mile after mile; there was no break or interruption in the cliff or in the beach.

Alix leaned forward and touched the pilot on the shoulder. 'What a marvellous beach!'

He turned a white, strained face to her. 'I know this place. We called it Wonderstrands.'

Alix was staggered for a moment. Then she rose to the occasion. She got up from her seat and leaned over his shoulder, her face very close to his, speaking into his ear.

'Donald,' she said gently, 'you dreamed about Wonder-strands. It was very wonderful, and lovely, but it was only a dream. This is a real place, Cape Cod.'

A stray wisp of her hair brushed his cheek. He said: 'I know. But this is the place we came to in my dream. Don't you remember?'

She shook her head. 'I wasn't with you in your dream,' she said, a little sadly. 'It was Hekja who was with you then, Donald. It wasn't me. All I know is the present, that we're in a seaplane, and we're rather near the water. Don't you think we might fly a little higher?'

He said: 'I wanted to see it as we saw it then, just to be sure.' He eased the wheel back, and climbed to three or four hundred feet.

Lockwood stirred and was about to say something; his daughter motioned to him to be silent. She crouched beside the pilot, her head very near to his, her hand upon his shoulder. They flew on down the immense beach for another ten minutes; it seemed endless and unchanging. Presently

Ross said uncertainly: 'There was a little sandy island, where we found the honey-dew. I can't see it yet.'

Alix said gently: 'You can't expect everything to be quite the same as in your dream, Donald.'

'I suppose not.'

A minute or two later they came level with Eastham. Looking ahead, the girl saw a series of wide stretches of inland water separated from the sea by sand-bars, calm and inviting. She said quietly: 'We could land on one of those lagoons. Why don't we put down there? We could have lunch on shore, and see if we could make sense of it all.'

He turned to her, smiling bitterly. 'I daresay you think I'm off my head. I'm quite all right, Miss Alix. But I'm telling you—this is the place I came to in my dream.'

'Wouldn't you like to land?'

'I'll land if you want to. But I'd rather go on, myself, and see the whole of it.'

She hesitated, and then said: 'All right.'

He flew on down the coast past Pleasant Bay and Chatham, the girl crouching close beside him. They turned the corner of the land and began to follow the shore westwards on the south side of the Cape. They flew on down the low-lying, sandy coast for a quarter of an hour, past Harwich and Hyannis; presently the country got a little bolder, and the shores more thickly wooded. Suddenly the pilot put the seaplane into a steep turn above a harbour entrance between sandy spits, leading to inland water.

He said to Alix: 'This is the place where we went in. I'm going to go down low again to have a look. Don't be afraid.'

She smiled, and said: 'Don't go and hit anything.'

'I won't do that.'

He throttled back and circled out to sea. The yellow sea-plane sank towards the water; presently he opened up again and flew towards the harbour entrance about thirty feet above the water.

'This is the place,' he said.

They passed the sand-spit and flew on above the placid inland water, with Osterville Grand Island on their right hand and Cotuit on the left. They passed on between the wooded shores into the Great Bay and turned to the north. A narrow, river-like stretch of water led inland with wooded country to the west and fairly open, park-like country to the east. They shot up this at ninety miles an hour; it opened out into a still, inland lagoon completely surrounded by the woods. The pilot took the seaplane up to about three hundred feet, and circled round.

'That's where we came to,' he said quietly. 'We made our camp down there, under that little knoll.'

They stared down at the lagoon. It lay still and attractive in the morning sunlight; the woods cast bright reflections in the calm water. There were two or three shacks or summer cottages clustered at one end of it and one or two large houses dotted about among the trees, not very near the shore. Otherwise it was deserted.

Alix said: 'Are you sure about it, Donald?'

He said: 'There's nothing changed here since we came before. Only those houses in the woods have come. Would you get back into your seat, Miss Alix? I'm going down to land.'

She slipped back into her seat. The pilot closed the throttle and put the seaplane into a wide gliding turn. He came in over the little shacks at the east end of the lagoon, slipped down towards the water, and flattened out with a little burst of engine. The floats touched gently and bit down into the surface; the seaplane slowed, sank down into the water, and came to rest before the little cove. Ross turned and taxied in towards the beach.

The floats touched on the sand, and the machine came to rest. The pilot cut the switches and the propeller stopped; silence closed down upon them. He turned to Lockwood. 'This is the place we came to in my dream,' he said. 'I'm sorry, but I had to land.'

He got out of his seat and pressed past Alix, opened the cabin door, and made his way along the float. From their seats the don and his daughter watched him as he splashed through the shallow water to the beach, as he stood upon the sand looking around.

The girl said uncertainly: 'Daddy, what ought we to do? Do you think he's all right?'

Her father said slowly: 'I think so. He's had a curious experience, and he's been living under a great strain. I think he's quite all right.' He turned to her. 'We don't know everything there is to know,' he said. 'There's nothing to be afraid of in that.'

She said: 'I'd never be afraid of Mr. Ross, Daddy.'

'Of course you wouldn't.'

234

She stirred uneasily in her seat. 'I don't think he ought to be alone.'

Her father said: 'You go to him. You're nearer him than I shall ever be.'

She got out of her seat, got down on to the float, and went along it to the beach. Lockwood followed her a minute later. She reached the pilot. 'Donald,' she said gently. 'Is it the place you thought it was?'

He nodded. 'It's the place, all right. We made our camp up there, at the top of the beach.'

He turned to meet the don as he came up. 'I suppose you think I'm mad, sir,' he said evenly. 'Probably I am. If so, I'm not fit to fly for you any more. But you're all right here, and the machine's safe enough. You'll only have to walk a mile to find a telephone. Ring up the Boston airport, and they'll send a pilot down to take her away.'

Lockwood said: 'Do you mean that you want to resign the job, Mr. Ross?'

The pilot said: 'That's right. I've flown enough for the time being, evidently. There comes a time when you've just got to stop. It may be I shall never fly again. In any case, I'm chucking up the job.'

'You're doing nothing of the sort,' said Lockwood.

There was a momentary silence.

The don faced him squarely. 'If you are ill now—and I don't think you are—it's just because you've worked too hard to make this journey a success. I'm not going to let you give up your job like this. I'll get someone else to take the seaplane down to Baltimore by all means, if you like. But I want you to come back with us to England.'

The pilot said: 'I don't care, either way.' Nothing seemed to matter now. There was a bitterness in his voice that made the girl's heart ache.

He turned away and moved up the beach; she followed a little way behind him in the soft sand. Lockwood hesitated, and let them go alone.

The pilot stopped at the edge of the woods and looked around. 'It's all very like it was, as I remember it,' he said. 'Only, the trees are smaller—it's all second growth, this stuff. It's a shame, that. It was so pretty then.'

The girl said gently: 'This place means a lot to you, Donald, doesn't it?'

He said: 'I was very happy here.'

He turned towards the little knoll. 'That's our hill,' he said. 'Would you come up there with me?'

She said in a low tone: 'Of course.'

They turned, and left the beach in silence. In silence they climbed up the little knoll above the quiet lagoon; the ground was soft and springy under their feet. At the top the girl stood for a minute, looking around. The still water lay beneath them, mirroring reflections of the trees and of the sky; the yellow seaplane lay below them on the beach. It was very quiet.

'It's a friendly place,' she said at last.

'Why do you say that?'

She turned to the pilot. He was on his knees beside a rock, covered in lichen and half buried in the sand. He was staring up at her. 'Why did you say that?' he asked again.

She shook her head. 'I don't know, Donald. Some places are happy places. This is one of them.'

'I know.' He glanced at the rock. 'Do you remember this?'

She knelt down on the turf beside him. 'I'm afraid not, Donald,' she said quietly.

He laid his hand upon it. 'This is our stone.'

'You mean, this is the stone you dreamed about?' she asked.

He nodded. 'This is it.'

Lockwood came up the knoll to them; the pilot raised his head. 'I dreamed that we put a stone up on this hill, sir,' he said evenly. 'Well, here it is.'

The don put on his spectacles and said: 'Let's have a look at it.' There was something very soothing in his practical acceptance of the fact. He dropped on to his knees with them beside the stone, and passed his hand over it. Then he got his knife and scraped a corner of it with a sharp tool. After a time he said: 'It looks like a tertiary basalt—an augitite.'

He raised his head and stared out over the lagoon. 'If that's the case,' he said, 'it can't be native to the cape. It's all sand and silica formations here. There's no basalt in these parts. Somebody must have brought it from some other place.'

Ross nodded. 'We got it from the hill above our camp at Brattalid. That's where we got all the ballast for the ship.'

They all stared down at it in silence for a time.

'That's a possibility,' Lockwood said at last. 'You get this sort of basalt there, all right.'

The pilot got to his feet. 'Let's lift it up and have a proper look,' he said. 'I think it's got some more to tell us, if it gets a chance.'

It was half buried in the turf; with some difficulty they heaved it from its bed. The buried face was cleaner than the top part; there were marks cut deep into the stone that ran under the lichens of the part that was exposed. They bent over it and scraped the lichens clear, working in silence.

Presently the don said: 'These are runic carvings.'

He brushed the dust away, and stepped back to see them in full view. The marks were quite clear where they had been covered by the ground, weathered and less distinct above. They made a pattern:

$$\ast \, \uparrow \, \mathsf{P} \, \mathsf{I}$$

$$\ast \, \mathsf{M} \, \mathsf{P} \, \mathsf{I} \, \uparrow$$

'Haki and Hekja,' Ross said softly. 'And it's been here all this time.'

Lockwood glanced at him. 'That's what it seems to mean.' He stooped and traced the markings with his finger. 'Haki and Hekja. So this is where Leif came to.' He stared out absently across the lagoon, and was silent for a minute. Then he turned to Ross. 'This ought to set your mind at rest,' he said. 'The Norsemen must have come here, as you thought.'

He got to his feet, and went down to the seaplane to get a camera to photograph the stone before it was disturbed again. The pilot stood up, and stared across the woods towards the west, towards the gently rising foothills of the mainland. 'It's turned out a good country,' he said thoughtfully. 'We told Leif that it was the best land in the world. And so it was.'

The girl was still crouching down beside the stone, fingering the runes. He knelt down again beside her. She ran her fingers slowly over the lines.

'I know these marks,' she said at last. 'I've done this before, some time . . .'

She raised her eyes to his. 'You were very much in love with Hekja, Donald, weren't you?'

He nodded without speaking.

The girl said gently: 'Tell me, what was she like?'

237

He said: 'She was like you.'

He took her hand in his. 'We were very much in love in those days,' he said softly. 'We could be again. Leif said our names would be together, for as long as this stone should endure.'

'I know, Donald.' There was a little pause, and then she said: 'The names of two young Scots, who should have been remembered for the work they did, who have been quite forgotten.'

He said: 'Not quite. We shall remember them.'

Available by Nevil Shute
In the Uniform Edition

MARAZAN

SO DISDAINED

LONELY ROAD

RUINED CITY

WHAT HAPPENED TO THE CORBETTS

AN OLD CAPTIVITY

LANDFALL

PIED PIPER

PASTORAL

MOST SECRET

THE CHEQUER BOARD

NO HIGHWAY

IN THE WET

THE FAR COUNTRY

ROUND THE BEND

REQUIEM FOR A WREN

A TOWN LIKE ALICE

THE RAINBOW AND THE ROSE

ON THE BEACH

BEYOND THE BLACK STUMP

SLIDE RULE

Also

STEPHEN MORRIS

TRUSTEE FROM THE TOOLROOM